THE DENIVAN EXILE

Book 2 of

The Saga of Terminus Mundus

Michael Mazzaro

SIGNALMAN PUBLISHING

The Denivan Exile:
The Saga of Terminus Mundus
by Michael Mazzaro

Signalman Publishing
www.signalmanpublishing.com
email: info@signalmanpublishing.com
Kissimmee, Florida

Cover design by: Kate Danailov

ISBN: 978-1-940145-32-7 (paperback)
978-1-940145-33-4 (ebook)

Library of Congress Control Number: 2014953226

Printed in the United States of America

SIGNALMAN
PUBLISHING

To God, Family, and Country

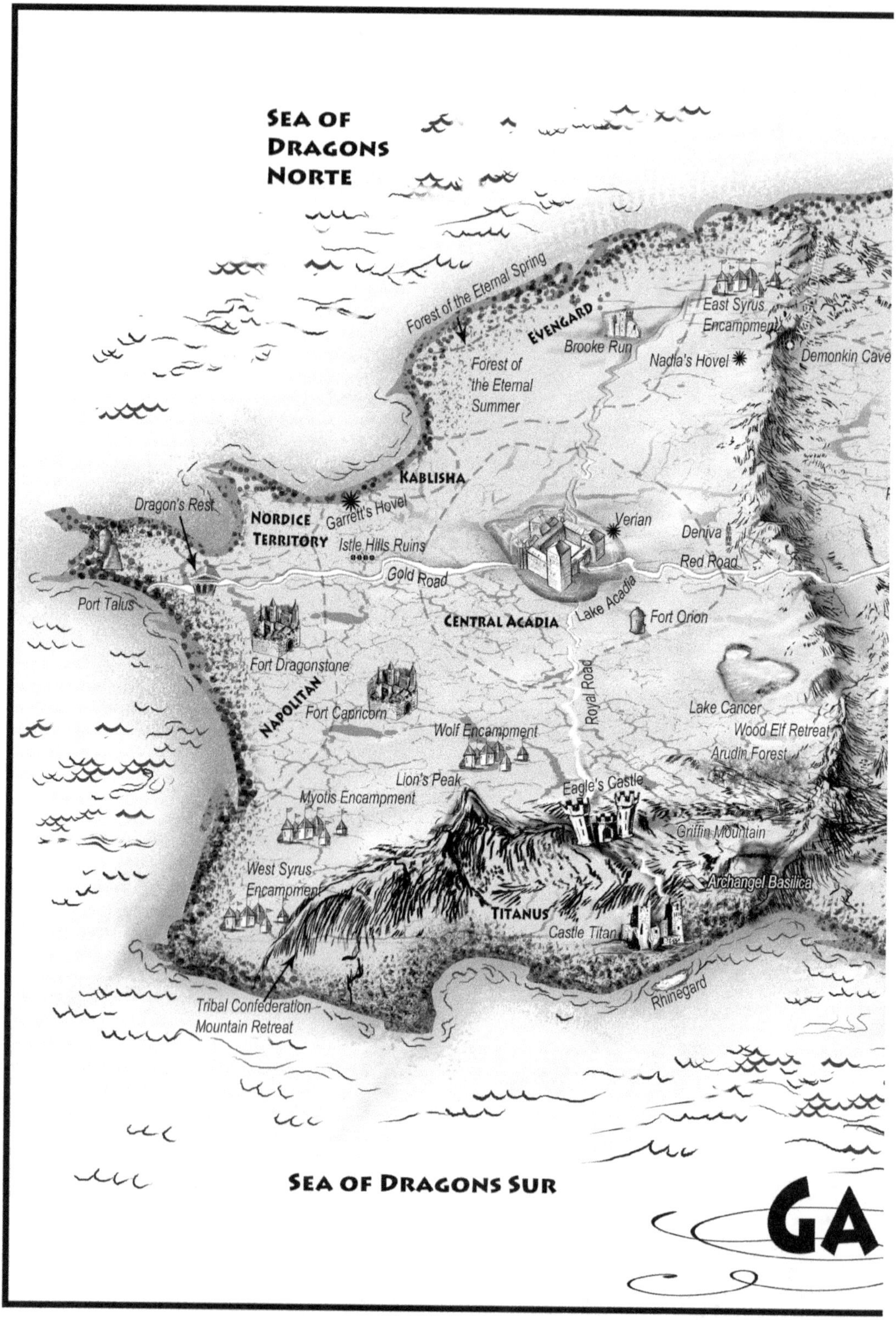
SEA OF DRAGONS NORTE
Forest of the Eternal Spring
EVENGARD
Brooke Run
East Syrus Encampment
Nadia's Hovel
Demonkin Cave
Forest of the Eternal Summer
KABLISHA
Dragon's Rest
NORDICE TERRITORY
Garrett's Hovel
Istle Hills Ruins
Verian
Deniva
Red Road
Gold Road
Port Talus
Lake Acadia
Fort Orion
CENTRAL ACADIA
Fort Dragonstone
NAPOLITAN
Fort Capricorn
Royal Road
Lake Cancer
Wood Elf Retreat
Arudin Forest
Wolf Encampment
Lion's Peak
Eagle's Castle
Myotis Encampment
Griffin Mountain
Archangel Basilica
West Syrus Encampment
TITANUS
Castle Titan
Rhinegard
Tribal Confederation Mountain Retreat
SEA OF DRAGONS SUR
GA

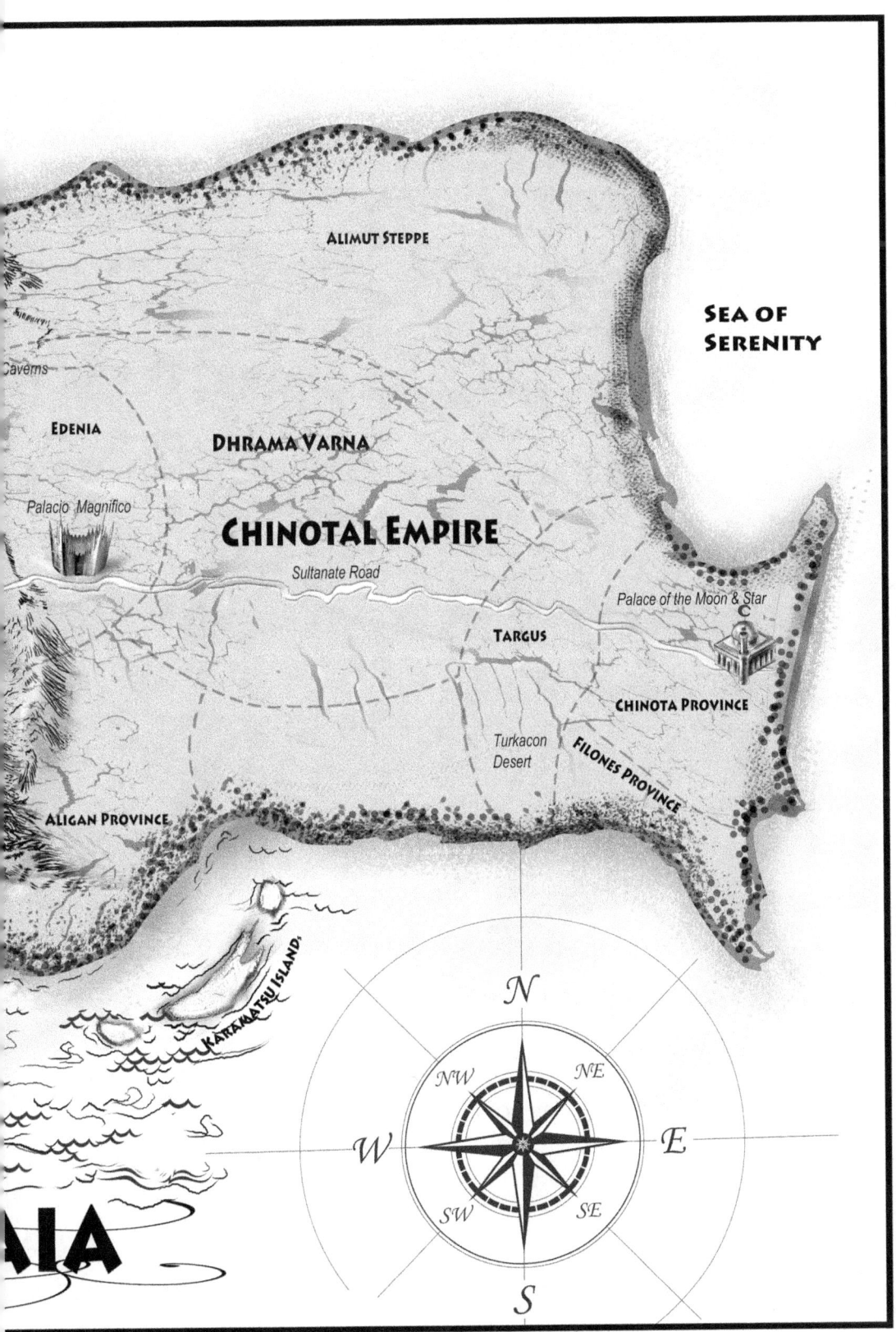

ALIMUT STEPPE

SEA OF SERENITY

Caverns

EDENIA

DHRAMA VARNA

Palacio Magnifico

CHINOTAL EMPIRE

Sultanate Road

Palace of the Moon & Star

TARGUS

CHINOTA PROVINCE

Turkacon Desert

FILONES PROVINCE

ALIGAN PROVINCE

KATAMATSU ISLAND

N

NW   NE

W   E

SW   SE

S

...IA

ACADIAN DUNGEONS, CASTLE ACADIA, VERIAN

Lord, hear my prayer, in your faithfulness listen to my
pleading; answer me in your justice.

Do not enter judgment with your servant;
before you no living being can be just.

The enemy has pursued me; they have crushed my life to the
ground. They have left me in darkness like those long dead.

My spirit is faint within me, my heart is dismayed.

I remember the days of old; I ponder all your deeds;
the works of your hands I recall.

I stretch out my hands to you;
I thirst for you like a parched land.

Hasten to answer me, Lord; for my spirit fails me. Do not hide
your face from me lest I become like those descending to Hell

At dawn let me hear of your kindness, for in you I trust. Show
me the path I should walk, for in you I entrust my life.

Rescue me, Lord, from my foes, for in you I hope.

Teach me to do your will, for you are my God.
May your kind spirit guide me on ground that is level.

For your name's sake, Lord, give me life;
in your justice lead me out of distress.

In your kindness put an end to my foes;
destroy all who attack me, for I am your servant.

Psalm 143: A Prayer in Distress

Echoing across the vast plains of Terminus Mundus, the *Legend of the Last Knight* resounds for all men and women of good will. In the 25th revolution of the reign of Stephen Acadia, King of Justice, Acadian conspirators lead by Count Maximilian Luminas succeeded in their bloody coup. Forging a diabolical alliance with a fallen angel named Abaddon, they exchanged the life of Stephen's daughter Cassandra for the crown. However, a group of elite warriors led by the three Marshals of the Alliance Army infiltrated the Castle in a daring rescue operation. After fighting their way through countless troops, Cedric Rhone rescued Cassandra and brought her to the only escape route out of the Castle. Trapped between the wrath of the Dark Angel and the dangers of the Royal Crypt, *La Morte Angelus* sacrificed himself to stave off Abaddon from his friends.

Abaddon charged at Cedric, and the two began a fury of swordplay. One sword each put them on even terms, and the two struck each other's sword on ten different occasions.

"Why? Why can't I kill you? You're a mere Divikin!"

"It's faith, Abaddon. I'm not fighting to die; I'm fighting to live for Cassandra!"

Three more deflections and the two foes pressed their swords together a last time. Abaddon hit Cedric with a third "fury of hell" attack. There was nothing left in his arsenal to stop it; the magic broke pieces off his armor and tore at his skin. The strap on the Rising Moon Helmet broke and the helmet bounced to the ground. Abaddon reared back and struck Cedric through the center of his chest.

"I will bleed you like a stuck pig!"

Gasping for air in cardiac arrest, Cedric mustered his strength and tried to pull himself off the sword. Failing to do so, his vision faded away. Abaddon was finally starting to savor his victory, though it had been much harder than he had anticipated.

"No more snide remarks or quips? Let's face facts, Cedric Rhone, you gambled and you lost. You may have delayed them from being in my hands temporarily, but I will hunt them down. There's nowhere on this planet that Cassandra can go where she will avoid me. Die knowing that you didn't have the strength to defend the woman you gave everything for. What do you have to say to that?"

Spitting blood into the eyes of the dark angel, Cedric murmured something. Laughing at his weakness, Abaddon taunted him again.

"What was that? Speak up!"

"Join me... in hell!"

Awed by the statement, Abaddon's mind failed to register the taunt of his bloodied opponent. It was over; he was dying!

"I hold the light and the darkness in my heart!" chanted Cedric.

Infused with the powers of dark and holy saber magics, Ragnarok erupted with golden power. Lifting his head, Abaddon stared into Cedric's brown eyes burning with holy fire. As the dark angel backed away, the divikin grabbed him at his throat. Squeezing the life from him, Abaddon struggled for air.

"You may have studied the divikin, but never the beauty of how we die. As we approach death, we become less human and more like our divine selves. This is my duel blade, the master technique of my race and class."

"You baited me?"

"After I drew your poison from Cassandra, I could never beat you on normal terms, but, as you implied, I gave up everything to save her!"

Striking upward with Ragnarok, Cedric broke Abaddon's blade. The piece lodged in the sword master's body fell to the ground.

"God, give me the strength!"

Shoving Abaddon to the ground with the strength of an angel, Cedric twirled Ragnarok in his hands once and fell to one knee. He drove the sword into Abaddon's chest where he had previously made the hole in his armor. The sword went all the way through and pinned the dark angel's body to the ground. Penetrated with the holy and dark magic infused in Ragnarok, Abaddon felt his body burning from within. Convulsing on the ground, Abaddon's countenance took on a fearful inevitability. Finally the attack subsided, and Cedric's blood dripped down on the dark angel's face.

"Looks like I lost again, Dad," admitted Abaddon as he stared at Cedric. "Permaneo Eques Ordinares. Hell, you've earned the knight's title: La Morte Angelus. I salute you."

A white light shot out from the center of Abaddon's body. Decomposing to ash before Cedric's eyes, all evidence of the dark angel faded from the history of Terminus Mundus. Exhausted and mortally wounded, Cedric vomited blood. He crawled to a pillar, and using his sword tried to hoist himself back to his feet. It was to no avail as he collapsed on the pillar.

"Father in heaven, my body is broken, but my soul is still strong!"

Cedric tried everything to move, but found his body wouldn't respond. Accepting his fate, the sword master sat himself up against the pillar and reached for his flask. He drank the last of his brandy and smiled.

"The sweetest taste in the world—one last swallow of brandy for one last victory. In nomine Patris et Filii et Spiritus Sancti... "

Summoning his will, Cedric blessed himself after three failed attempts.

"God... I never prayed for selfishness in my life... I knew I could win because You are always with me. With your will and power, anything is possible. Father, I am not embarrassed to submit myself to you. I can't die until I see her again... into your hands, I commend my spirit... thy will be done!"

Cedric closed his eyes and stopped breathing. He lay against the pillar as a calm, peaceful smile came across his face. His hand, holding the brandy flask, fell to the ground.

* * *

Clanking of armor came from the stairs. Eight Halberdiers cautiously held their weapons forward as they descended the final steps into a collapsing chamber reeking of blood. Overcome with terror, some of the soldiers vomited as they surveyed the damage to the dungeon and the burnt corpses of their former comrades buried in the rubble. Stunned by the disappearance of the blue light of runes burned on the stone door to the crypt, one of the Halberdiers noticed a larger prize. Cedric lay helpless against the pillar, Ragnarok at his side. Two of the Halberdiers took the initiative and ran towards the Prince, holding their spears out in front of them just in case.

"It is Cedric Rhone!" exclaimed the first Halberdier. "What the hell could do this to him?"

"Where are the others?" asked a second soldier as he scanned the room.

"Who cares! We've got *La Morte Angelus* in a compromised position. Hey, we take him out and I bet Luminas gives us a boon!"

"I could always use the extra coin."

Measuring the place to put their spears, the two signaled to their comrades to cover the room. Just as they were ready to strike, four arrows raced through the air and struck one of the Halberdiers in his chest. He stared in shock before falling over dead. The other Halberdier turned to see Duke Wilhelm von Angelhardt standing behind him, his crossbow resting on his armored forearm.

"What are you?" cried the Halberdier.

Saying nothing, the duke drew his spear and launched it into the Halberdier's chest, killing him instantly. Screaming, the remaining Halberdiers charged Wilhelm. Swiftly drawing Devil Slayer from his waist, Cedric's mentor engaged his enemies in melee combat. The first soldier went down after a thrust into his armpit as Wilhelm grabbed the second beneath his tower shield and broke his neck. Deflecting the attack of a third, a quick sword thrust was all it took to dispatch him. Parrying the fourth's attack with Devil Slayer, the duke head-butted his foe to the ground and crushed his throat with his steel-toed boot. The last two Halberdiers dropped their weapons to retreat, but Wilhelm showed them no mercy. Four more rounds of crossbow bolts left his foes dying on the stone stairs. The distraction resolved, Wilhelm ran over to Cedric. After observing his condition, his mentor pushed the palms of his hands together in prayer and chanted.

"One to shed salvation's light, one as black as darkest night!"

Markings of black and white light glowed from his arm to his shoulders. As tornadoes of black and white feathers swirled in the room, four wings burst from Wilhelm's shoulders and back. While there was nothing unnatural about his first layer of white wings, the black wings below were covered in mucosal fluid. Every few seconds the mucus would flash, and the duke would wail in pain. Checking Cedric's pulse, Wilhelm put his ear down to the sword master's heart. The faintest murmur of a heartbeat in his prince's chest brought a smile to his face.

"God, this one is strong! Your Excellency, I must ask you to hang on just a little longer."

Laying his hands on his wounds and drawing from his angelic essence, Wilhelm invoked a powerful version of heal light. His wings radiated sheer energy which transferred directly into Cedric's limp body. Even with his power amplified, fear and trepidation flooded the duke's mind.

"Come on, your Excellency, it's not like you to give up so easily. I need you to breathe."

A slight cough and the drooling of blood reassured Wilhelm with hope that his prince may actually pull through. Carefully staring at Cedric's eyelids, the duke actually believed him to be undergoing some form of REM sleep. Eventually, a smile crossed the Titan prince's face.

"That's it, I knew you weren't ready to die. Whatever kind of dream you're having, I'm sure it's a good one," teased a laughing Wilhelm. "It's not your time yet, your Excellency! Let me save you for once."

Alerted to a magical presence entering the room, Wilhelm lifted his head. A purple portal with a burning magic circle appeared bearing a young man and a young woman. Relieved at their appearance, the duke recognized them to be Quirinus Ophion and Mesmara Lorelei of the Kablisha tribe. Quirinus, or Quinn to his friends and kinsmen, scratched his mop of ruddy hair and focused his brown eyes on the fallen prince. His average height and athletic body was covered with a vanadium breastplate marked with a cross, brown gloves, quilted pants, and boots. A long sword was attached to a black belt and a crossbow was on his back. Mesmara swept back her long blonde hair to reveal her captivating genetic trait that left her with one sapphire blue eye and one emerald green eye. She was average height and athletic wearing a silver-colored battle dress, boots, and vanadium armor over her chest shaped to her anatomical features. Mesmara had a saber on her belt. Bowing to Wilhelm, they had promised Bishop Peter Wulf to follow his every order.

"Mesmara, help me!"

"Yes, great duke."

Rubbing her hands together, Mesmara knelt beside Cedric. Casting a second heal light on his body, the bleeding finally ceased. Quinn was drawn to the sheer beauty of the silver light that covered Mesmara. Despite her warrior appearance, she was one of the finest healers in all of Terminus Mundus.

Drawn away from the sight by the rustling of armor, Quinn grabbed his crossbow. The automatic crossbow was a closely guarded secret of the Kablisha tribe. The weapon was activated by releasing a red safety button on the side of the handle. A round of fifty bolts could be loaded into the bow and each would be set in place without the need to pull or crank the drawstring. Taking his aim, Quinn killed the first soldier coming down the stairs with a bolt to the neck. He held the remainder of the soldiers at bay with a rapid succession of shots.

"I think we're going to have company real soon," Quinn said as he continued to fire.

"You'll have to hold them off; if we don't stop the bleeding he'll die!" commanded Wilhelm.

Falling back, the Kablisha warrior got down on one knee at the feet of Cedric Rhone. Spotting Ragnarok on the floor, he tried to pick it up. His first attempt to lift the hilt with one hand failed. He proceeded to use two hands but it was to no avail. Frustrated, Quinn spit on his hands and grunted, yet he could only manage to drag the blade a few millimeters.

"Damn! How heavy is this sword?!"

"Don't fool around!" chided Mesmara.

"This isn't a joke," retorted Quinn. "I've wielded claymores before, but I've never experienced anything like this. What good is a sword that can't be lifted in a battle?"

"Ragnarok is one of the Legendary Weapons," lectured Wilhelm. "When the weapon is given to its wielder, the Dwarves use an ancient craft to balance it in such a way that no one but that wielder can use it."

"That's one way of not allowing your own weapons to be used against you."

Carefully examining the prince's body, Mesmara focused on his four wounds. Clotted blood and the slight reformation of skin made the healer breathe a sigh of relief.

"I think we stopped the bleeding."

"That's good," praised Quinn.

Licking her right index finger, Mesmara traced her hand along each of the wounds. She studied the nature of the incision intently and tasted the results on her tongue. A part of the beautiful young warrior wondered what indomitable will existed in this divikin to remain alive despite all of the pain. A foul taste in her mouth detected the presence of a poison and further treatment was necessary.

"Lord von Angelhardt, we can't do anything else for him here. The wounds are deep and I detect a poison ravaging his internal organs. I thought it impossible for a divikin to be susceptible to such poison, but this foul craft is weakening him."

"You're right, child, only the healing power of the Holy Grail can save him now. Now that we've stopped the bleeding, we can move him. We'll have to take him back to Bishop Wulf."

Mesmara removed an amulet from her neck and placed it on Cedric's body. Accidently, Quinn managed to drop the hilt of Ragnarok onto Cedric's wounded stomach. Mouthing a curse, he felt the burning, incredulous stare of Mesmara upon him. Apologizing with his eyes, the warrior maiden took his sincerity as enough. She chanted a spell in the ancient language as her hand held the amulet. Golden light shined from the jewelry when she ended the chant with "return." Waves of energy consumed the four present and they disappeared in the wink of an eye.

More Halberdiers ran down the stairs checking on the condition of their fallen comrades. They shook their heads as they found no pulse on any of the bodies. Proudly stepping down the stairs, Jonas Marimon grasped the hilt of his sword. Templar knights flanked him, alert to any danger. The Halberdiers in the room pushed on the door to the crypt, but couldn't budge it.

"What in the name of the saints happened here?" barked Jonas. "Where is the princess and the others?"

"There is no way out; I had men covering both stairways," reported a Halberdier commander. "The Runes are missing from the door. I believe they used Princess Cassandra to open the crypt. Since we can't get through, we have to assume they sealed the crypt from the other side."

"Good riddance, then! As long as this barrier holds, we're invincible."

Scanning the room, a glint of light caught Jonas's eye. He marched towards an object lying next to the pillar in a puddle of blood. Bending down, the templar commander lifted the Rising Moon Helmet off the ground.

"The Rising Moon Helmet, the legendary helm of Cedric Rhone," reported a smiling Jonas. "I'd know it anywhere. Abaddon must have killed the Titan bastard!"

Disbelief silenced all of the Acadians in the room. It couldn't be true—the most formidable enemy of their coup could not have simply died. However, they wanted to believe that Cedric Rhone was gone and all of the circumstantial evidence confirmed it. The Halberdiers and templars shouted for joy and exchanged high-fives.

"Spread the news: *La Morte Angelus* is dead!"

Eastern Acadia Plains, Independent Fiefdom of Deniva

Whereas there must be an exchange between the cultures of the east and west, it is hereby resolved that the Border Fiefdom of Deniva shall have its independence guaranteed by both the Kingdom of Titanus and the Chinotal Empire. Both parties are limited to a single garrison apiece and there is to be an unrestricted exchange of goods between our peoples in times of peace.

Paragraph Ten of the First Treaty of Deniva

Weary from their long and perilous journey, the heroes and heroines trudged towards Deniva. Remaining vigilant on point, Christian and Colin kept their eyes open for any signs of danger. The remaining riders in the column formed a shield around Amuro and the sleeping Cassandra.

The Trade City had long been an area of contention because of its advantageous position near the Kaiser Mountain Pass. At the peace conference of the War of the First Alliance, Nicholas Acadia proposed the construction of a trade city between the empire and the alliance, in the hope that the exchange of goods would avoid future wars. The de-Milly family, who had risen to prominence in one of the fiefdoms of Edenia, was chosen as the compromise candidate to serve as the Margrave of the Border Province. In spite of the three wars that followed between the west and the empire, the trade city had remained prosperous under the shrewd reign of Dennis de-Milly. Dennis had successfully played the two power brokers against one another to get what he wanted.

16

Nicknamed the "tortoise" by the engineers that designed it, Deniva was enclosed with stone walls and a reinforced gate. At the rear of the city was a large, western-style castle with a giant golden spire reaching into the sky. It was the city's patriotic symbol of wealth and trade that could be seen from both Verian and Palacio Magnifico in Edenia. Spouting liters of water every second, a marble fountain was at the center of the market circle surrounded by the major trade and commodity exchanges. Brokers and tradesman made the vast majority of their fortunes moving commodities from the east and west. Cobblestone roads extended like eight spokes of a wheel from the center to the surrounding, reinforced wall. While traders were in the majority, the city also had its share of craftsman, artisans, and specialty stores. Just before the castle gates, two barracks flanked the northern road. One was marked with the flag of Central Acadia but with three golden lion emblems on the shield instead of the traditional single lion. The other flew the flag of the Chinotal Empire with two stars surrounding a crescent moon on a banner of sandstone and sapphire blue.

Slowing their pace, Christian and Colin casually rejoined their comrades. Since they didn't go for their weapons, Amuro determined it was for talk and not battle. Breathing a sigh of relief, the elf marshal received the report of her new subordinates.

"I guess you had nothing to worry about, Christian."

"We can't be too careful, marshal. There's no knowing how far this conspiracy flows, and they have Acadian Knights here in Deniva."

"I still have difficulty coming to grips with everything myself. However, command doesn't allow me to dwell on the past. You keep your eyes open; I don't want to lose Cassie after sacrificing so much to rescue her."

"Yes, marshal, and take it from someone who knows—you're doing a great job under the circumstances."

"Well, the marshal isn't the type to panic in such situations," reassured Malcolm.

"Thanks, sweetie pie!" teased Amuro.

"Please, don't start this again, marshal."

"You don't need to be so formal, Malcolm. Lighten up a little. That goes for the rest of you—just because I'm in command doesn't mean I have to be reminded of it every second. Hey, Christian, didn't a Denivan attend the Titan Military Academy?"

"Yes, Ethan de-Milly—he is the son of the Margrave Dennis. Queen Civilia didn't want to offend our relations with this government so she allowed a foreigner the high honor of attending the school. The only restriction was that he wouldn't be granted landed title in Titanus."

"Don't tell me I'm going to deal with another spoiled, rich brat seeking military glory!"

Cecilia's antennae went up and she turned her head away from Amuro. The Vanadis brought Myst up from the rear to the front. The she-elf wondered what she could have said to invoke such a reaction from Cecilia.

"He's a good guy," explained Christian. "Ethan adapted to the Titan lifestyle rather quickly and we found him to be very good with a battle-axe. In fact, he even developed a crush on a certain Titan princess who shall remain nameless."

Upon hearing that juicy gossip from Christian, Amuro got a devious smile on her face. As the she-elf observed her friend, the blush in Cecilia's cheeks grew bolder. Despite Cecilia's embarrassment, this was too much for Amuro to pass up, especially if it gave her some level of control over the hot-headed Vanadis.

"Really!" teased Amuro.

"It's not what you think," retorted Cecilia. "That parasite stayed so attached to me I thought a precision strike with my spear would be the only thing that would separate him from me."

"I'm actually quite shocked," commented Saria.

"What exactly are you shocked about?" asked Cecilia, her blood boiling. "A beautiful maiden such as me always has dozens of suitors."

"Well, princess, you don't seem to be the type that would fawn over someone!"

Expecting the worst from Amuro, Cecilia was caught off guard by Saria's unsuspecting rib. Despite the sincerity in the way she asked the question, the Vanadis wondered half-heartedly if the younger elf maiden's past performances were merely an act.

"The Vanadis fawns over no one! Especially for one who is without honor!"

"Without honor?" asked a puzzled Saria "Did the scoundrel attempt to kiss you without your permission?"

"As a good Christian, I would have forgiven that. However, he did something far worse; he offered to buy me a drink!"

"That's why you're still single, Cecilia," responded Amuro, shaking her head.

"Titan military custom is quite clear," explained Cecilia. "The highest ranking officer must buy the drinks. The impertinence of a cadet to make such a gesture to the Commander of the Valkyries! If I didn't do it someone else might have killed him!"

"You didn't have to knock him out cold!" retorted Christian.

"In her excellency's defense, it was much to the delight of a raucous crowd," chimed in Colin. "It was the first time I ever saw a man smile from ear-to-ear while unconscious."

Amuro wondered if Cedric and Cecilia really were related. She was certain if it had been Cedric and young female cadet the results would have been very different. Hippolyte and Minerva were chuckling at the entire conversation, but carefully tried to conceal their laughter from the angry Cecilia.

"They're pretty funny," commented Minerva.

"I never would have expected this," said Hippolyte as she saw her sister sigh. "Is something the matter?"

"I don't know, sis. I'm starting to doubt that we made the right decision."

"You wish that we had gone back home instead."

"Definitely."

"I do too."

"It just seemed so right at the time to help the Prime Eagle."

"I tried to think about what grandpa would have done in that situation. I felt that if we just ran away, it would be as if we were letting those creeps get away with murder. I couldn't deal with that."

"Well I guess it's not all bad."

Minerva stared longingly as Walker rode by her while Hippolyte blushed at Colin riding on his horse. The girls turned to each other, blushed, and started giggling. Valentine just stared at them and rolled his eyes, but a quick slap on the back from Cagius told him to lighten up. Passing by the outer farms and plantations surrounding the trade city, the group stared ominously at the sight of the city drawbridge coming down.

"Let me do the talking, marshal. Ethan doesn't have a lot to do in Deniva and gets a little excited about his duty," cautioned Christian. "It's best if we leave it to someone who knows how to handle him."

"Okay, but I think we should send Cecilia out instead based on what you've been saying," teased Amuro. "If he tries anything she can just punch him out again."

The she-elf laughed as Cecilia just gritted her teeth and hung her head. Undeterred by the ribs, the Vanadis took out a compact, cleaned her face, and reapplied her makeup. Sighing, Amuro moved her lips to Cassandra's ear, whispered and roused her.

"Wake up, sleepyhead, we're here."

Cassandra blinked a few times and stretched her arms. Smiling as if waking from a pleasant dream, the princess felt as if she had been asleep for hours. When she felt Amuro's gloved hands along her waist, Cassandra's face turned dark red and she looked around quickly. The raven-haired maiden angrily demanded some answers.

"Amuro, what did you do to me?"

"You needed to relax, so I used a sleep spell on you."

"I wish you hadn't."

"How do you feel, Cassie?"

"I guess I'm starting to finally come to grips with what happened, but I'm still shaking."

"No one is going to expect you to get over what happened anytime soon. We just want you to know that we're all here for you now, your majesty."

The news hit Cassandra pretty hard. So much had happened to her that the princess actually forgot her father's final proclamation. She was Queen

Cassandra of Central Acadia, the first of her name. In accordance with the Alliance Charter, she was properly recognized by Titanus, Evengard, and Napolitan.

"Cassandra Acadia, the *Pauper Queen*. I am about to have my first royal visit and I don't even have any shoes on."

Amuro realized Cassandra was still dressed in her nightgown with Cedric's cloak wrapped around her. Laughing hard with her elven friend over her predicament, Cassandra pulled the riding cloak tighter over her body.

"Well I guess my first official act as marshal is procuring the queen a new wardrobe. It's good thing we're headed for a trade city."

As they neared the Deniva gates, a warrior on horseback left the city. Even from his horse he was observed to be about six-foot-five inches tall, and broad-shouldered with much more muscle than body fat. Brown eyes focused on the approaching party, the wind passed through his short, ruddy brown hair. Adorned in silver plate mail, a giant, twin-bladed, silver war axe hung on his back. Glowing in blue light from the runes on its handle, it was a not a weapon for a man of small stature. Without an insignia to mark his breastplate, the warrior was observed as a free knight without landed title. Recognizing it was Ethan, Christian broke from formation to greet him. Upon seeing the Titan spymaster, Ethan opened his arms in welcome and Christian reciprocated.

"Hey, Ethan, it's been a long time," Christian said in greeting.

Ethan de-Milly was the fourth son of Margrave Dennis. Born premature, no one expected the runt of the litter to amount to anything. Seventeen revolutions later, Ethan towered over all his brothers and sisters, and his father knew only one career would suit him. A few well-placed bribes and Ethan became the first foreigner to graduate from the Titan Military Academy. Upon his return, Dennis would make his son the marshal of the city and commander of its mercenary Nordice defenders. Gifted with the legendary ax, Odin's Judgment, the first knight of Deniva never shirked his duty.

"Christian, what the hell is going on? We got a report from Queen Civilia a few hours ago to expect some company and then we see that blasted light emerge out of Central Acadia. We tried to send out a message to the other kingdoms but we've got no radio contact with anyone west of the city. It might as well be the end of the world and my people need answers."

"It's a long story, Ethan. The short of it is we're in trouble and we need help."

"Is Cecilia all right?"

"Cecilia's fine, but I can't say the same for Cedric."

Swallowing hard, Ethan listened to the words muttered from Christian's lips in disbelief. Panicked, he didn't understand what he was saying.

"Where is he? If he needs medical attention we can get doctors to him right away."

"He's gone, Ethan. Cedric stayed behind to cover our escape. He's gone."

Tears streaming down his eyes to match those of Christian DeVries, Ethan muttered curses from his mouth.

"How's Cecilia holding up?"

"I don't know, Ethan. Cecilia's convinced Cedric is still alive... to be honest I am not ready to completely lose hope yet either."

"Did you see him die?"

"No."

Ethan perked up and chuckled.

"Then I don't think you have anything to worry about. *La Morte Angelus* is always raising hell in one way or another. I wouldn't be surprised if he's now sipping a brandy on the Central Acadia throne as we speak."

"It would be beautiful. I'm sure Queen Civilia explained the dire nature of our situation."

"Only that you're harboring the dejure Queen of Central Acadia and that you have nowhere else you can go."

"Up until a couple of hours ago it would have been true, but King Stephen abdicated in Cassandra's name before they killed him."

"Well, isn't that the icing on the cake. It might be best to keep that information to yourselves unless you want to cause trouble for my dad. It took me a lot of effort to haul that wine and salt to the gate so I figure it would be a waste of time not to let you gain entrance now."

"God bless you, Ethan."

"Hey, Titanus took me in and treated me like a citizen of the country. We know who our true friends are. My father would never do any less for you in your time of need."

Waving to the others, Amuro brought the command up. Longingly staring for Cecilia, Ethan couldn't contain his excitement when she closed on his position. As she trotted Myst past him, Cecilia merely flicked her fingers through her hair. For a moment, Amuro wondered if her friend was actually playing hard to get. Dismissing the silly notions, the she-elf maiden formally approached Ethan. The axe-knight nodded his head in respect.

"I am Ethan de-Milly, son of Margrave Dennis de-Milly of Deniva. On behalf of my father, I bid you welcome to the Trade City. We ask only that you adhere to one law. Deniva is neutral ground between the Alliance and the Empire. My father will not tolerate anyone breaking the neutrality. You will be evicted from Deniva if you do so. If you would follow me, I will escort you to the castle."

Positioning his horse, Ethan escorted the royals through the main gate. Servants handed them salt and wine as they passed by. Each took a drink of the wine and spread the salt along their hands to complete the hospitality ceremony. As the warriors rode through the city, Ethan dropped back to where Cecilia was riding. Captivated by the beauty of the Vanadis, Ethan stammered out his condolences.

"Christian told me about your brother. I'm sorry, I always liked him."

"Thank you, Ethan, but my brother isn't dead."

"Your word is good enough for me, but he is behind enemy lines and that's not good. Is there anything I can do for you?"

"Princess Cassandra is going to need a new wardrobe. I fear she only has the clothes on her back."

"No problem, a number of tailors in this city would be honored to dress a Queen. Now, what can I do for you?"

"Give me some time, Ethan, I'm sure I'll having something for you."

As Cecilia left him in her dust, Colin took position next to Ethan.

"You're out of luck; she remembers you," teased Colin.

"Are you kidding? That's great! It means I made a lasting impression."

"I'm trying to say that her excellency still remembers your insult."

"She still holds a grudge about that," commented Ethan with a grimace.

"Princess Cecilia has a very good memory and I suspect she will take her grudges to the grave."

Noticing the approach of Hippolyte and Minerva, Ethan wondered if the barbarians had actually formed a military alliance with Titanus.

"Hey, Colin, are you traveling with members of the Wolf Tribe or are they mercenaries?"

"They're the late Aramas' granddaughters Hippolyte and Minerva. Hippolyte is the Chief of the Wolf Tribe. However, she chose to come and fight with us instead of going home."

"A coup in Central Acadia and not one corner of the West is free from the stench of death. Aramas and Stephen, what in the name of God have we unleashed?"

"I fear we're only at the beginning. Trust me, God has nothing to do with this evil plaguing us."

Entering the central market, the eyes of many merchants immediately fell upon Saria. Showered with gifts of silk, satin, and jewels, Saria didn't know how to handle her newest admirers. The elf princess put up her hands and meekly refused their gifts. Growing more uncomfortable by the moment at the merchant's persistence, Cagius stepped in to defend his lady.

"That's enough, why don't you move along to more interested customers?"

"But the lady is so beautiful!" shouted a merchant. "She must wear this!"

"I know she's beautiful but she's just not interested. She's tired!"

Cagius noticed the pin of a guild leader on one of the merchants. Sliding off the side of his horse, he whispered into the guild master's ear. The merchant nodded eagerly and Cagius smiled back at him. The Guild

Leader took charge of his subordinates and moved them away from Saria to her obvious relief.

"Thank you, Cagius."

"You've got to be careful out here, princess. We're not in the Alliance anymore; people aren't going to take 'no' for an answer just because you're an elf princess. I wouldn't recommend going anywhere without an escort."

"All cities have seedy areas and Deniva is no different," added Valentine. "There is also the added danger of the many cultures that exist in this city. Of course, there are some advantages to that as well, but I won't discuss those in the presence of a Lady."

"Okay," responded a confused Saria.

Continuing on their route the castle, the riders approached the two barracks. Tensions rose as Amuro and Cagius stared at the Turk Pasha Selim Yazar. The imperial captains rushed to join their commander as the Alliance command staff held their ground. Dressed in the sapphire Chinotal officer's uniform, the Pasha's turban proudly displayed a sapphire cockade. Selim was of average height and weight, suggesting his post was due more to his brains rather than his brawn. The commander had short black hair that was beginning to turn gray, a neatly trimmed black beard and mustache, and piercing blue eyes. Sensing no danger from the Allies, Selim and his officers moved the imperial troops out of the training grounds and back into the barracks so the Alliance members could pass without incident. Once they were gone, Walker dismounted outside of the barracks bearing the Acadian flag. A big smile crossed the face of the shield master as a young knight, Jean-Luc Robespierre, walked out of the barracks sporting a blonde crew cut and blue eyes. The knight wore steel plate mail under a tunic bearing three golden lions across it. Though shorter and less muscular than Walker, Jean-Luc's presence was still imposing.

"Robespierre, it's good to see a familiar face."

"Walker, thank God you're alive."

"Did you follow the protocol?"

"When we heard about the coup we feared the worst. Don't worry, we followed your late father's plan to the letter. The commander of the garrison has been confined to quarters and the Order of the Lion is at your command."

"The Order of the Lion is at the command of Queen Cassandra Acadia!"

"Stephen finally relented in death. I can't believe you got her out."

"We paid for it in blood, but we managed to get her safely out of the city."

"Thank God, we needed some good news here today. What about Princess Marie?"

"We couldn't get her out."

"I fear for the girl. She is not as strong and worldly as our new Queen; I don't know if she'll make it behind enemy lines."

"We can only pray at this point."

"The Order plans to remember King Stephen at sundown. We'd be honored if you would bring her Highness."

"Absolutely. I owe the late King more than I could repay. I hope that keeping his daughter safe until she can return to her throne would be enough."

"I'll let you return to your company. We'll see you later."

Walker got back on his horse and joined the group. Valentine seemed a little wary.

"Are you sure we can trust him?"

"We'd better. Robespierre is my mother's maiden name and Jean-Luc is the son from her real husband. The Order of the Lion are free-knights cleared by my father to serve as the true honor guard of the king."

Laughing, the two joined the others in the castle courtyard. Walker dismounted as well-dressed servants took his horse. Walker bowed before Cassandra as he offered to take her down. Cassandra gracefully dropped into his arms. As her shield carried her into the castle, she ordered him to stop.

"Put me down, Walker."

"Your highness, under the circumstances I believe I am acting in your best interest."

"I appreciate your compassion, my brave shield, but I'm the Queen now. I'm not ashamed of my appearance."

"As you wish, your Highness."

As soon as her bare feet hit the ground, Cassandra began to shiver. Regretting her moment of pride, she pulled the scarlet and black cloak of Cedric Rhone around her tightly. Ethan spoke with one of the servants quickly who smiled and nodded. The prince gave him some gold pieces before returning to Christian.

"We were able to get some rooms ready for your group. I'm sure you would like to get cleaned up. I'll also see what I can do about some appropriate clothes for you, your highness. My father would like to have an audience with all of you this evening if that's possible."

"Thank you," Cassandra said.

"I leave you in the capable hands of our castle staff. I've got to make a report to my dad, but don't hesitate to contact me if you need anything."

The allies huddled themselves together.

"All right, we have rooms at the castle," informed Amuro. "Follow the servants to your quarters. Those of you that have your royal uniforms with you may want to turn them over to the servants to be washed. Also anyone that needs armor or weapon repairs should send them over to the smith. If anyone needs to have a uniform or other courtly outfit made, you'd better give me a list so I can pass it on."

The group followed the servants. Ethan walked over to Cecilia.

"Princess, if you would follow me, please."

"Why?" asked Cecilia.

"I believe you may want to review the last message your mother sent."

"Christian would be far better suited to review the message."

"Your Highness, it would be best if you went," said Christian. "Keiko, please accompany her."

"Yes, sir, Christian."

"Christian, I don't think I need that sylph following me."

Christian had left with the others leaving Keiko and Cecilia behind. Keiko smiled at the Vanadis, but Cecilia wanted no part of it.

"What is so pressing in this message that it requires my personal attention?"

"Your mother had a private message encoded at the end of the transmission directed to you and Cedric."

Reality hit Cecilia like a ton of bricks. Her mother had no reason not to believe that both her son and daughter were safe in Deniva. Tears streaming down her face, she offered Ethan a mea culpa in the only way she knew how.

"Ethan, I need that help now."

Ethan took the warrior princess in his arms as she pressed her head tightly into his chest.

"Why do you bother, Ethan?"

"How could you say that?"

"You owe me nothing."

"Cecilia, it's very difficult to find someone with a combination of strength, beauty, and grace, yet you fill the bill quite nicely."

"If I wanted to hear prose, I'd let Cagius read it to me."

"I know you're going through a difficult time. I don't expect you to seek my shoulder to cry on, but there are things I can do to help."

"I don't doubt that. You've proven more than once how capable you are. I should have known since you were always by the book, even at the academy. All right, show me to your receiving room."

"Follow me, princess."

Ethan and Cecilia entered the castle. Staring into the face of his goddess, the knight detected sorrow and trepidation beneath her solemn countenance.

"How many did you lose?"

"We lost Julius in the castle and Cerwin in the crypt."

"My God, you went into a hostile enemy city with only a handful of soldiers and made it out with only two dead and one missing in action. I knew about the fighting prowess of the Alliance military but I never expected this."

"If it wasn't for my brother, it would have been all of us. Overmatched and outclassed, it didn't matter to him. That's why I know he isn't dead. He definitely had one last ace to draw to make his royal flush."

"It took me a while to figure out why Amuro always called him the 'Riverboat Gambler,' but it fits him perfectly. We'll do our best to be as hospitable as possible but I'm sure we can't suit every need. You know if you need something, you only need ask. I'll take care of it."

The two stopped at the communications room.

"Here we are, princess. I'll leave you in privacy."

"Thank you, Ethan."

Cecilia gave Ethan a quick peck on the lips, surprising the Denivan. Leaving him with a full view of her seductive gait, the Vanadis gracefully bounced into the communication room and closed the door behind her. In sheer delight, Ethan grabbed poor Keiko and hugged the little sylph tightly.

"She loves me—I know it!"

Keiko broke free and slapped Ethan across the face.

"What?"

"Only Lord Cedric may place his hands on me without my permission!"

Keiko fluttered away and Ethan went about his business.

Castle Titan, Rhinegard, Titanus

"I've heard the joke a million times now but I doubt that there is not one officer that believes it to be true. We all know that if His Excellency was to die while we were there, we would have to die too because none of us is brave enough to bring the news home to his mother."

Freigraf Marshal Horace Irvine on the "Matriarch of Destruction"

In sharp contrast to the other major cities in the west, Rhinegard was the largest walled city in the world. The sprawling metropolis at the heart of the Kingdom of Titanus was nestled neatly between the Titan Heartlands and the Sea of Dragons-Sur. The ancient capital of the Kingdom of Titanus was founded by the Patriarch of the Royal Family, Ulysses Rhone. Stone towers climbed forty stories into the sky and each of the seven sections of the capital were divided by stone gates adding to the impenetrability of the city. The surrounding heartlands outside of the city grew grain and sugar.

Passing the first set of gates would take a citizen into the highly industrialized lower district. Massive fusion power plants, heavy industrial factories, smelting plants and weapon smiths were interspersed with towering apartment complexes. The second section of the city was the Burgher district as it transitioned to the development of ranch and two-story houses interspersed with corporations, schools, hospitals, restaurants, and trendy clubs. The city divided into two more sections at the next gate. The sprawling Titan Academy campus was a city unto itself housing all levels of higher learning and the source of Titanus' greatest wealth, Titan Technologies Corp. The Port District was attached to Rhinegard via causeways to a natural sandbar. The home base of the extensive Titan Naval Port consisted of two hundred "first rate" galleons, fifty Archipelago frigates, and fifty transport brigs, which were currently in port. In the port section was the area known as the Shtetl, where the remaining Worshippers of the Divine Father found comfort among the members of their own religion. Traveling from the academy through stone gates led to the upper district. Lavish gardens and sprawling estates housed the rich and high nobility. The main embassies of each foreign nation including the Kingdom of Edenia were contained in that district.

A separate fiefdom to itself was the Cathedral District. Archangel Basilica was built with gothic-inspired spires that seemed to touch the heavens themselves with stained glass windows all around the wide building. Archangel Basilica was commissioned by King Robert Rhone after Jesus Christ was raised from the dead. It was independent of both the city of Rhinegard and the Kingdom of Titanus, though one of the many Titles of the Arch Bishop of the Catholic Christian Faith was the Bishop of Rhinegard. A stone pathway led the way to the main entrance with statues dedicated to each of the Seven Sefiroth with Archangel Michael's statue in a position of prominence. The palatial residence of the Arch Bishop of Titanus was to the left of the Basilica while the Royal Crypt was to the right of it. An underground hover train ran from one section of the city to the next allowing access between the sections of the city. However, a special pass was needed to enter the upper class section unless it was for the Sabbath. While the other classes attended church in their own districts, the Basilica would swell during feasts. The Basilica was the seat of power for the Catholic Christian Church on Titanus, a position that had been held without challenge or controversy from the Kablisha Tribe, and the Kingdom of Edenia.

The final gate led to the castle on a hill surrounded by imposing stone walls and towers. A smooth roadway up the hill connected the Fortress of Rock and Steel, the stronghold known as Castle Titan, to the city of Rhinegard. The castle was protected by three towering walls built inside of one another. Drilling and training, the Scarlet Riders occupied the massive cobblestone courtyard in the shadows of the flanking military citadels. Just like Eagle's Gate, two stone eagles stood watch over the first of three reinforced stone gates. Ballista was on top of each of the eight castle parapets as elf mercenary archers patrolled her walls. Castle Titan was known as the "Castle that Cannot be Taken," though the old "jinx" had not been put to the test since no foreign army had ever penetrated Eagle's Gate.

The entrance hall into Castle Titan was lined with weapons and armor of every kind, a point of intimidation for guests entering its storied walls. Portraits of the great Rhone rulers—Ulysses, Marion, Gunther, Leto, Frederick, Robert, and Justin—were interspersed with other heroes of the Titan Kingdom, most notably Duke Wilhelm. The castle on its whole was quite plain and ordinary, not displaying the normal lavishness or aesthetics that the other castles possessed. However, there was great care taken to protect and preserve the large and ancient tapestries hanging in the atrium depicting the violent history that had given birth to the Kingdom. Contrary to the warlike personality of the Titan people, the audience chamber was distinctively out of place. Flowing from the entrance of the throne room to the steel throne of the monarch was a two-meter wide stream. Two carved eagle's heads made up the arms of the throne and Civilia sat on a red velvet pad. Blooming in the center of the throne room was a garden of red poppies. Ten Royal Guards, both male and female in their silver mail and disturbing eyes, surrounded the room with two flanking Civilia's throne. A crucifix hung directly over the throne and a portrait of a mother eagle looking over two nestlings hung directly above the entrance to the room so that the monarch always stared straight at the picture. Tensing her muscles, the queen sat straight up in her throne preparing to receive the reports of Martha Heinrich and Horace Irvine. Anxiety had overtaken everyone in the kingdom since the events of the night prior and it was a long, silent trip back to the capital on the hover train.

"Martha, why are we getting nothing but static from our allies?" asked the queen.

"As I theorized, the tachyon field is disrupting our communications," explained Martha. "We cannot send out signals to any other kingdom. The few operatives we left behind in Central Acadia have no means of sending any communications."

"God, we're blind, deaf, and crippled!" exclaimed Horace.

"For all we know, Abaddon could be marching an army right up to the barrier and we wouldn't even know before they arrived at Eagle's Gate," Civilia said, frowning.

"I'll start sending out patrols along the barrier around the Vale," said Horace. "It's not much but it'll give us some warning if we're under attack.

My queen, this barrier was developed to use all of the natural landscapes of Terminus Mundus against us. The mountains that blessed us with protections have become our prison."

"What about going over or underneath the barrier?" pondered the queen.

"We used the old trebuchets to shoot something over the projected end of the barrier but found it extends far into the upper atmosphere," lectured Martha. "The barrier also extends hundreds of meters deep into the ground. Doctor Tattenberg took into account every means we would use to circumvent this prison."

"Robotic bastard."

"If you don't mind, your Highness, I need to return to the academy. My scientists have already begun to check the backup systems for anything we have on Virgus' theories. We have to try to duplicate them in order to bring the barrier down."

"Why are you trying to leave my presence while holding something back, Martha?" asked Civilia.

"My queen, I believe this is the best briefing I can give you on the scientific situation facing us."

"The reason why I made you my chief advisor is because you've got a poor poker face. I know when you're hiding something. What is it?"

Martha hid her eyes. As tears fell from the scientist's eyes, Civilia wondered nervously what would cause her friend such distress.

"The Acadians threw the headless body of Felicia through the barrier some hours ago. If that wasn't enough, I detected obvious signs of penetration."

"Dear God, have they no decency?"

Martha called over one of the Scarlet Riders. Carrying a velvet pillow in front of him, the knight bore an object covered with the banner of House Rhone. Tensed and already in tears, Civilia gasped for air. Gripping the eagles on her throne until blood was drawn from her palm, she watched as Martha took the item from the knight.

"They found this with her."

Martha walked the object over to throne. The trembling Civilia pulled back the banner to confirm her worst nightmare. Bloodied and dented, the Rising Moon Helm instilled a fear in her greater than any intimidation her adversaries had used against her over the revolutions. Though she would not show it to those in the room, her eyes betrayed that the *Matriarch of Destruction* had been brought to her knees.

"Freigraf, would you please..."

Stammering to get out the rest of the sentence, Horace complied without having to hear his queen's orders. Inspecting the helmet in great detail, the war master found the Prayer to Saint Michael inscribed in the crown.

"There's no doubt, your Highness, this is Cedric's helmet."

"Were there any demands? Ransom?"

"None, your Highness," said Martha. "We found it as is. You know as well as I that when a helmet is presented like this, the bearer is dead."

Calming her storm, Civilia remembered her place. Though her grief was far too great, she was still queen and her emotions would not get the better of her.

"Martha, what are our options if we were going to send a message to Deniva? We have to assume at this point that they didn't make it."

"We can't do it by sea. The spy would have to land in an imperial port, make it through customs, then cut clear across the Empire, and finally cross back through the Kaiser Mountain Pass. The return trip could be even more dangerous."

"What if we sent a raptor, Martha?" asked Horace.

"A mountain journey is perilous for any of the birds, still... Andres might be able to do it."

"Andres?" asked the queen.

"He's a rare tufted condor, the only one of his kind in the core," explained Martha. "His mother determined him to be a worthless runt and chose to feed his brothers instead in the Royal Zoo. I took pity on the poor baby before he starved and brought him into the academy. Tufted condors are extraordinary flyers and make their homes in the high mountains. Andres is our only hope of getting over the peaks of the Griffin Mountains.

Once he gets to the Arudin Forest, he's almost home free. With his superior size and strength, the creatures that give those mountains their namesake will avoid him."

"It's the best we can do for now. We need to make sure that the party made it to Deniva and this radio silence simply won't do."

"Indeed, a helmet is not a body, your majesty," stated Horace. "We know the treachery the Acadians are capable of. I believe they might want us to lose our heads in this matter."

"We must be sure. Also, we need to know what happened to Duke von Angelhardt—he's overdue."

"I'll spare some riders and send them over to his estate," offered Horace. "I'm sure the duke has to get home some time."

"I'll head back over to the academy and prepare Andres for his mission."

"I'll prepare a message right away. Freigraf Irvine, short of the barrier falling, Castle Titan collapsing into the sea, or the Second Coming of Christ, I wish to be alone for a while."

"I understand, your Highness."

Bowing solemnly before the queen, Horace and Martha left the throne room. Her chief advisors were extremely concerned about the manner and disposition of the queen since they had given her the news.

"I didn't want it to come out like that," Martha said regretfully.

"There was no good way to say it," replied Horace. "However, I wouldn't give up hope so quickly."

"Why's that?"

"The jinx, of course; when they found the Rising Moon Helm, I half-expected them to be carrying the Wolf Demon Mail as well."

"Christian's armor? I don't understand."

"You think he would dare stay alive if Cedric had died? He's a smart man and would calculate that risk as too great."

Martha started to laugh.

"Thanks. I needed that. Well let's get old baldy ready."

Standing from her throne, the queen retired to the arched doorway behind, still holding onto the Rising Moon Helmet. Inside the archway was a lift, and a servant rode her up seven levels to her living quarters. Upon her arrival into the parlor area, her two maids bowed.

"I wish to not to be disturbed for the next few hours."

The maids nodded and left the room. Crossing the room to her office, the queen sat and opened her laptop. Reverently setting the helm on her desk, Civilia took a few moments to release her grief.

"It can't be true."

Slamming her firsts in the desk time and time again, the queen buried herself in arm in tears.

"Damn Wilhelm to Hell! He sent Cedric to his death!"

The seething rage of the queen was interrupted by a moment of serenity. Sucking her tears back, Civilia stared at a portrait hanging on the wall in front of her. Cedric stood behind a chair where Cecilia was seated, as the twins posed for a recent picture in their royal outfits. The uncomfortable smiles on their faces, from having to pose for such a portrait, caused the queen to burst out laughing.

"No, I won't accept the fact that my son is dead. Even if he is, I know that the others have made it to safety. Cedric would have made sure of that and no one is better suited to pull that rabble together than Cecilia."

Civilia proceeded to write a coded message.

"It's important we find some way to communicate with them. They need to know that they're not alone."

CASTLE ACADIA

"The Temple will never make an open declaration on who is the
rightful ruler of Central Acadia, for our duty is to the faithful.
As long as the faith continues to be practiced and our coffers
are full we will not interfere with politics."

Donos, First Patriarch of the Temple of the Divine Saints

Raging conflagrations, bloody canals, and ash-covered walkways had
reduced the marvel of architecture, Verian, to shambles. The floating
city on the lake had once drawn the admiration from ally and enemy
alike. Given priority to be saved from the raging fires, the Senate, the
Wizard's Tower, the Temple of the Saints, and Royal Castle were spared
the devastation of the city around them. Pikes with heads lined the entire
outside of the city—the unfortunate product of servants and peasants being
in the wrong place at the wrong time. In the center of the despicable act
was the head of King Stephen, adorned with the traditional jester's hat, a
final mockery the rebels bestowed upon him. Foul stenches rose from the
canals and streets as the pollution of headless bodies dragged by running
horses swept the ground. Cloaked in an aura of darkness, the radiance that
once emanated from Castle Acadia had been snuffed. Unlikely allies of
rebel soldiers and demonkin patrolled the courtyard with uneasiness on
both sides. Lined with loyal supporters of the new regime, Maximilian
basked in his own glory with his new bride. Sharon chose to stand at his
left side. Celius and the Wizards' Guild, nobles, burghers, senators, and
the bourgeois of Central Acadia had already pranced before the throne to
swear their loyalty. Still waiting his turn was Javos Mergovin, the Patriarch
of the Temple of the Divine Saints. The most powerful man in Central
Acadia not only determined the tenets of the religion but also controlled
the Templar Army and Saints. Short and plump, Javos barely squeezed

himself into his expensive silk garments. White hair and beard trimmed to perfection, the Patriarch swung incense in front of him.

"Patriarch Javos, I bid you welcome," announced Luminas.

"The Temple of the Divine Saints has always appeared before the throne of the new ruler to test his fervor before the faithful," explained Javos.

"I am prepared to submit myself to your judgment."

Luminas and his wife sunk to their knees at the bottom of the steps. Javos closed his eyes and murmured a prayer under his breath.

"Maximilian Luminas, do you swear fealty to the Temple of the Divine Saints, uphold the freedom of the faithful, and agree to destroy all corrupting cult influences?"

"I so swear."

"Then let the Temple bless you as King of Central Acadia and let all bear witness to your union with Sharon Fenidor."

Walking around the two royals, Javos spread his incense. Task completed, the Patriarch bent down and laid his hands upon Luminas' head. As he got close to Luminas, the vampire whispered to him. "I hope it wasn't too expensive."

"I find the herd is easily prodded to the desired field. The coin was not as necessary as I thought."

"A bit of good luck at last."

Crown presented to him on a purple velvet pillow, the pudgy priest placed it on the vampire's head.

"The old king is dead. Long live the king!"

Kneeling before their rising rulers, everyone in the room shouted repeatedly, "Long live the king!" A dark smile crept across Sharon's face as she reveled in the attention she felt she had so earned. Just as he predicted, Jonas and the Saints returned to the traditional position of guarding the king.

"Now that we are done with the formalities, what's our situation?" asked Luminas.

"Cassandra and her traitorous friends apparently escaped the castle by making their way into the crypt," explained Jonas. "My men tried to open the door but failed."

"My guild originally placed the barrier on top of the crypt," said Cerwin. "The seal could only be broken by one of royal blood. Our members have determined elf runes were used on the other side, but we have no craft to break through."

"It would be wonderful if Jacob and his undead legions took care of them for us," Sharon said hopefully.

"Not the Royals; it can't be that easy," said Luminas. "They must have had a definite plan when they went into the crypt. We have to assume Cassandra is lost to us, and the Alliance and our traitorous cousins recognize her as Queen of Central Acadia. While this barrier is in place, she can make no moves against us. What about the loyalty of our citizens?"

"We estimate three-fifths of Verian either evacuated the city before our attack started or left with the combined Alliance forces," said Celius. "Even the nobles who originally supported our cause have begun to get cold feet. Norville Warrington, some senators, and the families of House Huntington and House Reed have fled to the countryside. Norville believes we shouldn't have killed King Stephen and calls the coup a massacre."

"The senators who have sworn allegiance to us shall be our puppet government. All of Warrington's assets are ours already, so we don't need him or the others," proclaimed Luminas. "The middle class money that we lost in the initial evacuation concerns me more, and we may have to tighten the belt on some spending. What about the countless number of Nephilim and Demonkin who inhabit our city?"

"The way I see it, we saved ourselves some money," Sharon said in jest. "Basarabas is dead and Abaddon is gone. Therefore we don't have to spend a dime on what's left. I say we dismiss the rest of this rabble and rid ourselves of their taint."

"Is that so?" shouted Virgus as he entered the room flanked by Valadrim and the remaining Nephilim.

"Virgus, we thought you fled," surmised Luminas.

"To where, Luminas? I'm involved just as deep in this coup as you are. There is no sanctuary anywhere for the murderers of King Stephen now. This is truly the only place in the world where we are safe."

"I guess that's refreshing to hear, since we owe our protection to you," said a condescending Sharon.

"What are you here for anyway, scientist?" demanded Jonas. "Have you come to swear your loyalty to your king?"

"I'm here to remind you that the agreement between our parties still stands. We don't have any intention of going anywhere."

"Our agreement was with Abaddon and Basarabas; both of them are dead," proclaimed Luminas. "We answer to no one now."

"You will answer to me!" shouted the haunting voice of Abaddon.

Swarming from the floor, a mass of ethereal locusts began to morph into a definite shape. When the insects dispersed, the translucent body of Abaddon stood before the king's court garbed in black robes. All that remained of his wings were stubs. The dark angel's soul seemed to flow into and out of reality; at times his face would almost be flesh but it would quickly rot away and return to the ghost form.

"Abaddon?" asked a confounded Luminas. "This can't be possible!"

"Your eyes do not deceive you," corrected Abaddon. "I have returned."

"What happened to your body?" queried Sharon.

"Cedric Rhone destroyed my physical body, yet he lacked the abilities to bind my eternal soul. Thus I can continue to remain in this world, but only in this weak phantasm form."

The haunting admission of their fallen leader sent chills down the spine of every man and woman in the throne room. Were they truly spared the wrath of *La Morte Angelus*? A bloody helmet would no longer alleviate their fears. If a fallen angel could not defeat the Titan prince in battle, then the legends must be true. Every eye turned to the shadows and every sound made them jump out of their skin.

"How could he have survived that battle?" screamed Jonas. "We found his helmet and there was blood everywhere."

"I didn't say that he survived our battle! The evidence you found at the entrance to the crypt was my handiwork. His final attack could only have been released if he was at the brink of death. Cedric maintained his nobility and chivalry to the end; he gave his life so the others could escape."

"Cedric would give anything for Cassandra," offered Sharon. "He certainly put her beyond our reach now."

"We can't expect Amuro and the others to do something foolish and have the queen make public appearances," determined Virgus. "Instead they'll seek to increase their strength before Cassandra is reintroduced to the world."

"Millennia of planning done in by that damn boy!" exclaimed Abaddon. "Did you secure Princess Marie at least?"

"She's locked in the Wizard's Tower for now," answered Sharon.

"I sensed some abilities within her. Celius, did she receive any training in magic?"

"Since she's a pureblood human, there was no ability to use magic in her. However, purebloods can still use mana, so the Guild had educated her as a Sage."

"We don't need a Healer, they cannot unleash enough power."

A Lich of the Demonkin stepped forward. To the disgust of everyone in the room, the foul wizard took a few moments to adjust his jaw for speech.

"If I may, my lord, the Sage class has the ability to use conjuration magic. If we could procure a certain artifact, then I believe the princess would learn advance spells in that art."

"What do you need?"

"The Wizards' Guild must give us permission to use the Libro Mortuorum."

The thought of that book being unleashed haunted Celius to his core. The guild master knew that evil tome festers the mind and soul of its user to its core. Had he truly fallen so far as to willingly corrupt the young princess?

"That book has been sealed in the deepest vaults of our tower for centuries. It has been entrusted to us so we may keep it out of sight."

"The time for precaution is over, Celius!" ordered Abaddon. "You will surrender that book to me when I require it."

Begging Luminas with his eyes for help, the master wizard sought any means of not turning the book over. Overcome with rage at Abaddon's arrogance, the vampire sought to put the entity responsible for Cassandra's escape in his place.

"Abaddon, the last time I checked, I was wearing the crown of Central Acadia. What gives you the right to order me and my people?"

"The Nephilim and Demonkin still answer my beck and call. We outnumber your measly forces. If you wish the peace to be maintained, King Luminas, I suggest that we remain united against our common foe."

"You're the one that drove the ire of the Titan prince upon us with your designs on Princess Cassandra. They would have left us alone if you didn't take her."

"I didn't stand idly by while my subordinates recklessly murdered the one person we needed alive."

Tensions rose as Luminas stared Abaddon down but the fallen angel wouldn't give an inch. Though he didn't have a body, Abaddon still possessed a sense of power that terrified everyone else in the room.

"We're in this together, vampire! I am the one who put that crown on your head. You owe me everything and no one I work with is irreplaceable. My *prince* demands Cassandra and I will use any means necessary to further that goal."

Luminas said nothing but finally held his head in resigned defeat. He knew even in that form, he hadn't the power to challenge Abaddon. The vampire would dare not risk the full wrath of the other kingdoms if he broke his alliance with Abaddon.

"There is a little issue I need to have resolved, King Luminas," requested Virgus. "I have some work that needs to be done and I was wondering if you wouldn't mind giving me a few rooms."

"What do you expect of me?"

"Well, the dungeon that houses the crypt is off limits but the basement in the west wing would suit my needs."

"I guess we don't have a choice. What would you need such a space for?"

"I'm afraid that's a trade secret. I've had many difficulties with my inventions becoming subject to government control in the past. I didn't even realize the Titans were watching me until it was too late."

"I would greatly appreciate this gesture of good will on your part," teased Abaddon.

"Don't we already have enough of your foul presence in this castle?" asked Sharon.

"A small band of well-trained warriors were able to overcome both of our armies; I believe it's time we went back to the drawing board."

"I will grant you your space as a gesture of good will, but you'd better not do anything to threaten the safety of the people living here."

"Excellent. You needn't worry; I don't bother to experiment on humans anymore, King Luminas. I found it much easier to tamper at the genetic level."

Uneasy glances aside, Abaddon decided that he'd had enough for the rotation and his visit served its purpose. He nodded towards Valadrim who quickly turned with his soldiers. With the contingent following behind him, the Acadians who had been so jubilant when the ceremony began were now beside themselves with fear.

"This deal just keeps getting worse," observed Luminas. "Now, before we end this session, does anyone have any business before the king?"

A smile finally crept onto Sharon's face again. Luminas looked at her and clearly saw her twisted mind had something special in store for the court. Luminas resigned to giving her whatever she desired at that point.

"My husband, we have one last matter to deal with concerning the prior regime."

"You may do as you wish, Sharon."

Walking behind the throne room steps, Sharon grabbed the leash of a chained and naked Penelope. The late king's second wife fought kicking and screaming as she was dragged by the she-elf to the center of the room.

"Sharon, please let me go! I have a daughter just like you! I don't care about the damn throne—I just want my daughter back!"

"Your father has cast his lot with Warrington and the others. We're making examples of all those who defy the crown."

"I never moved against you. Please, you can't do this. Just give me my daughter!"

"You not a queen anymore, Penelope, you're just a pathetic, little broken doll who has outlived its purpose. We're taking out all the trash!"

Summoning Jonas to her side, Penelope turned her head in absolute fear of the man once sworn to protect her. For revolutions, Penelope had lied to herself that his reputation couldn't be true, but in that moment all of her fears were realized.

"Jonas, I believe you were never properly rewarded for your loyalty in these matters," congratulated Sharon as she handed the chain to Jonas. "She's yours to do with as you please."

"So I get full carte blanche?"

"Absolutely."

A sick smile crossed Jonas's face. One of the Six Swords, Sir Gavin, stepped forward. Gavin's reputation was well known among the Saints as being the most devoted to the Temple. Known for backing down from Jonas when a confrontation presented itself, Gavin did nothing even though he was disgusted at Stephen's murder.

"My liege, she was the Queen of Central Acadia. You cannot subject her to the treatment of a common slave."

"You are not kept in our service for your counsel, Sir Gavin," replied Luminas. "Your request is noted and denied."

"My liege, this is not the action that should take place on a rotation when we crown a king."

"You've got a problem with me, mister?" admonished Jonas.

Pleas falling on deaf ears, Penelope turned to Gavin for help. Not wanting to challenge Jonas, Gavin returned to his place. Another one of the Saints, Sir Roland, walked over to him and put a comforting hand on his shoulder. Jonas lifted the panicked former queen from the ground.

"We're going to have some fun, little girl. I just hope you're a screamer—it makes everything taste better."

Jonas threw the queen over his shoulder and walked out of the room. In the corridors, Abaddon was gliding next to Virgus and the other Nephilim commanders.

"I have a feeling they weren't too happy with our proposals," said Virgus. "Of course, there were other methods of persuasion at our disposal."

"We have no choice but to lie with them for now," said Abaddon. "We can't afford any more deaths."

"The conditions do call for us to be good neighbors."

The two laughed, but Valadrim walked uneasy. Revenge was burning in his mind for the death of his leader and friend, Basarabas.

"Lord Abaddon, what are your orders?"

"First, I have to find Krystos. There were some details that he left out when I asked him for his report. So, I am going to pay Lady Nadia a visit. If anyone knows his whereabouts, it's her."

"Do you suspect Lord Krystos?"

"Let's just say that someone taught that boy how to fight like an angel. My first suspicions run to the traitor that once served as a War Master of the Powers Choir. I recognized that style of combat."

"As you wish."

"Anything else?" asked Virgus.

"We need to ascertain some information about Princess Marie. If I am to assume physical form once more, I am going to need a catalyst. While in this form, I am subject to binding spells."

"Well, I guess that just about does it."

"You just pull your end of the bargain."

"If my place is not with you, where is it, my lord?"

Abaddon nodded and turned back to Valadrim.

"Send out your scouts; use any means at your disposal to find out where Cassandra is or if there are any enemies we haven't accounted for."

"As you wish, my lord."

Royal Castle, Deniva

"Jonathan, I am trusting you with a great secret, for I fear
for the life of King Stephen Acadia and the reign of the true
Acadian Kings. In Deniva, I have been secretly forging the
Chivalric Order of the Lion to replace the false Temple and
their Templar guardians. If anything should happen to me, I
ask you to use my journal and continue my work to appoint
the right young men to train in the Margrave. When the time
is right, these knights will form the true protectors of the
crown, and the stranglehold of the Temple on the throne will be
broken."

Hector Reed to Walker before the Battle of the Ruins of Istle Hill

Attended to by a bevy of servants, Cassandra was dressed in a gown
quickly prepared for the occasion. Though she had to sign away the
rights to every future gown she was going to wear, the young queen knew it
was worth it when she saw the final product. The gown was made of black
silk with a hoop design around the waist. Her shoulders and neck were
exposed. Around her shoulders was placed a white and blue cape marked
with lions and white rabbit fur held in place by a white and blue sash
marked with a lion. Imagining in her mind that Felicia was still dutifully
attending her brought some comfort to Cassie. Willpower alone held back
her tears and the thought of her handmaiden scolding her for ruining her
makeup. Rapping on the outer door caused one of the servants to answer
and announce Walker's presence before the queen. The Lord Protector had
only intended to borrow a uniform from the Order of the Lions barracks,
but apparently his father had left a last gift for him. His new uniform
consisted of a white military jacket with a blue lion insignia on the right

side of the breast over a white shirt and white coif. His pants were navy blue, his boots black, and the long navy cloak on his back was attached by a gold chain with a lion's head medallion hanging down. Walker clicked his heels together and bowed fully before the queen.

"Your Highness."

"Yes, Walker."

Getting the first look at his queen, the Lord Knight was awestruck. Walker hadn't seen Cassie in this light since he was first assigned to her as a bodyguard. He swore a vow then that he would allow no man to ruin the princess until they had first bested him in combat. His pledge would only last two short revolutions when Cedric Rhone unhorsed him at the Knights tournament on Cassandra's Quize. Now Cedric was gone and the duty of the queen's protector had fallen on his shoulders again. The only question left in his heart was whether this was Cassandra's true calling, or if she was only the illusion of an elegant queen.

"The garrison has prepared the memorial for your father. It would be a great honor if you would join us in celebrating a man to whom we owe so much."

"Thank you for your kind words, Walker. I will certainly attend. I must compliment you on your promotion. Your uniform is that of a true Lord Knight Commander of Central Acadia."

"Thank you, your Highness. I have something from your father that now belongs to you."

Moving his hands from his back to the front, Walker revealed a large black box. Slowly the knight opened the box revealing a gold crown with a large garnet stone in the center of it surrounded by twelve diamonds, representing the twelve districts of Central Acadia. It rested on a black velvet pad with a white silk veil attached to the back of the crown. Walker's heart broke when he saw the expression change on Cassandra's face. She lost it at that point and started to cry.

"King Stephen gave me orders to always protect this. Your father had it made for you; he feared that Marie might not be able to handle such responsibility if anything happened to him. He always knew that Central Acadia needed you."

Willing herself to stop crying, Cassandra permitted the servants to reapply her makeup. Walker handed the crown to another servant and they placed it delicately upon her head. The servants took the time to properly set her hair within the crown and drape the veil along the back of her head. When they finished, Walker knelt once again and muttered the ancient blessing of his country.

"Le Roi est mort, vive le Reine."

Rising to his feet, Walker took Cassandra's hand as she stepped off her pedestal. Grabbing the edge of her gown to walk correctly on her heels, Walker took her left elbow. The queen made him stop near the door and take Cedric's neatly folded scarlet rider cloak. Putting her right hand to it gently, she closed her eyes for a moment before continuing on their way. Apartments departed, the two walked down a set of ivory stairs within the ornate halls of Deniva Castle. The spiral atrium that was part of the golden spire towered into the sky as far as the eyes could see. Art decos and tapestries covered the spire on the inner walls.

Passing through the castle, they made their way outside to the Acadian barracks. The Acadian flag flew at half-mast and the whole garrison dressed in full regalia presented themselves with Robespierre standing out in front. Delighted to see all of her comrades, Cassandra noticed each of them dressed as if it was a royal ball. Hippolyte was tugging uncomfortably at her brown dress but Minerva beamed proudly in her own. Dressed in a rose gown, Saria was singing another elf lamentation for Stephen. Cecilia tapped the priest standing next to her to move forward. Father Michael Giovanello, originally of Napolitan, was of average height and thin build. Bishop Arthur had reassigned the fiery preacher when the Temple in Napolitan ordered him arrested for speaking out against their heresy. He wore the green robes of a priest, had short brown hair, brown eyes, and glasses. Flabbergasted, the queen witnessed Pasha Selim and his honor guard in attendance at the ceremony. Upon her arrival, everyone present snapped to attention and bowed. Cassandra was speechless at their attention and devotion to her.

"I know that you follow the Elf Traditions of the Divine Worship of the Father, your Highness, but like your Shield Master, many members of the Order of the Lion are members of the Catholic Christian Faith," explained Robespierre. "Thus I requested that Father Michael Giovanello prepare a prayer that will respect both of our faiths."

"Thank you."

Opening the scriptures, the priest read aloud.

"The Lord is my shepherd; there is nothing I shall want. In green pastures you let me graze; to safe waters you lead me; you restore my strength. You guide me along the right path for the sake of your name. Even when I walk through the valley of the shadow of death I fear no harm for you are at my side; your rod and staff give me courage. You set a table before me as my enemies watch; You anoint my head with oil; my cup overflows. Only goodness and love will pursue me all the days of my life; I will dwell in the house of the Lord for years to come."

Sharp sounds of every knight of the lion drawing their swords in final salute echoed through Deniva. Each of them knelt in succession and put the tip of their sword into the ground.

"Stephen Acadia, the first of his name, known forever in the hearts of the true Acadians as the King of Justice," began Walker, "we salute your noble spirit, for you continued to fight against the rebels until the moment of your death. Every knight stands ready today to give our lives and sacred honor for the protection of Queen Cassandra Acadia and the dear land that we love. Le Roi est mort, vive le Reine."

The knights and the royals joined the chorus of "Vive le Reine." Two knights stood, walked over to the flag and took it down. Joining them, four more knights carefully folded the flag over eight times to symbolize Stephen's heroic death. They handed it to Robespierre, and the captain approached the queen.

"There are many Acadians that owe everything to your father's actions. He tried to bring justice and pride to a nation that never looked past its own sycophants. The members of this order dedicated our lives for the time that we would replace the false Templar Guards that ultimately betrayed him. While I know that there is no comfort that we can offer for the loss of your father, I pray this symbolizes our devotion and love for you, my queen."

Presenting the flag to his queen, Cassandra held back her tears as she took it from the order.

"Lord Knight, what is your name?"

"Jean-Luc Robespierre."

"Your sword, please."

Robespierre drew the weapon and handed it hilt first to Cassandra. Kneeling before her, the queen tapped him on both shoulders with the sword.

"Jean-Luc Robespierre, forgive my inability to confer upon you a proper landed title befitting your new rank, but mark my words that all of Count Luminas' lands shall pass to you upon our reconquest of Verian."

A smile crept across Cecilia's face at the thought of mentioning victory over their enemies. She was beginning to understand what her brother saw in this girl.

"I knight thee, Lord Captain of the Order of the Lion, and Commander of the Garrison."

"I will serve you faithfully, your Highness."

"Rise!"

Returning his sword to him, Cassandra kissed him on the cheek, which caused the young captain to blush.

"With your permission, your Highness."

"Robespierre, thank you for all of this. I'll never forget it."

"Thank you, your Highness." Robespierre turned to his men. "Dismissed!"

The knights returned to the barracks. From one event to the next, the royals prepared for their audience before Margrave Dennis de-Milly. As Ethan led them to the audience chamber, the tribal girls were once again overwhelmed by the statues and fine art. In the back of her mind, Minerva started to wonder if all of the best art in the world was locked up in these castles. Amuro and Christian were sharing a laugh over one of the paintings. It appeared to show Sultan Ahmed Khan in a heroic charge on Eagle's Gate.

"A bit of a revisionist history?" teased Amuro.

"If history serves me correctly, Sultan Khan was commanding the battle from the safety of the Palacio Magnifico Dining Room," explained Christian.

"Give us a break; we have to maintain some semblance of neutrality. Therefore we have to take art decos provided by the Empire as well as the Alliance. I'll head inside and see if Dad is ready for you yet."

Ethan walked through the door and it was closed behind him. Given a moment, Cassandra approached Cecilia.

"Cecilia, I thought it was appropriate to give this back to you."

Cassandra extended Cedric's cloak to Cecilia. After a few moments of awkward silence, Cecilia grabbed Cassandra around both wrists and pushed the cloak back towards her with a smile.

"My brother gave that cloak to you, Cassandra. It wouldn't be appropriate for anyone to take it back except for him."

Staring into the Vanadis' eyes, the queen wouldn't believe it, but his twin sister truly believed Cedric was alive. Overcome with hope, Cassandra jumped into Cecilia's arms catching her off guard. Embracing her tightly, the Titan princess endured the awkward situation before silently walking away. Three deep breaths composed Cassie once more as she paced back and forth.

"Don't tell me you're nervous, your Highness," teased Cagius.

"A few more minutes and the butterflies in my stomach will turn into bats."

"Nothing to worry about, it's just the most important thing you've ever done in your entire life."

Cassandra started to laugh at the ridiculousness of Cagius' statement. It drew a smile from the daunting cavalier and everyone else in the room.

"Thanks, Cagius."

"Making others laugh is one of my many secret techniques! You're going to do great!"

Unnerved by the opening of the throne room door, Ethan's smiling face reassured the royals. Escorting them forward, Cassandra took the lead flanked by Walker and Robespierre. Amuro walked behind them, while the others took their place among the court. The Margrave's throne room was filled with over two hundred nobles, burghers, and merchants. Parading down a red carpet, the queen approached three ivory pedestals and two golden thrones. Seated on the right was the Margrave Dennis himself. Despite his age, Dennis maintained a well-trimmed mustache and gray hair, with his blue eyes focused on the approaching dignitary. Dressed lavishly and seated next to him was his pregnant wife Henrietta. The shapely young woman had long red hair and blue eyes. In contrast to the kings and queens, the margrave and his wife wore silver circlets on their heads. The chamberlain hit his staff to the floor twice and spoke.

"Margrave Dennis de-Milly, Margravine Henrietta, may I present her Highness Queen Cassandra Acadia of Central Acadia, Steward of the Western Alliance of Kingdoms, and Princess Marshal Amuro Jenitzen of Evengard."

Rising from his throne, Dennis bowed before the queen. The court followed suit, but due to her pregnancy Henrietta remained seated.

"Margrave Dennis de-Milly, I regret that much has been asked of you in these difficult times," announced Cassandra. "However, I must beseech you to grant us sanctuary in this our hour of need, though I fear that it will put great strain on the relationship you keep with the Empire."

"Everything your father ever spoke about you was true," said a welcoming Dennis. "It's quite refreshing to hear a real royal address placed in such a refined and elegant way. Sultan Khan barely manages a wave to me anymore. I have offered my margrave to you and extended the graciousness of our hospitality. As for Sultan Khan, you need not worry. Pasha Selim of the Imperial Garrison has informed him of the situation. They understand that you are my guests and I've made the appropriate bribes to make sure that they understand. I feel nothing but contempt for what has happened to my friend King Stephen, and it would be my pleasure to have you as my guest to insult the vampire who stole his throne."

"I thank you."

"I rarely get the pleasure of entertaining a queen, so please indulge me. The servants have prepared a royal meal to welcome you here to Deniva. You'll find some of our favorite local dishes being served. I have no doubt you will enjoy it."

"We thank you. I know my father sent his felicitations but I too wanted to congratulate you on your recent wedding."

"Yes. I loved my wife very much, but I was still a man with needs when she died."

"I was honored to become to the wife of the margrave, and I have great hopes for the child that now kicks in my womb," said Henrietta.

"Can you believe it? I already have thirteen children and ten grandchildren with four more on the way. I love them all—ministers, merchants, lawyers, doctors, and a knight trained in the ways of the Titans, the finest soldiers in the world. I enjoy a good war story. I hope to hear them over dinner. We'll speak then."

Nodding her head, Cassandra made a swift exit. Her escorts were more than happy to join her amidst the incredulous and apprehensive stares of the court. Ethan led them out and the doors closed behind them.

"I'm glad that's over," announced a relieved Cassandra.

"Why, that performance was fantastic," Amuro said encouragingly. "I guess all of those protocol lessons you complained about paid off."

"Worthy of the position of the Queen of Central Acadia!" chimed Walker.

"Well, at least that means we won't have to pack up and head into the woods," teased Colin.

"Too bad!" pouted Hippolyte.

Angry stares focused on the Wolf Tribe Chief, but the state of her younger sister seemed to burn the hardest. Minerva was obviously looking forward to some more pampering.

"It was just a joke, sis."

"Speaking of jokes, Ethan, what did your father do?" asked Valentine. "Henrietta can't have seen more than sixteen revolutions. You're almost twice her age!"

Ethan had a sour look on his face when Valentine mentioned that.

"My father loved my mother very much and when she died he locked himself in his room for a lunar cycle. Henrietta was a young courtier and took pity on him. She took care of him in that time and my father showered her with love in response. I just want my dad to be happy."

"I'm not judging him, Ethan. I'm just impressed at the old man. He did me one better."

"Come on, I have something special for your troubles," retorted Ethan, eager to change the subject.

Following Ethan into a study off the main hallway, everyone took a seat in the comfortable chairs of the library. The Denivan went to a liquor cabinet above a wet bar and took out a well-aged bottle of Acadian Whiskey. A servant entered the room with a small glass for everyone on a silver tray, including Joshua and Minerva.

"We've got a few cases of the one-hundred-twenty revolution aged whiskeys in the castle. I thought since that this was a special occasion, we could open one."

Snickering to himself, Christian wondered how they could drink such a fine whiskey without Cedric. Ethan poured and the servant walked over to each of the royals. When the servant reached Cassandra she politely refused.

"Your Highness, is there something wrong?"

"I'm embarrassed to say this, but I get sick on whiskey."

Cassandra's confession was a bit of a surprise. They thought she only took martinis at events to appear sophisticated but now found out it wasn't simply a rouse. The stares caused Cassandra to blush a little and Cecilia murmured something about being a "light-weight" under her breath. Joshua, however, decided to take the initiative.

"Lord Ethan, would you happen to have any gin in that bar over there?"

"Of course, bottom shelf."

The rest of the room watched in awe as Joshua put ice in a stem glass along with cold water. Taking out a cocktail shaker, Joshua tossed in a few ice cubes and vermouth. Discarding the vermouth down the sink, he poured gin in, and shook it up. Ice and water dumped, Joshua strained the martini into the glass. Lastly, he garnished it with a single olive.

"What? I worked at the smith in the day and the castle bar in the evening. Mom didn't want me working royal ceremonies, however, because of the suspicion it would raise."

Joshua brought the drink over to Cassandra.

"Why, thank you, Joshua."

She gave him a peck on the cheek causing the second young man to blush in her presence this evening.

Ethan cleared his throat.

"I would offer this toast to Prince Cedric Rhone, *La Morte Angelus*, wherever he is, but I damn well know that he's raising hell there. In the traditions of Titanus, to the heroes of the past and the soldiers of the future, God bless the warriors because sure as hell no one else will."

Everyone laughed and raised their glasses with cheers of "to Cedric." Upon drinking, Hippolyte and Minerva's faces turned immediately. Joshua started to choke. Amuro and Malcolm had a sour look on their face, but Cecilia put hers down in one gulp. Not standing on ceremony, she took the glass Cassandra initially refused.

"How can you drink that stuff?" asked Hippolyte.

"My throat's burning," commented Minerva.

"It's an acquired taste," boasted Cecilia.

Everyone seemed to finally be relaxing for a moment in the company of one another. However, Valentine was still working at full speed and took Ethan's relaxation as an opportunity to get some information.

"When was the last time the Empire took up shop here in Deniva?"

"Not recently, probably almost two revolutions ago. The Sultan prefers to remain in Palacio Magnifico and send his envoys out here to Deniva. I doubt Khan will show his face now that you're here."

"Is your father certain the guarantee of neutrality will hold?"

"Sultan Khan has faults, but he wouldn't dare break the treaty. Nothing is absolutely sure, but the Empire can't afford to lose us. My dad is personally responsible for thirty-five percent of imperial revenues. How could he replace that?"

Valentine looked to Christian who swirled his glass with unease. The Napolitan agent smiled as he recognized his Titan counterpart was deeply concerned about Ethan's words. Catching the time, Ethan knew it was time to leave.

"Dinner will be soon; I ask you to be prompt because I'm certain there will be a soufflé and that simply can't wait. I have some inspections to make before dinner, if you would excuse me. If you guys are going to talk behind our backs, we're not offended. This room is soundproof so scream your heads off."

Ethan left the warriors to their own devices. As he left, Christian closed the door for some privacy.

"Was there anything on the message, Cecilia?"

"My mother had personal messages addressed to me that I prefer not to discuss with anyone else at this time. The queen was quick with her message to Deniva so that our distress call would be received and they were well prepared."

"Is there any way we can send a message?" asked Valentine.

"I tried every frequency and code; it's no use." Cecilia shook her head. "That barrier is not only messing up our transportation but our communications as well. We're deaf to the Kingdoms."

"What about the Griffin Mountains?" offered Cagius. "Can we cross over them?"

"There's no passable mountain path unobstructed by the barrier," Christian said. "Even if we attempted to traverse the mountains via the Arudin Forest, we'd be writing our own epitaphs."

"Then I guess we are trapped," surmised Amuro. "We dare not try to enter the Empire—try to take over a port, and sail around."

"I wouldn't recommend it," Valentine said. "What about Edenia, Christian? Don't the Titans have friends there?"

"There is no navigable port resting on the borders of Edenia. That is part of the reason the Empire was able to conquer them so easily."

"It seems for now that we're going to have to accept this Denivan Exile," Cassandra said regretably. "Let us hope that their hospitality does not dry up quickly."

"That's the problem with merchants, my lady—their only love is the coin," stated Valentine. "Pray that the coffers of Dennis do not dry up so easily."

"What is your proposal, Valentine?"

"It is imperative we get better intelligence on our situation."

"The path back to Acadia is sealed," interrupted Cagius.

"Acadia is a problem of secondary concern. We need to ask some important questions of Dennis tonight. Am I right, Christian?"

"Yes. I think I understand what you're getting at."

"I didn't expect you to disappoint me."

"I guess we should make our grand entrance for dinner," observed Cecilia as she stared at the clock. "It would be rude to allow Prince Ethan to keep making excuses for us."

"Of course, you don't want to make Ethan look bad," teased Amuro.

"I have no ulterior motives, Amuro!"

"Down, girl! I didn't mean anything by that."

Everyone finished their drinks and placed their glasses by the bar. As they left the room, the royals formed a shield around Cassandra. The new queen was getting irritated at the overprotective behavior. Meanwhile, Minerva tugged on Walker's cape.

"Walker, what is in a soufflé anyway?"

"There are many ways that it can be prepared, however, since her Highness is the guest of honor tonight, my guess is chocolate and eggs."

Minerva gagged a little. Walker smiled.

"Trust me, just taste it! You'll love it."

Nadia's Cottage

"No, I won't kill you. I can't help but pity you as you are now,
a beautiful creature torn between Heaven and Hell. I pardon
you, and if you wish I will never stop trying until I find a way
to bring you into the Promised Land."

Duke Wilhelm to Nadia upon her defeat

Nadia was sitting at her table studying some books. She kept turning
her attention from one book to another as if she was cross-referencing
some factors. Suddenly startled, the beautiful demoness could hear the
gargoyle on one of her banners screaming. Moving her hands, the sorceress
expertly placed all of the books back on their respective shelves. Nadia
took a few moments to straighten up her appearance, but chose not to
appear in her true form. Rather than use the front door, Abaddon appeared
through a portal in his ethereal form. Stunned at his defeat at Cedric's
hands, Nadia had to use every ounce of self-control to stop from beaming
with pride.

"You know it's not appropriate just to pop in unannounced in a lady's
quarters. What if I were dressing?"

"I suspect you have other means of my detection. No one possessing
your powers would ever remain this far out in the wilderness without some
means of protection."

Savoring Nadia's appearance in her human form, Abaddon took the
time to decide whether he preferred this illusion or her true form.

"So this is the form you choose when you are among the humans?"

The demoness did a quick pirouette so that Abaddon could take a good
look at her. She knew it was the best means of keeping the jealous fallen
angel off of his game.

"What do you think?"

"I can see that it doesn't matter which form you chose to take. I didn't think it was possible for a human woman to be so beautiful."

"Well, just remember that you're free to look at the goods, but you can't touch. For a proud individual like you, it must hurt to know that you'll never have me."

Seething in anger at her taunts, Abaddon was overrun with jealously at the mere thought of Krystos holding this beautiful prize in his arms.

"Did you lose weight?" asked Nadia.

"This is the unfortunate consequence of my recent encounter with a certain Titan Prince."

"Prince Rhone did this to you?"

"You should see what I did to him!"

Abaddon was brazen with his boasting. Nadia knew that Cedric could never have survived the encounter with Abaddon no matter what Wilhelm believed. She knew better than to dare show any signs of weakness concerning Cedric in front of the dark angel. Reassured that her daughter was safe made his sacrifice worth it.

"He is dead then."

"Yes, it took everything I had. A Divikin should never have been able to push their body to the limits that this one did. I was sure I had killed him at least three times but he still managed to destroy my body."

"What of this princess that you were after?"

"That girl is safe for now, but won't be for long."

"Why did you come here?"

"I need you to summon Krystos for me. I demand his presence."

"Why?"

"You need not give him a reason. I expect him to contact me when beckoned. Do you know his whereabouts?"

"Have you forgotten the task you assigned him? He is attempting to kill Duke Wilhelm von Angelhardt. However, the Duke is well protected."

"I see. Will you relay my message to him?"

"Of course, my lord."

Preparing to leave, Abaddon stopped for a moment and stared carefully at Nadia. Focusing in particular at her face, eyes, and nose, an impossible thought filled his mind.

"It was the oddest thing that happened to me. When I was in the Royal Castle, I managed to have Princess Cassandra as a prisoner for some time."

"Yet you didn't manage to hold her. I'm sure my father will be very disappointed with you. Did you tell me this so I could soften the blow?"

"It was so strange how much she reminded me of you."

"In what ways?" said Nadia, flattered.

"Though your eyes are not the same color, the shape is indistinguishable; you both have the same figures, same temperament, and based on my studies, I have no doubt her magical abilities were equally impressive."

"Now you're trying to charm me by comparing me to a royal princess. It's no use, Lord Abaddon, my heart has already been won."

"I think you need a little reminder of what you really are, my lady."

As Abaddon's eyes glowed, Nadia felt a fog coming over her mind very quickly and soon she had her head bowed in submission towards the Dark Angel. Blankly, the demoness would obey any request the dark angel made of her. However, Abaddon canceled the spell and Nadia snapped out of her trance.

"You needn't worry, my lady, I was under orders from your father to simply give you this reminder. He fears that you have spent so much time in the temporal realm that you have forgotten your true home is Hell. I could control you so easily and take you back to him, but I would gladly deny that order even if it would mean an eternity of punishment. Who is the one that is going to protect you in the end? We can't control Krystos because he's not one of us; you, my Lady, belong with your own kind."

"Leave my home! I will not be a toy to sate your perverted desires!"

"Chose me, Nadia! I serve your father, but I have never asked anything of him. He intends for me to assume his mantle as the dark sefiroth of pride when he ascends to the Throne. Once I hold that office, the 'Prince' can deny me nothing. You don't have to return to Hell if you don't want to—I'll prepare a place for you here. I just ask that you return the love that I have for you."

"Krystos made me the same offer, while you continued to simply serve as my father's lapdog. Do you remember what we did to the last daughter that my father spawned? She was a rebel who tried everything to escape her place in Hell. We brainwashed and tortured that girl to give into the same despair we all suffered. When we broke her, she had more in common with the animalistic lost souls than a true princess of Hell. Yet, I would never have believed an angel would be brave enough to come into the deepest circle after her. The responsibility for breaking her and bringing her home was mine. I failed my father—there's no place for me at his side now. Krystos is the only one fool enough to defy him now."

The news sickened Abaddon. He cursed himself for his inaction during this time and failing to see what the demoness was looking for. His anger towards Krystos grew and he once again swore vengeance when all was over.

"Just remember, when our hour of glory comes, would you rather be a pawn or a noble?"

"I've made peace with my choices. Good luck with your search for the princess."

"Would you do one last thing for me?"

"That depends on the favor."

"Don't bother to transform into your succubus form in front of me anymore, I find this much more pleasing."

"That's one favor I'll be happy to comply with; the horns really hurt when I pop them out."

"Farewell, my dear."

Abaddon opened a portal and left. Breaking down, Nadia crumpled herself into the corner of the room. Crying and burying her hands in her face, she muttered prayer after prayer.

"I'm not one of them. I left that life behind!"

After a good cry, she calmed herself down.

"It's strange that I hadn't thought about poor Eva until just now. Maybe I deceived myself when I observed Cedric Rhone. A warrior with the unbridled bravery of Teman and the unconditional compassion of Krystos was the only one who could keep my daughter safe. There has to be something I can do to repay that."

Driven by her courage, Nadia went back to work.

Royal Castle, Deniva

"The beauty of the guarantee of neutrality for Deniva has been that I've been allowed quite a bit of discretion in political matters. In some ways, I am the most powerful man in the world because I am the only man with influence in the East and West. However, if I were to abuse or flaunt such a power, I wouldn't be Margrave for too long. That being said, I will continue to do in my heart what I believe is right, even if it acts against the interests of one of the parties."

Margrave Dennis de-Milly

Dennis was sitting at the head of a long table that featured all of the exiles from the west. Henrietta was at the opposite end. Ethan and Selim sat at the table along with other courtiers of Deniva. Already finished with their meals, the only food that remained on the table belonged to Minerva. The young wolf girl was eagerly helping herself to another portion of her new favorite dessert, chocolate soufflé. The Alliance members did not take many after-dinner libations due to the presence of the Imperial Turk and the fear of any slight. It was important in everyone's mind to maintain the neutrality of the city. Being spoiled by Ethan, Cecilia did not share in her friend's temperance. The Vanadis received as many after-dinner cordials as she desired. Amuro laughed again but quickly stopped when Cecilia glared at her.

"Well, based on the stories you've been telling, it's amazing that any of you are still alive."

"No one wanted to believe the stories the Titans were telling us," regretted Cagius. "Yet we couldn't deny what was right in front of our eyes."

"Demons?" asked Selim. "Fallen Angels? You really saw these things?"

"Saw them!" exclaimed Amuro. "We engaged them in combat."

Terrified by the thought of demons scaling his walls, Dennis watched as his young wife shook with fear at the tales that were told.

"We've had our problems with dark elf raiders, but never anything like that."

"Dark elves?" asked Amuro, her face suddenly becoming pale.

"There are some geologists who theorize that the entrances into the Underdark are in the caverns south of the city. However, the raiders we deal with are mostly exiles or scouts that are easily dispatched. It's not like they've ever launched a full-scale attack against us. I'm curious, what was it like to fight these new enemies?"

"The Demonkin fight in erratic patterns," explained Malcolm. "They prefer to overwhelm with massive amounts of force rather than rely on combat training. It can leave them in bottlenecks from time to time granting a smaller force a distinct advantage."

Selim took the data in with some uneasiness.

"How many of these creatures do you estimate to be in the west?"

"We've never had an accurate count," answered Cecilia as she finished her drink. "We estimate that the Demonkin could number in the hundred-millions."

"They are overwhelming Central Acadia right now," seethed Cassandra. "It would take hundreds of thousands of trained soldiers to lay siege to Verian."

"Well, you have nothing to worry about as long as you're in my care," reassured Dennis.

Ethan leaned over to Cecilia.

"Would you like another?

"Yes."

Ethan signaled the servant who poured Cecilia another cordial. Ethan seemed to be a little worried for a second but Cecilia simply smiled and teased him.

"You do know that Titans have a higher tolerance with alcohol. If you're thinking of compromising me with drink you're going to be disappointed."

"Cecilia, I saw your brother down five bottles of beer, two bottles of brandy, and he still carried eight people home from the bar we were at. I know there are no limits."

"That's my brother."

Ethan thought to himself that Cecilia once again did not use the past tense when it came to her brother. The Denivan Knight knew they were twins and had a special bond with one another. He just wondered how a single man could hold out against such overwhelming odds. Dennis raised his glass towards Hippolyte who acknowledged the honor.

"I am honored as well to sit with the granddaughter of Chieftain Aramas."

"I am thankful for the opportunity, Margrave Dennis."

"Believe it or not, I had some dealings with your grandfather. There were many different spices from the east that he purchased in bulk. Your grandfather was a shrewd one and he always pinched me down to the last penny. Those were some epic battles."

"Grandpa only started to discuss business with me after my father died, so he never mentioned any dealings with you."

"Well, don't let my hospitality towards you now make you soft in my dealings with you later. A good merchant loves nothing more than a good challenge. Your sister, however, seems to have taken a liking to our culinary expertise."

Hippolyte looked over at her sister who was happily munching down on her third helping of chocolate soufflé.

"My sister seems to be enamored with every cuisine of the Kingdoms of the West."

"I know you had two helpings as well," teased Minerva. "Besides, I'm just trying to keep pace with the queen."

Everyone broke out into laughter.

"We're very happy that you enjoyed the hard work of our chefs," said Henrietta.

Valentine and Christian exchanged looks with one another. Signaling Cecilia with the scratch of his nose, the Vanadis took the bait.

"Margrave Dennis, your generosity is most kind, but we all fear the delicate position we've placed you in. What if Sultan Khan were to visit?"

Smiling, Dennis was well prepared to the answer the inquisition placed to him. However, he had expected Christian to ask it instead of Cecilia.

"You don't have to worry about that. Right, Selim?"

"Yes, his Imperial Majesty prefers to spend his time in Palacio Magnifico, especially when the desert heat gets unbearable for his gout in the summer. The Kaiser Mountain Pass is a treacherous crossing, and with the dangerous conditions you describe, he will not risk coming this far west."

"I'm satisfied with that answer," interrupted Cassandra. "However, I believe we would prefer to draw up a contingency plan in case Sultan Khan comes for an unexpected visit. I didn't escape prison from the Acadians just to become a prisoner of the Empire."

Christian and Valentine signaled to one another again. Selim took no offense to Cassandra's concerns and understood her caution. Dennis signaled for the servants to bring dessert wine over to the table and poured a glass for everyone. He stood from the table.

"Allow me the privilege of toasting my guests one more time."

Everyone raised their glass, including Minerva who had to stop inhaling food for a moment. Walker couldn't help laughing at the irony of a girl who abhorred the thought of a dessert she couldn't stop inhaling it.

"I wish that our great reputation for hospitality is only exceeded by our actions, and that the peace between the Alliance and Empire maintains in these difficult times," Dennis said. "I also honor your fallen."

The cheers of "here, here" were heard. Cecilia stood for a moment.

"If you would indulge me, Margrave Dennis, the Titans must always toast 'the heroes of the past and the soldiers of the future.'"

A second round of cheers began to rise from those seated in the room.

"Is there anything else we can do for you?" asked Dennis.

"Yes," said Minerva as she held up her plate. "More, please!"

Everyone laughed as Hippolyte covered her face.

CITY OF ANTIQUITY, FOREST OF THE ETERNAL SPRING, SEVEN ROTATIONS LATER

"I urge you therefore, brothers, by the mercies of God, to offer your bodies as a living sacrifice, holy and pleasing to God, your spiritual worship. Do not conform yourself to this age but be transformed by the renewal of your mind, that you may discern what is the will of God, what is good and pleasing and perfect."

Letter to the Kablisha 12:1-2

The trees of the old forest towered into the sky, for these woods were almost as old as the first generation of elves that walked Terminus Mundus. A single forest road cut naturally through this path of trees leading to a large clearing. The scars of a large army marching across this road with siege weapons withstood the test of time. In the clearing was a large, stone-walled city surrounded by numerous farms against the city walls. The people working in the fields were dressed rather modestly in clothes that were made out of wool, cloth, and hemp. In the area surrounding the farms were livestock pens consisting of dairy cows, chickens, and sheep. The farm fields themselves consisted of grain, fruit, and vegetables. Surrounded by protective large stone walls manned by crossbowmen, the city was laced with tall buildings consisting of single-floor family apartments. Numerous market stands were positioned outside of mercantile buildings making shopping easy. In the center of the city was the most impressive building, a rather large gothic cathedral built with the traditional three doors in front. The Cathedral of the Martyrs had been designed with a variety of idiosyncrasies such as the asymmetrical design and the varying height of the two spires. The five angels on the roof were all in different positions and the stain glass windows were all of different sizes. Adjacent to the Cathedral was the two-storied Bishop's residence. In one of the upstairs rooms, Cedric was sleeping peacefully in a hospital bed. He had intravenous fluids going into his arm and other devices monitoring his bodily functions. The readings were slow but stabilized, and the sword master was breathing without the aid of a respirator. A deep scar in the right deltoid and left pectoral were clearly visible on his bare chest. The wounds continued to ooze with unnatural black pus. Carefully entering the room as to not disturb their patient, Mesmara and Quinn checked on the houseguest.

"The powers of Grail should have healed most of the damage to his body by now," observed Mesmara. "I'm amazed at the rate of his cellular regeneration; I would have imagined we'd be bandaging these wounds for almost a revolution."

"I really just wish he would open his eyes," said Quinn, worried. "Bishop Wulf knew it was going to take time, but he shows no sign of being in a coma."

"Quinn, as much as we both hoped, he's not the warrior of legend. That damned poison in his body has been tearing his organs apart. He's not going to just shrug off those deep wounds."

"I don't know, Mesmara. I know he's alive—that's better than anyone has ever done before in a battle against Abaddon."

The Kablisha beauty pulled Cedric's chart and examined the morning schedule.

"According to his chart, Florence came in already and checked on him. Apparently, she also took the time to bathe him."

"I'm a little worried about that cleric. I've heard stories that she doesn't allow anyone else to check on him but her—"

Quinn stopped mid-sentence as he glanced at Cedric's body. Whether it was real or only his imagination, the Kablisha warrior believed that Cedric moved his hand. He jumped back and instinctively put his hand to the hilt of his sword.

"What's wrong?"

"His hand moved!"

Mesmara looked over Cedric from head to foot. She didn't see anything on his body move. Annoyed at her companion's behavior, she brought her fingers to the bridge of her nose and shook her head in contempt.

"The nerve endings in his body are slowly regenerating; his muscles are bound to twitch now and then."

"You're right, I'm just paranoid with a guest of his stature around. We'd better be going, your uncle is going to want a report."

As she replaced the chart, Cedric grabbed her wrist with his right hand. With inhuman speed, the Titan prince grabbed Ragnarok stashed under the bed and spun Mesmara into his chest. Quinn was caught off-guard and found the tip of the legendary blade at his throat before he could get his sword out of his scabbard. With Mesmara trapped in his large arms, both Kablisha nervously anticipated the prince's next move. How was it possible that they could have been so easily deceived? A wounded patient clad only in his boxer shorts had subdued them.

"What place is this?" demanded Cedric.

Terror prevented the two from speech, much to Cedric's consternation.

"I know I'm not dead, so that rules out Heaven, Hell, and Purgatory. I'm not in Verian, Titanus, Deniva, or any place that I know. Where am I?"

"You are in the residence of Bishop Peter Wulf," responded a nervous Quinn.

"This is the city of Antiquity, the stronghold of the Kablisha," stammered Mesmara. "If you could find it in your heart to please let me go, I would most appreciate it."

"So it is to my distant cousins that I am eternally indebted."

Nodding, the sword master lowered his weapon and released Mesmara. A few more moments was all it took for the Titan prince to place his weapon back under the bed. Quinn took Mesmara in his arms and embraced her. Glad to be free of her predicament, Mesmara held him tightly. Stretching out his arms and shoulders, Cedric removed the pulse monitor on his hand.

"You have to admit that was pretty impressive for a guy as injured as I was. I could have killed both of you before you even knew what was going on, but I didn't. As you undoubtedly know, my name is Prince Cedric Rhone of Titanus. I would appreciate it if you gave me your names."

"Quirinus Ophion, but mercifully everyone just calls me Quinn."

"Mesmara Lorelei."

"Bishop Peter Wulf will be quite happy to know that you're up and well."

"He insists on seeing you immediately."

"Well, if you don't mind calling Florence, we'll get this needle out of me. Hey Quinn, you wouldn't happen to have my clothes, would you?"

"Of course. We took the liberty of cleaning the clothes you had with you in your saddlebag. Your armor was sent to the armorer for repairs; unfortunately, we haven't been successful in repairing it yet."

"It's been especially difficult finding a vein of gold to repair the pauldrons, but we're mining some out."

Quinn opened the closet door in his room. The prince's dress shirt and uniform were hanging in the closet. His boots on the floor were shined and polished.

"Thank you so much. At least I'll have something appropriate in which to meet your bishop."

Mesmara pushed the call button. In a few moments, Florence Polazzi entered the room. The Napolitan national from a noble family thought she was originally called to be a nun at a young age, but she failed out of the convent just before taking her final vows. Her proficiency in medicine and healing allowed Florence to transfer to the clerical school of Titan Academy. Lacking the necessary discipline for classroom work, the noble finished at the bottom of her class. With the ranks in Titanus full, Queen Civilia arranged for her to be assigned to the Kablisha. Florence was Cassandra's age, and the olive-skinned beauty focused her big green eyes on the sword master. Her long blue dress was covered by a white smock with tight, starched, white cuffs exposing her bare hands. A short white-and-gold miter, marked with a cross just above the brim symbolizing her office, held her long brown hair in place with a tight bun. Not missing an opportunity, the young noble took every opportunity to flaunt her fine assets to Cedric. With the precision of a surgeon, Florence removed the needle without spilling a drop of blood. A quick healing spell and the cleric closed the wound.

"I hate to be a pest but this is my room. How about a little privacy when I get dressed?"

Quinn and Mesmara were both embarrassed at Cedric's scolding and left hurriedly.

"He certainly is impressive!" commented Quinn.

"I wonder how many hours a rotation he works out to keep up a muscular structure like that."

Quinn shot an incredulous stare at Mesmara, who suddenly realized he meant something else. Blushing to a deep shade of purple, the maiden deflected her previous comments.

"What I meant to say was that I don't understand how he could have maintained his vital signs like that when he was awake."

"I wonder what that was all about."

"He seems all right."

"Your uncle is not going to be happy. The prince was on top of us before we could do anything. I hope he doesn't hear about it."

"Prince Cedric did have the element of surprise."

A glow in her face, Florence came out of the room humming happily.

"His Excellency should be ready soon. I just took the time to wrap his shoulder and chest again. He was afraid of bleeding on his dress shirt. I hope you weren't too offended by our little prank."

"What prank?"

"His Excellency awoke early this morning and asked for food." Florence chuckled. "We spoke at length concerning his situation, and he was happy to see a familiar face. Knowing how paranoid the prince is, I promised not to tell anyone he was awake until he could confirm his location."

Florence gave them a little wink while the two Kablisha angrily stared at her.

"Why, that no good Titan bastard!" cursed Quinn.

"Oh and Lady Mesmara, I should warn you of the prince's flattery. After I drew him a bath this morning, he asked if a cute cleric like me had found a boyfriend yet. When I told him no, he said that the men of the Kablisha must be really stupid not to date someone like me. If it was only anyone else but Princess Cassandra…"

Quinn reacted worse to the cleric's words than Mesmara did. Mesmara simply smiled as Florence quickly waved her left hand to fan the warmness in her face.

"I didn't realize it was so warm in here…"

"So the rumors are true! He is the worst womanizer in the whole of Terminus Mundus. You'd better be careful around him, Mesmara."

"Don't be so upset. How can the prince help it if he finds young maidens extremely attractive? After all, he already swept me up against his bare chest and arms…"

"Mesmara!"

Mesmara and Florence laughed harder.

"Jealousy is not one of your better traits, darling."

Opening the door to his room, Cedric came out dressed in a white dress shirt, black tie, kilt, and boots. Ragnarok slung over his shoulder, he refused Florence's futile attempts to give him a cane. Her work done, the cleric curtsied to Cedric before she returned to her room.

"Mesmara, Quinn, I guess its time to take me to your leader."

"This way, your lordship."

As they descended the stairs of the residence, Bishop Peter Wulf held court on his wooden throne in the palatial reception hall. The bishop wore white robes marked with the insignia of a lamb interposed with a wooden crosier. A white miter sat on a wooden table next to the throne, but he continued to hold a wooden crosier in his right hand. Wulf was old but not aged, with white hair and a long white beard. His blue eyes held a middle-aged divikin in his vision. Argus Kinkade, the Commander of the Kablisha forces, paced back and forth in room. Constantly running his hand through his jet-black hair, his brown eyes swayed with trepidation. His chest armor was made of ring mail tied over a cloth shirt and pants. He had a five-guarded saber at his side.

"Argus, you must calm yourself," recommended the Bishop.

"Forgive me, Bishop Wulf, I am uneasy with the way events have transpired over the past rotations. I'm still worried that the Dark Angel may have traced the prince back to us."

"I share those concerns. However, I am troubled by the many prejudices you harbor over the Titan prince. Cedric Rhone has proven his goals by his actions against Abaddon."

"I'm just not certain if it was right to use the Holy Grail. Perhaps we should have let him try to heal himself; it would have given us insight into our goals. Such power should not have been placed in the hands of one of his kind."

"It is impossible to know what the Will of God was in that situation. Garrett would not have sent Wilhelm to us unless there was a reason. I have not the power to deny the request of the Holy Sentinel of the Lord. There was no reason not to use the Grail's power since he was certainly still alive when he was brought to us."

"A Titan prince, born of the same warmongers that deserted these lands and your values for thousands of revolutions, could hold the greatest power ever bestowed on a being in creation. You cannot possibly believe that this is the most desirable path."

"I will not say that it does not trouble me that a country that prides itself on military strength may have been given a gift of otherworldly power. I simply trust in the Will and Judgment of God."

"I've done a lot of digging into his background. In some ways he's just as bad as Abaddon!"

"It depends on the authors of those accounts," added Cedric.

Startled, a mortified Argus witnessed Cedric's escort into the room.

"Prince Rhone, I didn't expect you to be up and about so quickly. I am Bishop Peter Wulf, the leader of the Kablisha. I bid you welcome."

"Bishop Wulf, I am honored to make your acquaintance. I was told that I owe my life to you and by my honor I will repay that debt. If you have any request you need to be fulfilled, I will act within reason."

Approaching the Bishop, Cedric knelt to kiss his ring.

"I've always admired the Titans; despite everything that's said about them, they always show respect to men of the cloth."

Rising, Cedric confronted Argus, not leaving more than a few millimeters between their noses.

"And do you bid me welcome?"

"I am Argus Kinkade, in your tongue; you could say I'm the Marshal of the Kablisha."

"You avoided my question. Do you bid me welcome?"

"I am not one to shun the ancient laws of hospitality; I give welcome to all of our guests despite what I may believe of them."

"As you are a guest in this country as well, I don't expect you could show anything less."

"I'd like to understand the meaning of that statement."

"It's not hard to spot a guard dog among the sheep. Prince Gustav Archibald of Edenia, you were the last person I expected to find among the Kablisha."

Quinn, Mesmara, and the bishop felt the tension in the room rise. Not only did Argus have to suffer the Titan's insults, but the revelation of his identity as well.

"Yes, Marshal Kinkade. I am well aware of your past: Richard Archibald's youngest brother, disgusted at the lack of fighting spirit among his kinsmen. I went to great trouble trying to hunt you down for my planned liberation of Edenia. I see even Wilhelm wouldn't reveal the secret of your self-imposed exile."

"Not everything is always as black-and-white as it seems, Prince Rhone. Edenia has chosen its own path as I have chosen mine. I know you've meet Quinn and my niece Mesmara by now."

"Yes, we were introduced," explained Quinn.

"I just wish it was under better circumstances," said Mesmara regretfully.

"You are in the City of Antiquity, the stronghold of the Kablisha," lectured Argus. "Would you care for a history lesson?"

"I am well aware of the great history of this city. I know during the Great War that the chief priest invited King Hayden and his people into this fortress to lead their final defense against Emperor Dondarion and the Dwarves. The walls helped delay the siege until the warrior Joab and Cerwin Faulkner could secure alliance with Ulysses Rhone and the Titans. You could say the only reason you're standing here today is because of my ancestors."

Argus gritted his teeth at the smug comment of the Titan prince. Cedric turned back to the bishop.

"Despite my love of it, I did not come here for a history lesson. I need to know everything that happened since I passed out after the battle with Abaddon."

"Wilhelm von Angelhardt brought you here from the castle. You were alive, but your bodily functions were poisoned. We used the powers of the Holy Grail to restore your internal system to normal. None of us can believe what indomitable will you possess to remain alive despite all of your suffering."

"Bishop, you know I'm not concerned about what happened to me. What happened to my sister and the others?"

"Your friends arrived safely in Deniva by traveling through the crypt. Cassandra is currently beyond Abaddon's reach."

Cedric pumped his fist in the air, celebrating his victory.

"Unfortunately, I must bear sorrowful news as well. Cerwin Faulkner did not survive the journey."

"Looks like God remembered you, grandpa," said Cedric as he muttered a silent prayer and blessed himself. "Bishop, what can you tell me about Abaddon?"

"What do you want to know?"

"His body burnt to crisp in front of me, but something shot out of it before his remains became ash. What was that?"

"Unfortunately, Prince Rhone, the light you saw was Abaddon's soul itself."

"While you were able to destroy Abaddon's body in the duel, you were not able to bind his soul," extolled Argus. "Since you lacked that ability, Abaddon was able to escape to an astral plane rather than return to Hell. He appears now as nothing more than a phantasm whose flesh rots the second he tries to take definite form."

"What happens now?" asked Cedric.

"Abaddon is severely limited in his current form," explained Argus. "He can manifest himself on Terminus Mundus but cannot maintain a field of stability for long. Thus he must return to the astral plane to rest and recharge his magic. Weapons and magic are useless in this form and any means of tracking Cassandra has been lost to him."

"Even though his powers are limited, his minions are still fanatically loyal to him and he holds much power over the rebels in Central Acadia," continued the bishop. "He will continue to haunt us until we can use the spell to bind him to Hell."

"What spell is that?"

"A craft developed by the Angels of the Powers Choir when the Lord God charged them with guarding the gates between the Celestial Realm and the Temporal Realm."

"All right then, tell me why Wilhelm von Angelhardt can't cast the spell and finish this once and for all."

"If we only could," interjected Argus. "When Krystos was cast out, he was cursed. The spells of binding are rendered useless to him."

"Before I fought Abaddon, Garrett Greensage gave me a book on the history of the Ragnarok War and the subsequent events. Abaddon gravely wounded Duke Camael of the Powers Choir and God had to seal him away in order to heal those wounds. He turned over command to his executive officer, Cassiel, and put himself into a long, deep sleep so his wounds would heal. If Garrett is correct in his history, then it is possible that Camael was incarnated in this world. Since his primary duty would be to battle and bind Acolytes, he wouldn't enter the world as a Sentinel, but rather an incarnated being. This way, he could covertly have all his powers at his disposal when the forces of the prince enter this world. I think we both suspect Camael is already here."

"Yes, your powers of deduction are impressive," said Bishop Wulf approvingly.

"We observed your assault on the castle," said Argus. "We know that Abaddon tried to bring out the Demoness sleeping inside of Cassandra Acadia. Did she utter anything to you in the ancient tongue when she saw you?"

"She called me Permaneo Eques Ordinaris, and she also called me an abomination which was pretty hurtful even if she was enslaved at the time."

"The Last Knight, the mistranslation that has haunted this world for revolutions."

"Mistranslation?"

"The Sentinels wrote everything down in the Divine Language, the elves translated it into their language, and now we have the modern unified tongue which was based on the elf tongue," pontificated the bishop. "Somewhere along the line, the prophecy was corrupted so it was translated as the 'Knight of the Last.' Our suspicion is that they messed up the elven word for *omega* or *end* with the elf word for *Lord*, which is *Adonai*. When the Sentinels spoke of the prophecy, they're actual words were 'Deus Eques Ordinaris,' translated as the 'Knight of God.'"

"Camael Incarnate is the Knight of God!" exclaimed Cedric.

"Yes," taunted Argus. "You may share similarities with this mistranslated form of the Last Knight, but it was a being that was never meant to exist. You simply are nothing more than a Knight who used the powers of his racial blood to defeat Abaddon. Only the arrogance of your people would make you foolish enough to believe a warmongering Titan could be the 'Knight of God.' You didn't even know you had to bind his soul."

"I'm sorry to disappoint you."

"On the contrary, we are quite pleased. Your defeat of Abaddon has given us precious time. Our agents seek the true Knight of God as we speak. We will find the individual with the power to bind that soul and Abaddon will be defeated."

"Your honor debt to us has been paid off for all of our lifetimes," praised the bishop. "It does not matter the circumstances upon which you took up your sword. Your selfless act saved Cassandra and Terminus Mundus. God blesses you and we have great hope for you."

"I'm sure you have your work ahead of you and you don't need me to foul things up any further. If I could ask one more favor of you, it would be to send me to Deniva."

"I'm afraid that request isn't possible at this time."

"Fine. If you're still concerned about my wounds, I will wait for the appropriate time."

Sensing no response from his "captors," Cedric pressed the issue.

"If not Deniva, then send me home! They have the facilities to treat my wounds. I have a lot of work that needs to be done."

"Prince Rhone, you have proven far too reckless to be left to roam Terminus Mundus. The enemy thinks you are dead. It is advantageous to allow that lie to continue so they will not disturb our agents from their mission."

"The problem with your plan is that our allies think I'm dead! The nations of the West just got cut off from one another, Constantine's beloved son is dead, and the Tribal Confederation is without a leader. This is not the time for cloak-and-dagger operations. If we can just provide a spark of hope, it will get us through these difficult times."

"You will return to your people eventually," said Argus. "I will not hand the enemy a lightning rod. If you head for Deniva, they will know the princess is there. If you return to your homeland, the Titans will act before the time is right. You will remain here, anonymous—that was the condition that Wilhelm von Angelhardt had to agree too if we were to use the Holy Grail."

"You think merely changing your allegiance has stripped you of your Edenian identity? When was the last time your people actually died for freedom? For the love of God, I implore you to have the decency to tell my mother I am alive!"

His "prisoner" seething with anger, Bishop Wulf reassured the prince he would pray on the situation and see what could be done. Argus decided to take a profoundly different approach and appeal to Cedric *the warrior* instead.

"We are prepared to make you an offer. You're good, Cedric; in fact, I've never seen a warrior more skilled in the martial arts. Yet, you have the potential to be better. You are currently at the limits of your training as a sword master. The Kablisha possess spells, techniques, and skills beyond what even von Angelhardt or the Titan Church can teach. If you give me the time and you're willing to put in the work, I can show you ways to turn your white magic into a force of holy destruction. Would that alone not be worth your time here?"

Cedric's rage slowed down. Barely surviving the first encounter with Abaddon made the sword master eager to find an edge against the Fallen Angel.

"A tempting offer, especially since you believe I was simply lucky last time."

"It was more than luck! Outside of Camael, you are the only swordsman to ever best Abaddon in battle. If he manifests his body before we find the Knight of God, you will have to fight him once more."

"A warrior never fights someone the same way twice."

"Good, then we have an agreement."

"You saved my life; though I accept with great reservations, there is wisdom in what you say. If you agree to train me, I won't make trouble for you… temporarily, at least. However, the length of time you make my mother suffer will try my patience."

"Thank you, Prince Rhone," reassured the bishop. "I will take the time to review the matter."

"Quinn and Mesmara will serve as your attachés," ordered Argus. "If you require anything while you are here, please ask them. You'll find that they are among our finest."

Cedric's stomach growled loudly, surprising the four Kablisha.

"Yeah, I know stomach, take care of me or else there'll be problems. Do you have anything to eat?"

"We'll take you down to Cookie!" interjected Quinn. "He always has some extra food available."

"Bishop Wulf, Argus, I'll take my leave."

Cedric left with Mesmara and Quinn.

"Seven rotations to heal what it would take most a revolution to do," observed Wulf.

"He is an interesting character if nothing else. I can't say I was very happy to see the rage in his eyes when we told him he was our prisoner."

"I fear it will be impossible for him to adjust to our ways. Always keep a pair of eyes on him, Argus."

Argus nodded as Cedric strode down the hallways with his escorts.

"Lord Cedric, if you don't mind us asking, how were you able to control your pulse in the room?" asked Mesmara.

"I used magic from the domination branch to create an illusion. The two of you saw what you expected to see."

"The domination branch?" pondered Quinn. "Isn't that branch extremely dangerous? I heard you can take over a person's mind against their will if you chose the right spell."

"Yes. I wouldn't recommend picking it up; the temptation for corruption is too great for most to handle."

"I heard a rumor that those powers of charm are the reason you're so popular with the ladies," teased Mesmara.

"I don't need any parlor tricks for that. Courting is a highly refined and developed skill passed on by Titan officers for ages. A couple of rotations with your boyfriend over here, and I can show him more than enough to sweep you off your feet in no time."

Quinn and Mesmara both blushed.

"How did you know?"

"You don't need to hide it, so you don't. Quinn, you have a bad habit of wrinkling your nose and squinting at every word Mesmara says to me. Girls won't like you if you act too jealous."

Cedric playfully hit Quinn in the middle of his chest as the Kablisha warrior gnashed his teeth. Mesmara simply laughed at her boyfriend's actions and changed the topic to cool his anger.

"We're all still in awe at the fact that a Divikin was brave enough to take on a divine being."

"There was no choice. I saw what Abaddon's corruption did to Cassandra and I knew I'd never let that happen to her again."

"That was true blue hero action right there!" praised Quinn. "You're well on your way!"

"To what?"

"Becoming the hero of legend, of course."

Stopping in his tracks at their comments, Cedric was puzzled by their meaning.

"Is something wrong, Lord Cedric?" queried Mesmara.

"Let's get one thing straight, I'm already a hero. I was a hero long before I fought Abaddon. If you two think your people can simply wait safely behind these walls for some hero to show up and save you, you're sadly mistaken. Quirinus, Mesmara, you both better think long and hard about what you are prepared to do."

"You're not joking, are you?" wondered Quinn. "You really believe that we have what it takes to do what you did?"

"People embrace the moment or are devoured by it. Speaking of devouring, I thought you said something about food."

The two attachés moved Cedric towards the cafeteria. His companions pondered silently, but Cedric took the time to review what had happened and what he had said. He came to a single conclusion: *Who are you kidding? When you fought Abaddon, you believed you could fulfill the prophecy. Now you know the truth; it was only the devil's luck that drew that ace. What makes you better or more devoted than Walker? He did the same exact thing.*

The three entered the dining area. A gruff, overweight cook in a white apron and a chef's hat was standing over a pot.

"Hey Cookie!" shouted Quinn.

"Quinn! Mesmara! You already had your meal! What are you bothering me for now?"

"We need you to fix something for our guest," said Mesmara.

Quinn put his arm around Cedric. Cedric grimaced from the pain in his right shoulder.

"You see this guy! This guy… is the guy who killed Abaddon!"

"I don't follow."

"Cedric Rhone is a guest of the bishop," explained Mesmara. "Can you fix him something to eat?"

"Sure, if soup's okay."

"Soup is fine," agreed Cedric. "I'll take some bread if you have it also."

"Have a seat and be prepared for the best food in the City of Antiquity!"

Taking a place at table, Cedric was waited on by Mesmara and Quinn. Mesmara poured him a glass of wine while Quinn got him bread and cheese. Cookie brought a steaming hot bowl of soup over to Cedric.

"You need anything else?"

"I could use some utensils," suggested Cedric.

"What do we have here?" Cookie laughed. "A noble? I keep a couple of sets around."

Bringing over utensils wrapped in a napkin, he watched as Cedric carefully opened the napkin, placed it on his lap, and meticulously set the utensils.

"There you go, your highness!"

After a quick blessing and prayer, Cedric broke the bread in front of him. He sliced a piece of cheese with his knife. All the while, Mesmara and Quinn watched him from across the table.

"You do know that your uncle didn't mean you had to keep your eyes on me every second."

"Oh, well you see, we don't have training until later, so we don't have anywhere to be right now," Mesmara said.

"Besides, don't attachés attend to every need of their superior officers?"

"We don't have attachés in Titanus and the marshals always liked to rotate cooking duties. I'm used to be serviced by trained servants, not my contemporaries."

As Cedric tasted his soup, his brow furrowed.

"I didn't realize it was a holy day. How long was I out for? I thought it was only a full rotation."

"I don't understand, Lord Cedric."

"There's no meat in this soup, not even in the broth. I know it's Lent, but abstinence is only required on one rotation."

Nervously, the attachés stared at each other.

"Don't worry, I'm not going to throw over the table or anything. I'm just curious about your methods of cooking."

"The Kablisha don't believe in eating flesh," stated Quinn.

"All throughout Lent?"

"No. We *never* eat flesh."

"I thought Catheri was a heresy."

"We're not pure Catheri; we don't believe in eating flesh but acknowledge the Edenian Creed, the authority of the Arch Bishop of Titanus, and the spiritually-inspired teachings of the Magesterium," explained Mesmara.

"This arrangement isn't going to work if I'm not going to be able to eat meat."

Despite his objections, nothing would stop Cedric from devouring every last crumb of food placed before him. He took a sip of wine and was pleasantly surprised.

"This wine isn't half bad. You make this yourself?"

"Yes," said Mesmara. "We have a few wineries and fertile vineyards."

"Is there anything wrong, sir?" questioned Quinn.

"Sorry I'm snapping at you two. I just long for a good t-bone, fried potatoes, and a lager right now."

"I'm afraid I can't help you with that, sir. Well, maybe the fried potatoes if you don't object to peanut oil."

"No, it's just not the same without the steak. Well, is there any way I can persuade either of you to let me out of here?"

"Not as long as we're under orders," replied Mesmara.

"Good soldiers—I like that. Well then, can I ask you for some more wine?"

"Absolutely!"

Mesmara poured another glass for Cedric, who raised the glass.

"Here's to hope! Every rotation is Lent here in the Kablisha! What about fish?"

"No, we don't eat fish because fish is flesh."

"You don't eat meat, you don't eat fish. What could you possibly eat around here that would get this mundane taste of vegetables out of my mouth?"

"Actually, Cookie makes this dish called pizza," offered Quinn.

"Pizza?"

"Bread dough rolled out thin and crispy, topped with tomatoes and cheese. Sometimes we add mushrooms or other vegetables to it."

Cedric shrugged his shoulders and smiled.

"Hey Cookie, whip me up one of those pizzas of yours."

Mesmara and Quinn gave the okay signal to Cookie, who got to work in the kitchen.

DENIVA CASTLE

"Contrary to the many opinions about me, I am not a heartless killer. My father squandered all the money and property my noble family had. I have a mother, three sisters, and two brothers to take care of. I learned at a young age that my only chance to keep them in the lifestyle they are accustomed was to distinguish myself in the military. I have chosen to use any means possible to achieve my goals, and I prefer the company of a good brothel to ease my pains. I don't want your pity and I don't want you to understand. I just want the respect due me because I fight for Napolitan."

Lord Antonio Valentine to Prince Julius

Seated at a table with Walker guarding the door, Amuro, Cagius and Cecilia prepared to listen to presentations from Christian and Valentine. The exiles were taking precautions even inside a friendly castle out of fear someone would interfere with their own private plans. This was a military briefing that was currently being hidden from Cassandra for the purposes of plausible deniability.

"All right, you two, what are you proposing?" asked Amuro.

"Marshal, we've come to the conclusion that we are safe in Deniva for now," explained Christian.

"I guess that is a relief," joked Cagius.

"Just because we are safe doesn't mean that we shouldn't see to our defenses," suggested Valentine.

"What defenses are those?" questioned Amuro.

"Marshal, we know from Dennis and Selim's lips that Sultan Khan is 'throwing his weight' around Edenia and Palacio Magnifico," said Valentine.

"Valentine and I concur that we need to send spies into Edenia to gather what intelligence we can on the Empire."

"While we don't know how deep the barrier has gone, Christian and I have mathematically determined that if we can make it to an imperial port, we can sail back to Rhinegard and Port Talus. We won't know if we can do this if we don't have intelligence."

"I agree with their assessment," Cecilia said. "I fully support the plan; however, it would be too much to risk both Christian and Valentine. One of you is going to have to remain behind."

Valentine and Christian looked at one another.

"Cecilia's right. So who's going to go?" queried Amuro.

Valentine and Christian both shouted, "I will." Cagius shook his head as if he knew the answer before the question had been asked.

"Christian DeVries is an excellent operative, but many of his skills lie in diplomacy and in all honesty he simply doesn't have the same field experience that I do. I am an expert in infiltration and bribery. If I take the mission it will cost us less coin, which we are running out of quickly. You also know that I have no qualms about doing what is necessary to complete the mission. I know that brothels are excellent sources of intelligence. I have agents in all of the finest Edenian Houses. I'm more expendable than Christian; I should go."

"What say you, Christian?" demanded the marshal.

"This mission requires higher level contacts than a mere brothel. You need the more sophisticated diplomat in this matter because my allies have infiltrated the highest levels of the Edenian government. I have the advantage of working with the Wood Elves in the past. They can safely move me across the Kaiser Mountain Pass. Titanus has many favors to call in from our Edenian friends. Colin Wilkins works very well with me and is a fast learner. Our contacts can get us legitimate lodging, papers, and employment in Edenia. We can move in and out of Palacio Magnifico at will. Besides, Valentine is needed here much more than I am."

"Why? I told you that I'm more expendable than you are."

"You'll need to train Joshua."

"Walker and Cagius can do that better than an assassin ever could."

"They can't train him in the way of the Paladin. Only one who trained with a Paladin can do so."

"I'm no Paladin," laughed Valentine.

"You were going to be. Don't be angry with me, but I kept files on everyone in the West. Valentine, I know you trained with Darius in the ways of the Paladin. However, when your family went broke, you went into intelligence. You knew it was the only way you could gain coin and fame fast enough to keep them off the streets."

"Bravo, it seems I underestimated your ruthlessness," mocked Valentine.

"Joshua has great potential in him. He's proven himself to be a natural sword fighter already. He has a chance to be better than his father. He'll never get that chance if we miss the critical training age. Valentine, you may be more than qualified to lead this mission, but let's do things my way this time."

"I guess it's settled then." Valentine sighed. "Even though I'm sure you'll find some way to foul things up."

The operatives shared a laugh.

"All right, Christian, you have my approval," agreed Amuro. "Please don't make me regret this. When can you be ready?"

"I'll need three rotations to call in our contacts."

"You've got it."

"I'll go tell Colin the news."

As they moved to leave, Valentine stalked DeVries.

"You won today, DeVries, but don't think I have to like it. You were right in there, you know; I'm the only chance Joshua has."

"Despite what everyone may think, we still do need men who are willing drop down into the trenches and do all of the dirty work to keep us safe."

"You take care of yourself out there!"

Valentine smiled before hitting Christian on the shoulder.

"If you need a good brothel while you're there, I can arrange for some prime entertainment. Just tell me your pleasure."

Christian put up his hand up and Valentine observed his band.

"No thanks. This is business, not pleasure."

"Well, to each his own."

Outside on the castle plains, Hippolyte and Colin were riding. A large boar thundered ahead of their horses as the two communicated to each other with hand signals. Hippolyte got on the side of the boar to drive the animal while Colin took stride in front of the beast. The tribal leader pointed in a circular motion to the assassin. The Lunar Falcon responded by taking an arcing sweep with Deathbringer. Colin cut a large ridge in the ground with his sword and quickly maneuvered out of the boar's path. As the boar slowed, Hippolyte got her spear ready. She took aim and struck the boar on the shoulder. The boar took a few slow steps before tumbling into the crater. The huntress jumped from her horse and drew a knife. Murmuring a slight prayer, she drove the blade into the neck of the beast. The boar struggled for a few moments before dying.

"The farmers of Deniva aren't going to have to worry about this one ripping through their crops anymore."

"What would you estimate his size to be?" wondered Colin.

"The biggest one we've got yet; I think it weighs about six hundred kilograms."

"I guess I better get the carrier assembled."

Colin assembled the metals bars on the side of his horse. Hippolyte playfully grabbed him from behind and nuzzled her face against his.

"Minerva and I could have never taken down one this size. You're a great hunter, Colin."

"It feels nice to hear that as a compliment. I'm used to that line being used in a negative connotation."

"What did you do for Cedric, anyway?"

"I was an assassin. The people of Titanus didn't think it was appropriate for their crown prince to do his own dirty work. My job was to eliminate enemies of the state in accordance with the legal process."

"How is killing legal?"

"Certain killings can be justified before a magistrate if a writ is issued by the sovereign of a country. Certain conditions have to be met in these circumstances and the sovereign will have to answer for them. Master Cedric used his writs to mainly take down Nephilim and their agents. Thus, no one ever questioned them."

Colin's explanation went right over Hippolyte's head.

"Your ways are very confusing."

"I guess they would be to an outsider."

"I don't understand how you could completely devote yourself to killing."

"I told you, I was pretty messed up when my family was murdered. It used to be easy to suppress these emotions. Master Cedric always said something about offering me a position as Graf if I would give up the path. I never thought I'd take that offer but I guess I'm starting to grow soft."

"Then I must be a good influence on you."

Colin snickered.

"I got Colin Wilkins to laugh!" exclaimed a smiling Hippolyte. "You wouldn't happen to have a girlfriend?"

"That wouldn't have been good in my line of work. Besides, I always used to get embarrassed around girls; I even insulted Marshal Jenitzen once and I didn't even know it."

"So that's why you were blushing as hard as me back when you rescued me. You know, I never properly thanked you for that. I would have never made it down that wall without you. You saved my life, Colin."

"Well, I am glad we made it in time."

"Though you have to admit it was a terrible rescue."

"Well, Christian and I had to improvise. If you're not busy tonight, Cagius recommended that I take you to see a movie that's playing in the city."

"A movie?"

"It's difficult to explain—it would be easier if you saw it yourself. It involves moving pictures on a screen."

"Yeah, I think Minerva mentioned something about that. I'd love to go with you."

"All right then. Let's get this baby back! If Cagius doesn't get his ribs at the time he wants them, he'll be bellyaching all night."

Colin grabbed the rear and Hippolyte took the head. Throwing the boar on the carrier, they hauled the kill back to the city. Hippolyte and Colin chose to walk the horses to put less weight on them. Inside the central market, Saria roamed the high-end stores with a single guard. As she exited one of the dress shops, a well-dressed, handsome, and distinguished-looking man approached her.

"Excuse me, Miss, can I have a moment of your time?"

Studying the man intently, Amuro determined him to seem okay.

"Yes."

"Are you the famous singer from Evengard, Amuro Jenitzen?"

"I don't know if I'm that famous, but I have trained in voice."

"I see. Well I happen to run a high-class entertainment establishment. Perhaps you've heard of the Siren's Club."

"I'm afraid I haven't," negated Saria as she shook her head.

"That's all right. I've witnessed your various talents first-hand and you are quite a beautiful young lady. Perhaps you wouldn't mind... performing at my establishment as a special attraction?"

"Do you perform any operas or ballets?"

"No, dear, however singing and dancing are two required skills that the young ladies in my troupe must have. Perhaps if I were to show you my establishment, you would get a better idea of what I'm offering."

Sensing danger as they entered the market, Colin left Hippolyte to protect Saria. The guard watching her shrieked in fear as Colin appeared as if he was derelict in his duty.

"You've got somewhere to be, buddy?" shouted Colin.

The man looked up to see Colin staring coldly at him. Even without his skull mask, the duelist was very intimidating and the gentleman that stopped Saria wanted no part of the assassin.

"Here's my card, your highness. Contact me if you're interested."

The man handed a card to Saria. On it was the man's name, Calderon, and in the corner was picture of a mermaid.

"Come on, your highness, I'll give you a ride back to the castle."

"Thank you, Colin."

Carefully lifting the princess onto his horse, Saria easily positioned herself on one side of the horse due to her elven grace. Hippolyte was pretty impressed by the show of strength from Colin but was quite unhappy at the length Colin had gone to assist the beautiful princess.

"Your highness, you shouldn't fraternize with men like that."

"He didn't meet Lord Valentine's descriptions."

"Trust me, that's exactly the type of shark that Lord Valentine is talking about. I'll emphasize again that you shouldn't go wandering around without one of us escorting you in this city. We don't know who we can trust yet."

"I'm sorry. I just got a little lonely in the castle."

Hippolyte and Colin looked at each other not believing the blissful ignorance of the princess. Neither thought that Saria understood what they were talking about. The two walked their horses back through the castle gates to the safety of the courtyard. Butchers were already waiting to take the boar from the two hunters. Colin helped Saria down from his horse before he gave a big hug and kiss to Hippolyte. The clearing of Christian's throat startled the two.

"I hope I'm not interrupting."

"Christian, I didn't see you," reported Colin.

"Hippolyte, if you don't mind, I need to speak with Colin about something."

"Of course, Christian."

Hippolyte knew something was wrong but didn't want to challenge the operative.

"Princess Saria, I wasn't aware that you were outside the grounds," said Christian.

"Good afternoon, Christian. I wanted to do some window-browsing this morning. Is Cagius done with his meetings?"

"Yes."

"Thank you."

Saria hurried into the castle. Hippolyte walked her horse and Colin's horse back to the stable.

"What's up?" questioned Colin.

"You and I have a mission. We're going to ride for Palacio Magnifco in three rotations."

"Why? Is Sultan Khan threatening to attack?"

"We need intelligence on the Empire's activities and an exit strategy. You and I are the best suited for the job."

"I was hoping that I could remain…"

"Need I remind you that you are still in the service of the Kingdom of Titanus, therefore you serve at the behest of Princess Cecilia Rhone?"

"I know my duty, Christian."

"It's not easy to love someone in our line of work. However, Hippolyte is a warrior—she'll get over it. The important thing is you don't get distracted on this mission."

"I won't."

"Good. I intend to use our contacts to get us into the Ranger unit. That way we'll be able to move freely in the Empire without worry. This is a very important mission and it might be our only means of getting home."

"Well then, we've got to do what we've got to do."

"We'll take Calvary with us, he can help us."

"How should I handle telling this to Hippolyte?"

"Wine and dine her for the next three rotations because you won't be seeing her for a while. When in doubt, be honest with her, but don't tell her anymore than she needs to know."

"You sound experienced in these matters, yet I've never seen you hanging around with anyone."

Christian simply walked away. Colin sighed and hung his head.

"Wonderful!"

Castle Titan

"A bird uses an astounding eighty percent of its brain; my invention exploits the other twenty percent."

Martha Heinrich

Martha, Horace, Queen Civilia, soldiers and scientists gathered around a large cage. Inside was one of the ugliest birds on the planet. The raptor was very large with golden-colored feathers and a large tuft of white feathers around its neck. The head, like all condors, was devoid of feathers, the red and yellow beak looked like it could swallow a human hand in one bite. Disinterested with the attention, the condor nestled itself in his tufted feathers like a pillow.

"Doctor Heinrich, I usually do not doubt your judgment in scientific matters, but this creature," observed Horace, "is this the best the mighty raptor core of Titanus has to offer?"

Martha looked at Horace with the same pained look a mother had when her child was insulted.

"He needs his rest."

"This is the ugliest condor I have ever seen," commented the queen.

Horace nodded in agreement and many of the other soldiers standing there regurgitated the sentiments of their queen and commander.

"Really, he's good!" defended Martha. "No other raptor in the core has undergone the intense training and scrutiny as this one has."

"Was he imprinted on humans?" asked the queen

"Of course he was, your highness. I personally served as his surrogate mother."

Civilia and Horace looked at one another with a furrowed brow, which accelerated Martha's depression.

"You'll see. I just need to adjust his attitude a little."

Taking a small microchip, Martha attached it to the back of the bird's head. Andres suddenly woke from his sleep and remembered his position. As the cage was unlatched, the condor hopped out of it, spread his wings, and bowed before Civilia. Many were astounded at the wingspan of Andres, and even the queen was impressed at the display of the condor.

"You see, your majesty! I told you one that I raised would never let us down!"

"I have a feeling that chip has more to do with it."

"Even with the chip, he has a definite love of Titanus."

An odd look came over the condor's face and suddenly he defecated right on Queen Civilia's boots. As her subordinates covered their mouths to contain their laughter, the ire of Civilia rose to the point where fried condor was going to be on the menu that evening.

"Oh Martha, I can't tell you how safe I feel that Andres is participating in the most important mission in the history of the Titan Raptor Core."

Martha was so embarrassed that she wanted to cry. She bent down and attached the electronic message to the leg of the condor and hugged the bird. She gently nuzzled her nose and face against the feathers of the bird in order to simulate a mother condor's behavior. Those gathered were afraid that the brilliant scientist of Titanus had lost her mind.

"Come on baby, you've just got to get over those mountains and get this message to Deniva."

Andres nodded his head.

"Make momma proud!"

Horace puffed his cigar and closed his eyes. He thought to himself, *It might be good idea for Martha to finally get married and have her own children.* Martha backed off and Bishop Arthur stepped forward. He blessed the bird with holy water. The bird shuddered every time the water hit him.

"May the Patron Saint of Animals bless this bird on his journey. May the currents be swift and the journey uneventful. You carry a large burden, my feathered friend. I will pray for you."

Andres spread his wings. Beating them rapidly, the condor rode the warm air currents. Spiraling high above Rhinegard, he set course for the Griffin Mountains. Civilia watched with unease and gripped her rosary tightly.

"Well, just when you thought it couldn't get any worse, my scouts came back with an extra rider last night," offered Horace.

"Who is it?"

"Duke von Angelhardt rode in with my men. He insisted on seeing you this morning."

"I don't know if I'm in the mood."

"All I know is that he requested a pot of tea, a lot of sugar, and requisition forms. I didn't understand the third one."

Civilia shook her head.

"He's waiting in your chambers, your highness."

"You're my advisor, Horace—what do you think?"

"I think you should meet him. I could see in his eyes that he had an important message for you."

"I trust your judgment both on the battlefield and the home front. Thank you, Horace."

"You're welcome, your majesty."

Civilia departed silently away from the rest of the soldiers. Horace barked out some orders for the Scarlet Riders while puffing away.

"All right, ladies and gentlemen, we've had our ceremony, now let's get back to work! I want the Valkyries on one side and the Knights on the other. On the double!"

The group went back to drilling while Martha and her group traveled back to Titan Technologies. Passing through the rooms of the castle, Civilia answered the salutes at every turn. Reaching her apartment, she quickly removed her boots so her servants could remove the fruits of Andres' labor. Standing behind a desk with his hands at ease, Wilhelm had his sword laid across the table. The duke saluted her until Civilia had taken a seat at the desk. Wilhelm began his defense:

"At the time of your ancestor, Ulysses Rhone, it was traditional that when an officer was subject to judgment he would first surrender his sword and remain at-ease before the sovereign. The Uniform Code of Titan Military Justice adopted all of the traditions of the First King. Despite the many revolutions, the laws and codes of our military have gone unaltered and I will abide by them."

"Why do you sit in judgment before me?"

"I believe the charges should have been preferred already. The whole of Titanus thinks that I should be held for treason since I am directly responsible for the death of Crown Prince Cedric Rhone."

"It is a capital crime to cause the death of the royal heir."

"I am prepared to face that as well."

"All right, you traitorous angel, how much longer are you going to hold me in suspense?" mocked Civilia.

"I'm sorry, but certain formalities have to be established in a Titan court martial. The reason I had to bring you here is because what I'm about to tell you is going to get me in a lot of trouble both on Terminus Mundus and perhaps even in the Celestial Realm. However, some information needs to be shared no matter the cost. Cedric is alive and well."

Filled with relief, the queen clutched her heart and took a few deep breaths.

"Thank God."

"Cedric was critically wounded by Abaddon in Castle Acadia. He gave Cecilia and the others the time they needed to escape through the crypt. I was able to get to him in time and start the healing process. Unfortunately, in my current condition, my magic wasn't strong enough to restore his health. I had to bargain with the Kablisha for the use of the Holy Grail. Bishop Wulf was reluctant to part with such a power. In exchange for saving his life, the Kablisha essentially are holding him prisoner in the City of Antiquity."

"Did Cecilia and the others make it to Deniva?"

"Yes. I'm sending Nadia to Deniva to serve as a mentor to Cassandra."

"I don't think that's a good idea."

"We have no choice; Jacob's Revenant killed Cerwin in the crypt. She has no one to guide her in the arts of magic. I heard about what happened that night at the victory ball and I don't think anyone wants another repeat of the frozen ice wine incident. Trust me, my queen, we're going to need Cassandra at full power if we're going to defeat this darkness."

"It should be our darkest hour that we rely on a demoness to give us hope."

"Nadia is no longer our enemy."

"Your feelings for her aside, I will not forgive her for her actions against my grandfather. She invaded Rhinegard."

"I understand."

Civilia was suddenly struck with the severity of the dietary situation that had befallen her son. The Titan rulers had loss all respect for their Kablisha brethren after they rejected King Frederick's call for aid against the Empire.

"He is a prisoner of the Kablisha, but they're Catheri! He'll never survive!"

"That's the reason why I asked for the requisition forms. I have no restrictions concerning traveling back and forth between the City of Antiquity and Rhinegard. I can bring him whatever you wish to send him."

"Raid the slaughterhouses, Wilhelm, whatever it takes!"

"Sounds like a mother sending her son over to the Titan Academy."

"What about an extraction? Could Evengard aid us in getting Cedric out of the city?"

"For now, your majesty, it might be to our advantage to leave him among the Kablisha. There are certain fighting and magical techniques they are willing to teach him if he remains there. No outside help can get to Cedric at this time. The City of Antiquity is protected by a powerful magic barrier that seals it off from the rest of the world."

"Are these techniques they'll teach Cedric worth it?"

"Yes."

"We'll play Bishop Wulf's game for now. However, he'd better pray that he doesn't have to face my wrath if anything goes wrong."

"Don't worry, I will pull Cedric out well before anything like that happens. You know Cedric being there works both ways... your son has brought out the best in a lot of people; he may change the Kablisha for the better."

"Why all the theatrics, Wilhelm?"

"I've sat as a judge many times in the military court, but it's been a long time since I stood accused. I wanted it to be fun for both of us."

"Wilhelm, how did you ever betray God?"

"I'm sorry milady, but some information must be kept confidential," said Wilhelm with a quick wink. "Just remember, while we angels can't break a rule, we are allowed to ever so slightly bend them."

"You're acquitted."

Wilhelm took his sword back and placed it at his side.

"Had he died, I'm not sure if I would have been able to hold back my rage to kill you."

"You're a mother, it's understandable. If it were my child, I would have reacted the same way."

"Wilhelm, you never told me you had a child."

"Nadia and I committed a grave sin. Now I fear the whole planet and perhaps Creation itself will pay for that sin."

Civilia stood and kissed him.

"Make sure he gets ample supplies. There's an unopened case of brandy in my closet, send it with my compliments. He has earned it!"

"I'm sure he'll appreciate it."

Civilia sat down and began to sign all of the requisition forms that Wilhelm had laid out for her. Wilhelm went to get the brandy out of Civilia's closet.

Deniva, Two Rotations Later

"Eagles mate for life."

Old Titan Proverb

At dusk, Cecilia, Ethan, Hippolyte, Christian and Colin gathered outside the city gates. Dressed as rangers, the two were prepared for any danger on their mission into the wilderness. Hippolyte was very upset and hung her head though she wouldn't dare show her tears to Colin.

"All right, Christian, we're counting on you and Colin to be our eyes and ears," ordered Cecilia.

"I won't fail you, your Highness," answered Christian.

"We're going to be at a severe disadvantage without you here, but such expenditures are necessary. If we can do anything to get back to Titanus, it's worth the risk."

Nodding, the operative knew his place; he had served the brother and now would serve the sister.

"We've given you more than enough supplies to work your way there," explained Ethan. "I don't know how you intend to get through the Pass but I'm sure you have a contingency plan."

"I'll worry about the Pass. You just take of her ladyship."

Ethan blushed, but Cecilia gnashed her teeth. A smile came across Christian's lips.

"If everything goes correctly, we'll ride back in about three or four lunar cycles with a report. That is if we even succeed with the infiltration."

"I have faith that there won't be any problems," stated Cecilia.

"I had enough unreasonable expectations dealing with your brother, I don't expect the same from you, your highness."

Christian turned back to see Hippolyte and Colin kissing deeply.

"Should we be happy about this?" wondered Cecilia aloud.

"I don't know why, but I think I like it," teased Christian.

The two broke from their kiss.

"Why do you have to go, Colin?"

"It's my duty. Besides, Christian really is helpless by himself. He prefers to delegate all the meaningless tasks to me."

"I guess," said Hippolyte giggling.

"Hey, I'll be back before you know it."

The Wolf Tribe Chief wasn't too reassured by her lover's comments. The Titan operative wanted to move the love affair along.

"Colin, I'm sorry but you're going to have to wrap this up."

"Right, Christian."

Colin kissed Hippolyte once more. He turned his horse and rode over to Christian. Calvary flew down and landed on the assassin's shoulder.

"What are you doing?"

"I think he's mistaken your shoulder for a tree branch."

Calvary snickered, making the assassin feel even more uncomfortable.

"Well I guess if I don't make it as a soldier, I'll at least have a career as a coat rack."

"Good luck, you two."

"Thank you, your Highness."

"Let's not lose the advantage, Colin."

"Back to keeping time with our heartbeats again!"

As Colin positioned his horse on the road, he turned back to Hippolyte. The two waved goodbye to one another one last time before Christian and Colin broke down the road. The three watched from the castle until they disappeared from view. Crying, Hippolyte sucked her tears back. She found Cecilia's hand come down on her shoulder.

"You don't have to hide your tears, Hippolyte. Always remember that a woman's tears are precious."

"I have to admit, I never thought I'd hear something like that coming from you."

"They'll be fine; those two have gotten out of a lot of tough situations these past revolutions. My brother always knew no matter what kind of mission he sent them on, they'd always come home."

"I know; it's just I wish I had his back on this one."

"There are plenty of eyes that will be watching them; if I know Christian he'll head right for the Wood Elves."

"The Wood Elves? Do they even exist anymore?"

"The Wood Elves are loyal vassals of Titanus," Cecilia snickered. "Christian may have personal reasons as well."

"I guess I'll head back."

Hippolyte sighed heavily as she trotted her horse back into the city gate, leaving Cecilia and Ethan alone. They weren't really alone because Keiko was sitting on a large rock in front of the city gate. Though Cecilia and Ethan weren't really paying attention to the sylph, she was biting down on a handkerchief with a nervous look in her eyes. Ethan got off of his horse first and handed it over to a servant standing near the gate. Offering his hand, he helped Cecilia down from Myst as well. Ethan bit his lower lip in anger.

"Christian would pick a night without the shine of one of the three moons to leave. Here I have you right where I want you, Cecilia, and it's not even romantic."

"What makes you think that I need a cliché like a moon to be romanced?"

"I just thought it would be nice to go for a moonlight walk."

"Well, apparently nature didn't agree with your plans, but it's okay. Perhaps I've been a little too cruel to you, Ethan."

"A little?"

Laughing, the two walked down the road in front of the city. Keiko left her position and started to follow them at a respectable distance.

"Are you aware of the mating rituals of golden eagles?" asked Cecilia.

"I got killed in one biology course with Martha Heinrich; there was no way I was going to take ornithology with her after that."

"That's a pity, you'd find that Doctor Heinrich's lectures are very interesting. The male courts the female by engaging in elaborate flying displays. He follows with posing behaviors and may after a time even bring her a gift of food. The female will fly away and wait for the male on another bluff. If the male fails to pursue her after an appropriate period of time, she will spurn any further displays. Persistence and commitment are as important to golden eagles as to the Titans themselves. It's one of the reasons we took the animal for the Coat of House Rhone."

"Are you saying what I think you're saying?"

"Unfortunately for my mother, King Stephen would not agree to a matrilineal marriage and broke her heart. Thus, she would never again accept any further proposals from him. I wear the badge of honor as proudly as my mother did when I tell you that I'm an eagle."

Cecilia smiled and faced Ethan for the first time. Keiko was crying harder now with a large smile across her. She landed on another rock and kept wishing for Ethan to take the next step.

"Eagles mate for life!"

"Thank you, God!"

Ethan grabbed Cecilia around the waist and lifted her up in the air. Though not used to being so physically manhandled, the Vanadis playfully laughed as she bent down and kissed him. The two held onto each other tightly as Keiko nearly slipped off of her position trying to contain her excitement.

"I can't tell you how long I waited for that, Cecilia."

"Nothing good comes easy! I had two choices the first night we meet either punch you out or slip a dagger in between your ribs to negate the insult. If I had only been any other girl---you're not the only one who's been waiting a lifetime for this Ethan. Now it's your turn."

"Are you sure you're okay with this? I didn't even ask your mother."

"I've waited long enough, Ethan, and you were always her favorite suitor."

"Well, if we're doing this, I'm going to do it right."

Ethan put Cecilia down and got down on his knees. He pulled a ring out of his pocket, a beautiful large diamond surrounded by three opals set on a band of pure gold.

"Princess Cecilia Rhone of the Kingdom of Titanus, will you accept a matrilineal marriage to the fourth son of the Margrave of Deniva?"

"Yes, Ethan de-Milly of Deniva."

Cecilia curtsied to Ethan as he put the ring on her right ring finger. He stood and kissed her again.

"I don't want to seem too pretentious, of course. Your mother will have to offer the final blessing."

Cecilia shook her head.

"Cecilia, the Titans have strict laws concerning the courting period. I can't offend the honor code I swore to at the Academy."

"Don't worry about it."

"Your brother adhered to them so strictly. I thought…"

"Just because my brother believes all those silly traditional Titan ceremonies need to be observed doesn't mean that I do. I spoke with Father Giovanello and we can be married at the end of the lunar cycle. I trust you can make all of the necessary preparations for a gown worthy of my grace and beauty."

"You'll have the finest."

Keiko's excitement had turned to fury at this point. She screamed at the lack of respect that the Titan princess had for her own customs. Cecilia grimaced as the sylph flew down.

"My lady, words cannot describe my happiness for you but I cannot allow such a blatant disregard for tradition. If your brother was to know of this…"

"Keiko, if you don't shut up, you're not invited to the wedding."

Keiko sighed and started to cry silently.

"I miss Lord Cedric!"

Keiko looked to the heavens as if to mutter a prayer when she spotted something moving against the canopy of the sky.

"My lady!"

Cecilia sighed as she had to break another kiss from Ethan.

"Keiko, I swear, if you interrupt me, I will personally use you for target practice."

"Look!"

Staring into the night sky, Cecilia pulled a pair of scopes from her waist. She turned on the night vision and stared. Andres was soaring down an air current to the castle. A big smile crossed the face of the Vanadis.

"What is it?" asked Ethan.

"It's one of ours!" exclaimed Cecilia. "All right, Martha!"

Andres soared down to a rock in front of Cecilia. It performed the same bow to her as it did towards Civilia earlier, except without the defecation.

"Is that a tufted condor?" pondered Ethan.

"Andres was Martha's little pet project. It looks like the good-for-nothing runt of the litter does have a talent."

"He made it all the way here from Rhinegard?"

Cecilia took the recorded message from Andres.

"You'd better follow us back, that is if you want to get your reward."

Andres nodded happily.

"This is the break we needed, Ethan. With any luck..." stammered Cecilia before stopping herself. "I'm getting ahead of myself. Besides, we need to bask in some congratulations!"

They walked back to the city. Keiko flew close to Cecilia almost as if to use her body as a shield. Andres appeared to be staring at her hungrily.

"What is it?"

Keiko pointed to Andres. "He's scaring me!"

"I can see why," said Cecilia. "Come on!"

The group headed back into the city.

Port Talus, Napolitan, Two Rotations Later

"A soldier who is not prepared to die in war is a fool. The sovereign weighs the necessity of conflict with this heavy burden in mind. Yet we fall into the trap time and time again believing that there is an 'invincible warrior.' It is these high-profile deaths that are the hardest to take."

Journal of General Darius

The streets of the trade city were silent. Tens of thousands of mourners lined every street in the capital. Everyone was dressed in black and many were crying into black handkerchiefs. The Praetorian Guard marched in full ceremonial garb with all pomp and circumstance down the streets of Port Talus. Behind them was a wagon bearing a coffin with the body of Prince Julius inside of it. The coffin was open so the peaceful, serene face of Julius could clearly be seen by all mourning his passing. Replicas of Excalibur and the Sacred Shield were placed over his chest and folded in his arms. The wagon's pace was slow and deliberate. It was on its way to a special open mausoleum on the eastern hill of Dragon's Rest. Children and women hung their heads in abject sorrow. Former members of the Legion saluted the coffin of the First Tribune when it passed them. After some time, the wagon would reach the mausoleum. Constantine, Marguerite, James, Matthias, Vincenzo, and Marcus Polonius stood with members of the Legions. The wagon stopped at the mausoleum and the Praetorian removed the coffin. They placed it in the middle of the tomb. Constantine had tears streaming down his face. It was painful for him to even stand there and watch. He knew it would be the last time he would the see the beautiful face of his son, the son in whom he placed so much hope, and the son he thought would one rotation rule the Alliance. James and Marcus stood next to one another. The battle-hardened legionnaires were not comforted by the slobbering of their Caesar.

"Not Julius—after revolutions on the battlefield, I would have never expected that he would die like this," said James. "I always thought this would be Cagius' fate."

"You were the one who warned us legionnaires not to fall into the trap," suggested Marcus.

"And still?"

James wept from his one eye.

"Julius is dead, Cagius is missing, and the royal family is broken," said Marcus. "Napolitan has fallen on hard times indeed. Are we to be eternally cursed for bringing Draconius to justice?"

"It's not over yet. We didn't find Excalibur or the Sacred Shield, and not everyone can carry those weapons. There may still be a Paladin who can save us."

"As unbelievable as it may seem, I can't imagine that Valentine lost them both."

James shook his head. Suddenly he broke into a coughing fit. He put a handkerchief to his mouth and Marcus noticed blood spilling onto it.

"What's wrong, James?"

"My stomach's been bothering me lately, and this news has been trying on me. I guess I'm due for a physical after all."

Constantine and Marguerite walked towards the coffin, each carrying a lily. The two them dropped the lilies on Julius' body.

"Julius, you would have made a grand Caesar. The line is now broken; the House of Imperia was short-lived."

Marguerite was disturbed. In her heart of hearts she still believed her son Cagius was alive. If so, the House of Imperia would carry on, but her husband treated the moment as if they both had been lost.

"We've had no word about Cagius."

Constantine didn't answer but Marguerite saw a clench of anger in his eyes. She thought at first it was at the sheer mention of the name of his other son. However, her husband was coming to grips with something else.

"He should have been buried with his sword and shield! It is the right of all Paladins! Where are his weapons? How dare they send me back his body without them? Our enemy truly has no honor."

"What if Cagius has them? Perhaps he carries on the fight in his place."

"It would be just like him to leave his brother behind. That boy never knew his true duty. Then again, what could I ever expect of a simple grunt?"

Marguerite cried harder. It was as if her heart had been torn out twice. She not only had to deal with the death of her son but also the scorn of her husband for her only living son.

"How could you?"

Marguerite bent down and kissed Julius. She covered her face with a black handkerchief before she left the site. Marcus immediately went over to her and led the wife of the Caesar back to the palace. He whispered something in her ear that comforted her. Matthias approached the coffin.

"Caesar, it is time."

"No father should live to bury his son."

Constantine kissed his son.

"This was all for you! Why didn't you do as I asked, my son? Perhaps then you would have had it all. Damn that bitch of a servant to hell!"

Constantine left the coffin. The mourners approached the mausoleum and paid their respects. It took many rotations for the stream of mourners to honor their beloved Napolitan Prince. In death, Julius had finally received the praise he deserved.

Arudin Forest

"Anton DeVries, you must take Dulles away from here or else he will surely die by the usurper's hands. I give you the Promissory Ring of House Landon; when Dulles comes of age make sure he gets this. She'll be waiting for him. Now go."

Cerwin Faulkner to the Ranger Anton DeVries

The trees of the Arudin forests did not have the same towering and mystic powers as those in the Forest of the Eternal Spring. The forest canopy, however, was thicker and more lush in these greenwoods. The sounds of a rolling stream and the songs of thousands of birds echoed along the forest roads. Colin and Christian were trotting through the woods on a dirt path with Calvary flying over them.

"This reminds me of the movie I took Hippolyte to," said Colin.

"In what way?"

"Well, one character got the other character out in the wilderness in order to kill him."

Christian shook his head.

"Of course, if you choose to dance with death, I will certainly oblige you."

"I'm not letting you watch any more movies!"

"What are we doing here anyway? The Kaiser Mountain Pass is in the other direction."

"We need help to cross the pass, and our vassals have promised to provide them."

The two heard noises.

"When do you suppose they'll make a move? They've only been watching us since we entered the forest."

"The Wood Elves always had bad timing."

Stopping, Colin sighed as Christian decided to shout into the middle of the forest.

"All right Gerard, enough fooling around! Show yourselves!"

The two heard the rustling of trees and branches. They looked around to see an army of a thousand wood elves dressed in ranger outfits standing on tree branches. These elves were shorter than their high elf cousins, with larger black eyes. They did not share the same thin and graceful complexion either, but were slightly stockier. This was due to their breeding with mortal man. All carried bow and arrows on their back and daggers on their brown belts. A single elf walked down the path, with a bushy blonde beard and long blonde hair. He was a bit stockier than his other companions and dressed in the same garb. The larger bow on his back allowed him to draw with much more power than his companions.

"You shouldn't have gone to this much trouble for an old friend," said Christian.

"I just wanted to make you feel slightly uneasy," said Gerard. "We can't take too many chances with demonkin and duco-matios lurking in the forest."

"They've never pushed this far south."

"They're searching for Queen Cassandra. A female Acolyte passed through the woods recently towards Deniva. Five of us attempted to stop her but she cast a spell on them all and put them to sleep. It was unusual for a creature of that power not to devour their souls."

"Christian, you don't suppose that's Nadia?" asked Colin.

Christian gritted his teeth.

"If Nadia has thrown in her lot with Abaddon we're in a world of trouble, but still, she is a magus. I'm starting to wonder if the Duke is working against us."

"I assume you wish to speak with her highness," suggested Gerard.

"It would help."

"Queen Civilia's here?" asked Colin.

"No, he speaks of Judge Landon."

Colin looked puzzled.

"I'm ready when you are, Gerard," said Christian.

"Follow me!" said Gerard.

The two followed Gerard and his warriors into the middle of the forest. Overwhelmed, Colin witnessed the huge city of the wood elves built entirely in the treetops. The residences themselves were made of wood, with mud covering the outside of them. Wood planks layered with clay tiles served as the roof. Hemp was used to hold the wood in place. Magic encased globes served as the power source and light for the individual homes and plank bridges. Occasionally, the elves would simply swing from a hemp rope from home to home.

Colin was surprised to see an extensive aqueduct system bringing in clean water from the river. The assassin took notice of a drilling army of twenty thousand elves consisting entirely of rangers.

"So the Titans do keep the true strength of vassals under wraps."

"We've been given the sanctuary and promise of protection from the Titans since the time of the Dark Elf rebellion," said Gerard. "This city of the trees is all that is left of our people."

"DULLES!" shouted a sweet female voice.

Christian grimaced at the sound of the name. High above, a high elf maiden stood at the edge of one of the platforms. Judge Rosa Landon was more muscular and heavier than most high elves due to her revolutions living out on the woods. A silver circlet held her dyed, fiery hair, and she was garbed in a long green dress and brown boots. Her eyes were bright green and shining with love. Towering over her comrades, the she-elf jumped onto a rope, slid, and twisted her body down effortlessly to the dirt. Leaping at Christian before he could dismount, she grabbed him around the neck and planted a big kiss on his lips. Christian lost his balance and the two went tumbling to the ground. Colin decided this was a good time to get off his horse as well. DeVries was lying flat on his back with Rosa on top of his chest.

"You nearly killed the both of us, Rosa!"

The she-elf got embarrassed as he tried to lift her off of him. The two of them sat on the ground for a moment facing each other.

"I'm so sorry. It's just that when I heard what had happened to Prince Rhone I feared the worst. I'm so happy to see you."

To ease her tears, Christian gently hugged her and kissed her on her head.

"It's all right. I'm okay."

Rising to their feet, Colin terminated his laughter.

"Colin Wilkins, may I present Judge Rosa Landon, the leader of the Wood Elves."

"Your ladyship."

"He's very well-mannered for an assassin."

"Pardon me, my lady, but why do you call him Dulles?"

Christian swallowed hard.

"I'm so sorry, Christian, I guess I overreacted when I saw you."

"It's all right." Christian sighed. "Colin, it's only right that you know since there has to be a level of trust between comrades. My real name isn't Christian DeVries, it's Dulles Marisol."

Colin thought that Christian was joking for a moment. When DeVries didn't smile, Wilkins knew that he was telling the truth. The rumors had already flared up for revolutions that Gwendolyn Marisol had a child, he just never suspected that child would have been right under his nose.

"You're Gweyn Marisol's stillborn child?"

"The assassin cut my mother deep but Cerwin was still able to deliver me prematurely. He deemed it was safe to put me in the care of the Edenian ranger Anton DeVries. It was the time of severe religious persecution of Christians by the Temple. It was easy for Anton to seek sanctuary in Titanus claiming to be a religious refugee. Since Wilhelm knew of my true past, he allowed me to stay with him on his plantation. When Cedric went to train with Wilhelm, I met him there."

"And Judge Landon?"

"My family spoke out against the murder of Gweyn Marisol and for that we became enemies of Camdem Jenitzen. Our families had agreed ahead of time to form a union with a Marisol male and Landon female. My father finally decided it was no longer prudent to stay in Evengard and decided to declare our house rogue. We came under the protection of King Justin Rhone, and were established here in the Arudin Forest as the leaders of the Wood Elves. My mother and father died here. Only my sister, Vanessa, and I are left of the Landon line."

"Now I know why we came here first. Don't worry, Christian, I won't get in your way."

"There's more to love than mere carnal pleasure, Colin!"

Colin snickered.

"To think I was assisting in the harboring of the most wanted man in all of Evengard. Does Amuro know who you really are?"

"I trust Amuro and love her in my own way. However, it would be best if I didn't declare myself in front of her. Though she constantly complains about him, she loves her father with all her heart and I doubt she'd believe me anyway."

Christian put his arm around Rosa and started to walk with her.

"Rosa, have you done as I asked?"

"Of course, Christian," acknowledged a smiling Rosa. "Minister Nuncio has been made aware of your coming to Palacio Magnifico. He will meet you at the Kaiser Mountain Pass in two rotations. He said that he hopes that you didn't forget about his fee."

Christian rolled his eyes.

"What a greedy bastard!"

Rosa signaled to some of the servants.

"Please take Prince Marisol's equipment up to my manor."

"At once, my lady," said the servant.

Christian stared at Rosa for a moment and she started to laugh hysterically. She patted him on the chest two times.

"Don't worry, I'll put you in the guest room."

"And my associate?"

"Yes," said Rosa as she looked Colin over. "Colin Wilkins, the famous Lunar Falcon! Since you were named after a bird with such grace, I didn't expect you to be a flesh and blood tank."

"Deathbringer is a sophisticated piece of weaponry; only those with significant gifts may take up the dance with death."

"Is he always like this?"

"Please bear with us."

"Absolutely."

Rosa took the time to pull Christian down to her lips. She hugged him tightly and started to speak softly to him.

"I am terribly sorry for the loss of your friend. Everyone loved Cedric very much. Despite whatever the horrible rumors said about him, Cedric would always give everything for this planet and its people."

"Cecilia doesn't think Cedric is dead."

"I would imagine it hit her the hardest, next to Cassandra of course. We all knew that Cecilia believed her brother was some kind of divine warrior. She'll never believe he's dead."

"There's a powerful bond between twins, Rosa. If she can sense something…"

"I understand. What is the word of our new queen?"

"Cassandra is still shaken up over what transpired. However, she seems to be getting stronger every day."

"She'll be fine—she is an elf, after all—at least the better half of her. I can't tell you how delighted I am that one of our own has ascended to such power."

"Really? You know what they say about half-elves."

"Well she's got the better half at least, unlike you! Come on, I'll make you dinner."

"Well, no squirrel this time."

"Squirrel is a woodland delicacy!"

Christian and Rosa grabbed on a hemp rope and pulled it once. A pulley system lifted the two into the air and safely onto a plank leading into the large residence of Rosa Landon.

Calvary stared from Colin's shoulder as the assassin fed him a piece of raw meat.

"What do you think, Calvary?"

Calvary sounded a long call.

"That's what I thought."

As Colin and Calvary walked towards a rope, Colin heard a faint lamentation. It was not as artistic and beautiful as the one that Saria had first sung for Cedric on that fateful day, but even though he couldn't understand the words, Colin could feel the strength of Cedric's deeds within the lamentation.

"Gerard? What's that music?"

"A lamentation for Prince Cedric Rhone. We honor the true heroes. Tonight we will sing of the deeds of the Divikin who will not yield even before the angels of Hell."

Colin stood for a moment and absorbed it all. He began to pray silently that Hippolyte wouldn't be singing the same lamentation before this was all over.

BISHOP'S RESIDENCE, CITY OF ANTIQUITY

"All right son, here's the deal! I know you're used to a life of luxury and safety in Rhinegard, but in order to reach your potential I've brought you here. Get ready for the worst training you could possibly imagine, but if you persevere, you'll become the greatest warrior this world, and perhaps creation, has ever seen."

William von Angelhardt to a young Cedric Rhone

Muscles writhing in agony from the poison, the Titan prince grimaced every time he wrapped the bandage across his shoulder and chest.

"So much for being a fast healer. I really wanted to avoid this, but I guess there's no choice."

Cedric pushed a button and the sound of heels clicking along the tile floor was instantaneous. Slightly out of breath, the dutiful cleric smiled and curtsied before her charge.

"How may I serve you, my lord?"

"Florence, you're a nice girl and honestly the personal service is greatly appreciated. However, you do realize I practically gave up my life for Cassandra, and am really looking forward to continuing that relationship."

"Of course, my lord. However, you must realize that serving as the personal cleric of the Permaneo Ordinaris Eques is the greatest glory I could hope to achieve. Those mean little twits in my graduating class said I would never amount to anything and now I have the last laugh. Besides,

I would never seek to tempt you away from your chaste virtue; it would be a terrible sin for a cleric."

Cedric thought the answer was rehearsed and wasn't sure if Florence actually believed the words she was telling him.

"Of course, if a handsome, powerful, Titan prince would happen to return the deep affections that I share for him, well, I couldn't imagine a more suitable form of courtly love."

"Now I believe you. Florence, would you please change this bandage for me?"

"Oh dear, Lord Cedric, you shouldn't have tried to do that by yourself."

Conjuring healing magic in her hands, the cleric treated the wounded areas. She quickly wrapped fresh bandages around his shoulder and chest. The abdomen wound was left unbound, since it healed faster than the others. Interrupted by a rap on the door, Florence stopped her investigation.

"Come in," shouted Cedric.

Quinn and Mesmara approached. Florence assisted Cedric in putting a t-shirt over the bandages. The two Kablisha warriors were not surprised to see the cleric so attentive to her charge. Both suspected some funny business going on, but allowed it to pass.

"How are you feeling, sir?" asked Quinn.

"Slightly better. Florence only drew two vials of poison from my blood this time."

"Uncle Argus wants to see you—he says he has something for you," declared Mesmara

"I guess I'm up to it."

Standing and stretching, Florence gave Cedric the once over again. Flashing a thumb's up, she gave him the go-ahead to follow Titan and Mesmara.

"Cookie is puzzled with some of your habits," said Quinn.

"He says he's never seen someone eat so much food who complained about it so much," added Mesmara.

"First rule of survival: you eat all you can get, no matter what."

"You can't mean that you'll eat anything?" inquired Quinn.

"Absolutely. You learn to live off of what's in the land if your supplies run out. There is one particular species of locust that tastes just like chicken."

"You eat bugs?" Mesmara gagged.

"It's pure protein; just make sure you crunch the head hard because you don't want it crawling back up your throat when you swallow."

Mesmara sprinted out of the room. Cedric and Quinn heard the sound of gagging and a toilet bowl flush.

"I think you went a little over the top with your joke, Cedric."

"I was serious."

Returning to the others, Mesmara regained her composure.

"Please, Lord Cedric, during your time here, I would appreciate it if you do not discuss any more of your culinary expertise."

Reaching an octagon-shaped room, the three entered. Stacks of books surrounded the single entrance of the bishop's library. The central repository featured rare books, some as old as the founding of the City of Antiquity. Argus stood at the southern end of the room with his arms crossed behind his back.

"I'm glad to see you've finally arrived. Mesmara, Quinn, I wish to speak with Prince Rhone alone, please."

The two nodded and closed the door behind Cedric. Darkness overtook the room and the Titan prince was forced to adjust his eyes to see Argus.

"I know of your prowess with a sword, Prince Rhone, but what are your abilities with magic?"

"I have full mastery of saber magic, proficiency in the healing branches of white magic, and full mastery of domination magic."

Argus dropped his book. Focusing his narrow eyes on the Titan prince, the Edenian exile had assumed that domination magic was a weapon of the Nephilim alone.

"Did you even consider the dangers of learning that branch? Perhaps that was your plan all along. Why bother to waste countless lives in conquering an empire when you could simply manipulate the minds of its leaders to kneel to you!"

"What do you know about me, Argus? You make blatant assumptions denigrating my character, yet you never bother to seek an answer to the question. Had I not studied that branch, I would have never discerned Abaddon's plans."

"And what were the results of your actions? I bet the Nephilim you interrogated was nothing more than a vegetable when you were finished with him!"

"This is a war and I made a choice! Whether you believe it or not, I hold the light and the darkness in my heart!"

"That's a dangerous road, Cedric, even for one that can take down a Fallen Angel. What makes you think that you're immune to its seduction? I'll test you!"

"What test?"

Disappearing from Cedric's line of sight, the sword master went into a fighting stance. Knowing his body wouldn't respond as quickly as his mind, the prince favored his wounds. As he wondered the extent of Abaddon's damage, the sharp pain from a blow to his shoulder broke his train of thought. Argus landed a punch right on the wound.

"Not as perceptive as I hoped!"

"Why don't you try that again, Argus?"

"I'll give you your fill, my warmongering friend."

Argus kicked Cedric in the side but the sword master grabbed his foot. The prince swept Argus's other leg out and both men landed on the floor. Fresh blood dripped from Cedric's wounds and a slight hesitation allowed Argus to disappear from his sight once more. As the prince lumbered to his feet, he experienced another painful blow.

"What's the matter, Cedric? Did Abaddon take so much out of you?"

Grimacing from the pain but too stubborn to accept defeat, Cedric tackled Argus at his waist. Driving the captain into the ground, Argus felt one of his ribs break. Dumbfounded at how the wounded Titan managed to gain the advantage, he understood how Abaddon must have underestimated his foe. Despite Cedric's persistence, Argus wouldn't concede defeat and was determined to knock the arrogance out of the Titan prince. Perspiring profusely, both men stood and Argus vanished once more. Holding his ground, Cedric closed his eyes. Just as Argus came upon him, the Titan prince rammed his right fist upward. Hit in the nose, Argus collapsed in a crumpled heap. Kneeling down, the sword master put his forearm across the captain's throat.

"I win!"

"Why did you let me linger for so long? You beat me in one punch!"

"I never fought you before, so I wanted to see what you had. Don't feel so bad, I put Wilhelm down the first time I fought him as well."

Releasing his hold on Argus, Cedric extended his hand down and lifted the captain up. Mesmara and Quinn rushed into the room with their swords drawn but their commander ordered them to stand down.

"How did you detect me, Cedric?"

"Your sandals make too much noise on the hardwood floor. I just needed the time to memorize your patterns. A true warrior uses all their senses when fighting his opponent. If it wasn't sound, I would have found something else. Trust me; trying to hunt down my buddy Christian when he puts his cloak up is much more difficult."

"I'm not easily impressed, but that was really good."

"Is this what you wanted?"

"Yes. I wanted to know if you were ready for this."

Removing a heavy tome from a bookshelf, Argus presented it to Cedric.

"I'll bet it's been a while."

"I had law books that were smaller than this. Just how many spells do you expect me to learn in here?"

"In this tome, you will find the spell for holy war. Unlike other small-scale holy-based magic attacks, this spell opens the full power of creation to the hands of its caster. If you master this power, you'll be able to annihilate entire divisions of the forces of darkness. Yet, there is one caveat—no person born in creation has ever learned it."

Opening the cover, Cedric skimmed columns of words, runes, and diagrams. As his eyes widened and lips curled, the prince shook his head.

"I don't even know half of prerequisites on this page for the spell alone. I'm going to have to raise my white magic level to even start the basics."

"I didn't say that it wouldn't take time. Even if you do learn to cast it, it will be done in intervals. You'll start off only being able to use it as a weak attack but it will get progressively stronger. I look forward to measuring your progress from the tome."

"Well, I guess I have some reading to do."

"Good luck; we'll spar again. I'll get you next time."

Laughing, Cedric gave Argus a hearty handshake. As he left with Quinn and Mesmara, Argus stomped his foot in disgust.

"There's no way that the duke taught him all this!"

With each step, the pain accelerated throughout his body. Determined to keep up his false front, the prince hid his agony from Quinn and Mesmara.

"That was really impressive," acknowledged Quinn.

"I wish you could teach us how to do that," pleaded Mesmara.

"It's easy, just be more wary of your surroundings. Battles aren't always fought under optimal conditions. You may find yourself fighting foes on a moonless night. That's when you have to be very careful."

The two just stared at him amazed and Cedric couldn't help but laugh.

"You can do it. Now, if you don't mind, I have some reading to do."

The blissful aroma of a long-lost treasure filled the prince's olfactory canals. Dismissing his two attachés, Cedric entered his room to find Wilhelm von Angelhardt grilling two thick, T-bone steaks on a charcoal grill. Not even the distraction of Florence changing his linens could sway his focus from the steak.

"You still prefer medium-rare, your excellency?" teased Wilhelm.

"Just don't overcook it, Wilhelm. Florence, could I trouble you for some of your services?"

"It's not trouble, Lord Cedric."

Dropping what she was doing, the cleric removed the bandages.

"There was nothing in school that prepared me for a wound like this."

Wilhelm's curiosity got the better of him and he closely observed Florence drawing vials of poison. The purple ooze was eating the new skin away from the prince's body. Once Florence contained the poison, she tended the wounds.

"Anything else, my lord?"

"I think I need some ice."

The cleric went outside and brought a fresh icepack from her medical tray. She cracked it twice against the dresser and handed it to Cedric.

"That's all, thank you."

Florence curtsied and departed. Wilhelm assisted his liege by wrapping a second bandage around the ice pack.

"How are those wounds?" asked Wilhelm.

"I'm in excruciating pain in all of the wounds and it won't stop throbbing. It didn't help that Argus decided to use me as a punching bag today. I'm sure Abaddon must have coated his blades in some poison. His magic bored right into my body so the poison had ample access to ravage my system."

"The Divikin do have a weakness to the darkness affinity. I'm not surprised that it's lingering. Still, you did take Argus down—that's worth something."

"So can I go home yet?"

Silently, Wilhelm tended to the steaks on the grill. He set the food down on the table and the two offered a quick prayer. Like a predator voraciously tearing into flesh, Cedric savored the first bite as it melted into his mouth.

"I'm afraid that's going to take some time, Cedric."

"Historically, the Kablisha aren't easy to placate. I never imagined prison to be like this."

"It's complete with all of the various forms of torture. The food stinks and they torture you every rotation by sending in an adorable cleric to take care of you. Have you let her down gently yet?"

"I have explained courteously and she is head over heels in love with me. She knows I won't hit a woman, so beating her over the head won't work either. So besides dinner and the checkup, what do I owe the pleasure? I'd offer you something but I'm a little short right now."

"Actually, I came here bearing gifts; there's no way you're going to heal those wounds of yours on vegetables alone."

Portals started to open around the room. A generator, refrigerator, chest, and crates appeared. A big smile came across Cedric's face.

"I guess you told mom."

"Civilia didn't think that Kablisha cuisine was agreeing with you."

"Well, eating pizza twice every rotation can't be healthy for me."

Reaching into a case, Wilhelm pulled out a bottle of brandy. He threw it to Cedric who opened it immediately.

"Consider this a reward for taking the action none of us had the courage to do. This might help dull some of the pain."

Licking his lips, he poured two glasses. They toasted and Cedric savored his first drink.

"I really thought I drank my last swig of brandy right after the battle with Abaddon. The odd thing is, it doesn't taste as sweet now. So, did you spread the word?"

"Unfortunately, I think it's best that only your mother knows for now. Oh, and I believe you misplaced this."

Wilhelm dropped the Rising Moon Helmet on the table.

"Abaddon's magic broke the strap and I had to battle without it."

"It was my fault, I made an amateur's mistake leaving it behind. They dropped it outside the barrier next to Felicia's headless body, I didn't expect humanity to have grown colder than angels in hell. It had a flag draped over it to play with morale. Titanus doesn't know if you're dead or alive. Napolitan is completely devastated by the loss of Prince Julius. All of the heirs are exiled in Deniva. There's just so little hope now among our allies. It wasn't until I broke the news to your mother that a spark of life returned to her."

"Hope is a funny thing. It can be so easily snuffed out at first, but when it spreads it leaves a conflagration nothing will stamp out. I'm not doing the West any good as a prisoner."

"Just try to learn what you can for now; I promise we'll get you out of here. That refrigerator is stocked with enough food to get you through the next two lunar cycles. I'll continue to visit and replenish you as I can. If you ever need anything, don't hesitate to tell me."

"What about Cassie? How's she doing?"

"Cassandra is still coming to grips with everything that happened. Nadia's on her way to Deniva now."

"I understand the choice, but Wilhelm, you must understand my concerns. I looked into Cassandra's corrupted form and I didn't like what I saw."

"She needs someone skilled to complete her training. You're going to need all of Cassie's powers when we take down the rebels. I know no one believes Nadia can be reformed."

"She's still a daughter of the prince! I know she has free will but…"

"Do you doubt my judgment?"

"You have a tendency to be too compassionate at times. You know when it comes to Cassie, I am going to be overprotective."

"There are other reasons why she needs to be there."

"Don't worry, Wilhelm, I'm sure it's for the best. I just don't think my sister will be as understanding."

"I know. Cecilia seemed to be a lot warmer towards Nadia when she was training with you at my plantation, but then again I don't expect anyone to forgive her for what she's done."

"Well, since you dragged yourself all the way out here, you can't leave me here drinking alone. One for the road!"

Cedric filled the two glasses again. Wilhelm held his glass in the air in salute to Cedric.

"No fooling around, Cedric, you did really good out there. Taking down an angel, that's something to be proud of!"

"Thanks, Wilhelm, but I used a lot of what you taught to win."

"Yeah, but I didn't expect you'd get stuck with a situation like this when I trained you."

"I don't believe that. There is a reason for everything."

"When I first started training you, I thought it was to be my successor; I just thought I'd be there with you."

"You were there when I needed you."

They both took a drink.

"I'm going to attempt to infiltrate what's left of the Nephilim and get what information I can. However, Abaddon is not likely to let me in on any important details."

"Well, just get what you can and get out of there. Consider it an order."

"I know. Do you have any other requests?"

"Yeah, I need another cloak. Cassandra still has mine. I also need copies of any book we have in Titanus that discusses these Kablisha. I think it's time I brushed up on my jailers."

"That shouldn't be a problem. Eat up! I'll see you soon!"

"I'll keep you in my prayers."

"Thanks, I need them all. Farewell, your excellency!"

Wilhelm disappeared in a portal. Cedric went back to finishing the steak on his plate.

CASTLE DENIVA

"Then he turned to the woman and said to Simon, 'Do you see this woman? When I entered your house, you did not give me water for my feet, but she has bathed them with her tears and wiped them with her hair. You did not give me a kiss, but she has not ceased kissing my feet since the time I entered. You did not anoint my head with oil, but she anointed my feet with ointment. So I tell you, her many sins have been forgiven; hence, she has shown great love. But the one to whom little is forgiven, loves little.' He said to her: 'Your sins are forgiven.' The others at the table said to themselves, 'Who is this who even forgives sins?' But he said to the woman, 'Your faith has saved you; go in peace.'"

The Napolitan Evangelist 7:44-50

Seated at her desk, Cassandra intently studied the Book of Rune. Unlike her previous attempts at casting, the queen held a spinning ball of fire in her hand. Walker announced Cecilia's presence behind her.

"Your Highness, Princess Cecilia is here."

Breaking her concentration, the gyro of fire dissipated. The Vanadis couldn't hide her uneasiness over the power Cassandra was using to generate the spell.

"Do you have to be so formal, Walker?"

"I know, I walk in and out of these rooms about six times a full rotation," complained Cecilia. "I'm getting tired of being announced."

"I take my duties seriously," responded Walker.

"If you don't mind, Walker, I'd prefer to see Cassandra alone."

A lump growing in her throat, the queen wondered what her haughty companion needed to speak of privately.

"As you wish. I was about to head down to the training room anyway," noted Walker. "Valentine wants a second when Joshua starts training. Do I have your permission, your highness?"

"Of course."

"Just make sure Valentine doesn't kill him!" teased Cecilia as Walker left. She turned her attention back to Cassie. "Does he know that was a joke? Then again, with Valentine you never know."

Unwilling to respond to the jest as she deemed Cecilia's actions bizarre, Cassandra sat petrified at her desk. Grabbing a chair, the Titan princess plopped herself down in front of the young queen.

"I've successfully decoded the message. I have to hand it to my mother—she never gives up."

"Was there any news of Cedric in the message?"

"There was no word, which isn't the worst thing in the world. If he were truly dead our enemies would be blasting trumpets from every parapet. They would have sent one of his body parts to Deniva as a message at least."

"You're right."

"I always am. I checked thoroughly through my mother's message. She wrote it in the ancient tongue just in case it got intercepted. I had to break out the codebook, so it took me a little while longer to read it and then it was a matter of sending a response. Amuro, Cagius, and Hippolyte all wrote something to put in the message. Would you like to add something to it?"

"Thanks, Cecilia, but I don't really have anything that needs to be added at this point. I'm sure the rest of you can handle the logistics of our current situation."

"That's fine. Perhaps anonymity would serve us best for now. The less attention drawn to this location, the better. We've already dealt with two duco-matios."

"If that's all, I bid you good afternoon."

"Not necessarily. It's been bothering me for a while over how I've been treating you."

Enraged by the smugness of her understatement, Cassandra stared at Cecilia with scorn. Ever since the two had been formally introduced, the queen had been walking on eggshells.

"Really?" replied Cassandra, taking a sarcastic tone.

"Hear me out, Cassie, this is hard enough for me. I've been doing a lot of thinking since the night I wanted to bury my ivory dagger deep in your throat."

"That's encouraging."

"It broke my heart to see you break down like that outside the crypt. Part of me wondered if you were really going to kill yourself. Your entire world came crashing down, and look at you now—regal, attentive, and desperate to do anything to win back your home. You're someone I'm willing to charge into war with, and I don't say that about most. I love my brother dearly, and he saw something in you. Cedric knew what it was going to take to save you and just to be willing to give everything up for you makes you worth fighting for."

Observing her target sniffling sweetly at first, Cecilia knew what was coming. It would start with single tear dripping down her left cheek, but the waterworks would be in full force. Annoyed by her companion's countenance, the Vanadis continued her apology.

"I feel I haven't treated you honorably, and for a Titan that is a grave sin. The fact is that I should have embraced you like a sister. Will you forgive me?"

"Of course."

Cassandra willed herself into Cecilia's embrace and dropped her tears onto the Vanadis's shoulder. Rolling her eyes, the Titan princess pulled her in tightly.

"Why did you wait, Cecilia? Why couldn't you tell me all these things before something happened to him?"

"Just as Cerwin always said, you're too quick to cry. Don't you realize that a woman's tears are precious?"

"Just because I well up fast doesn't mean they're not for a reason, sister."

"Okay, are we square?"

"Well, I do have one thing I've been meaning to ask you."

Searching through her desk drawer, the queen pulled out Cedric's rosary.

"How do you pray on these?"

Cecilia bit her lower lip.

"I guess Cedric probably should have thrown his prayer book with the rosary also. I think you and I have to pay Father Michael Giovanello a visit. I think it's about time we started you in RCIA."

"That was what your mother wanted me to go through before I married Cedric, right?"

"Yes. Besides, I want you in the Church so you can serve as the maid of honor at my wedding."

"Ethan proposed?"

A quick smile from Cecilia answered the question. Cassandra hugged her companion tightly once more in congratulations. The tender moment was interrupted as Cecilia's communicator buzzed. The Vanadis grabbed it.

"What's the matter, Ethan?"

"One of the guards called me down, we've got someone approaching the city. She's like nothing I've never seen before. It seems to be some kind of Magus; I'm worried she's part of the Guild."

"Don't do anything, I'll be right down."

Cecilia shut off her communicator. To alleviate the queen's newfound concern, her companion winked at her.

"Cecilia, you don't suppose…?"

"Stay out of sight up here, if worse comes to worst, we'll have Walker get you out of here."

"Okay. Be careful, Cecilia."

At the Castellan Gate, Ethan was on his horse with three other guards. Selim rode up as well.

"What's going on?" asked Selim.

"We think a Magus is approaching the city," replied Ethan. "Since there is great sensitivity between the Acadians and our exiles, we're taking every precaution."

Spotting Nadia's approach through his binoculars, Selim couldn't place the woman. Her nonchalant gait confused him and there was something about her that left him uneasy.

"She isn't an Imperial."

"Pull your men back, Selim, you've got no stake in this."

"I'm curious, Ethan. It's my prerogative to investigate all threats to the city."

"Please, I don't want to threaten the neutrality of this city. If this concerns the queen and something happens to you, we'll have an international incident."

"All right, Ethan, if you insist. This is your city after all."

Signaling to his imperial troops to retreat, Selim and his men returned to the safety of their barracks. As they departed, however, Cecilia came tearing through the city on the back of Myst. Many of the merchants and people on the street had to get out of her way quickly as the Vanadis was not stopping for anything. Ethan already had his hand to his head at his fiancée's blatant disregard for the safety of the civilians.

"Is the mage still coming?" demanded Cecilia.

"Yes."

"I'll meet her!"

"Wait, Cecilia—"

Ethan reached out to grab Cecilia, but she had already ridden off. Gritting his teeth, Ethan ordered his men to remain behind as he chased after her. About two hundred meters from the city, Nadia observed the Titan princess's break-neck approach and knew trouble was approaching. Pulling her spear out from behind her back, the Magus thought to herself: *Did Wilhelm think this through when he asked me to come to Deniva?*

Submissively, Nadia staked her staff in the ground and put her arms up. Before she ran her over, Myst stopped just short of her position.

"I knew an agent of darkness would come for us eventually; I didn't realize Lucifer would send one of his best!"

Placating the enraged princess with a cute and innocent smile, she acknowledged Ethan coming up behind her. Desperately hoping that the Denivan might be a little more reasonable, the magus breathed a sigh of relief.

"Jesus, Cecilia, don't do that to me!" shouted Ethan before he turned his gaze to Nadia. "That isn't guild standard equipment, if you can even call those clothes!"

"We would have been better off if a guild member had shown up," explained Cecilia. "This creature before us poses a greater threat than all of their powers combined."

"Really?" asked Ethan.

The knight was never one to judge a book by its cover and did suspect that this woman before him harbored some powers. However, there was no way she could be as bad as Cecilia was exaggerating.

"Don't be so naïve, Ethan!" scolded Cecilia. "She's one of the daughters of the prince himself."

Remembering his theology courses from the Academy, Ethan dropped his horse back a few feet behind Cecilia.

"I will not deny my origins," explained Nadia. "While I am his spawn, you should know that my father and I stand apart."

"How do you know her, Cecilia?" asked Ethan.

"She's Wilhelm's woman!"

"I prefer the term 'paramour.' It sounds less possessive."

"What business have you here, devil?" demanded Cecilia.

"I come on behalf of Wilhelm von Angelhardt. I bring word that he will not travel openly to Deniva because demonkin agents are following his movements. We have to keep Abaddon blind to Cassandra's presence in this city."

"As far as I'm concerned, a Nephilim is already here! Wilhelm could have easily sent me a message rather than letting his paramour play messenger girl."

"Abaddon still thinks I'm on his side. Therefore, if I come here and make no report on Cassandra, he will think to look elsewhere."

"I wonder what side you're really on. What is your intention?"

"I'm here for Cassandra. We dare not take her out of the safety of this city for now, but there is much she can learn from my powers."

Cecilia twirled her spear above her head before thrusting the tip of it to Nadia's throat. Shivering with fear, Nadia believed the Vanadis made no idle threat.

"Be gone before I put your head on a stake!"

"Come now, Cecilia, you're a good soldier! Would you dare cut off your right arm before you go into battle? Cassandra is a sorceress of tremendous talents. Cerwin Faulkner recognized those talents and placed her on the path of the Rune Mistress. I have the power to finish what her uncle started. There's no one left among you who knows the true power of magic. The Red Wizard is impressive in her own right but Cassandra's true potential would be wasted unless she is fully immersed in the black arts."

As his fiancée grinded her teeth, Ethan didn't know what to do. A part of him wanted to grab Cecilia's spear and put it away from the woman. Yet, the knight feared greatly for his home and the prospect of this woman entering at will.

"I'm a sinner, Cecilia! I've accepted that, but I was given a second chance on the condition that I wouldn't sin anymore. Whether you believe it or not, I love Wilhelm deeply and I would never do anything to betray that love. Yes, I have personal reasons, but I want to see the revolutionaries defeated just like the rest of you. Let me help!"

"I saw what happened to Cassandra the last time someone immersed her in the black arts. My brother isn't here to save her again."

"I agree, the creature cannot be unleashed on this world again."

"What do you think, Ethan?" asked Cecilia.

"While the decision is ultimately yours, I trust Wilhelm. My recommendation is we let her finish what Cerwin started."

"I knew you'd say that. Perhaps the scriptures were right."

Replacing her spear, Nadia curtsied to Cecilia.

"All right, Nadia, you can plead your case to the queen. However, if she refuses your help, I will not hesitate to throw you out. In fact, I may even relish it."

"You have my word that if she rejects my help, I will leave peacefully."

"I'll give you a lift. I don't want a daughter of the prince running wild in the city." Cecilia pulled Nadia up on her horse. The magus spotted the ring on her finger and on Ethan's finger as well. She genuinely smiled.

"Congratulations on your engagement, princess! I have some gifts still about me and I can tell that your children will be very good for the cause."

Blushing as they headed back, both lovers couldn't help but maintain a sense of pride over Nadia's prediction. Inside the castle, Walker and Cagius were standing in one end of a castle training room. Joshua stood with a wooden sword in one hand and a shield in the other. Valentine held a sword made out of bamboo. The assassin seemed irritated while Joshua was bewildered.

"Do you understand what's going on here?" asked Valentine.

"No," answered Joshua.

"This is a bamboo sword. Every time you fail to deflect my attacks, it's going to hurt like nothing has ever hurt you before. You'll be bruised and covered with welts in no time. That pain will be a reminder of the importance of keeping your guard up."

"Why?"

"Because a Paladin is a shield; he defends the weak! The shield you carry is more important than any damn sword you would ever use. The rank is about sacrifice! Julius Imperia understood that when he took up the class. That's why his body lay sprawled out in Castle Acadia. If you're not willing to make that commitment, then don't waste my time!"

Assuming a fighting stance, Joshua raised the ire of his trainer by leading with his sword and not his shield. Valentine relished the lessons he was going to teach this boy. As he came at the paladin-in-training, the assassin knocked him off balance. Joshua maneuvered his shield but was unused to its weight. Staring at the situation before them, Cagius and

Walker knew it was only a matter of time. They barked out instructions in the hope it would buy him some time.

"Keep the shield at shoulder level!" yelled Walker. "Never let it drop lower!"

"Remember the sword can also be used as a shield," suggested Cagius.

Valentine swatted Joshua in the back. Joshua never felt pain like that in his life, but managed to get back into a fighting position. Though he was impressed at his recovery, his instructor would not let such a mistake pass.

"If this was a real sword, you'd be dead! I put a clean wound right into your liver. You'll thank me some day when you make that block! Get ready!"

Coming at him again was too painful for Walker and Cagius to watch. Joshua was beaten so badly that Walker went for the hilt of Sigmund in case he had to stop Valentine from killing him.

"Valentine's going all-out against him," observed Walker.

"I think he partially blames himself for my brother's death," explained Cagius. "Valentine's emotions are hard to read at times. We're just used to seeing him kill but there's more to it. It was highly unusual for a person of his rank, but my father never let him take on anyone as a ward and Valentine sees Joshua as a hope for my country."

The two heard another thud and Joshua's resonating scream. Cagius shook his head and put his fingers to bridge of his nose.

"Move your feet!" ordered Cagius.

"When I sparred with the Acadians, they would attack me, at least! How can I win if I just defend?" screamed Joshua in defiance.

"How can you attack?" lectured Walker. "You won't be fighting second-class Acadian halberdiers anymore! If you don't learn how to use that shield, you'll die quickly. You're letting your anger make you stupid—don't fight angry!"

Leading with another attack, Valentine nailed Joshua right in the middle of his chest.

The boy fell to the ground gasping for air and cursing in pain. Walker and Cagius could make out some of the wounds through Joshua's shirt and were disheartened.

"That is a kill shot, boy, there is no recovery from a wound to the heart," taunted Valentine. "Not that I'm sure you have much of one anyway. All of those brawny muscles and you don't have the slightest sense how to use any of them. We're going to need a lot of work."

Silently praying in her room with closed eyes, Amuro prayed for Joshua's safety. In part, she was trying to drown out Joshua's screams from the room below her. However, every time she heard the sound of a whap she closed her eyes tighter and prayed harder. After a few moments, she gave up praying and poured herself a glass of elven sweet wine instead. About to savor the first taste, she was interrupted by gentle rapping at her door. Putting the glass down, she opened the door and found her sister. Saria had her hands folded, shoulders slumped, and eyes facing downwards. The older sister had seen this look before and wondered if her baby sister had done something wrong.

"Saria, what's wrong?"

"Can I talk with you, sis?"

"My door is always open," offered Amuro as she let her sister in. "What's the matter? Is that guy from the club bothering you again?"

"No, I believe dear Cagius made his point quite clear."

"Probably from the tip of his trident, but I know something's bothering you. You can't hide anything from me."

"Sister, I fear that I'm a bit of window dressing here."

"Well, you shouldn't feel too badly. After all, there's not much any of us can do as long as this Denivan Exile is upon us."

"Actually, I was hoping you could teach me how to fight."

Laughing at first, Amuro's apprehension grew when her sister didn't join in. The elf marshal wondered what she was thinking. The mere thought of Saria in battle horrified her. Determined to defuse this little inconvenience quickly, the red wizard didn't want her sister getting any romantic ideas about battle.

"Oh no, you were serious."

"I'm not offended by your reaction, dearest sister. You've always been the stronger of the two of us, but I thought maybe there could be something I could do to help."

"No offense, sis, but singing and dancing aren't exactly considered martial arts. I think you would be better off sticking to what you're best at."

"I'm stronger than you think; dancing does take a lot of physical exertion."

"I don't doubt that, and I've seen some of your dancing. I know you're a lot more flexible than I'd ever be. However, that is very different from handling a weapon."

"Isn't there some type of test I could take?"

In an attempt to quickly squelch Saria's desires, Amuro drew Enhancer. Since it was balanced for her body, Saria would never be able to wield it and this fantasy would be over. Handing it to her sister, the younger elf took it eagerly.

"Try and lift it to the level of your eyes."

"Okay."

Instantly burdened by the weight of the weapon, the young she-elf tried to lift the sword. Persevering, ignorant of her sister's trick, she managed to finally get it close to her eye level after failing eight times.

"This is a pretty large room, try and take a swing with it."

Saria nodded and struggled. She lost her balance as soon as she swung, but Amuro dutifully caught her before she fell down.

"Are you okay?"

Saria cried.

"Come on, Saria, not everybody is cut out to be a soldier. Someone like you, however, would be perfect for propaganda promotion and troop entertainment."

"I don't want you to think of me as a doll."

"Hey, don't ever sell yourself short like that! You're just talented in a different way."

"I didn't want to come here, Amuro. I was trapped and everyone has worked so hard. When Cedric did what he did, all I wanted was to get out alive. I'm such a horrible person for wanting to live while he died!"

Grabbing her sister by the shoulders, Amuro made her younger sister look her in the eyes.

"No. Don't even think that! Cedric knew what he had to do! You don't bear any responsibility for that. You're right, you didn't ask to be part of us, but you shouldn't worry about that. We'll take care of you."

"But isn't there anyway I could fight? I know some magic."

"Who taught you magic?" asked Amuro.

"I learned some magic in the illusion branch while I was training in singing and dancing. They train us so we can have greater effect on the crowd before us. I can use some status effect spells."

Feeling bad about the trick she pulled, Amuro decided to placate her sister a little.

"Status-effect spells? If you can use that, there might be a more elegant weapon for you."

The devious smile crossing the face of her older sister made Saria nervous. After she had left the room, the young elf could hear the sound of rummaging through a chest. She closed her eyes a few times when she heard her sister cursing when she couldn't find something. Finally, a loud crackling made her jump. Amuro reentered the room holding a long leather whip. Saria gulped when she saw it.

"What are you doing?" screamed Saria.

"It's for you," said Amuro as she shook her head.

"Cagius and I... we haven't... I don't even think I could, but if you think it would help."

Amuro stared at her stammering sister and wondered what she truly thought. It hit the elf marshal and she blushed. It was an embarrassing moment with both sisters wondering what was going on in each other's heads.

"What you do with Cagius on your own time is none of my concern!" exclaimed Amuro. "The only military force I ever witnessed using a whip are the female members of the Myotis Tribe. However, I've seen you dance with a ribbon before. I believe you could properly use it to its true potential."

"I'll certainly try, sis."

"We'll train every other rotation. Get ready to work because it's not going to be easy. That type of weapon is going to cause a lot of pain at first, so be prepared."

"Thank you, sister."

Bubbly and happy, Saria hugged her sister. Amuro was pretty happy at being doted on by her sister and playfully held her back.

"I knew everything Daddy said about you wasn't true."

Amuro grimaced at her sister's statement. She knew her father had not approved of her joining the army or commanding Alliance forces in battle. However, she didn't know he had been saying things about her behind her back.

"What do you mean, what Father said?"

"Daddy usually refers to you as a warmongering, unattractive tomboy who he wishes would just get married so she would settle down and stop embarrassing the family."

Amuro became enraged, but one look at her happy sister ended the rage. She was determined, however, to have a long talk with her father when she got home.

"Yeah, this will work out fine."

Amuro suddenly shuddered and grabbed her head.

"What's wrong?"

"I just felt a tremendous amount of magical energy come into the castle. I don't think it's Cassandra, so I'd better check it out."

Upstairs Cassandra was sitting at her desk when she heard a loud and impatient knock at her door. Carefully approaching the door and examining the peephole, the queen spotted Cecilia standing with her hands on her hips and impatiently tapping her foot. Cassandra opened the door.

"What happened?" inquired Cassandra.

"I have a guest that insists on seeing you."

Eyes cast downward, Nadia trailed Cecilia. The overwhelming joy of finally seeing her daughter in the flesh needed to be contained. A sense of pride and accomplishment flowed through her whole being that she and Wilhelm had produced someone as beautiful as Cassandra. Yet, there was overwhelming sorrow for the suffering Cassandra was meant to endure because of their sin.

"Who is this?" asked Cassandra.

"My name is Nadia, I am the paramour of Duke Wilhelm von Angelhardt. In the many classes of magic users, I am a magus and I am here to complete your training."

Seeking Cecilia's advice on the matter concerning this mysterious woman's intentions, the Vanadis remained silent until prompted.

"Well?" asked Cassandra.

"Well, I don't trust her, but that's just my opinion," said Cecilia.

"My intentions are noble," offered Nadia.

"So she keeps saying," countered Cecilia. "I've always believed that actions speak louder than words. Nadia's checkered past always makes me feel uneasy around her."

"Your Highness, it is my intention to finish your training. I respected your uncle as a mage, but there were limits to his powers. We're all in grave danger right now and each of us has a part to play. I've been looking for my chance at atonement and the time has come. Let me help you become the greatest sorceress this planet has ever seen!"

Cassandra sighed and looked to Cecilia one last time, but knew her friend expected her to make the decision.

"Cecilia, if you don't mind, I'd like some time to speak to our guest."

"If you have any problems with her, just call me or Walker! I'll send the message back to my mother now."

Cecilia strutted past Nadia, gave her one last intimidating look before leaving, and closed the door behind her.

"So Duke Wilhelm von Angelhardt sent you?" asked Cassandra.

"Yes."

"The Duke and I have not spoken often. However, I do know that he loved Cedric very much. It was in the midst of the Senate Inquisition when he told me to watch Cedric's reaction carefully. He said only then would I know if I really loved him. You know, he was right. When Cedric held to his principles despite the overwhelming pressure to turn over those girls, I knew then and there he would never let anything happen to me!"

"That is the most wonderful feeling in the world."

"Are you one of the Nephilim?"

"I'm afraid I'm far worse than a Nephilim. I am actually a being known as a daughter of the prince. Since I am of his genetics rather than his magic, I'm almost an angel."

"I find that hard to believe."

"Don't judge me simply by my appearance. I came to Terminus Mundus to retrieve something for my father. After Wilhelm defeated me, I swore my fealty to him in exchange for the gift of free will."

"You don't have to answer this if you don't want. I'm sorry, but I have to know. What is Hell really like?"

"Think of all of the worst things you can imagine about this world and then couple that with the knowledge that there is no salvation from God. Abandoned, desperate, lonely, and bound to the will of Prince Lucifer for all eternity, it is no wonder why lost souls claw at each other in the Lake of Fire. Of course, we nobles are above the common rabble, but we still watch."

Looking at the eyes of her daughter, Nadia witnessed tears of compassion welling up. The young queen embraced her and the warmth within the chest of the magus was beyond any elven empathy she had been gifted in the past. A bright smile soon came to her face and she continued.

"It's amazing how quickly people use the cliché *it's Hell on Terminus Mundus*. They are such misguided fools, and could never comprehend utter despair. Yet, there was one among us who changed everything, and that's why I am so fortunate to be here now."

"What happens to you now?"

"I'm on probation now. That's part of the reason why I'm here. Wilhelm von Angelhardt gave me the chance to get out and I took it. I have free will now, and if I'm good little girl maybe I will see the 'City of God.' Wilhelm speaks about that place with such fervor that sometimes I see images of it in my dreams. I still have so much to do, but right now I have to be here for you. Will you let me help you, your Highness?"

"If we're ever going to get out of this mess, we're going to need to start trusting each other. My home fell because of mistrust. The Acadian nobles never saw past such bitterness, and even those loyal to me became blind to the dangers. My uncle left my training incomplete, so I would gladly become an apprentice to one with such talents."

"Thank you, your Highness."

"Well, you can call me Cassie."

"Very well, Cassie," Nadia corrected herself as she noticed the open Book of Rune on Cassandra's desk. "The Book of Rune—I wasn't aware that your uncle bestowed this treasure to you. I hope you understand how precious and unique this gift was. There are only four like it in all of Terminus Mundus."

"He never told me that. However, Uncle Cerwin always had a habit of spoiling me with rare and exciting gifts."

"He obviously thought very highly of you. The Rune Mistress is the most difficult sorceress class to ascend to. Its level three spells have the power to both injure and cripple your enemies. I don't want to get too far ahead of your level, but there is a spell in this book that will make you impervious to any foul craft a mortal wizard may lay upon you."

"I've got a lot payback on my mind and I wouldn't mind seeing that Celius suffer for what he did to my father."

"A good attitude for this line of work; there's little nobility in the realm of sorcery. However, you shouldn't focus too much on the revenge factor as it has a habit of consuming young magic wielders."

"I promise I won't go too far, but I want to know when we can get started."

"As soon as you'd like! I'm so excited to see what creeps in the darkness of your very soul."

Remembering the situation with Abaddon, Cassandra nearly fainted at Nadia's words. The magus realized she went too far and eased her pain. Cassandra might have been her daughter genetically but she was raised to be a prim and proper princess.

"Sorry, Cassie, I was just kidding. Trust me, Abaddon and my father want to make you into their evil pawn, but I'm just curious about all of your abilities."

"That's a relief. I spent a matter of moments as a succubus and I never want to go back to being one of those again."

"I hate to say it, but you still are one."

"What?"

"The spell Abaddon used on you only brought out part of your inner being, but don't worry, we succubus aren't all bad. We have to deal with the pangs of uncontrollable lust at times, and once you get the taste of soul inside of you it's very hard to crack that habit...delicious soul energy..."

For a moment both women slipped into a trance of sorts thinking about the sweet taste of a soul. The queen broke free first. Despite her ramblings, Nadia could see Cassandra was overcome with horror at the thought of being taken over by such a creature again. Fearful that the queen may summon Cecilia, the magus shook her hands in front of her.

"You know what, forget I said that. We are going to have to do something about your outfit, though. While that gown is most becoming on you, you certainly can't train in that."

"Unfortunately, my wardrobe is quite limited for the time being. It's very expensive to get anything tailored in Deniva right now. I just hope you don't make me wear anything as embarrassing as the leotard my Uncle made me wear. I felt like I had next to nothing on."

"Well, when you become a true sorceress, you're going to actually be wearing a similar outfit to mine. Since it takes such a long time to cast a spell, the key is to keep your targets distracted. Skimpy outfits are often the best means of teasing the male mind."

Pirouetting in a circle, Nadia modeled her skimpy outfit. Flushed at the idea of wearing something so embarrassing, the queen covered her face and shook her head. Nadia picked up the phone in the room.

"Yes, I would like the number for the best tanner in the city. I'm in need of some leather."

Dietrich Rhone Memorial Science Hall, Titan Academy, Rhinegard

"Rhone was cunning when he joined us in battle. He didn't ask for money or tribute. His price was knowledge. We didn't know it then but the Titans had grand designs for the West and we were desperate. This University stands in Rhinegard today as a testament to King Ulysses Rhone, and I enjoy the honor of being the first Commencement Speaker for its graduating class. After all, none of you would be here this hour without me."

King Hayden Marisol's address to the first graduating class of Titan Academy

As the sun rose over the Griffin Mountains to the east, the first signs of life emerged around Titan Academy. Cadets from the Military Academy had woken at reveille and ran their ritual three miles across the grounds. Students were either headed to the dining hall for a morning meal, taking an early morning workout, or busy heading to their first classes. Bustling with activity was the Dietrich Rhone Memorial Science Hall.

No building at the Academy had been torn down and built up again as much as this particular structure on the campus. Named after Leto Rhone's brother, who preferred science to politics, this incarnation featured an exterior of interlocking steel beams and glass windows. Steel hoods covered the windows to provide extra protection in case of attack and to prevent bird crashes during migration season. A large sculpture of the atomic mass of Hydrogen was on top of the building. Though considered to be the most developed building in the world, it was the subject of constant jokes and ridicule. In the infinite wisdom of the architect of the University, the science hall was the only building on the campus made to face the backside of the statue of King Ulysses Rhone.

Martha Heinrich had the entire fifth floor filled with her staff, graduate students, and undergraduates searching for files in cyberspace. Martha Heinrich was the University Provost, but instead of taking up her office in the Administrative Building, she chose to remain at her old office in the Science building. Her office had mahogany paneling around it and was completely soundproof. Martha had a large computer on the right side of the room with ten monitors so she could work and observe every lab at the same time. The right side of the room had three lab hoods set up with different chemicals. The provost had her desk in the direct center of the room with two laptops on either end of the table. The scientist was so adept she was able to search and type on two laptops at once. As her irritation level rose, Martha's typing speed increased. In an instant she pulled up multiple files and scanned them for anything useful. Grunting endlessly at her futile attempts to conquer her mentor Virgus, Martha greeted a scientist as she continued to work.

"Please tell me you have some good news. I'm really in the mood for some good news."

"I'm sorry, my lady, the archives are empty. Doctor Tattenburg apparently took all of his files with him and set up viruses and dummy files to cover his tracks."

As she banged her head against her desk, her subordinates remained bewildered at the stability of the woman leading them. Though she was the chancellor of Titanus, Martha began her life as a nameless babe at an orphanage in the Titan heartlands. Believed to be the illegitimate love child of some Titan noble, the sisters were shocked to discover the extent of the infant's aptitude. Seeking to take advantage of her gifts, she was sent to the Titan Academy at her fourth revolution of age. At the time Virgus Tattenburg was the provost and served as a mentor to his brilliant young charge. He probably would not have survived the chemical explosion that cost him half his body if not for the brilliant and decisive actions of Martha. Though she could replace his damaged limbs and organs with cybernetic components, she could never heal the damage to his mind. Abhorred by his experimentation on humans, Martha usurped his position as provost and forced Civilia to exile him from Titanus in the place of her ailing father. When she became queen, Civilia raised Martha to chancellor, but Martha always remained a child at heart. Her antics were often looked down upon, despite her superior intellect.

"I think I need a break," announced Martha as she sat back and cracked her fingers. "Anything else on the agenda?"

"You have mandatory appeal from a student, Martin Kruger, honor code violation."

"This is just what I needed to relieve some of the tension! I'm going to rip him a new one. Stay here and take notes!"

The scientist signaled to an undergraduate in the hallway. Unlike most Titans, this individual was on the motley side. His hair was uncombed, and his uniform tie was loose. Entering the office, Kruger knew he was in for it when he saw the provost smiling at him with her hands folded under her chin.

"Mister Kruger, we finally meet. Have a seat!"

The undergraduate said nothing, but chose not to antagonize the provost any further because of the bad mood she was in.

"You were charged by the honor board with plagiarism. This is your mandatory appeal; let me say first that I am surprised you did not bother to send paperwork concerning your defense to me beforehand. Now, tell me why I shouldn't throw you out of this university, and don't waste my time with a sob story about what your parents would think. I've heard that so many times I could use something original."

"I didn't plagiarize anything," argued Kruger defiantly. "I don't want to sprout some lunacy about a conspiracy against me, but I am the victim."

"Really? Why would anyone be after you?"

"The graduate student teaching the course didn't approve of my topic for my physics paper. He called it heresy despite the fact it had nothing to do with anything religious. If anything, he's the one who should have been dragged before the honor board for the false testimony he gave."

"What exactly was this heretical topic?"

"I was studying Doctor Tattenburg's theories on tachyon fields."

Martha's jaw dropped. How the hell could what she had been searching for tirelessly fall right into her lap?

"Son, I'm warning you right now that this better not be a joke! I will literally call Marshal Irvine and have him use you for target practice!"

"I'm telling the truth, ma'am. I know he's a pariah around here, but Doctor Virgus was once a great man. Didn't you always teach us to explore every possible solution?"

"Do you have a copy of that paper?" Martha nearly shouted.

"Unfortunately, I was forced to surrender all of my documents to the honor board and they destroyed it. I did, however, email the paper to a printer a few times. There may still be a copy on the university server!"

"Bring it up now!"

Martha allowed Kruger access to her laptop. The student worked quickly and was amazed at the processing speed of the computer. In no time, he was able to bring up the files.

"Here it is. Now provost, if you're going to kick me out I wish you would just get it over with. I'll take up a career in the Titan navy and be fine."

"Shut up!" ordered Martha as she scanned the paper. "Where did you get this research?"

"I'd rather not say. It may open me to self-incrimination later."

"Listen to me—this is a matter of life and death! I have the ear of the queen and I guarantee that if I like your answer, you'll have an ironclad royal pardon. Please, Kruger, where did you find the research?"

"I went through the black market in Deniva. I was able to get three journals Doctor Tattenburg published, second-hand, of course, but all of his theories were there. I also hacked into the Wizard Guild's computer system; they apparently had a few of his lectures on video. I know it was forbidden by treaty... there you go, now I've done it."

"You still have these materials?"

"Yeah, I managed to save these."

Reaching into his backpack, Kruger dropped the journals on her desk. He went back on the computer and brought up the lectures from his file share. The provost startled the young man and kissed him.

"Thank God. I never thought a journal could be so beautiful."

Signaling to the other scientist in her office, Martha opened her office door and barked out orders.

"All right! Run these papers downstairs and make about a hundred photocopies! Start passing them around to all of the department heads in physics, chemistry, computer science, and engineering; I want proposals on my desk tomorrow morning from each department! I'm sending copies of Virgus' lectures to your servers. Order whatever food you need and I'll have cots brought in. Also, I want the graduate student that teaches Physics 101 fired and escorted out of the building. Don't let him take anything with him. Let's look alive, people!"

"Well, I suppose I'm not getting expelled."

"Mister Kruger, report to Doctor Shen in the physics department immediately! As your punishment for ethical violations of the honor code, you'll be working on this project."

"Wait a second, you just agreed with everything I just did. How could I be in violation?"

"You still wrote on a topic that was strictly forbidden by the teacher of your course," declared a smiling Martha. "We still have to recognize the chain of command. If you fail me on this project you're going to be my personal guinea pig for the next fifty revolutions! Capiche?"

"I avoided the military for this! I'm convinced Marshal Irvine would not have been as harsh."

"You a gamer, son?"

"Of course."

"Guardian Realm, right? What kind of character are you?"

"Paladin."

"You get your next hundred hours free on Guardian Realm; I'm picking up the tab. If you want to join my party I play as the wizard Heintha. I'm always looking for a good tank."

"Thank you, Doctor Heinrich."

"Don't worry, son, I have a feeling you and I are going to have a very prosperous relationship in this building."

Kruger left for the physics wing. Plopping herself back at her desk, the five department heads reported for work.

"Now, let's see what my old mentor has to say about tachyon fields. The queen needs some good news."

"But, provost," interrupted one of the scientists. "You've been working yourself to the bone. Now that we have a break, you really should rest."

"What do I always preach in my classes? No notebook today, no sleep tonight! Unfortunately I'm going to have to cancel my class again; my students are really going to hate me when they have all those make-up evening courses."

Kaiser Mountain Pass, the Gateway to the Empire, One Rotation Later

"We repealed them three times; the wall held! The old proverb was true—the Edenian walls defend themselves. The Imperials were undeterred, they came back and the walls crashed to the ground. Emperor Linus did nothing; he sat on his hands while the Turks poured through the wall. Some begged him to rally his men! To fight! To call on Titanus for aid! But he did nothing. He simply walked out to the Sultan and surrendered. The greatest city on Terminus Mundus, the "City of Dreams," conquered without shedding a drop of blood. We fled here to protect the Ark, but you will find many friends still in Palacio Magnifico, King Frederick."

Rabbi Levi upon arrival in Rhinegard after "The Fall"

On the western end of the Kaiser Mountain Pass, Christian and Colin surveyed the landscape. The pointed tops of the mountains cast shadows upon them and the jagged, narrow pass lay at their horses' hooves. The pass might very well have been the salvation of the west. Sultan Assad Khan's plans were to cross the pass and attack Titanus shortly after the fall of Palacio Maginifico. However, an early snowfall made the Kaiser Pass unavailable, and Frederick Rhone had the time he needed to gather his allies in the First Alliance. Garbed in their ranger gear, the eagle Calvary remained perched on Colin's shoulder despite his discomfort.

"Your friend is late," chided Colin.

"Nunzio is not a friend, he's a business partner," corrected Christian.

"Who is he anyway?"

"He's the undersecretary of the Chancellor of Edenia. Nunzio comes from a very powerful aristocratic family who disagreed with Emperor Linus's decision to surrender. Since they lost the majority of their holdings to the Imperial Crown, they've been very close with the Titan Government for revolutions. Nunzio, unfortunately, is a mercenary and cares little for family honor."

"Gold?"

"Can't get enough of it, and we're just better at paying him off than the Empire is."

"I guess we have no choice," said Colin as he shook his head. "I'd prefer we didn't have to place so much trust in a man of loose moral standards."

Scanning the pass again, Christian recognized Nunzio's approach with his slightly balding dark hair and brown eyes. He had a neatly trimmed mustache and goatee. Dressed in noble Regalia, the undersecretary was flanked by two Eastern Dragoons. Unlike Cagius, these dragoons wore cloth military uniforms under a light armor breastplate with a helmet designed to serve as a riding hat. They had long jousting spears in their hands ready to defend. DeVries waved and Nunzio laughed when he saw the two men in ranger garb.

"So, you are Mister Wint and Mister Kidd?" asked Nunzio. "I've heard much about you."

Despite his initial confusion, Colin determined the cloak and dagger to be part of Christian's greater plan. Used to improvising since his comrade rarely shared his plan, the assassin took on the role of the strong and silent type.

"Secretary Nunzio, I understand that King Archibald is recruiting rangers. We would appreciate a contract."

"Yes, the Empire is in a perpetual state of war with the West and always needs good intelligence. From the descriptions I received, you and Mister Kidd are quite skilled in what you do. The king has graciously decided to hire you."

Nunzio held out a piece of paper stamped with the seal and signature of the king.

"Of course, there is a franchise fee."

"How much?"

"Let's see, the services of Mister Trediak in preparing the document come to about three thousand, and then there's a supplemental fee of ten thousand for myself."

"If Mister Trediak did all the work, what's the extra ten thousand for?" demanded Colin.

"The seal, of course!" taunted Nunzio. "You wouldn't imagine how greedy the captain of the watch is."

"I'm sure your cut is significant as well."

"You need this more than I. Do you have the payment or must I send you on your way?"

Christian tossed Nunzio a large bag of coins. Unaware Christian had been smuggling such a large sum of money, Colin decided it was a question best left unanswered.

"That is greatly appreciated, Mister Wint. Please follow me through the pass, and welcome to the Edenian Rangers."

Colin and Christian followed Nunzio and his guard into the pass. Stroking the eagle on his back, Colin signaled Calvary to fly through the pass. The trip allowed for limited visibility and rocks underneath the hooves were long and slippery. Even at a trotting speed, a rider could get easily tripped up. As Christian watched Calvary fly, he noticed how effortlessly the eagle navigated the pass. The strong eyes of a Titan golden eagle caught sight of the treacherous curves and turns before they became an obstacle. The hour-long journey gave way to the sight of Palacio Maginifico, the capital of the Kingdom of Edenia.

The "City of Dreams" shined with a white light, its wall apparently a combination of mortar and ivory. The tops of each of the city towers were made out of gold. Ballista guarded the parapets and archers manned the walls. A stone gate marked the entrance to the city with the carvings of the Christ and the Great Prophet of the Ancient Scriptures on it. Although smaller than Rhinegard, Palacio Magnifico was a city exclusively of middle and upper classes. The lower serfs lived in farms and towns outside of the main city. Gardens and fountains lined the walkways of the city, giving an aura of sophistication and luxury. The bustling markets and sophisticated populace complimented each other well. Museums and libraries appeared at different points throughout the city. In the center of the town was a large Oratory devoted to the Holy Virgin. It was made of out glass and reflected the sunlight, with a large statue of the Holy Virgin of Mercy leading the way. Across the way from the Oratory was the Grand Library of Edenia, the five-story white building housed copies of all of the great books ever written on Terminus Mundus. As they passed through the gates and city, Colin could not help but stare in awe at the beauty of the Oratory. The assassin thought it more beautiful than the Basilica itself. The duelist snapped back to the harsh reality of Edenian life when they came to the palace courtyard. He saw the banners of the Empire flying prominently, the moon and star present everywhere. The city was lost without a fight and in the end it truly didn't have the means to defend itself. In the mind of one raised by the Titans, the only thought that could come to mind was that of cowardice. *Why would someone surrender all of this without a fight?*

Nunzio turned to Christian.

"Mapes runs a boarding house three streets from the palace. It would probably be best if you remained there. Many Rangers board there and I made sure she had an available room."

"Thanks for everything!"

"No problem; you just make sure Cecilia gets home alive. The only hope some of these people have left is Titanus. Got it?"

"I know. We're still with you."

Turning from the palace, Christian and Colin traveled to the boarding house. After a short ride, they got off their horses and put them in the attached stable. Entering the tavern area, the elder Mapes was working the bar. Rangers were at many of the tables in the main room taking in a meal. Mapes had graying hair and wore thick glasses. She was slightly hunched over and walked with a limp. One look at the two and the wary old innkeeper approached.

"Mister Wint, Mister Kidd, I'm Mapes, the proprietor of this boarding house," she said with a wink. "I was told by the government that you needed my assistance."

"It would help," replied Christian.

"All right, room five on the second floor; you get two squares a day. The rate is two hundred a week, payable up front."

"Okay."

Setting down the money, Christian signed the book under his alias. Mapes tossed Colin the keys and gave him another wink. Ignoring the crowded room, the two operatives ascended the stairs to their room at the end of the hall. As they entered the room, the two agents observed two beds, one closet, one drawer, a small desk, but fortunately a private bath. Colin sighed at the thought of spending as much money as they did for this.

"Well, we didn't come to Edenia for the luxury," taunted Colin.

"It's more than we need," corrected Christian.

"I don't know. It seems like all we've done so far is waste an awful lot of money with zero results."

"Why do you think I'm always begging the queen for more money? It's not cheap trying to deal with all our enemies. Now, we'd better unpack."

Christian put his bags down on the desk. Removing radio and computer equipment from his back, Christian built a makeshift transceiver. Colin kept busy by unpacking their clothes and equipment.

"So, Christian, what's the plan?"

"The first thing we have to do is establish contact with Cecilia in Deniva. I'm sure she wants to square things with us. Then we'll hit the streets and check out the populace."

"I guess we'll be making the alleys our new home."

Playing around with the buttons, Christian licked his lips as the right frequency came across. The spy master was concerned that the interference from Virgus' barrier might interfere with communications in Deniva.

"I've got them, Colin! This is Wint calling Eagle's Nest, what's the outlook? Over!"

"Eagle's Nest is secure for now." Cecilia's voice crackled over the radio. "Glad to hear you're okay. Unfortunately, we had an unexpected bogey in the feeding zone! Over!"

Christian and Colin looked at each other, worried.

"A *bogey?* Over!"

"Yes! Arrived the other rotation on behalf of the Sentinel in order to help with the rearing of our chick! Over!"

"Check! If you don't hear from us in three minutes, send the lover's present! Over!"

"Roger! Over and out!"

Christian flicked off the radio.

"Who's the bogey?" asked Colin.

"Unless I missed, my guess, Nadia."

"Oh dear God, just what we need. I think every single wild card showed up on Terminus Mundus save for the one we need, the boss!"

"Yeah."

"How are you doing? Everyone has been so concerned about everyone else; I don't think anyone wondered about you. Cedric was your best friend, it couldn't have been easy."

"I'm fine."

"I wish I could believe that. Are you in Cecilia's camp? Do you really think he's dead?"

Determined to avoid an answer, Christian clapped his hands.

"Let's take a walk!"

"What about Cecilia? Don't you have to call her back?"

"Titan code three, Colin; three minutes translates to three rotations."

"It would be nice if you told me these things."

"You see, you just learned your first lesson. I guess you'd better get a codebook to study."

Pecking at the window, Calvary startled the two agents. Colin signaled the eagle to meet them downstairs. When the two hit the streets, Calvary returned to Colin's shoulder. The streets were bustling with people in the middle of the rotation.

"So this is the City of Dreams." commented Colin.

"Yes, Palacio Magnifico is well named because it is the aesthetic and cultural center of the entire planet. Anything you could ever want on Terminus Mundus is found and traded in this city, a crossroads of Divikin, Elf, Dwarven, and Human cultures."

The two heard Colin's stomach growl.

"That sounded like an explosion," teased Christian.

"You forgot that I didn't take well to your girlfriend's cooking. I've never been that sick on meat in my life."

"I knew she used too much seasoning, but Rosa can get a little flighty at times. I'll make it up to you. Come on!"

Hitting a fruit stand, the fresh smell was pleasing to Colin's nose. Christian did the negotiating with the vendor.

"Rangers, what can I get you?" asked the merchant.

"Two slices of watermelon, please," said Christian.

"Right away!"

The trader took a watermelon behind his counter and a machete. Hacking off two wedges, he passed the melons to Christian as he dropped some coins on the table.

"Much obliged!" offered the merchant with a wink. "Come back for all of your culinary needs!"

"I'll keep you in mind."

Christian handed Colin a slice. Scampering up a fire escape, the two operatives took a seat on a building ledge. It provided a perfect view of the city.

"What is this, Christian? It smells delicious."

"Watermelon; it's grown exclusively in the southern Imperial territories. It's a delicacy in the West. However, since Cedric hates it passionately, Civilia keeps it away from the dinner table."

"This is the first time I've seen it."

"Just taste it, and mind the pits."

"I see."

Savoring the first bite, Colin chewed it and spit a pit out.

"This is really good. How could Cedric have hated it? This tastes like sugar."

"It's pretty expensive so don't get too used to it. I just figured I owed you a treat for coming out here with me."

"Come on, buddy, I wouldn't leave you alone on this one. Even though I miss Hippolyte so much it hurts."

"May you always keep that feeling! Now, here's your second lesson; tell me what you see."

"No sign of Imperial presence and no advance Imperial agents watching for the security."

"Good, which means we beat them here. Remember, we have to keep appearances up, so we head down to the Palace each morning and check the board. We take missions in the East and not the West. Got it?"

"Don't worry, I'm not turning traitor yet."

"Good."

Reaching into the rind of the watermelon, Christian slipped out what appeared to be some form of microfilm.

"Christian, was the vendor one of ours?"

"Yes. Just a little update on the current state of the Empire, but I really did have a hankering for watermelon."

The two ate and laughed as Christian loaded the file into his PDA.

Wizard's Tower, Central Acadia

"I've found humans to be very receptive to temptations.
However, you cannot simply overtake them right away. Most
of them must be broken very slowly and delicately. Especially,
since I am usually trying to influence a gentle spirit!"

Abaddon on the throne of the Locust King

Guided by the light of Celius' staff, a party of wizards and Nephilim descended a stone spiral staircase. Feeling uneasy at the presence of the Lich leader of the demonkin, the master wizard carefully counted his steps. Abaddon's otherworldly appearance constantly faded in and out between manifestations. The dark angel had no intention of allowing Celius to keep the Libro Mortuorum from him. Even the eerie, robotic smile of Virgus rattled his bones. He didn't know which of his new allies he feared more at this point, but there was little hope for fulfillment of the original promises made to the guild.

"I'm still not sure about this," cautioned Celius. "The powers of the Libro Mortuorum shouldn't be handed over to ordinary mortals."

"Considering the mistakes you've made, you're not in a position to advise us right now," replied an angry Abaddon.

His grunt was the wizard's final protest. Reaching a portal marked with a glowing purple magic star, Celius waved his hands in a few patterns to open the pathway of the portal. Every individual carefully stepped through the portal and moved into a stone basement, forty stories underneath the ground. The vault of the guild was kept in total darkness save for the light of the staff and Abaddon's radiation. Empty pedestals were everywhere, covered with a faint blue magic light.

"Magic shields?" asked Virgus. "What was this room meant to contain, Celius?"

"We built this room in hope of containing the Legendary Weapons."

The Nephilim shook their heads. Abaddon could not believe the arrogance these wizards exuded. In his battle against Cedric and his friends, he noticed the weapons they carried. During his intense preparations for the invasion of Terminus Mundus, he made himself well aware of the weapons made by the unknown ore of the Dwarves. Abaddon wondered if Celius truly believed that such powerful warriors would simply hand over the great treasures they had been entrusted with.

"Let's see, where did we put the Libro Mortuorum?" asked Celius rhetorically.

Examining the logbook, Celius moved his finger until he reached the entry. Three paces forward and two steps sideways, the master wizard reached a chest. Magically prying the lock open with his staff, the Libro Mortuorum floated in the air. The demonic book was bound in human skin and its cover art depicted skeletons and demonic creatures devouring body parts. The demonic face in the center of the book featured an open mouth. As Valadrim stepped forward to take the book, the Lich grabbed him on the shoulder.

"Wait, this book is very dangerous. Pick it up and you'll lose a finger," cautioned the Lich master.

Opening his arms, the Lich secured the tome in a force field.

"Bound in human skin and written in blood, the Libro Mortuorum will give a sage with the proper training the ability to summon legions of undead hordes," lectured the Lich. "An army we can use against the royalists. Quantity of forces is the only way we can protect ourselves against their superior quality. I shall invoke a few simple spells to dispel the harmful curses placed on it."

"Who are the royalists?" asked Celius.

"We decided to call those that are supporting Queen Cassandra's ascendancy to throne 'royalists,'" explained Abaddon.

"I don't understand," argued Celius. "The patriarch has recognized King Luminas. If anything, Cassandra is the rebel queen."

"Do you really believe the other nations will accept such a claim? No nation recognizes Luminas as king. This war is far from over, Celius! Now, I have to call on our special guest."

Vanishing from the room, Virgus knew that if he was going to catch up with Abaddon, he had to hurry up the stairs. Valadrim and the Nephilim left with him. As his Lich master read from the Libro Mortuorum, Celius' spying eyes looked on. The master wizard was thrilled to be examining such an ancient magic and believed his powerful magic could harness it.

On the twentieth story of the tower, Marie sat in her room doing needlepoint. Despite the superior skill her older sister had always complimented for, her hands were unusually calloused. Such trivial matters no longer mattered to the princess. The cheerful disposition of the young princess, the one that could instantly change the mood of Cassandra when she was most depressed, was gone. Her eyes were cold and her expression vacant. A closer examination of her wrists by the trained eye would notice the markings of an attempted suicide. With the news of Cedric's death, Marie tried to open her veins, seeing it as the only means of her escape. The wizards responded by placing her in a constant state of trance to prevent any further attempts. Even though he knew the princess wouldn't respond, Abaddon knocked on her door. The dark angel was embarrassed by the way he had handled Cassandra and was not about to repeat a mistake. Knowing it was futile, Abaddon entered the room and released Marie from her state of trance. It took three blinks for Marie to regain her senses. Seeing Abaddon before her, Marie went to the window, but bars prevented her from jumping to her doom. Desperately searching for a weapon, the princess accepted her fate and fell to her knees.

"Princess Maria Acadia, I am Lord Abaddon."

"I know you. You're the monster that killed my beloved Julius!"

Abaddon got closer to her and knelt down in front of her.

"I am here to beg your forgiveness, your highness. I did not know who I was fighting at the time. My subordinates had informed me that I was fighting Prince Cedric Rhone instead."

As the manipulative, dark angel lifted his eyes, he spotted an opportunity. Marie started to shake as she backed away. Could this princess be so naïve and trusting to think that he meant what he said? It was a long shot, but he needed to shift the blame for Julius' death completely on Cedric. Abaddon knew full well Marie would never betray Cassandra unless she thought her older sister was being controlled by a sadistic puppeteer.

"I can offer you the opportunity that you want," continued Abaddon.

"What are you talking about?"

"I can give you back what you want. Julius Imperia can come back to you."

"But Julius died—I saw you kill him."

"There are ways to bring someone back. You, your Highness, may have the talents to perform such a ritual."

"I could never do something like that. It is forbidden... but for Julius I... I wouldn't even know where to start."

"Of course, it would require some magical training," explained Abaddon as he moved to leave. "I understand you know some magic, but your levels aren't powerful enough yet. My associates can help you learn the necessary spells with a special book."

"Lord Abaddon, a moment please."

"What is it, your Highness?" asked Abaddon, knowing she had taken the bait.

"Why help me?"

"There is sadness in my heart for what I did, though I did believe my reasons were justified at the time. You didn't deserve this! An arrangement had been made long ago, but Cedric Rhone refused to honor such an agreement. Cassandra rightfully belongs with her own kind but the Titan prince wouldn't allow it."

"That can't be true! Cedric loved my sister. Then again, Cedric didn't come to rescue her. Julius had to rescue us. Why wasn't he there if he loved her unless..."

Marie grabbed her head as Abaddon left the room. Virgus was waiting for him, out of breath from his long climb. Smiling at his master, he already knew the answer to the question he wanted to ask.

"Well?"

"It is best to brainwash her slowly. Let's leave her out of her trance for a while and see what happens. If you're correct about this, Doctor Heinrich, we'll have plenty of time."

"Martha Heinrich was my best student; I know all of her strengths and weaknesses very well."

Valadrim and his men finally joined them. The Nephilim commander bowed before his Lord.

"Valadrim, what news?" inquired Abaddon.

"Lord Abaddon, Lord Krystos sends word that he will see you at Lady Nadia's cottage at the appropriate hour. He says that you know what that means."

"Excellent. Our friend owes us an explanation for all the events that have come to pass. I intend to press him this time."

"He gives word that her ladyship will not be present. Krystos demands that you refrain from further contact with her."

"Of course, why take the chance? The damned fool believes I would use my power on her. I want her love, not her as a puppet. However, I will acquiesce to his little tantrum for now."

"I suggest we send a guard."

"No, Krystos doesn't have anything up his sleeve. He still believes in the time-old principle of honor, and I always believe it's better to have an honest enemy than a false friend. If he's requested my presence, he wants to talk. I'll rest before my journey; keep an eye on the princess. Make sure she doesn't make another attempt on her own life."

Abaddon vanished as the Nephilim took up positions around the princess' chamber. Virgus peeked through the keyhole and found nothing but a very confused Marie.

CASTLE TITAN, TITANUS

"Princess Civilia, I know what your desire is. My opposition to this practice is well noted, but I love my country as well. Thus I will personally handle the experiment. However, you must meet my one condition: we must do this with one egg and the proper genetic material. I wouldn't worry, though, because my experiments never fail!"

Doctor Heinrich to Princess Civilia Rhone

Entering the throne room of the castle, a nervous Martha carried a folder full of the diligent and professional work of her department heads. While the brilliant scientist did not have any definite answers, she owed her liege something. It had been some time since she had come to the castle to visit her friend, and frankly she didn't know what reception she was going to receive. As the Royal Guards opened the chamber doors for her, the chancellor received the one response she never anticipated. Civilia was sitting on her throne wearing a smile and reading from her prayer book. Martha silently calculated how long it would take a mind like the queen's to crack under the enduring pressure. Her logical mind had acquired all the necessary facts, Civilia's beloved son was dead. As much as she prayed and hoped, he wasn't coming back. Noting the disheveled appearance of her chief advisor, the queen took pity on her friend. Civilia set her book down and greeted Martha with a kiss on both cheeks.

"What's wrong, Martha? I didn't expect to see you this morning."

At a loss for words for a moment, Doctor Heinrich shook herself to regain her place.

"My queen, we found the breakthrough we've been looking for!"

"What have you learned about the barrier?"

"Apparently one of our fine young physicists at the Academy was writing a paper on Virgus' theories."

"Finally a bit of good fortune."

"Maybe just a little bit! My department heads are currently working on the fastest method of duplicating Virgus' research. Since we scrapped all of his projects, we are starting from ground zero. We understand little about this tachyon field he created, but I've made everyone drop what they're doing to focus on this project. The bad news is I'll be accepting dissertations on tachyon theory for the next twenty revolutions."

"Can we bring it down?"

"That's the problem. I had my departments look into the theory last night. There's no way we can duplicate the results from scratch, so we're going to attempt to retro-engineer it first. We think we can duplicate Virgus' technology in approximately two revolutions. Then we can develop the weapon to take it down."

Martha flipped through her notes in order to give Civilia an accurate number. While prone to exaggeration, a solution to this problem needed to be as exact as possible.

"I believe it would take approximately eight revolutions to destroy the barrier."

"Eight revolutions? That's a long time."

"I can't promise you anything sooner. I'm sorry, your highness."

"We must endure. What do you need from me?"

"I need a lot of money. I'm afraid that this might be the most expensive war this country has ever fought. Our treasuries are going to be empty as a result of it."

"I knew you were going to say that. There are no spoils to be won from this war to offset its costs. I hope to God I don't have to bankrupt my country to save its very soul. I'll address the country in five rotations and make the case. However, you know they don't take kindly to new taxes."

"God bless you, my queen."

"I was thinking back to what you said to me before we chose to create Cedric and Cecilia."

"Are you speaking of my ethical objection?"

"No. You told me that your experiments never fail."

"I am the greatest genius on Terminus Mundus."

"Martha, I don't want you to be offended by my actions. I'm splitting the role of chancellor for the time being and am inviting Wilhelm von Angelhardt back to serve at court. Your priority is the to get the barrier down, Wilhelm can handle the rest. I'm sorry."

"I'm in absolute agreement, your Highness, and I'm not offended. I hate to say it, but I think Wilhelm is better suited for these times than I am. I'll leave a copy of our proposals with your servants for when you get a break from the other five thousand things you need to take care of."

"I guess I could do with some light reading," teased Civilia. "Now, what about radio transmissions?"

"We're still deaf and I'm afraid it's going to stay that way until I find some way to pierce the tachyon field."

"All right, then we're going to have to continue to use unorthodox methods to keep contact with what allies we have left."

"Do I detect her Highness is in a much better mood lately?" inquired Martha as she prepared to leave.

"Perhaps, but I prefer not to discuss it," said Civilia with a wink.

"Okay, we'll leave it at that! I'll be at the Academy if you need me."

Martha left the room and passed another member of Civilia's court on the way in. The distinguished and meticulous Taylor Yueh was dressed in a long scarlet coat over a white shirt and black vest. His pants and shoes were black as well. Hanging from his neck was his family's shield consisting of three eagles in flight on a white and blue background. A signet ring with the same shield was on his right index finger. Taylor's dark brown hair was combed back and his brown eyes never left the queen. The foreign minister of Titanus bowed before her.

"Your Highness, I await your command," pronounced Taylor.

"I have a mission for you. I fear it is grave and dangerous."

"I have become accustomed to such dangerous missions during your reign. What dire task is upon me now?"

"The advance weather reports show that the sailing weather will be good over the coming lunar cycles. You will leave with a contingent of two hundred and fifty of our riders led by Samuel Irvine. You'll also get one hundred landsknechts and fifty commandos. Admiral Grogan will command forty three-deckers and ten transport brigs on a mission to Port Talus. We're going to establish communications the old-fashioned way. You're going to disclose as much information as we have on this barrier. If they have any scientists that are working on this problem, bring them back here so we can coordinate. Our spies say Julius is dead, so I don't know if Constantine will receive you or not. We should pass on the information that Cagius is alive."

"I will try to deal with it as delicately as possible and make no mention of this Joshua. What about Evengard?"

"Let's concentrate on the safer course with Napolitan first before we worry about the elves. Their magic will keep them insulated from Nephilim intrusions. I thank you for undertaking this desperate mission."

"I am your servant, my queen. The preparations will be completed shortly. I was getting bored anyway. What's a foreign minister to do without any powers to communicate with?"

Taylor left to prepare for his mission.

Nadia's Cottage, the High Hour of Night

"My Prince, I do not trust Krystos' intention. I know many in the Powers Choir have turned on the Father, but this one was Lord Camael's Shield-bearer. I wish for discretion in dealing with this particular Incarnate. There are also personal issues between us."

Abaddon to the Prince on his reservations concerning Krystos

Disguised as a Nephilim once more, Wilhelm reclined at the table waiting for his guest of honor to arrive. Chuckling at how revolutions of history repeated themselves time and time again, the double agent reflected on his mission. Wilhelm had fallen from grace willingly and was not really sure what was going to happen if he died. While he served God, his soul could still belong to the prince, unless his wings were healed. He shuddered at the thought of spending an eternity in Hell, but was comforted by the fact he felt that way. The duke hadn't given into despair yet. Pouring a glass of red wine for himself, Wilhelm silently prayed before sipping it. The shouting gargoyles shocked him to reality, giving him precious seconds to prepare himself as Abaddon materialized in front of him.

The rivalry between Krystos and Abaddon was as old as the creation of the angels. Despite the principality's superior skill, Krystos was the more revered warrior due to his station in the Powers Choir. Seeking to prove supremacy, Abaddon was offered the opportunity to command the prince's army. Yet, he might have forgiven the Powers Choir angel if not for Nadia. Abaddon's lust for the prince's daughter was well known. It helped him bear the horrors of Hell and the isolation of his castle on the sixth plane. Nadia fell for his mortal enemy and that was an insult too large

165

to bear. He had begged the prince not to bring Krystos into the fold, but his humiliating loss to Cedric took away all of Abaddon's capital. He was crawling back to his rival on his hands and knees.

"Abaddon, you arrived punctual as always."

"You're getting too cute with your messages for my tastes."

"You're just upset that I made Nadia leave and decided to meet you alone."

"I'm a bit surprised, actually. I figured you'd keep her here since I would never kill you while she was present."

"I'm not afraid of you. I would easily defeat whatever Nephilim lackeys you brought with you, but I know you didn't."

"Why not?"

"You desire the pleasure of killing me with your own bare hands!"

"I guess you can read me like a book. Yet, this doesn't frighten you."

"I've been on Terminus Mundus now a very long time and many have tried to kill me."

"Like this Duke von Angelhardt perchance?"

"He is a thorn in the side of the Nephilim and the Demonkin. Yet for some strange reason, he doesn't bother me."

"What do you know about him? I clearly underestimated this warrior the first time around and I won't do it again."

"Wilhelm von Angelhardt came down from Heaven with the Sentinels. These angels eventually had offspring in this world and they formed their own nation in the Istle Hills. For a time they lived in harmony, but eventually there was a schism into three factions. Wilhelm remained with the Kablisha at first, but found their ways repulsive and cowardly. Thus, he turned to the Titan faction in the south. When Ulysses Rhone came to power, Wilhelm was named his War Master. Over the revolutions, his status at court was reduced until he became the guardian of Prince Frederick Rhone. Since his reign, Wilhelm has regained his stature at Court and served as guardian to Prince Cedric Rhone."

"I was told all of the Sentinels were gone save for that one fool Teman. I never expected to find one living in plain sight on Terminus Mundus. What choir is he from?"

"He belonged to the Powers Choir. Duke Camael had reserved for him a place of honor in his command."

"We killed so few of them; I find myself wishing one of them was him."

"Nadia said you've been looking for me."

"Yes."

"Why?"

"I need you to look into something else for me."

"What? Isn't there any work you can do on your own?"

"Something is lingering around the west, even though it is but a whisper. I killed the Titan prince, the 'Angel of Death,' yet where is the sorrow? Where is the saddened countenance? Are there any fallback points that I am unaware of?"

"I think if the prince was alive, one of the kingdoms would have given a signal. The warriors of the west win battles because of the quality of their military training and high morale. What greater boost to have the warrior who killed an angel."

"Yes, that does seem true."

"Though I understand your reservations, especially if I was the angel bested by a mere Divikin."

"Careful, Krystos, you are dangerously close to running aground in the shallow waters of my patience."

"Patience or competence, Abaddon! I'm certain the prince must be delighted you allowed the body he crafted for you to be destroyed so easily. Why come groveling to me unless you can't go back to the prince empty-handed? I can feel your energy dissipating; you grow weaker every moment."

"My greatest desire is complete my mission, but if I could drag you kicking and screaming into Hell at the same time, all my suffering would be well worth it!"

"I hate to disappoint you, but I've come to enjoy my time among the humans."

"That is why you're weak! You've taken a fancy to them and you wonder why I can't allow you to be part of the plan. I'm afraid you'd sell me out to save them!"

"I see them as more than chattel. In fact, I see them as we were: arrogant, stupid, and refusing to listen to their Father."

"Now you go too far, Krystos! How dare you compare our noble race with this excrement of the Father? He sent His Son to them, and what was their reaction? They nailed him to a tree! Is that the Central Acadia you want to save, Krystos?"

"I guess you could say I'm indifferent. It was painful to watch what happened on Calvary, but there was still honor among them. How easy would it have been for the Divikin nations to march on Central Acadia and lay it to waste for their sins—yet, they had more faith in God than we ever did."

"Indifferent? No, I think you're a loser."

"That may be true," responded Wilhelm as he sipped his wine.

"Now heed this warning, Krystos! You best start the toeing the line around here! The prince still believes you have value, but I have lost all patience. If I find out that you are playing both sides, I will not hesitate to bind you and sling you down straight into the pits, where the fallen ones will tear at your flesh and eat you for all eternity!"

"Let me show you something. I wouldn't want you to forget why I'm working with you in the first place. One to shed salvation's light, one as black as darkest night!"

Removing his jacket, Wilhelm's wings burst from his back. The Dark Angel had never actually seen Wilhelm's punishment. Abaddon could do nothing but stare in horror at the poison running into the angel's body from the blackened wings. Though he wasn't looking for his pity, the principality actually felt sorry for his enemy at the moment. Once again, the double agent was one step ahead of his enemies, the clever deception forced Abaddon to only see what was in front of him.

"I was a sinner, Abaddon! I didn't sin all the time, yet I am tortured every moment I remain in creation. I've made my own Hell here! I am banished here, completely separated from God. Fires and fallen ones are nothing compared to the misery, pestilence, and death I have witnessed in creation. I stood there and watched the Son struggle on that Cross for three hours. Do you know what it was like to see King Robert Rhone break down and cry like a baby when the Son bowed his head? I had to stand there and watch! I wasn't allowed to reach up there and bring him down. That's why I stopped caring because I'm helpless and I've got nowhere else to go."

Abaddon gritted his teeth. He lost the angry edge in his voice and ceded the battle to Wilhelm.

"I tire of hearing of your self-loathing. You had love!"

Wilhelm pulled his wings back in and replaced his jacket.

"Why did she choose you?" demanded Abaddon. "She had me! I treated her as the queen she is. You made her a human!"

"Maybe I'm so pathetic I make her laugh. Perhaps she feels the need to nurse my weakness. Perhaps she just longs for the same freedom neither of us can have!"

"No. I don't believe that. What if I told you that the next words between us never leave this room? I don't speak to the prince and you never say a word to Nadia."

"What do I have to hold you to this?"

"Even fallen, I still have my honor angel-to-angel. It's always better to be an honest enemy than a false friend."

Staring into the eyes of his foe, Wilhelm nodded and decided to take a leap of faith.

"All right, Abaddon. What's this all about?"

"I've been racking my brain over the prince's theories. He theorized that Eva was infatuated with Teman the second he rescued her from Hell. Then, in classic fashion, the brave knight debauched the pure princess. Teman was far too good a soldier to do something like that. A guardian angel would take his time and observe his prize to make sure it wasn't a trap."

"So far so good…"

"I observed Cassandra up close and personal. I studied her facial features, her body, and even her soul. She was everything the prince ever wanted in his granddaughter. Cassandra made a beautiful succubus and no mortal would ever resist her."

"And?"

"There was something else inside of her. The princess possessed a purity that allowed her to hold out against her inner nature to the last possible moment. Cedric Rhone exploited this purity, and as the darkness left her she was more concerned about his well-being than her own."

"Should I be flattered? If I ever did have a child, I would certainly be proud if she turned out to be like Princess Cassandra."

"I've played this game already, Krystos. There are no longer any pretenses between us. The prince used Lilith to create the 'daughters.' They were meant to be temptresses and their targets were the Sentinels living in Creation. The prince needed a 'granddaughter' to bridge the gap, a girl who would possess the powers of Heaven and Hell. Yet the prince was blind to the fact that the twice-turned traitor and his wayward daughter would deliver the weapon of victory."

Wilhelm shook his head to confirm the answer Abaddon already knew. The Dark Angel was enraged that his rival was the one who had violated the object of his lust.

"What happened, Krystos? I checked with Virgus, Cassandra is the legitimate daughter of Stephen and Sharon! How did she become the prince's granddaughter?"

"There are some secrets that I prefer to keep, if only for Nadia's sake. After all, if I told you everything, you might find it necessary to eliminate me. I will let you in on one detail: a daughter of the prince is amazing."

Abaddon screamed in rage, however he soon collapsed to one knee.

"For Nadia's sake... I will honor my vow... I'll keep your secret and I will not ask either of you to surrender Cassandra to me for now. This truce is temporary and changes nothing between us. I will accomplish my mission Krystos, I've been warned more than once of my fate if I don't."

Wilhelm watched as Abaddon ripped his robes away, revealing the gaping wound Cedric had given him. The pain was too much for the Dark Angel to bear and his spirit faded back to the sixth plane to regain his strength. Wilhelm waited for a few moments to make sure he was gone. The duke raised his glass.

"It would have been impossible to keep it a secret from Abaddon's prying eyes forever. However, it is in the best interest of all to keep it between us for now. The time is coming soon for Cedric to know the whole truth, because he's the only one left who can save my daughter. I salute your skill, Cedric Rhone; I did not know how gravely you wounded the Dark Angel. Your sacrifice may have just saved us all."

Kablisha Barrier, Forest of the Eternal Spring, One Revolution Later

"The Lord God created the planet Terminus Mundus to serve as the Gateway between the Celestial and Temporal Realms. In this way He created them. The planet was created to act as the first barrier between Hell and Heaven, for the second barrier stood at the Asphodel Fields themselves guarded by the Powers Choir. Thus the Sentinels were tasked with guarding this barrier. The Sentinels erected many other barriers in their time that were less effective than the Barrier of the Lord. For these barriers were not of the Lord and thus they can be penetrated."

Apocryphal Book of Sentinels 1:5-8

The tranquility of the Forest of the Eternal Spring was interrupted by the darkening skies above. Bathed in red, this disturbance covered but a minor area. It wasn't long before the birds, forest animals and Fae recognized the danger and fled deeper into the forest. Shifting their shape into a doorway, black clouds descended to the earth. The thin, pale light blue wall that served as the Kablisha's barrier against the rest of the world bent and folded. Transformation completed, eight-foot tall creatures with bodies similar to a gorilla stamped against the ground. Acidic saliva dripped from the fangs of their goat-like heads, mounted with two massive curved horns. Howling as they emerged from the portal, the forest cried out in fear.

In the City of Antiquity, Bishop Wulf led the morning rosary service on the first holy day of the month in the cathedral. Kneeling in the first pew flanked by Quinn and Mesmara, the Titan prince followed along. The ever-present shadows surrounding him no longer bothered the prince, for he was solely focused on leaving. The first revolution trapped in this backward country had been intolerable, and Cedric was ready to get back into the fight. As usual, Argus kept his ever-present gaze on the sword master.

"Glory be to the Father, to the Son, and to the Holy Spirit," started the bishop.

"As it was in the beginning it is now and ever shall be, world without end. Amen," replied the churchgoers.

Excruciating pain filled the bishop's hands and he was granted a vision of the forest. Peter Wulf's renown as a mystic was a well-kept secret. There was a movement among many to grant him prophet status, but the bishop would have none of it. He was merely a servant of God, and there were things that he was meant to see. In his sight, the five demons destroyed everything in their pace. Argus recognized the look on the bishop's face and knew it wasn't going to be good. As Argus rushed to his side, the bishop's bloody hands stained his clothes.

"Bishop?" asked Argus.

"They've breached the defenses."

"I understand," replied Argus as he called a server over. "Ring the bells immediately."

Nodding, the server nearly tripped over his cassock ascending the stairs. The boy grabbed the rope and chimed the heavy church bells. The entire populace gathered outside the cathedral. Crossbows at the ready, soldiers and militia took positions up on the city walls. Tormented by the panicked cries of the Kablisha, Cedric took a deep breath, blessed himself, and genuflected. Leaving the cathedral, the Titan prince pondered his injuries. Did he still have will, stamina, and skill to meet whatever was coming? His actions worried his constant companions.

"Lord Cedric?" queried Quinn.

Silently returning to the bishop's residence, Quinn and Mesmara awaited Argus' orders. A soldier came down from the walls to make his report.

"Captain Kinkade, we heard the bells and all our troops have taken position on the walls. What's the situation?"

"Bishop Wulf has detected a breach."

"There hasn't been one in over twenty revolutions," exclaimed the shocked soldier. "Do you think that Titan prince drew them here?"

"Possibly, but it isn't right to put this on him."

Sensing the growing fear among his soldiers, Argus agreed with their trepidations. Cedric was a nuisance and showed no signs of being the warrior they had prayed for. A sharp scream interrupted the captain's thoughts. Mesmara was restraining a woman whom he recognized as Kylie. The young Kablisha mother ran the grocery and was often assisted by her two children.

"Let me go!" screamed Kylie.

"No one leaves the city during the crisis!" ordered Mesmara. "You don't understand the ferocity of the creatures that are out there."

"My children are out there!"

Horrified by the prospect, the Kablisha maiden let the terrified mother go. Argus understood what caused her reaction under fire and sought further information.

"Kylie, how did this happen?"

"Their teacher took about twenty children in their class with him out on a field trip into the Forest. They're down by the stream."

A crowd of concerned parents stared down at their Captain, expecting him to do something about it.

"Don't worry, I'll bring them back," reassured Argus before he turned to Quinn. "Where's Cedric?"

"I think he went back to his room."

"He had that look in his eyes, uncle. I think he knows something."

"You keep him in this city no matter what happens. Don't let anyone come after me."

"Right."

"Where are you going?" asked Mesmara.

"Someone's got make sure they get back safely. Stanton! Nelson! Rivera!"

Three soldiers approached him bearing crossbows and swords. The first two looked like grizzled veterans and the last appeared to be coming into his prime. Nelson was lanky and tall and favored his right hand. Stanton was of average height and favored his left hand. Rivera was lanky and average height, yet was unfazed by the chaos around him as he favored his right hand.

"You three with me!" ordered Argus. "Stanton and Nelson, stay up and cover me. Rivera, hang back behind us three and close it out. The rest of you brace the Main Gate and keep the posterns open. We'll be back as quickly as possible! If you get a clear shot on any of the demons, take it! Let's go!"

Argus departed with his troops. The gates closed and beams were brought up to brace it. Quinn took command on the wall above as militia armed their crossbows into firing positions.

While this went on, Cedric suited up for the first time since his battle with Abaddon. He attached the new cloak Wilhelm provided for him to his shoulder plates. The Titan prince had half-remembered that he was the owner of Julius' gauntlets. Muttering a silent prayer for his fallen friend and others who had bravely given their lives, the sword master grabbed Ragnarok. Breathing deeply, the sword never felt so heavy in his hands. Was it possible with his injuries to even draw it? Resigned to the mission, Cedric hooked Ragnarok behind his back. His first attempt to draw the blade was a disaster. He failed a second time as well, falling to his knees in agony. Silently, Florence watched him suffer from behind the door. The Crown Prince chastised himself for his weakness.

"Who the hell are you really? You weren't the 'Last Knight,' but you are still Crown Prince Cedric Rhone of Titanus, *La Morte Angelus*. You have a duty to the woman you love to draw that blade."

Focusing on his open pocket watch resting on the table, the Titan prince drew inspiration from a smiling picture of Cassandra. He would not allow her to become what Abaddon wanted. No creature born of Heaven, Hell, or Creation would stop him.

"I have to endure this pain for her sake."

Yelling, Cedric drew the blade to the silent praise of his personal cleric. *I wouldn't want to be whatever is coming*, she thought to herself.

Out in the forest, Argus and his company sprinted down the forest trails. Covering the distance a mile from the city, the screaming of children caught the captain's ears. As they accelerated to the sounds, they saw the twenty children running with their teacher in tow behind them. Scampering across the ground on all fours like a wild beast, the demon closed on his prey.

Argus struck a match and lit the bolt in his crossbow, the soldiers with him followed suit.

"On my command!" commanded Argus.

Aiming, the Captain set his scope for a headshot. A quick adjustment for the wind, Argus smiled, squeezed the trigger, and shouted, "Fire!" Four bolts all hit the beast in the forehead. Dumbfounded at first by the attack, the demon cried and fell dead. Resetting the bow by yanking a lever on the side, the string was drawn back and a new bolt locked in place. Argus and his troop took up positions behind the children and sent them running for the City of Antiquity. The demon beasts roared as if they sensed the death of a member of the pack. The captain communicated with Quinn in the city.

"What do you see?" asked Argus.

"There are four more!" answered Quinn over the communicator. "They're heading down the path. The bishop used a spell from the altar to seal the breach. You don't have to worry about any more coming through. We'll come to assist you!"

"Negative! Hold your ground and cover us! We'll head for the eastern postern. Rivera, take point! Nelson and Stanton, drop back to the rear with me. Now, you kids stay close together! We've got a long run!"

Distracted by Argus, the sound of cavalry boots climbing the stone stairs caught the Kablisha soldiers by surprise. In awe of the Titan prince's decorative outfit, the militia was comforted by Cedric gathering information from each of them. A hand to the shoulder by the sword master eased the tense situation. Quinn was enraptured by the command skills of his charge and found himself saluting Cedric as he approached.

"Lord Cedric, can I assist you?"

"What's the situation?"

"Twenty children and their teacher were on a field study outside the city," offered Mesmara. "Uncle Argus went to retrieve them."

"What are we up against?"

"Five lower circle demon-beasts broke through the barrier separating Terminus Mundus from Hell." explained Quinn. "It rarely happens, but it's still a nuisance. Usually they prance around for a while and leave. Argus and his party took one down already."

"You let Argus out there alone?"

"It was his orders!"

Cedric let down the scopes on his helmet. Spotting Argus and his group, the sword master moved his line of sight to observe the four beasts in hot pursuit. Estimated at two hundred meters away by his tech, a red light alerted the Titan prince to two more demons coming hard on the flank.

"You missed two!" shouted Cedric as he cursed in the ancient Titan.

"What?"

"Ten o'clock! Two more beasts!"

Already under enough stress, Quinn surveyed the land with his scopes. Beads of sweat formed on his forehead as he cursed. Cedric closed his eyes for a moment and took two deep breaths. Reaching for a swig of brandy, the Titan barked his order.

"Give me your crossbow!"

"They're out of range!" protested Quinn.

"Just do it!"

As he surrendered the weapon, Cedric realized he wasn't familiar with this particular type of crossbow. Looking everywhere for the mechanism to wind it back in place, the sword master checked his cloak for a crow's foot.

"Where's the crank?"

Quinn gave Cedric a quick crash course on how to use the crossbow.

"It's automatic. You flick this lever back, the string draws back and new a bolt loads. That one has fifty rounds."

"This is very impressive weapon; I hope I can master it in time."

Unveiling his equestrian talisman, Cedric summoned Jericho.

"I summon the mightiest of the stable of Hayden Marisol! Ride now, Jericho!"

A blue bolt of light emerged from the talisman and Jericho materialized on the grounds below the gate in full armor. The other Kablisha stared in awe.

"*Is that a horse?*" pondered a soldier.

"That's the largest one I've ever seen," commented another soldier.

"I need everyone to keep me covered until I get out there." ordered Cedric. "I'll take care of the rest."

"What are you doing?" demanded Mesmara.

"I'm going to cut off the flanking demons for your uncle because they're not going to make it."

"Prince Cedric Rhone, I am under orders by my superior officer to keep you inside this city," warned Quinn. "I will not hesitate to order my troops to fire."

"Shoot me!"

Smiling, Cedric dove off the wall and landed perfectly in Jericho's saddle. Quinn cursed up a storm and threw his arms up in protest. Jericho snarled and nodded his head.

"Godspeed, Jericho! We're back in the game!"

Neighing in approval, Jericho took off at break-neck speed toward Argus and the others. Tenderly, Mesmara put her arms around Quinn's shoulder to comfort him.

"If anything happens to him, your uncle is going to kill me."

"Then we better pray nothing happens to him."

Wondering if everyone in the city was going to take up position at the wall, Quinn was startled by the arrival of Bishop Wulf.

"What's happening?" asked the bishop.

"Argus is trying to get those outside the city back through the postern but they're going to be flanked," reported Quinn.

"Lord Cedric rode off to help him," interrupted Mesmara. "We weren't able to stop him."

Opening his hands, Wulf blessed Cedric as he made his way across the field.

"Saint Michael the Archangel defend him in battle!" prayed the bishop.

Pursued by the beasts, Argus peeked to see the monstrosities closing on the slower moving party. Going for a one-in-a-million shot, Argus fired over his right shoulder. It struck first beast in the knee. The resulting tumble tripped the other three beasts with him. Momentary relief gave way to outright fear, as he heard a beast's howl from the flank. Two demons leapt from their cover, with fangs exposed to devour the children.

"God save us!" evoked Argus.

Just as the demon was about to strike, a bolt flew through the air and struck him in the head. Turning his head, Argus watched as Cedric fired a second shot from on top of Jericho. The chest strike put the beast down for good. With a scream of *Titanus*, the Titan prince reared Jericho with Ragnarok drawn. A slash underneath the throat left the second demon staggering. Clawing at its wound, the creature choked to death on its own blood—though not before, an awestruck Argus believed in the tales told of *La Morte Angelus*. Circling across the field, Cedric brought Jericho on the flank of the running children as they made for the postern. However, one of the girls tripped and fell to the ground before they reached the walls. She tried to get up and move but she couldn't. Noticing his sister was not at his side, a boy ran back to her. Kylie screamed for her children from atop the wall as the group entered the safety of the postern. Hearing screams, Cedric turned Jericho around and smiled.

"Of course!" joked Cedric.

"Cedric, you can't!" screamed Argus.

"You get the rest of those kids back into the city," ordered Cedric. "I'll see to these two."

The pleas of the Kablisha captain fell on deaf ears. In a matter of moments, Jericho reached the children. Leaping from his saddle, Cedric saw to the crying brother and sister.

"Be strong! We're getting out of here alive!"

Cedric examined the girl's leg and spotted a break near the ankle. Lifting her up to Jericho, he tied her into the saddle. Intimidated by the overwhelming presence of the Titan prince, her brother didn't know what to do.

"I know better than most what it's like taking care of a younger sister. I've got a feeling you're pretty much the same way. By my authority, you're now a soldier in my command. Your mission is to get your sister to safety; I'll take care of the rest. That's an order, son."

"Yes, great prince," stammered the boy.

With a little boost, the boy climbed onto Jericho. Following his orders, he held his sister tightly. The warmth between the siblings was obvious as she stopped crying. Jericho stared into his master's eyes and snarled.

"Get them back to the postern! Godspeed!"

Jericho nodded, turned and rode to the Postern. While Kablisha militia were assisting and treating the children at the postern, Argus dealt directly with Kylie's children coming in on Jericho. Noticing Cedric wasn't with them, the Captain tried to run to Cedric, but Nelson and Stanton grabbed him.

"Let me go! It's our mission to keep him safe!"

"You can't help him now, sir!" reasoned Nelson.

"Then just fire!"

"They're out of range, sir," said Stanton.

As three demon beasts moved to run him down, the arrogant smile of the greatest Knight on Terminus Mundus returned to the Titan prince's lips. Whatever confidence Cedric had lost when he was first told he wasn't the Permaneo Eques Ordinaris had returned to him. Breathing deeply, he staked Ragnarok in the ground and a holy aura surrounded him. Argus and Bishop Wulf could sense the power emanating from his body.

"What's that power coming off of him?" asked Mesmara.

"He's going to try to use the Holy War spell," said the bishop.

"There's no way he can use a spell that powerful this quickly!" shouted Quinn. "The Sentinels are the only beings who ever used that spell in creation!"

Chanting in the divine language at a whisper at first, the voice of the sword master ascended to a crescendo. The surrounding aura from his body expanded to a greater radius, and flames formed in his eyes. As he screamed *Holy War*, the white flames of the light of creation gathered in the palms of his hands. Thrusting forward, they created a shockwave so powerful that the targeted beasts were reduced to ashes in mere moments. Despite this awesome power, the wave subsided and neither the land nor a living creature was harmed save for the spawn of Hell. It was not a sight the Kablisha expected.

"He's mastered Holy War…in a revolution!" stuttered Wulf. "Who is this Cedric Rhone?"

Utterly exhausted from the force behind the attack, Cedric knew it wasn't over yet. As bushes rustled at his flank, Cedric grabbed Ragnarok once more. The first demon-beast, bearing the wounded knee from Argus' bolt, roared at the Titan prince. Refusing to back down, the sword master taunted to demon to come at him. Happy to oblige, the beast charged as Cedric infused saint saber into Ragnarok. Assaulting the demon, he sliced the creature first in its wounded knee. Spinning around, the second slice was across its abdomen. Dumbfounded, the demon fell to ground, clawing and scratching as it struggled to stand. With all the strength he had left to muster, the sword master brought his claymore down on the beast's neck ending its misery.

"Do you call this a challenge?!" screamed Cedric at a seemingly invisible opponent.

Yanking up the head of his foe, Prince Rhone staked it on a small, dying tree.

"If you plan on inflicting terror, chaos, and suffering on Terminus Mundus, then you sure as hell better up your game. I am Prince Cedric Rhone of Titanus, *La Morte Angelus*. Fear me, for I am this world's avenging angel, and to those who have poisoned it with darkness, I will bring an inoculation of fire and death! Abaddon, you will never have her!"

Staring in horror, the Kablisha wondered silently if this new demon they had unleashed was more dangerous than the torments of the Hell. To the last, they no longer doubted the might of the Titan prince. After wiping the purple blood from his blade against the fur of the beast, Cedric celebrated his victory with a swig of brandy.

"My God, everything they said about this one is true!" said Argus.

Theatrics aside and adrenaline drained, Cedric staggered weakly to the city. He didn't have to wait long for a company of militia came to carry him back. As he entered the city, the remaining military knelt before him in homage and the civilians chanted his name. Crying tears of joy, Kylie grabbed the Titan prince around the waist.

"God bless you, Cedric Rhone!" praised Kylie. "God bless you!"

Smiling, the Prince turned his gaze down to Kylie's children whose eyes were filled with wonder and gratitude. Cedric bent down so the two children could him hug him as well. Quinn and Mesmara ran to him.

"That…what you did out there…it was…" stammered Quinn.

"Quinn is trying to say that we're all amazed with what you did," explained Mesmara.

"There wasn't much choice, given the circumstances."

"Anything you want, man!" offered Quinn. "You've got it!"

"Right now, you can help by finding Florence."

Cedric collapsed to the ground. Not but a second later, Florence was at his side, tending to his wounds. For the first time, his jubilant comrades noticed the blood running down his right shoulder from the wound. As they removed his breastplate, they could see the wound on his chest and stomach had opened as well. Anticipating the worst, a tearful Florence pressed her starched cleric robes tightly against the open wounds. Invoking all of her white magic knowledge, she worked tirelessly to close the wounds. To her surprise, she was joined by Mesmara and Bishop Wulf. The Kablisha screamed out orders to give the Titan prince room. The children were getting worried that he was going to die there on the spot. Many parents began to shuttle them back to their homes just in case. It took some time, but the worst of it passed, and the wounds closed. After a few moments, Florence opened her eyes and recited her diagnosis.

"You tore your deltoid and have a partially separated shoulder, my lord; we'd better get you back to bed."

"I'm in no position to disagree with you," replied Cedric.

He tried to stand, but Quinn and the others would have none of it. They brought a stretcher and carried Cedric back to the bishop's residence.

"That is a very impressive weapon you carry, Quinn. I wouldn't mind having one crafted for myself."

"I told you, anything you want."

Wincing in pain, Cedric still received many thanks, blessings, and gratitude from his Divikin brethren. In their hearts, they would never treat this brave soul as an outcast again. Florence stuck her right index finger in her mouth, which had been inside of Cedric's shoulder wound.

"The poison in his body is gone," she diagnosed.

As Argus stood to the side observing all of the happenings, he was approached by Bishop Wulf, who leaned heavily on his crosier.

"I know what you're thinking," offered the bishop.

"He killed all of those demon-beasts like they were mere goblin fodder," said Argus. "Though I can't get over the look he had in his eyes when he finished that last one off. I had read so much about him but never did I expect to see anything like this."

"Do you doubt your original theory?"

"I don't know, but I can see now how he took down Abaddon. No angel would ever believe anyone born of creation could fight like that. We know how bad his right shoulder is and still he wielded that sword like a true master. He learned Holy War so quickly…it is possible?"

"What do you want to do?"

"I think Cedric and I need to have a talk divikin-to-divikin. There are questions I need answered."

"As you wish, Argus, but I don't want to discount what you did today. No one in this clan would have gone outside these walls if you didn't lead them. It was very brave of you to risk your life to save those children."

"You knew I always would have gone anyway. Besides, I had to try my best to keep that thickskulled Titan prince from doing something stupid."

"The barrier should be stabilized for some time now. Don't worry, they didn't come here because of Cedric. I analyzed the tear and they've been working on that for some time now. Though after this defeat, I doubt they'd get too many volunteers to return."

"Well, that's good news at least. All that running worked up an appetite; I think I'll go get something to eat."

"Stop by the residence, we'll continue our conversation over luncheon."

"Thank you, your grace."

The two left for the bishop's residence.

Royal Castle, Margrave of Deniva

"So then Jesus said to them clearly, 'Lazarus has died. And I am glad for you that I was not there, that you may believe. Let us go to him.' So Thomas, called Didymus, said to his fellow disciples, 'Let us also go to die with him.'"

The Titan Evangelist 11:14-16

The ever-resourceful exiles were not about to rest on their laurels in the first revolution of their predicament. Cassandra petitioned Margrave Dennis and received permission to remodel part of the castle dungeons to be used as a large training ground. Valentine was very excited because it gave him a chance to work with Joshua in a large area. Joshua was admittedly not as happy. In the morning, the royalists would gather in this area together and keep themselves battle ready. Sporadically returning from their Edenian observations, Christian and Colin made good use of the facility as well.

In one corner, Cagius and Walker watched helplessly as Valentine continued to train Joshua in the ways of the Paladin. With less enthusiasm, Amuro instructed Saria in the proper technique of using a whip as a weapon. Half of the training area was sealed off in a magic barrier, as Nadia and Cassandra practiced the art of spell casting. The other royals took to using the wood and metal training dummies strewed out across the basement. Malcolm preferred to fire his practice arrows at targets, but tired of the game quickly as he hit the bull's eye every time.

Cagius had placed Joshua on an intensive weight training routine and diet over the past revolution. His time spent at the blacksmith's gave him the proper foundation and the lad now towered over his comrades at two hundred centimeters in height. Now powerful enough to hold a kite shield and thus protect larger portions of his body, Valentine worked overtime to find new ways to torment Joshua. Cagius and Walker bit their lips as the assassin continued his aggressive posture against his charge. Two lunar cycles before, he switched from the bamboo sword to a blunted iron blade. In order to keep the trainee on his toes, Valentine would often use a second blade so Joshua would learn to block with his sword as well. The young paladin-in-training gritted his teeth and perspired underneath his protective helmet. It took almost everything he had to deflect the strikes. Cagius smiled at the hard work of his nephew.

"Could you believe he only started doing this a revolution ago?" commented Cagius.

"It's very impressive, especially since we tend to forget how young he is," observed Walker. "I certainly couldn't have held my own against Valentine when I was his age."

"I just wish Darius could have gotten his hands on him."

"Trust me, Cagius, with what he's gone through, he needed more than technique. Only Valentine can give him that."

Twenty minutes of constant fighting with a kite shield and broadsword took its toll on Joshua. Valentine finally got around his shield and whacked him with the iron blade. Agonizing from the bleeding welt already formed on his back, the trainee shifted into attack mode. Knowing he had him now, Valentine allowed the young man to flail wildly. Elegantly, the assassin parried each attack, until he spotted his opening. The teacher grabbed his student on his arm and brought him to the ground with a loud thud. Taking his sword, Valentine brought it down hard across Joshua's chest. As the young paladin moved to stand, his teacher shoved his boot onto his chest.

"You're already dead, so stay down! If you lose control and fight angry, you'll die. You'll waste your life just like your father did!"

Valentine grabbed Joshua and pulled him up. Joshua remained defiant though he would adhere to the proper protocols in front of his master.

"Do you think this is a game?"

"No."

"Really? You have some ability and strength but it's not enough! You can't keep letting that temper take hold of you; you'll never be a paladin."

"Do you think he's going over the edge?" asked Walker.

"We've got to trust Valentine," reassured Cagius. "He knows what he's doing."

"You're not encouraging me."

"I never trained to be a paladin. There was no way my father was going to allow me to usurp what he believed to be my brother's rightful rank. It was rough crawling up through the legions, but we never did anything like this. Valentine trained under Darius and I'm sure the old man put him through something worse."

Their conversation was interrupted by the sound of a loud crack, and a woman's soft cry. Knowing that soft and cute whelp anywhere, Cagius ran toward Saria. On the floor and holding her bleeding chin, the younger sister wept while the older sister stood condescendingly over her. Though her agility, discipline, and desire to use the whip as a weapon were unquestioned, Saria hadn't progressed as Amuro expected her. The intricacies of the weapon eluded her, and most training sessions ended with blood and tears. Comforting the young elf maiden, Cagius stroked her soft hair.

"What happened, Amuro?"

"She missed; on the crack she let the whip come too far back and struck herself in the chin."

Annoyed at Cagius' constant doting, the marshal wondered if the Dragoon placed all of the blame for Saria's ills on her. The dutiful older sister knelt down and put her fingers to Saria's chin. She used her healing magic on the wound. It not only stopped the bleeding but also removed the scar.

"There we go, all better."

Sniffling as the pain subsided, Saria felt her chin and was relieved there wasn't a scar.

"Thanks, sis."

"I won't tell you how many times I dropped my trident on my own foot," joked Cagius. "You just need to see Joshua's back to understand how hard this is. The important thing is to keep getting up. As long as you can stand, you can still fight. Are you ready to try again?"

Saria nodded. Inspired by Cagius' pep talk, Amuro thought to herself about how he'd probably claim later it was one of his many secret techniques. Gracefully rising to her feet, Saria kissed Cagius and accepted the whip from her sister. Eager to practice, the elf maiden jumped over a series of ropes flawlessly as she attempted to crack her whip at small targets her sister had positioned for her.

Focused only on her training, the other events in the basement remained foreign to Cassandra. As she trained, one thought burned into her mind over and over, how embarrassed she was to be dressed only in black leather clothing that looked like a one-piece swimsuit that fit too tight to her skin. Despite the reassurances of her new mentor, Cassandra would never feel comfortable wearing such clothes. The cold floor underneath her bare feet didn't increase her comfort level either. Grasping Nadia's staff for practice as she had done before with her uncle, the young queen awaited her next challenge.

"From your training, I see you have a natural affinity for fire spells that's why you've mastered Blaze Wall so quickly."

"Uncle's specialty was fire so he knew how to train me quickly in that discipline. It was also the easiest to manifest in my free time."

"I see. All right, I'm going to make you try Storm Bolt. I assume you've read the incantations in the Book of Rune about a hundred times."

As she was about to acknowledge her teacher, both women suddenly stopped. Even Amuro shivered outside the barrier. The evocation of a tremendous amount of magical energy crashed against Deniva likes waves on the shore. Not knowing its source but determining it not to be of Abaddon or her father's origin, Nadia ignored it and continued the lesson.

"Good. Get ready."

Opening her hands, Nadia summoned a demon from a created magic circle. The demon was about as tall as a human and had many human features. However, it had horns and bat-like wings.

"How did you do that?" gulped Cassandra.

"While I am haunted by my past, I never forgot what I learned. There's nothing like training on a moving target. Besides, I'm here if anything happens."

Filled with wroth and frothing at the mouth, the demon target screamed as it charged at the young queen.

"Oh shoot!" Nadia chastised herself. "I forgot that they love the taste of virgin blood more than anything."

As it swiped with its claws, Cassandra performed a back flip to avoid the strike. Impressing her mentor with her profound agility, the rune mistress thrust her staff into the demon's chest before bashing it on the head. Dazed and open to attack, Cassandra chanted in her ancient, native tongue. She held the staff away from her body in her right hand and pushed her left hand forward. In the palm of that hand, a magic circle formed as a yellow shimmer overtook her. As the demon recovered, the young queen finished her chant. The last words came out in the unified tongue, "storm bolt." A bolt of lightning flew out of the magic circle and shot into the air. It took a diagonal path towards the demon and struck the beast head on. Charring the skin from its skull, the beast frenzied. Cassandra was shocked she had unleashed such power, but Nadia understood her trainee was more than a mere prodigy. Her smile barely concealed, the young woman in her care had not only read the Book of Rune but comprehended all of the minor intricacies of each spell. Seeing physical attacks were useless, the demon chanted and prepared to unleash its limited magical arsenal. However, when it called for the attack, nothing happened.

"I don't understand, I didn't cast silence," stated a confounded Cassandra.

"The Storm Bolt not only damages the target but also silences them," lectured Nadia. "Its magic is going to be useless for the next few minutes. Do you understand its weaknesses?"

"Its bane should be holy magic."

Repeating her movements from before, Cassandra shimmered in silver light this time. Chanting for a shorter time, the young queen unleashed "Holy Ball." This spell sent white, hot light from her staff and tore through the body of her demon opponent. As ash fell to the basement floor, Nadia and Cassandra celebrated with a hug.

"Very good, my pretty prodigy. If you're willing to keep working on the Storm Bolt spell it will kill a demon outright."

"I have to admit I'd rather cast one Storm Bolt than go through a litany of spells trying to finish off an opponent. It's one thing to do it under perfect conditions, but I don't know about a battle."

"These are the powers of level three spells, and only the most advanced sorceresses can use them. The Magus Class cannot even cast the spells you are learning."

"Really?"

"Yes. I can use Blaze Wall but Storm Bolt, Stone Cloud, and Freeze Arrow are beyond me. There may be more spells I could teach you. You see there is a spell that you should be able to master even though it isn't traditionally in your class."

Giddy like a child receiving birthday presents, Casandra was eager to learn. Yet, her lecture was interrupted.

"Look out!" screamed Hippolyte angrily.

Wildly flailing at a practice dummy with his axe, Ethan accidently cut off one of the arms. The projectile whisked past the wolf tribe girl's right ear and she stared at her host with a look of death. Ethan had been off all morning in his training. It was as if something else was eating at his heart and mind.

"Careful there, Ethan! I nearly lost an eye in your last attack."

"God, I am sorry, Hippolyte," apologized Ethan. "I thought coming down here would help but my mind isn't all there."

"I can't imagine why," stated Malcolm. "Then again, I might want to get as far away from Cecilia as possible in her current state."

Pounding on the steps and heavy breathing caught the attention of everyone in the room. A servant stood at the base of the stairs leaning against the wall and bent over holding her ribs. Filled with fear in her face as if she had been berated, Ethan took pity on her. Running to the servant, the girl bowed before the margrave's son.

"Your highness," panted the servant. "It's time."

"Cecilia, I'm coming!" screamed Ethan.

Hooking his axe behind him, Ethan barreled up the stairs. The others watched the warrior flee in panic and wondered what kind of reception awaited him.

"Well, I guess we'll be one more heavy now," teased Cagius. "Is it a boy or a girl?"

"The Titans have very strict traditions concerning these matters," explained Nadia. "They refuse to perform any tests to determine the sex of the child. With Cedric missing in action, this child is heir to the Titan throne. Primogeniture trumps everything else in terms of succession."

"I'll put money on the fact it comes out ready to ride in the saddle," joked Amuro.

"Perchance, have any of you ever witnessed a Titan woman giving birth before?" proposed a laughing Nadia.

Everyone shook their head, though Amuro got a real devious smile across her face when she spotted the look in Nadia's eyes. Cassandra wondered for a moment if the two hadn't been separated at birth.

"If you have to witness one birth, this is the one," promised Nadia.

Everyone in the basement looked at one another. They stopped what they were doing and sprinted for the stairs. Not wanting to be left alone, Cassandra threw a cloak over her body and heels on her feet. Ethan ran as fast as he could before he reached the ward section of Deniva Castle. As he entered a luxurious hospital room, he spotted two doctors and five nurses attending to his wife. Two nuns were praying on either side of her. Despite her situation, Cecilia managed to keep some semblance of her normal appearance. Teased for a revolution about her and Ethan's "wedding night conception," rumors were whispered throughout the castle on how Cecilia had commanded a successful campaign though no one dared ask which spouse led the charge. Keiko had barely left Cecilia's side since she had entered the third trimester of her pregnancy and for once the Titan princess was thankful for the sylph's incessant nagging. Outside the room, a servant took Ethan's axe and had a green smock for him to put on over his clothes. Ethan took a moment to admire his wife under the circumstances. Taking the moment to smile at one another, the two kissed and embraced.

"I thought you'd never get here," teased Cecilia, relieved he made it. "I've been holding this child in for forever."

"They just gave me the word!" replied Ethan.

"Get over here and do your husband's duty!"

"I'm just hoping you don't break my hand."

"It depends on how many more snide remarks you come out with. Did you bring the holy water?"

Ethan took his spot next to Cecilia. As the Vanadis took his hand, the margrave's son pointed to the holy water vial next to the bed.

"I got Father Giovanello to bless it this morning," explained Ethan. "All right, let's get the rhythmic breathing going, just like we worked on before."

"I'll breathe when I need to," exclaimed Cecilia. "Who do you think knows my system better, me or that halfwit you made us see?"

Rolling his eyes, Ethan knew everything he feared leading up to this was going to come true. Suddenly startled by what sounded like a herd approaching, husband and wife observed all of their companions trying to get better view from the door. The nurses wanted to clear them away from the door, but no one was going to budge. Amuro snuck underneath the rest of them and managed to squeeze into the room.

"Look at my friends!" exclaimed Cecilia. "I guess I should be charging admission, come on in and treat the birth of my first child as the opening act of a circus."

"Under the circumstances, maybe you guys shouldn't be here!" argued Ethan.

"Are you kidding me?" demanded Minerva. "I've never seen a baby being born before and it's definitely something I want to see."

One look at Nadia, who was doing her best to keep herself invisible, was all Cecilia needed to confirm that the witch must have explained to her friends the unique nature that a Titan woman takes toward birth.

"Why don't you take a picture?" teased Cecilia. "It will last longer."

Valentine had the guts to do just that. He pulled out a little mini-camera he used for spying and took a picture of the proud mama and papa. The Vanadis would have killed him if not for the contraction at that moment. The doctor got into position.

"All right, your highness, the baby's turned and I see a head," explained the doctor. "Now I'm going to need you to push."

Cecilia composed herself with the same drive she would use to command her troops. Propping herself up on the bed, she took Ethan's hand and put her other hand against the rail on the bed. A deep breath later and Cecilia pushed. The royals were not disappointed at the show.

"Come on, little one, you don't want to be stuck in the womb! Get out here and see the world."

"You're doing great, your highness," encouraged the doctor.

Insistent on the next one, Cecilia pushed. Ethan knocked his foot against the floor in agony as his wife crushed the bones in his hand.

"One more time!"

Determined to finish the job, Cecilia let go of Ethan's hand and she grabbed the rails on either side of the bed. They literally twisted and bent, but the Titan princess did not offer one scream. A smile crossed her face as the soft cry of a young boy was heard throughout the room. The royals cheered and Cassandra was a welled-up mess. As Ethan moved to kiss her on the cheek, Cecilia grabbed him and pulled him in a deep kiss.

"Another fighter for the cause," teased Cagius.

To a chorus of laughter, the doctors and nurses took their time inspecting the young boy. The bending of metal caught their attention, as an aggravated Cecilia demanded they work faster until she finally reached a boiling point.

"Give me my son!"

The doctor worked very quickly cutting the cord and taking out the nose plugs. Ethan stared at Cecilia.

"How did you know it was a boy?" said Ethan.

"Titan mothers have a good instinct about these things," said Cecilia. "Legend has it that we know it's a boy because they kick harder in the womb. In reality, Martha taught me how to hear the inflection in the cry when they come out of the womb."

The attendants wrapped the child in a blue blanket and gave him over to Cecilia. Cecilia's mood immediately improved upon cradling her son.

"Mommy's here now," said Cecilia softly. "It's all right, little one."

Cecilia stared into the big brown eyes of the young boy. Ethan took the time to sprinkle the holy water on Thomas' forehead. The Titans did not treat this as a formal baptism but instead as a means of showing the parent's love of the child and their commitment to rear it within the faith. Everyone in the room fawned over the motherly instincts of Cecilia. Amuro was pleasantly surprised at seeing the side of her friend that Queen

Civilia had spoken so highly of. Hippolyte and Minerva recognized these instincts from dealing with Cecilia before.

"It goes to show you that all Titan females are truly mother eagles," observed Nadia.

"Why are you still here?" teased Cecilia.

The Vanadis took her son and handed him over to Ethan for the first time. The Denivan knight looked at his son with great pride and took some time to study him. Ethan was surprised to find out how many Rhone traits were present in the child. He stared at Cecilia and then back at his son a few times before starting to laugh.

"There's not a doubt in my mind," said Ethan. "This child is certainly more Rhone than de-Milly."

"It must be a little left over present from Martha's genetic tampering," explained Cecilia.

"Did you decide what to name him yet?" asked Amuro.

"His name is Thomas," offered Cecilia.

"I understand—you don't believe anything unless you see it with your eyes," guessed Cassandra.

"Actually, I always respected Thomas because the Titan evangelist wrote that of all the disciples he was willing to go back to Verian with Jesus even if he was going to have to die. Also he was apparently outside doing good works while the other disciples were hanging out in locked rooms. Otherwise he would have been in the room when Jesus returned to the disciples the first time."

Everyone contemplated this and realized that Cecilia would come up with a different reason from a scripture passage than everyone else in the world.

"I'll bring Thomas down to the nursery," proposed Ethan. "You can take some rest."

"Rest?" questioned Cecilia. "Are you kidding me?"

Cecilia moved to get out of bed.

"My great-great-great-great-great-grandmother actually gave birth on the battlefield, cradling the newborn in one hand and swinging a sword in the other. I dare not insult my ancestors by taking some mere bed rest when there's work to be done. I gave up all this valuable training time so I wouldn't risk the life of my son! I can feel my muscles starting to atrophy. What I need right now is to get cleaned up and get some food in me. Then I'm going to have to start my workout regimen."

"You really should rest, your Highness," ordered the doctor.

"Trust me, I know my body. I'll sleep well tonight," retorted Cecilia.

"You Divikin are so annoying" quipped Amuro. "If it was anyone else, I'd just cast a sleep spell and all our problems would be solved."

Standing from the bed, Cecilia stretched. A couple of the men in the room averted their eyes out of respect, but Joshua did peek a few times.

"Actually, Cecilia, you look to be in the mood for a little pampering," offered Cassandra. "The Royal Spa has a wonderful bath treatment that I'm sure you'd enjoy. It's my treat!"

Cecilia raised her eyebrow at this. Cassandra's idea did seem like a good one, but she didn't know if she wanted to leave her son alone. She turned to Ethan.

"The doctors have a battery of tests that they need to run, you can't rely on Martha's good judgment alone. I'm going to have to deal with a steady stream of my relatives that will want to see the child. Take the time to get yourself healthy; Thomas will probably need you in a few hours anyway."

As she started to leave the room, Valentine on the sly bent over to Joshua's ear.

"I'll bet Thomas can't wait to nuzzle those…"

Valentine didn't get a chance to get the last word out before Cecilia caught him with a right cross, sending the assassin flying to floor. She calmly walked out of the room with Cassandra as if nothing had happened. Joshua couldn't help but laugh after the torture his mentor was putting him through. Wiping the blood from his lip, the assassin smiled.

"I don't think any of her muscles atrophied," quipped Valentine as he picked himself off the floor. "Come on, Joshua, we've got work to do."

Bishop's Residence, City of Antiquity

"The prophecy of the Legend of the Last Knight has been studied by scholars from every country and every branch. No one truly knows all of its secrets; however, the ancients do believe that it was actually mistranslated and should read 'Knight of God.' However, some Elf scholars repeat a tale that a portion of the prophecy was lost when the Dwarves sacked the first Castle at Brooke Run. That particular prophecy also mentioned the 'Mysterium Finalis.' However, no such documentation exists as to what this truly means."

Introduction to "Deciphering the Legend" Elf Scholar Demetrius

Cedric was seated at the table in his room, dressed in a simple t-shirt and shorts. He used the sharpest steak knife he had to cut the remnants of the thirty-two ounce T-bone steak in front on him. The juices dripped from the beautifully cooked purple to pinkish inside. Cedric took the time to dip the meat in the juice. In spite of the extra effort it took to cut the meat, Cedric smiled each time the flesh touched his lips. A pile of fried potatoes were on a plate next to the steak. Occasionally, Cedric would pop one into his mouth with a loud crunch. His ears rose every once in a while to the sound of joyful music playing outside. Staring at the streets below, he saw the Kablisha had ignited a large bonfire in the center pit of the City of Antiquity. The children were singing and dancing around it. It brought a smile to the sword master's face as he drink ale from the stein on the table. A knock at the door drew his attention away from his meal.

"Come in," said Cedric with a sigh.

Argus walked inside the room. Wrinkling his nose at the smell he hadn't smelled in a long time, the Captain gagged twice. Cedric laughed as he continued his meal.

"I really wish Wilhelm would inform us when he decides to play grocery boy for his favorite ward," commented Argus.

"I decided to reward myself after my earlier heroics. The Kablisha are a good and righteous people, but your choice of diet leaves much to be desired."

"You know that you're the reason we are having a celebration out there tonight. My people would certainly not shun you, especially after what you did."

"You guys don't need me out there to have a good time. Besides, this is as good a place as any to hide from a love-struck cleric looking to dance."

"I must admit it was a bit disconcerting to witness your antics during your victory dance."

"The power of creation provides a great rush. I was loaded up on enough adrenaline that I felt I could take on the powers of Hell. It's a little side effect I'll correct the next time."

Cedric picked up the bone and started to gnaw the last pieces of meat off of it. Argus tried to hold back his disgust but realized he had no chance of containing this Titan prince. Cedric took another swig of ale.

"Can I get you something to drink?" asked Cedric. "Brandy? Beer?"

Argus put his hands up.

"Twenty-five revolutions among the Kablisha has hindered my tastes for flesh and libations. Besides, you Titans have nothing on the wondrous cuisines and brews courtesy of my Edenian forefathers."

"To each his own."

Cedric continued to pop the fried potatoes into his mouth. Argus was surprised to see Cedric using a red type of sauce to dip the potatoes in before eating them. He simply could not understand the eating habits of his guest.

"Can I sit down?" asked Argus.

"Absolutely. Are you sure I can't get you anything?"

"I'm fine, Cedric, but thank you."

"I'm not use to you showing such civility and deference towards me. I must have done something good."

"I don't think I need to tell you the good you've done. God, Cedric, I couldn't believe it myself. When I read the reports about you, I thought they were exaggerated. I thought Titanus was just trying to build up their Crown Prince and his mighty deeds. But today, I saw a true hero."

"I'm just trying to do what I can. You knew I wasn't going to be able to hold back once there were kids involved."

"I should have known…"

"Don't blame Mesmara and Quinn, they did want to stop me. I just told them to shoot me if they wanted too."

"You shouldn't set them up in a no-win situation like that. They're good soldiers and they take it very hard when they disappoint me."

"What do I owe the pleasure? I know you're not here just to praise me, though I do appreciate the compliments."

"I need to know something about you that's very personal."

"That depends on the question you ask." Cedric laughed and took another swig of ale.

"I had Wilhelm recount the means he went to in order to save your life," recollected Argus. "He said you called out the name 'Cassie' in your sleep."

Taking a long drink of beer, the Titan prince wanted to avoid the question.

"I could have, but I honestly don't remember a thing that happened to me after I lost consciousness. All I know is that I took a swig of brandy and said a prayer to God, and the next thing I remember is waking up in bed here."

"Please, Cedric, I'm begging you. The fate of Terminus Mundus may rest in what happened to you!"

"I'm not sure if what I saw was meant for the eyes of all or simply my eyes alone, Argus."

"I haven't been completely honest with you concerning the Legend of the Last Knight. It isn't just one legend, Cedric, there are four distinct interpretations of it."

"Why didn't you tell me?"

"I was afraid. I didn't want to believe that one of the Titans would be the one to bring us salvation. I harbor my own prejudices against the warlike nature of your people, which made me blind to the bravery and honor of your knights. I'm sure you've heard of the 'Bis Reginam' of the Titan legends."

"I am familiar with the stories of a queen who was blessed by two sources."

"The Elves have the version that Wilhelm spoke of to you. We have our own version and the Edenians have a completely different version that speaks of a 'Mysterium Finalis.' I was wondering if you saw anything in the time you were dreaming."

"There aren't words I can use to explain it to you. If you're hell-bent on seeing what's going on in my screwed-up head, I might have a technique that could allow you to discover the knowledge you seek."

"What technique, exactly?"

"I can create a bridge between our brains using my magic. You won't be able to affect what's going on but you'll be able to see everything as if you were there."

"I don't trust that brand of domination magic you use."

"Don't worry, this particular spell won't lobotomize or hypnotize you. I admit I don't have too much practice with this area but I've disciplined myself to use all of the proper spells of the branch."

"I guess my curiosity is going to get the better of me. How long do you need?"

"I just have to do one thing first."

Cedric finished his last fried potatoes and downed his beer. He walked into his private bathroom and emerged a few minutes later.

"I can begin when you're ready," said Cedric.

Argus took a deep breath. "Okay."

Cedric closed his eyes and opened his hands. Argus just sat there. After a few moments he wondered if anything was happening.

"Hey Cedric, when are we going to—"

He stopped midsentence as his surroundings completely changed. Argus wondered where the room he was in had gone. Lush trees and soft grass were everywhere around him. Animals of every kind bounded about him feeding off the abundance of the land. Argus could hear the roaring sounds of four rivers flowing down from a single head. The Kablisha Captain raised his eyes to single giant apple tree no more than fifty meters in front of him. It was in that moment that he realized where he really was. Turning his gaze to the east, he spotted a golden barrier protecting this beauty from the area around it.

Could this be Eden? thought Argus. *Am I dead? What does this all mean*?

The Captain raised his eyes to the north where there was a single ruin in the landscape. It looked like a forum that had lost its ceiling and half of its columns. Despite the beauty around him and willingness to stay where he was, Argus felt compelled to walk to this particular structure. He moved quickly and was able to run faster than he ever thought he could to reach this structure.

"Cedric Rhone certainly has some strange dreams. I just don't understand why he would warn me against viewing such a vivid site."

Argus walked up twenty marble steps until he reached the forum. Standing barefoot in a tattered black dress, Cassandra levitated in the middle of the ruin. Eyes closed and arms extended, she was surrounded by an ethereal blue light.

"Cassandra, the Royal Princess of Central Acadia; I heard she was beautiful, but now I know why Cedric longs for her so much. My God, she's almost like an angel herself."

Immersed in tendrils of dark energy before her was the broken and bloody body of Cedric Rhone. Remembering the agony and suffering when he was first brought to them, the Kablisha captain wept at the wounds the sword master was suffering from. Despite striking the infinite tendrils with Ragnarok, Cedric held his forlorn gaze on Cassandra. After what seemed like an eternity to Argus, Cassandra landed on the ground before her champion. Opening her eyes, she agonized at her betrothed's condition. The Princess let out a loud cry and for a moment Argus doubted his own eyes. Suddenly before him were two Cassandras. On his right was the most compassionate and tender creature he had ever laid eyes on. Wearing a dazzling white dress and spreading her white wings wide, an angelic Cassandra comforted the injured warrior with tears of mercy. The enticement to the left of the Kablisha captain was too much for his eyes to ignore, however. Created from all of mankind's lusts and temptations, the demonic Cassandra was stunningly beautiful in her skimpy black gown. The demoness' eyes stared hungrily at Cedric, demanding his attention by deliberately flaunting her enhanced assets. Yet, to the captain's surprise, this demonic apparition agonized over the Titan prince's condition as well.

"Cassie…" murmured Cedric.

The distinctions of succubus and angel made no difference. Both rushed to his side and placed a hand on his shoulder.

This isn't right. wondered Argus. *Why show him this?*

"This is my burden, Argus," said Cedric.

Argus was flabbergasted at being called out; Cedric had assured him that he couldn't interact with anyone in the dream.

"Don't be so shocked, Argus. This is my dream and I can chose to play it out as I wish. Here she is before you—Cassandra Acadia, by a cruel twist of fate a child of two celestial realms. How will she be perceived by those around her? The angelic embodiment of mercy set to bathe the world in the light of rebirth? Or the compilation of all our carnal desires ready to lead all creation on the path to destruction?"

The Kablisha captain breathed heavily. It was as if his blood was boiling inside of him, yet he could not remove his gaze from the demoness. She was just too beautiful, too perfect to be true. In her, Argus felt as if all of his desires and dreams could be satisfied. Entranced, he walked straight to her.

"Dammit, Argus! Are you so blinded by your own temptations?"

The captain snapped out of his trance. Ashamed, he slumped down against the pillar.

"She'll destroy us, Cedric. How can anyone resist her? Now I understand the prince's true plan. Cassandra was meant to turn creation against God."

"That's because creation is blind. They can't see beyond the physical."

"Her angelic form isn't strong enough to suppress this demon. Is that why this is your burden, because you choose mercy over lust?"

"No, it's my burden because I can hold the light and darkness in my heart."

Argus finally understood what the Titan prince meant. Like everyone else, he assumed the sword master was talking about himself, but the light and darkness in his heart represented his love for Cassandra. Cedric put his hands to both of their cheeks.

"I cannot love one part of her and forsake the other. Quick to cry, but strong enough to lead when called upon; powerful enough to level areas with her magic, but wise enough to train for countless hours in those powers; even when compelled to suck the soul from her victim, she still fought the temptation to the last moment. There's never been anything like her in creation, and I have been charged to love and protect her."

Elation overcame both forms of Cassandra and they came together in the single princess once more. She was dressed as a queen and radiated with otherworldly light. Overcome with joy and love, Cassie unleashed a blast of magic to destroy the tendrils tearing at Cedric. As Cedric collapsed, the raven-haired maiden knelt so she could catch the knight. Weakened by the ordeal, Cedric allowed himself to fall into her lap. Cassandra bent over and kissed him on the forehead.

"Rest now, my faithful knight, you've certainly earned it," comforted Cassandra.

Unlocking the powers in the depths of her souls, a golden glow healed the deep wounds of her unwavering protector. She took his agony from him and over time, Cedric could breathe easier.

"That's right, darling. Let me hold you in my arms and give you what comfort I can. I know that you believe it is your destiny to sacrifice yourself for my sake. I am so sorry, but the ordeal is not over—rather, our hour is coming soon."

Argus swallowed hard and wondered what she could possibly mean. He wondered if it meant that another battle was coming or did it mean that Cedric was destined to rule in the West as King or Emperor.

"No matter the distance that separates us, my dearest Knight, I will be with you and you are with me," promised Cassandra. "Only you had the power to save me from the darkness. Have comfort in the fact that I shall not hand you over to death so easily. Live for the future that we must build together. Let us end the strife that ravages Terminus Mundus and sets brother upon brother. We will drive out the Nephilim, the Demonkin, and their rebel allies to redeem this world in the light of creation for our children and all our heirs. However, I cannot do this without you! We are joined, my dearest love, as we were the day of that tournament when you crowned me against my father's will. This one at last is bone of my bones and flesh of my flesh; let us be one in our Solemn Hour! Cedric, I pray to see you in your glory."

At a loss for words, Argus held his head in shame. This maiden was blessed and cursed, and the blame he had laid on her for the sins of her grandfather were unjustified. Understanding the indomitable will of his prisoner, the Kablisha captain lifted his eyes to Heaven and his embarrassment was stolen from him. Cedric and Cassandra's act of faith filled him with hope. For a moment, Argus thought himself invincible. In an instant, a blinding light filled the entire area and the Captain shielded himself. A booming voice emerged from above and spread the dark green feathers of a Powers Choir angel upon him.

"The Divine Plan of the Lord God will be revealed to you in His time," echoed the voice.

"What must I do?" begged Argus. "Where is Camael?"

"Live your life according to the gift of free will!" said the Voice. "Leave the matters that concern God to God. You will know what needs to be done when the hour arrives!"

Despite the maze of spiraling feathers, Argus managed one last gaze at the two lovers. Four broken wings lie on the ground between the two. The Princess tilted her head toward the Captain and smiled at him with tears in her eyes. Argus screamed to her, but was already transported back into Cedric's room. The Kablisha captain fell off his chair but Cedric caught him before he reached the ground.

"More of a nightmare than a dream…" commented Cedric.

Calming his emotions, Argus turned from Cedric. Embarrassed and perspiring heavily, he graciously accepted the towel Cedric handed to him.

"I'm sorry," pleaded Argus as he wiped the sweat with the towel. "I just couldn't see beyond the succubus. How do you do it?"

"God never gives us a cross we can't carry. I could have easily given into my lust the first time I laid eyes on her, but I saw something more. I hope you found what you were looking for."

"I fear I found only more questions."

"Would you like that drink now?"

"Yes."

Cedric opened a bottle of brandy and poured two glasses.

"I'm glad for the opportunity to share a drink with someone besides Wilhelm. Here's to the heroes of the past and the soldiers of the future. God bless the warriors because sure as hell no one else will."

The two toasted and Argus took his drink, slightly choking.

"That's as strong as I remember," stated Argus.

"You know a good brandy is supposed to be savored, not swallowed," replied Cedric.

"Perhaps that's my problem. You know I have a few good cigars in my room; I think you've earned one."

"I'd appreciate that."

Argus left the room quickly to head back to his. Walking to the window, children were waving at him. The prince cocked his head to the corner of the room where he had a calendar. Cedric walked over and struck out the date with a red "X." There were many other rotations with the "X" marked through them.

"Though there are no bars and no guards, this place remains my prison. I know that God has a plan for me but I don't know how much longer my sanity will allow me to endure it. I toast my friends this evening; may you have strength to endure your Denivan Exile as well. And being that it is almost one revolution now, I swear to you I shall make this toast until my last revolution on Terminus Mundus. I offer you my thanks, Julius, those gauntlets saved my life and I pray every rotation that you receive the eternal reward you richly deserve for your sacrifice. Godspeed, my friend."

Cedric finished his drink on the toast and opened his pocket watch. He stared longingly at the picture of Cassie in it.

"Stay safe, and know I shall never forsake you."

Royal Castle, Castellan of Deniva, Approximately Four Revolutions Later

"No one ever said it was easy to follow the path of the Cavalier. First, you have to give up all of your needs. Second, you must find a lady suitable to defend. She need not be beautiful but rather kind and in some ways naïve. You do not take advantage of the woman but rather you seek to prevent others from doing so. It is not necessary that you fall in love with this Lady; rather you may consider this relationship completely amicable. As for me, let's just say that I've already broken the third rule."

Diary of Prince Cagius Imperia

Adjusting his riding gloves, Cagius strutted towards his horse in the courtyard. Valentine was already waiting for him on horseback. However, they were unable to make a timely exit as Walker and Malcolm blocked their path.

"Did you honestly believe you could hide this from me, Cagius?" asked Walker.

"I know what I have to do, Walker," said Cagius. "If you want to come with me, I'd appreciate your help."

"Someone is going to have to watch Valentine," offered Walker. "If you're going to do this, I've got your back."

Painfully, Malcolm took his place on a horse as well. Though he shook his head and muttered under his breath, the elf offered no protest. Just as

Cagius and others were ready to ride out, the faint sounds of quick steps stopped them. Sighing, the Napolitan prince spotted Cecilia's son Thomas running at them. Appearing eight revolutions of age rather than the four he had actually seen, the young Rhone's golden brown hair was spiked as his brown eyes bore into the man standing before him. Thomas was wearing a white shirt, black tie, and dress pants as if it was a Titan Christian school uniform. Cecilia's boy was short, thin as a rail, and had yet to inherit the physical frame or appetite of his parents. The Titan princess often wondered if it was the punishment for not informing her mother of her wedding or christening of the child.

"Lord Cagius, what are you doing?" inquired Thomas.

"Calderon has taken it upon himself to escort the beautiful and fair Princess Saria to his club with the aid of some rogue mercenary guards. There is no doubt in my mind that their intentions are dubious. Thus, my associates and I are going to have a gentlemanly discussion about the nature of intentional torts."

Snidely looking at his elders, the young Divikin was not fooled by Cagius' big words. In some ways, it was similar to elf blood and caused the boy to mature much faster than normal humans his age. Physical makeup aside, Thomas had an intuitive nature that made Christian DeVries take an interest in him. On Christian's advice, the royals eagerly took turns tutoring the boy.

"You're going to beat him up, aren't you?" reasoned Thomas.

"I told you we're going to talk," retorted Cagius. "At first, at least..."

"I may be a kid but I'm not stupid. Mom is going to hear about this."

"Thomas, all we ask is that you give us a fifteen-minute head start!" pleaded Valentine.

The four broke out on their horses to the city proper from the courtyard. Thomas shook his head.

"Why does the task of being the responsible one fall on my shoulders?

The young prince determined it was better to heed Valentine's request rather than suffer his wrath later. He was assured by the fact his mother was more than capable of making up the time deferential if needed. Taking his time ascending the stairs, the young prince attempted to stick as close to the time limit as possible. When he reached his mother's open door, he checked his watch and shouted.

"Mom!"

The always-attentive mother eagle leapt from her seated position and scooped her son up. Determining he hadn't injured himself, she probed further into his unannounced visit.

"What's the matter?"

"Cagius is going out with the others to beat up Calderon!"

"I knew it," commented Cecilia as she hung her head. "Had your father listened to me and properly vetted the new guards this wouldn't have happened. Well, I'd better get down there before Valentine starts slitting throats. How long did you give them?"

"Fifteen minutes."

Cecilia went to get ready.

"Thomas, don't you have lessons to get to?"

"Her majesty wished to be alone this morning. She's leaving today."

Sighing, Cecilia disbelieved it had been four-and-a-half revolutions since Nadia had offered her services to train the princess. The Titan princess still held the historical grudge all Titans felt for the demoness, but couldn't shake the feeling that the sorceress was indeed the right choice. Cecilia had watched the powers of her friend grow at an accelerated rate. The Vanadis was convinced the queen was now more than capable of handling the powers of darkness that sought her out. However, this growing power made the queen an even more attractive target and it was only a matter of time until the enemy came to claim her. Her motherly instincts caused her to notice the quizzical look on her son's face as if he was trying to reason out his mother's concerns. She smiled at him and changed the subject.

"What did you learn with Amuro yesterday?"

"She was teaching me the basics of the elf language."

"It's important that you learn the classics."

"I hate to admit it, but it's a little easier than learning ancient Titan."

"Well, when they created the unified language they used more elvic terms than ancient Titan, so I understand your plight. I had some trouble with it at first, too."

Cecilia said something in the ancient language to Thomas who immediately responded in kind. The two laughed at the little pop quiz.

"Now be on your way; mommy has to get changed."

"Right, mom!"

Cecilia embraced her son tightly and gave him a big kiss before sending him on his way. Closing the door, the Titan princess unbuttoned her blouse. While this occurred, Amuro walked into the courtyard as Maiden was brought to her. The elf princess flipped an apple up in the air and caught it behind her back. Stroking her mount on its mane, she slowly fed Maiden the fruit.

Spotting a full-armored Ethan in the courtyard, she assumed the worst.

"Hi, Ethan."

Grunting, the Denivan knight was furious and ignored Amuro in his anger. Normally, he had so much discipline with the hiring and training of the guards. However, his son was taking up a lot of his time and so he subbed out the duties to others. He didn't know what was worse, Cagius' actions or listening to the ribbing from his wife.

"So you've heard," joked Amuro.

"What are the odds of Cagius exercising restraint in this situation?"

"The odds aren't good. Cagius is normally a very respectable individual who would never do anything wrong. In fact, I would rate him as the most upstanding citizen of our wacky bunch. However, if he believes that he has the moral high ground, Cagius becomes an entirely different animal. Since my sister is involved, this will only further his resolve and most likely lead to some righteous display of justice."

"Oh, God."

The sudden thought of a massacre spurred Ethan to his horse. He paused but a moment as he heard the clanking of a familiar armor in the courtyard. Cecilia pulled out her talisman and summoned Myst in the same method that Cedric used. Without saying a word to her husband, she mounted.

"Cecilia, maybe it isn't a good idea if we both go," suggested Ethan. "This is my job and my negligence."

"Bone of my bone, flesh of my flesh—we said our vows together and we face our problems together from now on."

Ethan nodded while Cecilia leaned on him.

"A woman does not want to be protected by a man when she is capable. What she wants is an undying commitment to stand and fight with him to the last! No matter what end!"

Amuro stared and shook her head.

"I prefer the 'knight in shining armor'!" injected Amuro. "Can we get off this love fest before Cagius kills someone?"

The three followed the path Cagius had laid before them. It wasn't a long trip to the Siren's Club from the castle. The club was situated near the upper class section of the city and preferred to market itself to that type of crowd. The building was all brick on the outer façade with a large black door in front of it. Velvet curtains hung from the areas where the windows would be. The highlight on the outside of the building was an eighteen-foot marble statue of a mermaid with an exposed top, riding on a clamshell with a "come hither" look on her face. Two bouncers lay on the ground outside the building with blood and bruises all over their faces, victims of Valentine's quick handiwork. The inside of the establishment was much more exotic than that of the outside. Private rooms complete with velvet curtains lined the outer half of the room including a marble staircase leading to a second floor with eight rooms, partitioned by golden doors. An elevated stage large enough for six performers complete with three poles was situated in the center of the establishment. The area surrounding the stage featured long couches where patrons could watch the performers. Three performers were currently on stage dressed like mermaids. Translucent material forged into a clamshell covered their breasts while green silk flowed along their lower bodies to give the impression of fins in water. The one in the center was singing a tune while the other two danced. Pink and gold neon lights were flashing everywhere creating a calming effect for the patrons. Waitresses were serving the male patrons dressed in the same attire as the performers on the stage. In the corner of the room, two unsavory characters guarded a nervous Saria. She was carrying her whip on the side of her belt but didn't look like she had used it yet. Calderon sat at a table with six of his personal security standing behind him. He was dressed in a black robe over his white shirt and pants and had a smile on his face. Not intimidated by numbers, Cagius exposed his hands on the table. Examining his potential opponents for weaknesses, Valentine analyzed the guards. Meanwhile, Walker kept his eyes on Valentine. Malcolm sighed, surveying the room for a possible exit.

"Calderon, I'm going to ask you nicely," threatened Cagius. "Let Saria go now!"

"I don't think you understand the gravity of your situation," reasoned Calderon. "I need the girl to work in this Club. She will instantly triple the revenue I receive. Your Dad might have sway over the merchants in Port Talus, but I hold all the cards here."

"You don't seem to understand that you are treading very closely to the edge of my patience. I believe I've been more than reasonable, but I cannot condone this latest kidnapping. This is the third time now I've had to come down here! I'm not coming back here a fourth time!"

"Really? You know what I've become impatient with? The citizens of Deniva are sick and tired of giving you exiled Royals a free ride. You take our tithes to the King and live the life of luxury. Don't give me that garbage about defending us. If we have any problems here it's because you brought them on us. It's time you give us our fair share."

Composing himself with a deep breath, Cagius restrained himself. Walker noticed the guards behind Calderon open their jackets. A nervous look crossed Malcolm's face as he witnessed the same.

"You see the bulge on the pants of the guards standing behind him?" whispered Walker.

"They're either dirks or short swords, I can't tell from this distance," observed Malcolm.

"Oh boy, if a knife fight breaks out this could get ugly."

"We'd better be careful, I doubt that King Dennis could sweep this many dead bodies under the rug."

"Sir, my talents are not suited to participate in an entertainment establishment like this," interrupted Saria. "My talents are best suited for the opera, ballet, and classical works. Since we have no arrangement you have no right to hold me here against my will. I respectfully ask to be released immediately."

Saria's attempts to defuse the tense situation were fruitless as Calderon laughed. Everyone was resolved at this point that there was no way it was going to end peacefully.

"Listen to the little songbird, like I need a contract to enforce what I want. If you really want to do some good, honey, you'll get changed for the primetime crowd, and tell your boyfriend here to get out of here before it gets ugly."

Putting their hands to the dirks under their jackets, Cagius flashed a look at Valentine. The assassin had calculated the best course of attack. The probability of the Napolitan prince holding back his associate from killing everyone if they drew first was nil. Knowing he had only one course of action, Cagius grabbed Calderon by his head and slammed him into the table.

"You broke my nose, you bastard!" screamed Calderon as blood dripped down his face.

Valentine turned the table on the security guards and knocked them over. Two dirks went flying and the assassin went for one.

"Got a solution, Malcolm?" demanded Walker.

"Nothing."

"I can only think of one thing."

Walker dragged an innocent bystander out of his seat.

"Dude, I am sorry."

Walker punched the bystander in the face before the rest of the stunned crowd could react to the noise of the altercation. Walker furthered his cause by yelling "fight!" which set the patrons of the establishment against one another in the chaos.

"You humans and the pleasure you derive from pugilism," quipped Malcolm.

Malcolm grabbed one of the guards off the floor. He kneed him in the stomach and threw him against the wall. A second had already come at him but Malcolm gracefully stepped to the side. Using the guard's momentum, the elf ranger carried him straight into the wall. Valentine pinned a guard with two dirks on his shoulders as he pummeled a second one. Saria gracefully slipped past her captors into the chaos and grabbed Cagius' hand. Hustling to the bar near the entrance of the establishment, the cavalier made sure his lady was unharmed. As she smiled at him, Cagius turned back to see that Walker and Malcolm still needed help as most of the patrons in the establishment had turned against them.

"I'll be right back," promised Cagius. "I'm just going to make sure that no one ever bothers you again."

"Thank you, my Cavalier," said Saria as she kissed him. "What should I do if anyone comes over here?"

A patron was thrown near the two. He smiled eerily at Saria, who took a bottle at the bar and broke it over his head.

"Don't worry, dear," laughed Cagius. "You're a natural."

Rushing into the fray, the Napolitan prince pulled two guys off of his comrades. While Walker and Malcolm looked like they had some skill in pugilism, Cagius threw wild haymakers. Patrons were beating each other against the stage, the bar, and all over the establishment. Others were being thrown down the staircase or slammed into the surrounding walls. Walker picked up one patron and threw him through the weakened front door. Already attending the injured bouncers, Ethan picked the poor sod off the ground to interrogate him.

"What the heck is going on in there?" asked Ethan.

"It was a great fight, Pa, but I lost!" said the disoriented Patron.

The patron collapsed into Ethan's arms. Ethan looked back to his two beautiful companions who both shrugged their shoulders. Gently treading through the broken door, the three witnessed the utter chaos. Head hung low, the Denivan Knight knew this wasn't going to look good for either his father or his friends. Calderon still had a lot of pull in the city and the reparations for this disgrace would be heavy. Walker grabbed a bottle behind the bar and was about to smash it over someone's head. Cecilia spotted the label and screamed across the room to get his attention.

"Walker, no!" screamed Cecilia.

"What?" asked Walker.

"Not the brandy!"

Walker looked at the label and set it down.

"Oh, sorry," apologized Walker.

Walker grabbed a beer mug and smashed it over the guy's head instead. Cecilia smiled, walked over to a seat, and took the bottle. She found a clean glass on a rack on top of the bar and poured herself a drink. Ethan realized his wife intended on teaching him a lesson. The Denivan knight looked to Amuro, but she was captivated by Malcolm as he fought off his adversaries. When one of the guards jumped on his back, the Elf Princess was quick to react.

"Hang on, sweetie!" screamed Amuro. "The cavalry's a'coming!"

Amuro jumped on the guard's back and put him in a choke hold. She muttered a quick spell and put the guy to sleep instantly with green mist coming out of her mouth. Going back-to-back with Malcolm, she helped him get rid of his attackers with a series of different kicks. Malcolm was quite surprised to see her react so aggressively.

"Amuro, are you all right?" asked Malcolm.

"Malcolm, seeing you resort to barbarism like this is really turning me on," said Amuro as she smiled devilishly.

"Will you stop teasing me? I'm embarrassed enough already!"

Amuro pulled him up and kissed him hard on the lips.

"Sis!" screamed Saria.

Amuro broke her kiss and walked over to her sister at the bar. She noticed three bodies on the floor, all the apparent victims of broken bottles to the head. The two elf sisters actually smiled at each other for a few moments.

"Are you okay?" asked Amuro.

"Yes, but I'm not sure about the others," said Saria.

Saria pointed at Cagius who threw someone through a table. He looked like he was getting tired of having to fight off so many guys.

"I had a feeling in my gut that it was going to come down to this," recounted Amuro.

"I'm sorry, sis."

"You don't have anything to be sorry about! Stop apologizing all the time!"

Ethan shook his head as someone ran right at him with a tray in his hand. Ethan groaned, grabbed him by his coat, and threw him away. He scanned the room trying to get a handle on where his friends were so he could get them to safety and call in security.

"Hey, where's Valentine?" asked Ethan.

He heard a bystander scream out and saw him run away limping.

"This guy's crazy; he bit my leg!" shouted the man.

Valentine got up on one knee. He spit skin and blood out of his mouth before moving to one of the guards who still held a knife. The assassin grabbed his arm and snapped it.

"He's fine," griped Ethan.

Staggering and drunk, a patron was shoved into Cecilia and tried to grope her through her armor. Enraged, the Vanadis grabbed the guy, and threw him down the length of the bar where he flipped into the wall. Calmly returning to her libation, her husband stared disconcertingly.

Already bleeding from the nose, Calderon attempted to make a run for the safety of his private office. When he did, Cagius picked up a chair and threw it at his legs. The owner went tumbling to the ground as the Napolitan Prince slowly stalked him. Cagius lifted him up by a neck with a smile on his face.

"Have I made myself clear?" asked Cagius.

"My men will never bother Saria again," replied a nodding Calderon.

"Good!"

Cagius dragged him over to where Saria was sitting. Calderon screamed in fear of what the Dragoon might do to him. Cagius just stood him up straight and put his hand around the back of his neck. Calderon felt as if Cagius was ready to break it at any moment.

"Now apologize to this beautiful and sincere young lady!" threatened Cagius.

Calderon was barely able to get an apology out as Cagius squeezed the life out of him. He quickly bowed his head.

"My deepest apologies...for my treatment of you, young lady...it won't happen again," stammered Calderon.

"Thank you, good sir," responded Saria as she bowed her head. "Your apology is accepted."

"I seriously hope this little mishap hasn't strained the relations between Napolitan and Deniva. Now, you can go."

Cagius let go of Calderon who didn't take the Dragoon at his word. He slowly backed away never losing eye contact with Cagius. When he reached the safety of his office door, the group could hear the quick opening, closing, and locking of the door.

"Well, now that you're done with that, can you help me get control of the situation?" asked Ethan.

"No problem!"

As the Napolitan prince turned, one of the hired men came up on Cagius with his dirk drawn. Saria unlatched the whip from her side and snapped it in one quick motion. She effortlessly caught the armed man around the neck. Saria gave the whip a quick tug so she could recoil it without breaking his neck. The attack caused the armed man to drop his weapon and fall to the ground clutching his bleeding throat. Amuro clapped; she was so impressed. Saria closed her eyes and gave a cute smile.

"I guess all that training has paid off," commented Amuro.

"We've got to break this up!" commented Ethan. "By order of the margrave of Deniva, cease and desist immediately!"

A variety of objects were flung at Ethan who ducked behind the bar for cover. Cecilia laughed at him from the other side of the bar.

"That worked," teased Cecilia.

"Well, do you have a suggestion, my little eaglet? If I call in the riot squad, we may have a bigger mess on our hands."

"I think we need a magician's touch."

"I don't think my illusion spells will be effective in this situation," interrupted Saria. "I can only use them in a contained area."

"My sleep spells are only going to work on one person at a time," added Amuro.

"No, I'm going to use Cassandra," retorted Cecilia.

"She's never tried anything like this before," countered Amuro.

"You've watched her practice. We both know she's the only one of us that can cast a spell to contain the entire building. Someone go pull Valentine out of there before she's gets here!"

Walker and Ethan nodded.

"This will be fun!" teased Walker.

The two found Valentine with his knee on the chest of one man while driving the head of another into a table. His mouth and hands were both dripping with blood. Walker and Ethan grabbed him by his arms and pulled him away.

"What are you doing?" demanded Valentine.

"We're here to help," teased Walker.

"I don't need help!"

"Yeah, but they do," argued Ethan.

Pointing at the six men writhing on the ground in agony, they saw three of them were grabbing broken arms while the others were trying to stop the blood gushing from their bodies. Valentine took a moment to admire his handiwork. Cecilia took the last sip of her brandy and got her communicator ready.

"Your Highness, we have a situation, over."

In the Castle, Nadia and Cassandra were standing in her room. Nadia made Cassandra dress in her new battle outfit. The queen wore a leather one-piece outfit around her chest and waist. Across her waist was a black belt with a golden buckle that had a magic circle carved into it. On her back was a black cloak made of a thin material with a silken consistency; this was held in place by a gold chain with a medallion that had a cross on it. Cassandra's arms were covered in long black gloves made of the same material as the cloak, held in place by golden bands. The queen's legs were contained in fishnet stockings and knee-high black leather boots. The sorceress tiara she wore was made out of silver and had a garnet stone in the center of it. Despite her revolutions of training in such a uniform, Cassandra still blushed at the thought of wearing such a revealing outfit. Nadia was beaming with pride at how much her daughter had accomplished with her guidance.

"Well, Cassie, I can say whole-heartedly that I have nothing further to teach you. You know all of the spells that are known to the Rune Mistress and the Magus Class, but you must continue to work to master them."

"I will."

"I should have known that such words would not have been needed between us. It pains me to leave but I must, Cassie."

"Do you really have to leave, Nadia? You've taught me so much."

"I cannot stay. My presence here would be a danger to you now. I came here for a specific purpose and I am so proud that it has been fulfilled."

Nadia grabbed Cassie and hugged her tightly. When her mentor kissed her cheek, the young queen wondered why it felt so warm and comforting holding onto a woman she had only known for just four short revolutions.

"Now, I have a final gift for you," offered Nadia.

Stepping back, the Magus opened a portal. She reached inside and pulled out a long silver staff with a large crimson rune stone at the top of the staff. Cassandra folded her hands together and squealed with delight. She had dreamed of this moment ever since her uncle had promised to train her in the arts of magic.

"The presentation of the staff is the most sacred in the tradition of magic. You are no longer an apprentice of arts but a true master. I, Nadia, present to you, Cassandra Acadia, the Staff of Rune, thus cementing your legacy as a Rune Mistress, the most difficult of all of the sorcery classes to attain."

Nadia held out the staff so Cassandra could reach out and take it. The young queen took it with the reverence befitting the honor bestowed to her. She then playfully took it into her chest and hugged it tightly.

"When you master the full powers of this staff, you will be able to strike at the magic well of any false wizard. This technique may save your life one day. Your uncle was right to train you down this path; you will become the greatest sorceress of us all."

"Thank you for everything, Nadia!"

"Thank Duke Wilhelm for giving me the opportunity for my final redemption!"

Nadia opened a star-shaped portal in the center of the room. Though she did her best to hide it, the demoness couldn't stop the tears from coming. She had made a promise to Wilhelm, but just couldn't leave Cassandra behind without any knowledge of what was going on. She turned back to the queen once more.

"No matter what, don't stop believing that Cedric is still alive! You keep waiting for him to come back because there's no way he's ever going to give up on you—not with the love that I've seen you have for him."

The tears freely falling, her mentor stumbled into the one scenario she wanted to avoid.

"I'm sorry, Nadia, I can't control it."

"Not all tears are devoid of joy!"

"Will I see you again?"

"When this Denivan Exile is over, we will all need to come together to accomplish our ultimate goal! Godspeed, sweetheart, I love you very much!"

The Magus disappeared in the portal and as quickly as she had come into the young queen's life, she was gone. Snapping Cassandra back to reality and forcing her to dry her eyes was the sound of her communicator going off. Setting the piece in her ear, she was surprised to see it was from Cecilia.

"Cecilia, is that you? Over."

"Hi Cassie, we've got a little situation over at the Siren's Club that need's a woman's touch. Over."

"Cecilia, what's all that noise I hear going on in the background? It sounds like a bunch of people trying to kill each other. Are you in a battle or something? Over."

"Yeah, a big fight broke out at the club and they're tearing the place apart. We could use some of your magic if you're not too busy; over and out."

Cecilia tapped her communicator off just as a panicked Cassandra yelled at her for details.

"Well?" asked Ethan nervously.

"Oh, she'll be right over."

The same star-shaped portal that Nadia used to exit the Castle appeared in front of the bar, and Cassandra emerged. She tightened the grip on her staff when she spotted the situation before her. One of the more inebriated members in the fight came up to Cassandra and began to rub against her as if she was a performer. Abhorred by the situation, the young queen froze and cried. A sharp right hook by Cecilia dispatched her newfound admirer and Cassandra took a few deep breaths.

"Don't worry, your highness, I had three or four guys try to grope me as well."

"I think you could use more than a little magic, Cecilia."

"I don't think it's anything you can't handle."

"It would be best if you stepped outside. Otherwise I can't guarantee that you won't be affected by the spell. Cecilia, since you're Divikin, would you mind acting as my shield while I set up the spell."

"No problem."

All of the royals except Cecilia ran for the door as Cassandra raised her new staff over her head. The Vanadis took a position in front of her with her staff pointed out so no one would interfere with the cast. The Rune Mistress started to chant in the elven language and a green mist flowed out of her mouth. Staring down at her feet, the Titan princess could see the green mist slowly creeping up from the floor and over the bodies of everyone in the room. While familiar with the incantation, she never witnessed any sorcerer casting at this radius. When Cassandra finished chanting, the queen swung her staff forward and yelled "sleep." The eyelids of everyone in the room started to grow heavy and droop. In mere seconds, their eyes closed and with a sudden thud everyone hit the floor of the club completely asleep. Cassandra put two fingers to her lips and blew a kiss.

"Good night, boys!"

Cecilia turned back and tipped her spear to her war crown in salute. Ethan held the door to the club open so the two ladies could walk outside. Security forces and hospital workers were standing outside ready to enter the club and tend to the injured patrons.

"Well?" asked Ethan.

"All done," responded Cassandra.

"Go get them!" ordered Ethan.

The royals allowed the security and hospital personnel to pass into the club. They were surprised to see everyone unconscious but simply chalked it up to exhaustion. Calderon came out of his office and sought medical attention. Outside, Ethan shook his head and sighed. The Denivan knight was giving Cagius the evil eye.

"What a mess!" screamed Ethan.

"What?" retorted Cagius. "He kidnapped her!"

"You're not helping!"

"I did what I had to do! If your men would have done their job and kept Calderon off of Princess Saria's back, I wouldn't have had to resort to this. Do you think I enjoyed that scuffle in there? I almost got killed three times."

"Besides, you should thank us for acting so discreetly," offered Valentine.

"Discreetly?" demanded Ethan. "Valentine, I watched you break a guy's arms while spitting the flesh and blood of another out of your mouth!"

"Normally when people have the audacity to draw a weapon on me the coroner walks in with body bags."

"Come on!" quipped Amuro. "Calderon had it coming."

"Let's just say that my Dad doesn't necessarily have unlimited resources and the bribes are beginning to dry up," retorted Ethan. "I think it would be best for all of us if we all find a way to get home soon."

"From your lips to God's ears," commented Cecilia.

The group heard two horses race up behind them. They saw Hippolyte on one horse and Minerva on the other. The five revolutions had been very kind to Minerva who matured from a spunky teenage girl to a mature young adult. She had cut off her pigtails and now wore her hair exclusively in the braid Cecilia taught her how to make for combat. Though her sister remained a little more voluptuous, Minerva had gotten very curvy. The younger wolf princess still wore a million-dollar smile on her face and kept her adoring eyes on Walker.

"It looks like we missed all the fun," teased Hippolyte.

"What did you guys do?" asked Minerva.

"We were just here to back up Cagius and his eternal chivalric war," joked Walker.

"Well, I think it was sweet how my cavalier came to my defense," defended Saria.

"You would think so," teased Amuro.

"If you don't mind, I would prefer to return to the castle immediately," interrupted Cassandra. "I think we've made enough of a scene and caused Ethan enough trouble."

"Thank you, your Highness," said Ethan. "I whole-heartedly agree."

The royals got on their horses and went back to the castle. However, there was a man standing in the streets. He walked quickly outside the city gates and onto the plains. When he was a safe distance from Deniva, he reverted into his true form as a duco-matios. The demonkin hurried quickly for the mountains.

Bishop's Residence, City of Antiquity

"Of course, you know I will try anything to get out of here!"

Cedric Rhone addressing Quinn and Mesmara

The City of Antiquity had not changed much and the bishop's residence remained intact. Mesmara and Quinn walked down the wing past Florence's desk as she sat in constant vigilance for her one personal patient. Smiling at the two as they passed, the warriors were uncomfortable with the cleric's antics. Reaching Cedric's door, they found the same fresh-cut flowers that were left there every morning from the residents of the city. With one last look at one another to gain confidence, the two sighed and knocked on the door. Ever so gently, the door slid open, but no one was there to greet them. They wrinkled their noses at the smell of roasted flesh as they walked into the room and Mesmara immediately covered her mouth with a handkerchief. An empty bottle of brandy was on the nightstand, which Quinn promptly discarded.

"I think last evening must have been very important for Lord Cedric," observed Mesmara.

"Well, I guess I can understand how he feels."

"Really?"

"If I didn't see you for five revolutions, I might start drinking too!"

"That's sweet."

"His family and friends—I can't believe we've been able to keep him away from them for so long and he hasn't broken yet."

Quinn walked over to the lump on Cedric's bed and assumed the prince had yet to shake off the events of the previous evening. He signaled to Mesmara who shook her head and pointed back to him. The warrior roused the sword master.

"Come on, your Highness, rise and shine!"

"The bishop wants to see you and sent us to get you."

Quinn felt the sheet of Cedric's bed slip down. All that was there was a pillow and rolled up blanket. The two looked on in terror."

"God help us—not this morning!" screamed Quinn.

The two went for the hilts of their swords. Cedric's voice rang out over the room.

"Combat training!"

The two drew their swords and Cedric seemingly stepped out of the shadows. He had the two of them on the defensive immediately. Titan and Mesmara's sabers could barely handle the attacking power of Ragnarok and both were tripping over their feet. Cedric had a big smile across his face and looked as if he was handling the two of them effortlessly.

"You guys are getting better. I used to get both of you on the ground by now."

The two had to save all of their strength for the defense so they dared not speak. Cedric suddenly stopped swinging his sword and instead pressed into the two sabers. Even with their combined strength, the burly sword master easily bullied both of them over. The Kablisha lay on their back for a moment trying to form a plan. The two were furious just as Cedric intended. He raised his hand and offered to have them come get him.

"That's enough!" shouted Quinn. "We've had enough!"

"To hell with it all!" shouted Mesmara. "We're going to have to kill him!"

"Agreed! Maybe we can have a peaceful morning again!"

The two screamed as they stood up. They charged at Cedric who simply shook his head. The knight put his sword behind him and took a single step to the side at the precise moment. Quinn and Mesmara realized what was going to happen to them as they tripped over their own feet and fell to the floor. The Titan prince tapped them both on the back with Ragnarok and signified their total defeat.

"Why did you lose?" asked Cedric.

"Because you're better than us!" replied an angry Quinn.

"That is the truth. However, you should have been able to hold your own longer against me. The reason I beat you so quickly is because you attacked in anger. Emotion is an important weapon when battling a superior opponent, however, you mustn't let it destroy you before the battle begins."

"Yeah, Cedric, we know...you made us read your stupid book," countered Mesmara. "But will training under these impossible conditions really help us?"

"Yes. It's very important that you learn humility as well. Now, I'm afraid it's going to get worse for both of you."

Cedric grabbed both of them around their heads and put them in a headlock. Mesmara kicked and struggled to get loose.

"Not again!"

"Now, my dear little Kablisha brother and sister, will you please show me the way to go home? I am tired and long for my own bed. You see, I had this drink about an hour ago and I guess it went straight to my head."

"Come on, you know we can't do that!" pleaded Quinn. "We refuse— do your worst!"

"I'm impressed with you two. I figured after I did this two hundred-plus times to you, you'd actually give in. Argus sure knows how to pick them."

"We fear uncle's wrath more than yours," said Mesmara

"Good soldiers!" teased Cedric. "Up we go!"

The Prince grabbed his two subordinates by their shoulders and lifted them up with ease. The two were relieved that they no longer had to endure their "morning workout." Quinn stared at Cedric's shoulder for a second and noticed no new blood and tears.

"I guess your shoulder is feeling better," said Quinn.

"It sure took long enough," said Cedric.

"I've had our alchemists and apothecaries studying the blood samples we took from you," noted Mesmara. "However, since the poison was based in darkness, it's impossible to create an effective antidote. It's amazing you were able to survive after Abaddon filled you with so much poison."

"I guess the Holy Grail saved him," reasoned Quinn. "We might need to keep it close if it's the only way to repel Abaddon's magic."

"I doubt your leaders would agree," said Cedric. "So you said the bishop wants to meet me?"

"He wants you to join him and Argus for breakfast," said Mesmara.

"Cookie's making eggs and fried taters!" said Quinn.

"And bacon, perhaps?"

"No, Cedric! There is no bacon! There has never been any bacon! Besides, I think you eat enough meat as it is."

"I respect the fact you guys don't eat meat! Please respect the fact that I do!"

Cedric put his arms around the shoulders of his two hosts and lead them out of his room. Florence was waiting for him in the hallway with fresh linens. She curtsied before him and blew him a kiss before heading to work. Further down the way, there were some children leaving one classroom for the next. They saw Cedric and were captivated by him. They lined up like soldiers, saluted, and shouted his name. Cedric turned and answered the salute causing the children to cheer. The Titan prince marched them over to the next classroom like a drill sergeant. The nun waiting to teach the next class just smiled at the sword master as her class took their seats with perfect discipline. She patted him on his left shoulder as Mesmara and Quinn laughed.

"You really are what they say you are, Cedric Rhone," praised Quinn.

"I don't know if we can ever repay you for what you've done for us," commented Mesmara. "The counter-attack on the demons was one thing, but you've gone out of your way over these past three revolutions to help us whenever anyone needed it."

"Your people saved my life; the little things I do around here are the least I can do."

The three reached their destination, the bishop's private dining room. Bishop Wulf reclined at the table with Argus. Maids were waiting to serve the three as Cedric took his seat. Quinn and Mesmara left the three in privacy.

"Well, good morning, bishop," greeted Cedric.

"Good morning, Prince Rhone. I believe we need to have a little chat."

"I figure it can't be anything too good."

"Actually I think you'll find it quite to your advantage," interjected Argus.

"Really?"

The Maids took the time to carefully serve the three. Cedric went for the salt and pepper shakers. When he finished with those, he went for the hot sauce. After seven thousand complaints about the blandness of the food Cookie had made exclusively for him, the Titan prince used almost half the bottle. Argus still couldn't believe the level of spice the Titans preferred on their food.

"We have kept you informed over these past five revolutions that our search for Camael Incarnate has been fruitless," explained the Bishop. "Garrett has not received any further visions and our field agents continue to come up empty."

"We have discussed this scenario at length," recounted Cedric. "I am not one to lose faith, but I do believe it's high time we start trusting in ourselves to banish this darkness as God most likely intended."

"After much discussion and prayer, we have reached the same conclusion," agreed Argus. "The Kablisha have nothing further that we can teach you, Cedric. You have mastered the technique of Holy War and your white magic prowess surpasses even that of the Bishop's. Thus I believe keeping you in the City of Antiquity is no longer to your advantage."

"Argus and I have decided that we are going to allow you to return to Rhinegard."

Cedric got a big smile on his face as he shoveled in the eggs and taters. The news he had long waited for had finally come and at long last he was going to get back in the fight.

"You're right, that news is to my advantage. What, may I ask, brought about this sudden change of heart?"

"Abaddon's been silent these past five revolutions and all signs point to the fact that we are at a major impasse," explained Wulf. "Though he discovered her presence in Deniva, fear of the Empire's wrath keeps his armies at bay. The time is right for you to make your reappearance. We think it will cause Luminas and the others to lose hope and with luck turn on the leaderless Demonkin."

"I doubt that. Luminas has nothing to go back to and is quite charismatic. Every member of Central Acadia that stood with them will stand trial for war crimes, murder, and treason. That might be enough to keep them in league with the darkness."

"That's something that we will need to discuss," requested Wulf. "Luminas, Celius, Marimon, and Sharon must all pay the stiffest penalties for their crimes. However, I think it would be wise to grant clemency to the lower ranking officers. It would give incentive for them to rebel against their masters."

"Cassandra is legally Queen of Central Acadia and thus the decision would normally fall to her. However, Titanus is the only nation to have formally declared war on the rebel government. Thus sole authority to declare military tribunals for war crimes rests with the Supreme Commander of the Titan Army, namely me."

"Yes, but I don't doubt that you won't be looking to consummate a marriage with Cassandra very quickly," retorted Argus. "In that case, the decision would rest with her."

"Despite what you think, it's the furthest thing from my mind. Central Acadia has to be secured first or else Cassandra will look desperate to fulfill her claim and turn the advantage to our foes."

"Spoken like a Titan," teased Argus.

"Even though veiled, I do consider that a compliment. When do I get the hell out of here?"

"Soon. We've been calling back our scouts and when the last of them returns, we can make preparations for the duke to bring you home. Figure on less than a lunar cycle!"

"Sounds good, but I thought you felt that I was your final option."

"The things you have done for our people are nothing short of saintly," explained Wulf. "However, we should not be containing this great power any longer. You may think that your faith is your greatest strength, but the hope you give to others is a far greater power. The west needs you, Cedric Rhone, and we're very glad that we played our part with nursing you back to health."

"Hey, I told you I'm indebted to you. If not for the Grail, I'd be lying dead in the cold earth."

"You've paid it back many times over, friend," said Argus.

"That's why it's going to be very hard for many of those around here to see you leave," offered Wulf.

"I'm afraid that Florence is going to maim you so just so she stays on your personal cleric," teased Argus.

"As an aristocrat, I do appreciate having my every whim taken care of. Well, since we're all friends now, I'm sure I can count on your help when we retake Verian. I'm going to need every man of good will I can find."

"We'll help you as we can. However, our military prowess does not match that of Titanus. I fear our armies won't be as capable as the other nations. We can offer you very little."

"You don't do justice to your warriors. Your light armor warriors are skilled with the sword and bow. If I adequately protect your forces with heavy infantry, you'll be able to hold your own. Quinn and Mesmara have shown a lot of resolve putting up with my antics!"

"They're good soldiers."

Argus grabbed a package behind him and handed it to Cedric.

"Is this a going-away present?" asked Cedric.

"Consider it a sign of our appreciation."

Cedric opened the package. There was a much smaller version of an automatic crossbow in the package. The prince raised it up to his eye in order to test the mark and range. He was very impressed at the craftsmanship.

"Quinn never stopped bragging about how much you liked the weapon. We thought that a smaller version would be more appropriate for you to handle on horseback."

"I can't wait to test it out on some of those Demonkin bastards."

"Well, hopefully that won't be for some time."

"I don't know what that future holds, but outside of the fact there is no bacon, Cookie does make some good eggs."

CASTLE ACADIA, VERIAN

"The Royals are separated and dispersed. They are unaware that all of their plans must be spoken in the softest of voices—if more than a whisper, they will disappear forever. Patience, as they say, is a virtue. We have all the time in the world as long as we remain protected behind this impenetrable barrier. Eventually our enemies will make a mistake and that will be our time to strike."

King Maximilian Luminas personal journal

Five revolutions later and Verian was still in ruins. The only landmarks left standing in the fallen city were the Wizard's Tower, Temple, and Castle Acadia. The once brilliant Senate building was falling over into the canal. The remaining buildings had either been burned out or crumbled into the canals as well. Dead fish lay belly up everywhere and the magnificent flora and fauna that surrounded the castle withered and died. Decomposed heads still adorned the walls on pikes. Castle Acadia had become a symbol of decadence, debauchery, and opulence. The nobility, who remained loyal to Luminas, were living quite well in the central throne room and surrounding apartments. The Templar Army had gone about the surrounding fiefs and towns drafting every strong lad and pretty lass into a slave labor force. The nobles would gorge themselves on the food and drinks provided for them on the fields of this forced labor. The castle slaves suffered a far worse fate, as they became nothing but mere playthings for the elitists. This behavior had sickened one-third of the Acadian nobility who lived in a commune under the command of Norville Warrington. Sir Gavin remained as far from Castle Acadia as he could, patrolling the outer reaches of the dome looking for breaches. Even the proud Nephilim hadn't been seen in the city, outside of guarding Virgus' secret projects in the basement of the castle.

Luminas and Sharon sat on their thrones above the fray. They were sharing kisses and laughter at the many events. One of Sharon's favorite games was to have one of the nobles act like an animal on command. She especially preferred to see them truly make jackasses of themselves. The atmosphere of the room soon came to a grinding halt when the doors to the throne room opened. Abaddon entered with Virgus and the duco-matios that was in Deniva. Abaddon had avoided the presence of the court, secretly conspiring with Virgus on ways to forge a new body.

"Lord Abaddon, it's been some time since we enjoyed your company," announced Luminas.

"Nonsense, my dear friend, you prefer when I don't come around here," countered Abaddon. "You prefer not to face the reality of our grave situation, but continue to believe we are invincible behind this barrier."

"Your criticisms of our styles are not welcome," pronounced Sharon. "Yet I doubt you simply came here for mindless banter. What news do you bring?"

"I come here with news that concerns all of us," said Abaddon.

"Really?" asked Luminas.

Abaddon signaled for his duco-matios companion to step forward.

"My Liege, I have observed Queen Cassandra Acadia in Deniva," said the duco-matios. "Her magic has grown powerful."

"We can no longer delay. We'll need to muster our army quickly if we are to strike and bring Cassandra back here."

Luminas laughed at the naivety of his former lord and master. Cassandra could prance about all she wanted in Deniva because it was the one city beyond their reach.

"My dear Abaddon, are you trying to start a world war?"

"I do not appreciate your tone, Luminas."

"We've gone over this a thousand times. Deniva is a city protected by both Titanus and the Chinotal Empire. If we march on Deniva, Sultan Khan will consider it an act of war. He will send his armies to defend the Trade City that brings him much wealth. Our army is no match for the Imperial Janissaries and the likely Dragoon Cavalry that will arrive from

Edenia in support. If the Titans find some way to attack our southern flank while we are occupied in the east, Central Acadia will fall in a matter of rotations. I would dare not risk that."

"Your cowardice will not stop me from achieving my weapon."

"Feel free, Abaddon, to take whatever steps with your armies you feel necessary to attack the Empire! Central Acadia and her Templar Army will have no part in it."

"The Demonkin cannot repel an imperial attack, not with the losses we sustained securing this castle and country for you. You owe me!"

"Then I guess you'll have to find an alternative plan."

"Do not try my patience, you mere Demonkin!"

"I think you'd agree that I've taken an awful lot from you and your friends. I've been rather patient, but I will not opt for the suicidal path. It would bring a quick end to my glorious reign. If it had not been for your foolishness in battle with Cedric, we would not have been suffering behind this barrier for the past five revolutions!"

"You were the ones that killed King Stephen Acadia. If not, the royals would have had no claim to the throne and we could treaty with Deniva for the princess."

The two sides stared one another down. Abaddon calmed himself. He knew that arguing with the Acadians was getting them nowhere. They could never know the importance and strain of his mission.

"What is Khan's price?" asked Abaddon.

"You want to buy him off?"

"I don't see what choice we have. Sultan Khan controls everything we want."

"Cassandra is a liability for both of our sides. Her strength as a leader and connections to the late Cedric Rhone could cause problems for the Empire as well."

Luminas thought about it. There was a large paper map of the Western Acadian plains to the right of the entrance to the throne room. Abaddon turned to the map as well. The two continued to study the various terrains and the same idea crossed their mind at the same time.

"Considering the precariousness of our situation, a non-aggression treaty may be in our best interests," lectured Luminas. "If he was to lose Deniva, the Sultan would need an equitable source of trade income and only Port Talus could provide that."

"You're afraid to fight the Empire, and you propose attacking Port Talus. Your Templar army would be crushed by their legions."

"Abaddon, I'm not proposing attacking Caesar Constantine! I'm saying we have to make Sultan Khan believe that he could have it. Khan's price would be the territory west of the Kaiser Mountains. I believe we might be able to make him turn a blind eye if we were to offer him the Northeast territory. It is home to some of the easternmost villages of the Tribes who are cut off from their Western brethren."

"I'd prefer the royals have less allies, but are you sure Khan will deliver?"

"Khan's dream is Port Talus. He needs western resources to build an army necessary for a prolonged siege. We then agree to let him march through the barrier and assault the city. Napolitan is destroyed, Titanus has one less ally, Cassandra is yours, and even the Empire will be weakened from the attack. It works to our advantage so well, I curse myself for not thinking of it earlier."

"Good. I find that a man with a desire is easier to control! Luminas, I'll need you to spearhead an effort to get Sultan Khan to agree."

"What about you?"

"The ranks of the demonkin are thin, as you aptly pointed out. I, however, have other allies at my disposal. In fact, I know of just such an army that will be perfect for assaulting Deniva. I'm sure the Sultan will want his hands clean of the incident. I would appreciate it if you gave me a strong commander to lead them."

"I'll give you my best. Allow me to present Rene Palias!"

Rene Palias stepped forward from the crowd of nobles. The balding, white-haired man still wore his blue Acadian military uniform despite the slight limp in his left leg. Rene's uniform was decorated with at least sixty medals and commendations mostly won during the war against the Tribes. Palias might have been a good tactician but his insatiable desire for accolades and pride led him to be labeled as the "Peacock" by Walker among others.

"Yes, my liege," answered the marshal.

"You are to accompany Abaddon on his mission. I believe that you are best suited for a field command."

"My accolades precede me, my liege; I would be honored to bring the false queen to justice, and her 'shield' as well."

"Palias, I've changed my mind concerning the war criminal Jonathan Walker. Don't bother bringing the bastard home, the Oath Shield will suffice."

"As you say, my liege."

Palias turned to Abaddon and saluted him. Abaddon was a bit dismayed by the primped-up general, but he didn't have much choice. He wouldn't dare risk Valadrim's death in a forsaken place like Deniva.

"Is that all?" asked Luminas.

"Yes."

Abaddon turned and left with his group. There was almost a sense of relief on the Dark Angel's face as he no longer had to endure the pettiness of the court. As they exited the throne room doors, Valadrim was waiting for him.

"Lord Abaddon, may I have a moment please?" asked Valadrim.

"I'm very busy, Valadrim, I have an appointment with an old friend to keep."

"My appearance in this city means we have cause for great concern."

"What is it?"

"We found this one crossing our borders back towards the Northern Forests."

The Demonkin tossed down the body of a man that was obviously in the garb of the Kablisha. His clothes were torn to ribbons and many deep wounds covered his body. There was clear evidence that his skin had been seared in an attempt to interrogate him. Dismayed by the infiltration of the barrier that had taken place, Abaddon shook his head.

"He must be descended of the Ancients to endure our pain and interrogation tactics," determined Abaddon. "This man is no Titan so he must be of the Kablisha Clan."

"I believe so," agreed Valadrim. "He was no stranger to pain. No matter what we did to him there was no chance that we could break him. He never whispered a word about what he was doing here, even among his babbling screams."

Abaddon closed his eyes.

"Why do the Kablisha no longer cower behind their barrier? We were no threat to them. Perhaps their loyalty to Daddy is too strong."

"I believe they seek the Permaneo Eques Ordinares. Prince Rhone has already failed them. It must be someone else."

"You speak of Prince Rhone so calmly, Valadrim. When you make such a statement be bold, lest it not actually be true. I am impressed at the courage of our foes."

"If the Kablisha are allowed to join with the other kingdoms, we could have an army marching on us very shortly."

"Virgus isn't ready with the new army yet. Where did they gain the ability to break his shield? Valadrim, how do you believe we should handle this?"

The Nephilim bent down and ripped an amulet off of the Kablisha scout's neck.

"He had to get in and out of their barrier somehow. This amulet must be the key. Our hellish prophets say the City of Antiquity lies beyond a holy barrier. My lord, allow me to take my armies, cross this barrier with the amulet and we will crush the Kablisha threat once and for all."

Abaddon allowed himself to smile.

"The end of both the rebellion and the Kablisha menace in one fatal blow! The Empire properly compensated, the kingdoms leaderless, Cedric Rhone dead, and Titanus alone. Our time is at hand! Valadrim, prepare your army to march! You will launch your assault upon my return."

"At once, my lord! Where are you going?"

"Into the Under Dark. I have a favor to ask of an old friend."

Royal Castle, Deniva

"In the ancient times, while the fledging Kingdoms of
Evengard and Titanus fought against the Emperor Dondarion
in desperate battles, there was a powerful class of heathens
known as the Dragon Masters. These heavily armored
barbarians had the power to summon the Dragons and Drakes
of the West. While their clans usually fought against one
another, the Dragon Clans turned their attention towards
Evengard, forcing King Hayden and his army to flee Brooke
Run. In response to this threat, the Order of the Dragoons was
started in the West with the specific purpose of slaying Dragons
and the Clans. Four hundred revolutions ago, the armies of the
Dragon Clans were broken by the Dragoons and the Dragons
returned to their caverns. A powerful curse was placed on the
leader of the Black Dragons, Seres, by Elf Mages. Since this
time, Dragons have not been an influence on the West. "

The Dragon Wars, Elf Scholar Demetrius

Reading the Book of Rune at the desk in her room, Cassandra was distracted by the heavy falling mountain snow on the margrave. Bubbled over with joy by the white powder, she threw on a heavy coat and boots. In a matter of moments, she ran down the castle steps and out into the courtyard. The members of her Order found it a little strange to see their queen throwing the snow up in the air. Cassandra allowed herself to fall back into a white embankment and made a snow angel. She was laughing and the rosiness of her cheeks was clearly visible. Walking by, Cecilia pulled a fur wrap tightly around her shoulders and jumped up and down to stay warm. The sight of Cassandra left her absolutely confounded.

"How could you enjoy this blasted early frost?" asked Cecilia angrily.

Cassandra laughed and sat up. Cecilia had not seen her friend this happy in a long time.

"Come on, Cecilia, don't tell me you never enjoyed playing in the snow."

"Snow makes it worse for the horses! You're such a child!"

"I don't mind being a kid at heart," chuckled Cassie.

"What?"

"I can imagine little Cecilia and little Cedric running around the Castle Titan courtyard gathering up snowballs. Then the two little monsters would probably engage in tactical superiority before pelting unsuspecting guards!"

"In Titanus, we use snowball fights to train against range fighters, except the snow is packed around three-pound rocks."

Cassandra stopped laughing and swallowed hard. She had been told so much about the harshness of life in Titanus that she honestly believed Cecilia was serious for a moment. However, the Vanadis couldn't contain her straight face for too long and laughed.

"Got you!" teased Cecilia.

"I was scared because it sounds like something you would do."

"It hasn't snowed in Rhinegard in my lifetime, too far south! We're used to the rain but if significant snow did fall in the city it would cause a headache. Up, your highness!"

"Spoil sport!"

Offering her hand to lift her up, Cassandra took it. However, the devious queen caught her friend off-balance and pulled the Vanadis into the snow with her. Not amused by her friend's antics, the Titan princess calmly got up and grabbed Cassandra around her waist. She hoisted the queen over her head and carried her over to the Castle entrance before setting her down. Cassandra didn't stop laughing the whole time.

"You know, Christmas will be here in a few weeks," said Cassandra.

"Yes."

"Five long revolutions and no closer than where we started from."

"No. I'm starting to wonder if our only hope is going to involve an invasion of the Imperial lands and hijacking a boat back West."

"I guess I could count on you to have a backup plan."

Cecilia gritted her teeth in a smile.

"How are you able to keep such hope all this time?" asked Cassandra.

"Hope? I thought that was your virtue."

"Me?"

"I half-expected after your performance at the ruins that you would have locked yourself in your room for a revolution. Yet, you were right back out that night pleading our case before Margrave Dennis and the others. I wouldn't sell yourself short."

"Cedric became the embodiment of all our faith. He was prepared to fight Abaddon even though he was so wounded. I was a fool to think that he would die there. I know now that Cedric fully intended to survive that battle. The reason he gave me his rosary is because he knew I would cherish it until the time I could give it back to him."

"Then how are you going to tell him that you keep breaking it?"

"I didn't mean too," said Cassandra, grimacing.

"I'm just saying that he carried those beads into combat for thirty revolutions and you've had to get them repaired time and time again."

"I've never been good with relics."

"Anyway, don't you have somewhere to be?"

Cassandra looked at the large castle clock attached to the golden spire and saw the chiming of the hour.

"It's my turn to instruct Thomas, isn't it?"

"Please do not keep my son waiting," chided Cecilia.

Cassandra gave Cecilia a quick hug, one the Vanadis did not seem to appreciate. The Titan princess still hadn't forgiven her friend for pulling her into the snow. Cassandra walked quickly towards her room. Walker had already let Thomas in and he was seated at Cassandra's study desk. The young prince had a book open that showed illustrations of dragons. He stared at it intently and didn't hear the queen come in. Cassandra took the opportunity to remove her coat and change her boots.

"Do you see something you like, Thomas?" asked Cassandra.

Thomas looked up from his book startled. He immediately stood and bowed, drawing a chuckle from the young queen.

"Just looking at the history, your Highness," explained Thomas.

"Let's see."

Cassandra walked over to the desk and stared at the book as Thomas retook his seat. The prince focused on the pictures as Cassandra went to the text. She could tell it was written in Elvish immediately but even she could not decipher some of the text.

"This text is a little advanced for you, unless Amuro's taught you advanced elvish without my knowledge."

"I can still look at the pictures even if I can't read it."

"Would you like to know what the text is?"

"Of course!"

"Well I'm supposed to be teaching your protocol and courtly behavior, but what fun is there in that? How about we have a little history lesson today?"

Thomas got an excited look in his eyes. The royals usually stuck to a strict regimen when it came to his schooling, but Cassandra was always willing to go off on a tangent with him. He often enjoyed having her as an instructor more than the others. Putting the prince on her lap, she guided him through the text.

"This is a period in the West known as the Dragon Wars. The timeline for these events fall after Hayden Marisol and Ulyssess Rhone had defeated the Dwarves. There was once a barbarian tribe in the West that lived in the far northwest near the Kaiser Mountains. What made these clans unique was their ability to call dragons to serve as mounts in battles. The elves called them the Dragon Masters. My ancestors and scholars would tell tales of how their battles would darken the skies at times. Dragons would swoop down from the sky, and lift men and elf alike and then drop them to their deaths. However, their greatest disadvantage was the fact that the clans could never stay united for a significant period of time. After the betrayal of the Dark Elves had weakened Evengard, a new leader named Rathmor came to head the Black Dragon Clan. He convinced the leaders of the Fire Drake Clan and the Ice Drake Clan to turn their attention against the elves and Brooke Run. If these barbarians could rule both the forest and mountains in the north, they could create a grand empire and fill the void left by the Dwarves. The Dragon Masters led their assault against Brooke Run. The dragons' fierce resistance to magic and their range proved to be a severe detriment to the defending Elves. Hayden Marisol was forced to flee Brooke Run and the elves became refugees again in the City of Antiquity."

"How do you fight a dragon?"

"The elves summoned their allies, now led by Queen Marion's son, Gunther Rhone. The King knew that his main force of cavalry would be useless against the dragons as they swoop down and grab the horses. However, their Edenian kinsman had long been spear fighters. The Titans enlisted the Edenians help and they trained an order known as the Dragoons."

"Were these Dragoons similar to Prince Cagius?"

"Yes. Cagius is the last descendant of an order long forgotten. The Dwarf Craftsmen of Titanus determined that the best way to kill a dragon was to use the dragon against them. They made spears of dragon bone melded with silver and steel. These weapons were powerful enough to pierce the armored underbellies of their foes. The Dwarves also crafted a special type of plate armor for them made from a combination of steel, dragon bone and vanadium, making them impervious to dragon fire. Titanus and Evengard launched an assault in the winter catching the Masters by surprise. The Fire and Ice Drakes were the first beasts to be neutralized by the Dragoons. Teams of fifty would corner an individual Drake in a mountain path. The dumb and flightless beasts were easy prey for the Dragoons and their spears until they became extinct. The Titanus and Evengard armies rode in and finished off the barbarians, driving them into the South. The Black Dragon Clan proved to be a greater menace. King Gunther treated with the Lord Gilden of the Golden Dragons and explained the necessity of why he had to join forces with him against his own kin. Gilden agreed to his terms and took the fight to the Black Dragon Clans in the skies. Titan Knights on horseback funneled Elf Archers from one location to next. They picked off Dragon Masters from their mounts in the sky. Finally, the great elf hero Joab pierced Rathmor's heart with a shot fired from King Gunther's horse. When Rathmor died, the Black Dragons shook off their mounts from their backs and fled into the darkness of the world. Elf mages placed a curse on Seres and banished him into the mountains, where he hasn't been heard from since. Despite the fact they fought side by side, Gilden and the Golden Dragons had no trust of either Titanus or Evengard and they retreated as well."

"And the Dragon Masters?"

"They were scattered in the Griffin Mountains of the South where they wailed and swore revenge upon Titanus. These wild men plagued the west for revolutions until your Uncle Cedric met them in battle. They once said in the labyrinth of jagged rock, the wild men could never be conquered. Now they say nothing."

"Do the Golden Dragons and the Black Dragons still exist?"

"Yes. Every once in a while you can hear the call of a Golden Dragon in the skies, but mostly they left us alone."

"Would it possible for someone of the West to harness the power of these Dragons? They would make a formidable ally."

"There have been those who've tried. Unfortunately, they have mostly ended up as lunch. Dragons are almost impossible to tame; one would have to be trained and possess considerable skill with the sword and magic."

"I'd like to try," said Thomas as he licked his lips.

Cassandra was surprised at first to see such fire in the young boy. However, she did know who his mother was, and must have imagined Cecilia had the same passion for becoming the Vanadis at his age. The logical portion of her mind thought she might have taken this too far, but she was too excited to stop.

"Since you're a Titan, you'll be able to develop the necessary requirements in terms of mana. I believe your great-great-grandfather had a mother who was an elf so you should have enough of a magic well in you so I can teach you a few basic spells. However, I still feel that you'll need to discuss this with your mother first."

"She'll never go for it."

"Don't worry, I have a way with your mother," winked Cassandra.

"Are you going to throw her in the snow again? I don't think she liked that too much."

"Well, as long as we're learning about history, do you want know the story behind the Great War of the Elves and the Dwarves?"

"I've been waiting for someone to tell me that!"

"There's no time like the present."

Eastern Syrus Clan Territories, Kaiser Mountains

"In the land is heard the sound of moaning, of bitter weeping.
The mother mourns her children; she refuses to be consoled
because her children are no more."

The Woeful Prophet 31:15

For five revolutions, the Eastern villages of Syrus Clan were allowed to live despite the tyrannical rule of the Acadians. In spite of the pleas of Priestess Posha, the clan elders of the sect refused to join the other members of the Tribal Confederation in the safety of the mountain retreat before the barrier rose. They did not believe that the Acadians would do them any harm if they did nothing to antagonize them. Sir Gavin and Sir Roland of the Acadian Templars were on patrol in the region with Templar Cuirassiers backing them up. The two Templars rode up on a ridge and observed the peaceful clan village. Clan members were busy tending to their corn and soybean crops while the children were playing games in the square. The clan elders held their silent midday prayer in front of the village altar. They burned incense, asking the spirits to aid them as they endured the suffering and blight brought upon them by the Acadians. Gavin shook his head at all of this.

"What fools!" observed Gavin. "They should have gotten out."

"You can't paint the Tribes with one brush, Gavin," commented Roland. "This particular sect of the Clan believes in pacifism at all costs. They're willing to be sheered like sheep rather than resort to violence."

"I can't accept the fact that these people are a threat. Come on, Roland, we've got bigger fish to fry. I want to check out the eastern edge of the barrier and make sure there are no signs of weakness."

"Then you believe the rumors concerning the new powers of Cassandra?"

"I don't doubt them for a minute. I hate to say this, Roland, but I'm starting to believe we might not have gotten Rhone either. I'm having trouble sleeping as I keep picturing his shadow creeping upon us in the night."

The two could hear the sounds of horses approaching their position. Gavin had his command draw their weapons just in case. Relieved for a moment, he was happy to see it only his fellow Saint Sir Karstak. The large and hard man rode up with his large war axe on his back. Roland noticed two full divisions of Templar Cuirassiers behind him and wondered if they were moving to a battle. Karstak rode ahead of the column to get to Gavin and Roland.

"This is better than I expected," grunted Karstak. "It's good to see that my fellow brothers will be able to aid me."

Gavin stared at the larger Karstak with some uneasiness. He never liked Karstak and didn't care for his gluttony, whether it was with food, drink, or women. Despite the fact he had broken every vow that he pledged when he became a Saint, Jonas wouldn't strip Karstak of his position. Karstak was the Knight Commander's enforcer and often kept Jonas' hands clean.

"Is there combat?" asked Gavin.

"Nothing we shouldn't be able to handle," chuckled Karstak. "I bring an order from King Maximilian Luminas. These Eastern Syrus Clan members are in open rebellion against the Kingdom and we've come restore order."

"Surely you jest!" exclaimed Gavin. "These people wouldn't lift a finger to help their own; they'd never rebel against us."

"What's going on here, Karstak?" asked Roland.

"These people are a nuisance, but they're sitting on a very important patch of dirt right now," explained Karstak. "I can handle this mission without you. However, I thought you might be interested in a few spoils."

"We're Knights!" screamed Gavin. "Not butchers! I will no longer execute such madness!"

"You've been away from the Castle too long, Gavin, you're getting soft! Don't tell me all those lectures from the dead Titan Prince are getting to you, too."

"This isn't about the independence of Central Acadia anymore, Sir Karstak! I'll fight off the Titans to the last for my country, but I won't do this. Come on, Roland!"

Roland nodded as he left with Gavin and his command. Karstak smiled at the thought of not having to share the glory for this conquest with his fellow comrades. The Templar started to bark out orders to his men.

"Surround the village on all four sides. On my command, sound the charge!"

The Templars broke to their positions on the surrounding hills over the valley where the tribal village was. Karstak wore a huge smile on his face as he pulled his axe from behind his back. The Saint was very eager to get into the battle. He turned to the trumpeter standing next to him.

"Sound the charge!"

The trumpeter blasted. The Kablisha villagers stopped what they were doing and looked up. They could hear the sound of horses all around them. The Templars charged down the hill from the four sides. The villagers screamed and fled in terror. The first waves of horse archers cut down the few men that used themselves as human shields to protect their families. Karstak and his axe joined the battle next; he cleaved one man from gut to neck with a deranged smile on his face. Other Templars started to throw torches onto the huts that either burned the villagers out of their homes or burned them alive.

"Kill the men and elderly! Take the women and children! The king will want his share of new slaves!"

The Templars followed the commands to the letter and the peaceful villagers were no match. In less than an hour, the village was sacked, the men and elderly slaughtered, and the women and children carried off as slaves. Karstak rode proudly at the head of his column, with the clan elder's head on the handle of his axe. Blood dripped down the handle and the knight's armor but it didn't bother him. A scout rode to the head of the column and greeted Karstak.

"Sir," saluted the messenger. "I come from the train headed from Central Acadia to Palacio Magnifico. What news?"

"You can inform Knight Commander Jonas that the territory is secured," boasted Karstak.

Palacio Magnifico, Edenia

"Now that my succession is secured, I will build an army that the world has never seen. We will ride to the west and conquer all who oppose us. Even the mighty walls of Titanus will eventually cave to our power. My ambitions are limitless."

Sultan Assad Khan

The hustle and bustle of the Edenian marketplace was in full force. Christian and Colin walked down the middle of the marketplace continuing their observation of the city. Their riding clothes were clean, an indication they hadn't run a mission in a while. Colin was busy munching on an apple while Christian was finishing off the final pieces of an orange.

"What do you think about the last mission?" asked Colin. "You think we can get out by sea?"

"Since the Titans broke the blockade in the Sea of Dragons-Sur, Hamali may be our best way out," explained Christian. "However, it's going to require a lot of resources to get the Edenians to draft the necessary papers to get our people through the Pass."

"We've got to get out of here. If Khan hadn't gone to war with Titanus, we might have already been home."

"It would be just like that fool to start a meaningless conflict in the middle of this greater evil. We can't worry about that; our best bet is to make sure that the Edenians don't get too nervous."

"And Martha?"

"No progress."

"Looks like there is a problem even she can't solve. I never thought it possible."

"Don't give up hope yet on the self-proclaimed greatest genius on Terminus Mundus."

A foul stench hit Christian right in his elven nose. Covering his mouth and nose, he could see the reactions of others as the odor hit the streets.

"What?" asked Colin.

"Did you just pick up that pungent odor?"

Colin smelt the air. He wrinkled his nose and immediately started smelling himself first, but soon realized the smell was everywhere.

"Well, I'm good, but that really stinks."

"There's only one animal on Terminus Mundus that produces an odor with that type of dung. Come on!"

Christian and Colin made for the rooftop using ladders and windows to get where they needed to be. They stared from one building as Edenian Dragoons were busy clearing the central walkways. The ceremonial golden armor worn by these spear-knights proved to Christian that an important dignitary was on his way to see the king. His suspicions were confirmed when he spotted Imperial Mamelukes on camels and horses riding in front of and behind a three-ton mammoth with a large carriage on its back. The massive beast simply lumbered his way across the city streets, disinterested at everything else that was going on. A creature this size was not easily startled and simply followed its normal routine. The carriage carried Sultan Khan and his chief advisor Saladin. The Sultan was about average height but quite pudgy underneath his expensive sandstone-colored silk robes. He wore a turban with a large and bright ruby at its center. His gray hair was beginning to turn white underneath the turban but his bright blue eyes still showed deep ambition. The Sultan continued to wear a neatly waxed white beard and mustache. Khan reveled in the admiration that was being bestowed upon him by the citizens in the streets. Colin and Christian shook their heads in disgust at the behavior of the Edenian citizens; it was unclear if the admiration was genuine or the result of bribes from the king and guards. Saladin was about as tall as Cagius but he did not have his added girth. His eyes were deep blue with a black beard and black mustache. It was neatly trimmed and waxed as well. This man also wore a thin desert scimitar on his waist.

"I'd recognize Sultan Khan anywhere, but who's the man in black?" asked Colin.

"Saladin; he's the Imperial Chancellor subject only to the Sultan. There are many rumors surrounding him; some say he is a Master of Black Magic, others say he's one of the legendary eastern immortals."

"What do you think about him?"

"Cedric's met with him on occasion and I attended. Saladin is an honorable man and maybe one man we can trust within the Empire to advise against Sultan Khan's lust for the West."

"The Sultan and his advisor are headed to the palace. It must be a high-powered meeting. Do you suppose it could be an assault on Deniva?"

"Khan wouldn't do it alone, but there's another train approaching from the pass."

Christian focused his scopes on a train coming out of the pass. He spotted Templar Knights and Jonas Marimon leading the way. A new banner moved with the coat-of-arms of Central Acadia, featuring a gargoyle on a banner of black and scarlet.

"It's the Acadians!"

Colin pulled out his scopes.

"Looks like King Luminas made himself a new banner."

"What madness has possessed the Sultan to meet with the vampire?"

"I'd sure love to be a fly on the wall in that room."

The two operatives looked at each other with a smile. Colin cracked his knuckles.

"I guess we'll need to relieve some of the guards," joked Christian.

The two slid down a ladder attached to a building. They made their way quickly through the streets on their way to a desired target. The two picked up their isolated marks. Two Landsknechts were walking on the side of one of the palace walls on the way to the gate. Christian and Colin approached them head on.

"What are you Rangers doing here?" asked the Landsknecht.

"Wint and Kidd heading for our next assignment," explained Christian.

"No Rangers in the palace today!" said the other.

"Why not?" asked a sly Colin. "What's with all of the trains coming to the palace?"

The two put their weapons down.

"I'm not going to ask anymore," ordered the first Landsknecht. "Get your asses off of the palace grounds now or else you'll both be spending the rest of your rotations in the palace dungeons."

Christian put his hands up in a submissive posture.

"I meant no trouble."

Christian crunched down on something in his mouth and spit out a dart at one of the Landsknecht. Before the other could react, Christian quickly spit another dart at him. The two went down like a ton of bricks.

"What the hell was that?" demanded Colin. "It certainly isn't standard issue for operatives."

"I had Martha mix me a special formula that acts as a powerful sedative. I had the delivery method embedded in a false tooth near the back of my mouth. They'll be out for four hours and have no memory of the previous six. Take their clothes!"

Colin looked over the two Landsknecht and stared at his own body. He shook his head.

"There is no way that armor is going to fit me."

"Too many fatty meals from Hippolyte!"

"The food here isn't exactly heart-healthy!"

"Make do what with what we've got."

The two donned the armor. Colin was trying hard to get the armor around his chest. Finally he simply cut the straps and tied them together. Fortunately the elaborate cloaks and hollow skirts of the Landsknechts could be used to hide the alterations.

"Well?"

"I'll be okay as long as I don't have to move too much or breathe for that matter."

Christian whistled over to Calvary who was flying overhead. The eagle landed on one of the collapsed guards.

"Wait for us near the pass; we may have to make a run for it," commanded Christian.

The eagle nodded and flew off. Christian and Colin made for the palace gates. They didn't attempt to sneak in, but rather chose to move as if they belonged there. Christian moved directly towards one of the captains in the courtyards. The captain sighed heavily when he was coming over.

"Now I'm going to be stripped of my command," observed the captain. "I believe our people had been more than fair with you so far, yet you continue to take advantage of us."

Christian rolled his eyes and handed him an envelope. The captain took out a brown paper bag and put the envelope in it.

"I don't like it when others take a bite out of my lunch," explained the captain.

"I need a favor."

"I figured so much. Then again, I understand why you want to be here when you saw the trains approaching."

"What is going on around here? My friend and I were nearly attacked by two Landsknechts while asking for ranger assignments."

"You'll find out soon enough. Lower reception room, three doors down, three spiral staircases down and to the left! I want you to stay to rear of the room because my ass is on the line if you screw up."

"Thanks."

"To hell with that, the people of Edenia owe the Titans. However, we're all square after this."

Christian and Colin walked into the palace. The ornate ivory and gold columns greeted them as they entered the main forum. Colin had never seen this palace before and his jaw dropped upon seeing the opulence and magnificence of the aptly named structure. Fountains and gardens adorned the entire forum leading to four marble staircases. These were the only access routes to the royal reception chamber and apartments. However, this wasn't the destination for the two operatives. They proceeded down velvet carpets into the lower bowels of the palace. Christian surmised it would be the perfect place to hold an under the radar meeting. The two followed the captain's directions to a hidden strategy room. Landsknechts were already present in the room and formed up along a conference table. Colin and

Christian went right to the empty positions in the room in order to fill out the remainder of the guard. They remained silent as they heard footsteps approaching the room. Christian moved his left eye to see Sultan Khan and Saladin enter the room. Finally he caught the sight of King Richard Archibald, the ruler of Edenia. The same divikin blood flowed through the veins of the Archibalds and Rhones, but the similarities ended there. The still handsome king was no taller than Cedric but appeared lanky and kept his head hung submissively at all times. Richard had brown hair that was cut to shape his small head and a neatly trimmed brown beard. He wore gold and red robes matching the coat-of-arms of Edenia. Christian couldn't place it but when he looked into the brown eyes of the Edenian king, he felt something very familiar.

"Richard Archibald, I must thank you again for your welcome," pronounced Khan.

"Edenia is the faithful servant of the Empire," replied Richard.

"Indeed. I can't wait to sample some of your fine cuisine this evening. I haven't been able to enjoy myself since the end of the war."

"I hear your recent naval campaign against Titanus did not fare well."

"It didn't fare at all!" laughed Khan. "I sent my most decorated admiral out in the largest flagship ever built at the head of the largest armada to sail the seas. The fool allowed himself to be drawn into the Eagle's Lock where the Titan fleet tore them to pieces from both sides. The damned queen herself took command of that blasted ironclad, the *Sea Eagle*, and rammed my beautiful flagship. Civilia, of course, had the audacity to send my admiral home in a rowboat."

"We believe that our intelligence was compromised," explained Saladin. "There has been turmoil in Dhrama regions recently. It is possible that conspirators leaked the information across the mountains. What of the Rangers?"

"The Rangers are preoccupied with the dangers assaulting us from the West," lectured Richard. "The Demonkin are growing bold with their attacks. We've lost eight patrols in the past three lunar cycles. Some of those men can't be replaced."

"Hopefully that will begin to change," surmised Khan. "Have our guests arrived?"

"The Dragoons are clearing them now. We can't be too careful with the Acadians even if they come to us under a flag of truce."

"I was shocked at their offer," interrupted Saladin. "After five revolutions of almost zero contact, the Acadians have orchestrated a conference."

"It would have been rude not to accept their offer," said Khan. "I guess we owe them that much."

Christian turned his attention from Khan back towards Colin. Colin started to loosen something on his boot. Christian noticed a five-inch dagger sticking out of it.

"What are you doing?" whispered Christian.

"I have standing writ from Master Cedric to assassinate Sultan Khan if he presents himself as a target of opportunity. We may never get this chance again."

"Now is not the time, Colin."

"If I kill him now I won't have to kill him later. We're staring at a man whose limitless ambitions have nearly destroyed the West."

"If Khan were to be killed there would be chaos in the East. Revolutions breaking out in the East and West would play right into Abaddon's hand."

Colin eyes pleaded with Christian to take the chance, but he knew in the end that the elf would never agree. He replaced the strap on the boot and covered his knife. Christian was surprised at the disappointment in Colin's face.

"I just want the record to show this was my idea," whispered Colin.

"Stay focused on why we're here and stop thinking like an assassin," whispered Christian.

The door opened to the room as the shades were drawn. A procession of King Luminas, Queen Sharon, and Jonas Mormont arrived. Christian and Colin pulled down their ceremonial hats to cover their eyes from the sight of the Acadians. Christian's eyes betrayed a genuine surprise at the arrival of their enemies. Jonas stared at the two of them for a moment before joining the king and queen at table. While he had suspicions, the knight commander did not expect the enemy to expose themselves so bluntly.

"The vampire that would be king," jested Khan. "I can't help be feel uncomfortable sitting in the same room as the thing that killed his king and usurped his throne."

"The chess game we all play is a dangerous one," retorted Luminas. "I know you had no love of King Stephen Acadia."

"Love, no! However, I respected the man. He certainly did not deserve to be beheaded, have his head stuck on a pike with a peasant's crown, and body dragged through the streets like a broom! Have you no decency?"

"Many regrettable actions occurred in the culmination of my rise to power. I assure you no further misfortunes need to take place."

"Then perhaps you should learn to act more gracefully in everything," demanded Saladin.

The meeting started off poorly. Luminas and Sharon were disappointed they were not getting the respect they deserved as sovereigns of a nation as Khan had done with Stephen in the past.

"Why did you come to meet with us in Edenia?" asked Khan.

"We have a proposal that may attract your attention," responded Luminas. "We desire to perform an action that requires tribute."

"What would that be?"

"We wish to attack Deniva."

Christian swallowed hard. The blatant statement by Luminas could only mean the détente was coming to an end and Abaddon's lust for Cassandra had grown too great. The only hope Christian held onto was the laughter from Khan's oversized belly.

"Attack Deniva! You certainly are bold. Why should I give up my good friend Margrave Dennis? He makes me rich!"

"Princess Cassandra Acadia has taken refuge in the city."

"We have known for quite some time that Queen Cassandra Acadia was a guest of Margrave Dennis de-Milly," pronounced Saladin. "The margrave has provided more than adequate compensation for this favor."

Luminas furrowed his brow at the thought of the Empire being so easily bought off by their enemies. Jonas looked ready to pounce in attack but the vampire used his mind powers to keep him in a calm state. The last thing he needed was the negotiations to turn into an all-out battle. The Empire held all of cards here and he just needed time.

"Then you know that she is a dangerous revolutionary that must be apprehended immediately," commented Sharon.

"Queen Fenidor, I cannot condone such a tone used to describe your own daughter!" exclaimed a defiant Richard.

"Cassandra was well protected in the Castle. She chose to betray Acadia and flee with the rebels to Deniva," defended Sharon. "Great Sultan, we would appreciate your assistance in this matter."

"You have wasted my time," said Khan. "These negotiations are over."

Khan moved to leave with Saladin.

"We would, of course, be willing to compensate you for such an attack," interjected Luminas.

"What, Luminas?" asked Khan. "You don't have enough treasure to compensate me for the steady revenue loss of Deniva."

"What about territory?"

Khan stopped in his tracts. Colin whispered over to Christian.

"Is he offering to become a vassal?" asked Colin.

"Abaddon will never surrender Central Acadia to the Empire."

Khan sat back down.

"Are you willing to bend the knee? The vassalage of Central Acadia would be appropriate compensation for an attack this size."

Luminas shook his head and presented a map of the Western plains. He put his finger towards the Northeast Plains near the Kaiser Mountains.

"No, but we have recently come into possession of the northeast tribal encampments of the Syrus Clan," explained Luminas. "Six hundred seventy two acres worth of lands in the West! Supply lines! Trains! Resources! That would be everything you'd need for an attack on Napolitan! I believe the Imperium is more than enough compensation for the loss of Deniva. We will grant you access through our barrier, supplies, support trains, and the Titans will not be able to launch a counterattack. If Dragonstone falls, the city will be yours!"

"A worthy prize!" nodded Khan.

"My sultan, a moment please," advised Saladin.

Saladin pulled Sultan Khan aside and began to speak with him. However, it was still near enough for Christian to read his lips.

"What do you think?" asked the Sultan.

"It sounds too good to be true," commented Saladin.

"Land in the West—it's what I've dreamed of."

"Sultan, in light of the rebellions, we need Deniva to fund the cash flow into the Empire. We've enjoyed a great financial bump since Deniva started the embargo against Acadia. We can't afford to lose the money."

"We'll get by. The Edenians are miracle workers with the bureaucracy; we'll lean on them for a while."

"Tensions are high in Edenia! Sultan, if we desert Deniva now we may lose them to the West altogether."

"Titanus is contained! We have nothing to worry about."

"We both know the prowess of Martha Heinrich; they will not remain contained. The Napolitan Dragon Legions are the finest heavy infantry in the world; our casualties will be high and Dragonstone will not fall easily. I don't trust these people, my sultan."

Khan turned back to Luminas.

"My advisor is correct. What are my other guarantees besides the land?"

"A pact of non-aggression between our governments for fifteen revolutions with an option to renew for another five," offered Luminas. "We also agree to pay you fifty thousand pieces of gold in advance."

"I also want the safety of my garrison in Deniva guaranteed," demanded Khan. "If any of them is lost in the battle, I demand compensation as well."

"I will make sure our attacking force gives your garrison more than ample time to exit the city."

"Do we need a drafter?" asked Khan.

"I hope you are not offended but we took the liberty of drafting the document prior to our meeting. If Lord Saladin wishes to review the contract, he will find everything in order."

Saladin took out a pair of reading glasses. He took the parchment that Luminas removed from a box. He looked over the document with a very discerning eye. Colin leaned over to Christian.

"What do you think?" asked Colin. "Is it legitimate?"

"It's going to be flawless. In fact, I'm sure they've provided more caveats to the Empire. Let's go."

The two started to sneak out of the corner of the room as Saladin handed the document to Khan.

"Everything that you agreed is in this document," responded Saladin. "The other terms in this treaty are favorable to our side as well."

"You don't think I'm doing to right thing," commented Khan.

"No, my lord, but my duty is but to advise you. The final decision must be yours."

"My ambitions know no limit."

Khan signed the document. Christian and Colin walked out into the courtyard and removed their armor. They quickly put their Ranger uniform back on. They were both distressed and for the first time in his life Christian had no idea what to do. He kept shaking his head.

"I never thought that fat bastard would sell Dennis out," grunted Colin.

"Even if he didn't agree to it, I doubt Abaddon would have been discouraged from attacking Deniva."

"What are we going to do?"

"I'm thinking, but the most important thing is that we get the hell out of this city as soon as possible. We can't do anymore here. Our operatives will send word to Mapes to lock up our room and not let anyone in."

Christian and Colin got their gear together and went to the stables. Mounting their horses, Christian was still clearly troubled by what had transpired and kicked himself for not anticipating it. A hardy slap on the back from Colin was enough to get him to focus. He noticed the sly smile on the assassin's face that told him to focus on the bigger picture. The two rode their horses out of the city gates and headed for the Kaiser Mountain Pass. However, as they approached the Pass, they noticed Dragoons on horseback blocking all traffic into the West.

"Jesus, what now!" commented Colin.

"Be cool!" ordered Christian.

Christian rode up to one of the Dragoons. The elf began to manipulate his vocal patterns as to appear as if he was using an eastern accent.

"Wint and Kidd, we have urgent business in the West at the behest of King Archibald," announced Christian. "We tracked a band of demonkin that took out some of our men and we have some revenge planned."

Christian handed the Dragoon his papers. The Dragoon looked them over.

"These are in order, Mister Wint, but I have my orders. The Acadians have asked us to block the pass for the time being. Apparently that jerk Jonas Marimon and his Templar Knights want to inspect the area before they leave."

"Can't you make an exception? We need proper time to lay the ambush."

"You'll have to wait. I promise we'll get you through as soon as possible once their train passes. I'm sorry."

Christian turned around and went back to Colin.

"Well?" asked Colin.

"Looks like we're stuck!"

"Well, here comes trouble!"

The two looked up to see Jonas Marimon and his Templar Knights riding towards the pass. Jonas was ruthless but not stupid. He knew two of the Landsknechts in the room seemed a bit out of place and he wasn't prepared to pass up this opportunity. The knight commander signaled to some of his knights and went towards Christian and Colin. However, the two were not caught off guard. Despite his concerns, Christian continued to encourage his partner under the circumstances. Jonas showed complete disregard for the Dragoons stationed there and rode over to the Rangers.

"Eastern Rangers!" observed Jonas. "The wretched spies of a worthless kingdom! I'm proud to boast I killed my share of you in the past."

The Dragoons noticed this and were none too pleased by Marimon. The outright disdain of the Saint would not be tolerated by this proud military force.

"These Rangers are under the protection of the King of Edenia and the Empire! Please proceed with your inspection of the Pass. We have no time for your foolishness and the traffic is growing."

"You damn cowards aren't too observant," jested Jonas. "Our friends in Titanus often disguise themselves as Rangers when they go off into the wild in order to cover their footsteps."

"As you can see from our papers, I am Mister Wint and this is my associate, Mister Kidd," said Christian with his accent again.

"Your buddy is awful large for a Ranger."

"Strong as an ox with unfortunately the brain to match!"

Colin was not happy with the comment even if it was part of the act.

"You have quite a way with words, Mister Wint."

"You know of my love of prose, Mister Kidd."

"Enough of this foolishness!"

Jonas drew his sword. Christian put his hand behind his back and started to chant under his breath.

"Kill Christian Devries and Colin Wilkins!"

"I guess the charade is over. You might remember this!"

Colin shielded his eyes while Christian threw his jujitsu attack in front of Jonas' horse. The same flash bang effect from the palace took place. Jonas' horse and the horses of his surrounding knights were blinded and kicked violently. The knight commander cursed himself for falling for the same trick twice. Christian and Colin took off in the confusion. The two had the horses jump over the roadblock into the pass.

"I thought you said to stay cool!" teased Colin.

"That was cool!" exclaimed Christian.

"I hope you're not thinking of taking the Kaiser Pass at full speed because in those narrow passes this would be suicide!"

"If we don't make Arudin, we're dead! Besides, I've got an idea!"

Christian whistled hard. The two heard the call of Cedric's eagle as it descended from the sky into the mountains. Calvary flew over Christian and Colin and went into the pass.

"Turn on Calvary's movements!" ordered Christian.

"This is crazy!"

"They're crazier if they follow us!"

"After them!" ordered Jonas to his knights.

Four knights took off after the two Titan agents into the Kaiser Pass. Calvary took the lead in the narrow pass while Christian and Colin focused on the eagle's movements. The two often had mere split seconds to twist their reigns through the sharp turns. Bolts were flying over their heads from crossbows. However, without the guiding direction of the eagle, the knights truly had no chance to catch the agents. As they turned quickly, one the knights was thrown from his horse when he hit the side of the walls. This disturbed two of the other horses, and they stopped throwing their riders. The final knight held up just in time to avoid the fray.

"Damn!" screamed the Templar.

Christian and Colin made it through the pass. Christian signaled to the Guards on this side.

"Rangers coming in hot!" ordered Christian. "Acadian scum are trying to follow; don't let them pass! They have no authority from the king."

"Yes, sir."

Christian and Colin immediately rode into the forest. The knights returned from the pass pursuit. Two of the knights were on foot, one was still riding, and the one that had been thrown was now slung over the back of a horse.

"Are they dead?" demanded Jonas.

"We failed to pursue," commented the Templar. "I don't know what sorcery they used to get through that pass."

Jonas screamed and kicked the dirt.

"That's bad news for me and worse news for all of us if they made it to Deniva."

"With what? They have no army in Deniva; those two aren't going to be able to do anything."

"I hope you're right. I want you to gather some men and set up a patrol through the Arudin Forest. See if you can find them! I'll stay with the king."

The Templar gathered some knights and rode through the pass again.

The Underdark, Southeastern Acadian Plains

"The Underdark is the home of these evil cousins of the surface elves, known as the Drow. No one knows exactly how far the underground holdings of the dark elves extend, nor has there been an accurate census of their true power. They hate the light, and have researched ways to travel while avoiding the sun, which is an anathema to them. Though still possessing two separate sexes, the Drow have adopted a hive mentality and it is to their chief priestess whom the dark elves give their absolute obedience."

On Drow, the Elf Scholar Demetrius

Kilometers below the surface of Mundus rested an intricate series of limestone caves where water dripped from the supposed underground streams above. The eerie glow of the underworld kept the caverns strangely lit despite the fact no sunlight peeked through. Abaddon traveled a comfortable road carved in the deep caverns. Virgus and General Palias followed close behind. A fearful Palias held a torch, but an unnerved Virgus simply used a different lens on his robotic eye to light a path for him. At times, the appointed marshal swung his torch wildly, as if he was trying to fend off some form of darkness. He was frightened by a small mammal hanging on the cavern wall. An eerie, incandescent glow emanated from its white fur.

"What creature is this?" asked Palias.

"You have encountered *Mustela lucerna*," explained Virgus. "It is a rare creature commonly known as the Lamp Weasel."

Excitedly taking a picture with his telescopic eye, Virgus documented the discovery.

"The Underdark is a mystical place, my Acadian friend. There are many mysteries, discoveries, and wonders in these caverns below."

"Why the hell would anyone live here?" asked Palias.

"I am sure that as an Acadian you aren't familiar with the history of the Drow. They were among the 'Tribes' of the High Elves once. However, these tribes turned their back on the Lord and began to worship a demoness known as the Spider Queen. Thus, the Lord demanded these 'lost tribes' be dealt with. The rebels struck first and attempted genocide against those Elves that had completely intermarried with the primitive humans, the Wood Elves. The attack was so swift that only a few managed to flee the Forest of the Eternal Summer and run to the safety of the Kingdom of Titanus. Hayden Marisol rallied his Titan allies once more as the lost tribes moved against Brooke Run. The combined strength of these forces crushed the rebels. The Lord God put a terrible curse upon these elves, driving them from the 'promised land' and sending them underground in exile. They have stayed here for many revolutions and their hatred has grown as large as the population."

"What are we looking to collect down here?" asked Palias.

"I'm simply here to collect a favor," said a smiling Abaddon. "And, with that, an army!"

The three approached two male Drow standing at attention guarding a cave. Their skin had turned from the pale golden tint seen in the High Elves of Evengard to an ashen color from revolutions of living underground. Their hair had turned to a bleached white and their eyes had a glowing purple tint to them. These guards favored light armor in the form of chain mail vests and carried one-handed swords. They remained on high alert and drew their weapons on Abaddon's approach. Abaddon certainly wasn't welcome in these caverns even if he was an enemy of Evengard.

"There's no need for this!" said a calm Abaddon.

The Dark Angel summoned power in his ethereal form. He cast a spell that put an intense burning effect on the weapons of the guards. The blades heated to red and immediately became too hot to handle. The Drow dropped their weapons, but fearlessly remained ready for a confrontation. Palias grew nervous at the supposed inability of Abaddon to control this race. He had always heard rumors about the cunning and strength of Drow swordsmen and didn't want to challenge it.

"I didn't come here to fight," explained Abaddon. "I only ask for an audience with your queen. We are old friends and I need to speak with her."

The Drow guards remained defiant, but generally accepted the reasonable request. They proceeded down the cavern they were guarding and left the three adventurers wondering if they were going to return. Abaddon remained confident, but Palias was seeking more information.

"You seem to have many allies across the West. However, I am curious about your relationship with these 'creatures.'"

"I prefer to keep all of my options open. The Drow were cursed by God, and upon my arrival I felt it prudent to form an alliance just in case the need should arise. She knows where her loyalty lies."

"Who?" asked Palias.

The conversation was interrupted as the three could hear the sound of a chariot fast approaching their positions. Palias drew back in horror as hundreds of red glowing eyes could be seen coming from the dark cavern. Enormous hairy legs came out of the cavern first, followed by the bodies of two large spiders that pulled a golden chariot. The Drow standing on the chariot was Alia Drathan, priestess and queen of the Drow. Palias' first thought upon seeing her was that next to Saria this was the most beautiful elf he had ever seen. Her skin and eyes remained the same color as her kinsman but her hair was bright and fiery red set in place by a golden and obsidian twisted tiara. She wore a black dress that was lined with golden trim, accenting her features quite nicely, and black sandals on her feet. Alia held onto a large golden staff marked with a ruby at the top of it. Her disposition was one of extreme anger and she scorned Abaddon the moment she spotted him. Alia had served as a priestess of the Spider Queen faithfully, but she was ambitious. She was not content with her lowly position so Abaddon sought her out. The two conspired to murder the High Priestess and rigged the process so Alia would succeed her. Once she was in that position, the captivating Drow manipulated the Matriarchal Society to change the office of High Priestess to Queen. Five revolutions later, Alia regretted her decision and lived in fear of the rotation when Abaddon would return.

"You always knew how to make a grand entrance," teased Abaddon. "Good day, Alia."

The Drow Queen jumped down from her chariot and gently stroked her pets. Alia quickly turned her attention to Abaddon, and Virgus wondered how his master was going to control this wild girl.

"I have nothing to discuss with you, Abaddon."

"Alia Drathan, lowly priestess among the Drow of the Underdark! Did you soon forget the favor I did for you? I raised you up to a queen among your people. Alia, you owe me a favor and I've come to collect."

"Our business is through."

"No, my dear, you swore to make yourself available to me when I called and I am calling! I have need of your people for a minor task. You will lead the Drow in a siege of the Margrave of Deniva."

"I will not risk my people on such a fruitless endeavor! Deniva means nothing to us and the human traders there have always treated us kindly."

"Do you think I would only offer you Deniva? I full intend to aid you in your dream of assaulting Evengard."

"Evengard is a dream!"

"I can make that dream a reality! I can't believe that you still doubt my power even though I made you a queen. I cannot leave Evengard on the northern border forever. My Nephilim and Demonkin will march with you in a siege of Evengard. However, you will need to deal with this nuisance first!"

"Why Deniva?"

"There is a half-breed there of great importance to me! Her name is Cassandra. I want her alive."

"An entire city for one girl! Abaddon, are you desperate or simply in love?"

"The situation requires great caution. Royal Warriors from the four families are in the city and sworn to protect her. One of those protectors is Marshal Amuro Jenitzen—I know she is of great interest to you."

"As much as it would please the swords of my soldiers to slit the throat of that Evengard harlot, I fear that we must decline. The needs of my people are the primary concern. Even the most carefully planned assault on Deniva would cost us many lives and take away resources from our desired objectives. It would also bring the wrath of the Empire down upon us, and who will stop them?"

"I have dealt with the Empire, you have no fear of reprisals. I will hold our contract completed if you do this final task for me."

"My answer is no, Abaddon! Farewell!"

"I was hoping that you would have acted smarter."

"What are you going to do, Abaddon? Replace me with a duco-matios?"

"Not exactly; the connection of the Drow with the branch of mysticism would render a duco-matios useless. I know of the hive mind your culture has developed and how the high priestess or queen can control the minds of her people. My agent would be dead the moment he shifted into a dark elf body. What I have in store for you will make you much more agreeable to my scheme. You were so naïve to come to me alone."

"I don't understand."

Abaddon manifested his physical body for a brief moment to Alia's shock. He grabbed Alia and pulled her close to him, kissing her on the lips. The light in the Drow Queen's eyes began to fade even after the Dark Angel broke the kiss. Abaddon screamed as his physical manifestation rotted to ash but the transfer of magic was complete. Virgus and Palias witnessed a complete change in Alia's demeanor. The defiant look in her face disappeared. Alia was now docile in front the Dark Angel and immediately fell to her knees before him. Abaddon tore at his robes and opened them. His two companions stared at the great wound Cedric had inflicted on him. It throbbed repeatedly even on his ethereal body and took a few moments for Abaddon to recover. When he finally controlled the pain again, Abaddon turned his full attention to the kneeling Alia.

"What is your command, Master?" offered Alia.

"Rally your people, Queen Drathan, and lay siege to the city of Deniva. You are to take Cassandra Acadia prisoner; she is not to be harmed."

"How will I know her, Master?"

"I am sending the Acadian Marshal Palias with you, he will command your armies in battle so there are no accidents."

Palias stepped forward. He no longer was concerned and afraid of what the Drow Queen would do to him. The general was actually amused at the now docile beautiful she-elf before him. Palias had a few other thoughts run through his mind, but knew he'd better not anger his Dark Angel ally before the mission was complete.

"As you can see by these medals, I have many distinguished accomplishments," boasted Palias. "If your soldiers can fight, I can command them."

"I assure you, great marshal, that our fighting abilities should be the least of your concerns."

Alia stood and walked back to her chariot. She assisted Palias in getting onto it before turning her spiders towards the tunnel. Virgus went over to Abaddon to see if he needed any help. Abaddon put his hands up and refused any assistance. The two would follow the chariot on foot until the tunnel led them into the large glow of a thousand blue lights underground. An underground stream formed a crashing waterfall before the limestone city of the Underdark. The shock of Palias was beyond description as he never knew something so large and beautiful could exist this deep underground. While their craftsmanship was not on par with the Dwarves, the Drow had certainly outdone themselves in construction of their six-tiered city, complete with statues to spider gods and demons everywhere. A central domed temple serving as the seat of power for Alia Drathan was placed next to the crashing waterfall. All of the abodes were built out of limestone and the inhabitants were mostly outside. The females of the race seemed busy worshiping the gods. The men were practicing their swordplay or working the smiths. Armorers, sword smiths, and fletchers were busy making the weapons of war. Abaddon smiled when he saw the numbers were in the hundreds of thousands.

"This will do very nicely," commented Palias.

"Alia, inform them of our arrangement," ordered Abaddon.

Alia hit her staff into the ground. The sound echoed throughout the Underdark and all its inhabitants turned their attention towards the queen.

"Children of Lolloth, the path to our destiny has been shown to us. The God of the High Elves banished us from the light and cursed us to live in the Underdark. This curse will never be broken until we are able to wrest control of Brooke Run from their grasp."

Frenzy overcame the denizens of the Underdark, and their purple eyes glowed. Like the queen of a beehive or anthill, all subordinated themselves to Alia. Unfortunately, her will was controlled by the dark angel alone. Many voices were heard throughout the gathering crowds. They included "death to the High Elves" and "curse those of Evengard."

"I have aligned us with an ally that can make our dreams a reality. However, before we can deal with our enemy at hand, there is a nuisance we must take care of. Our allies have tasked us with the destruction of the Margrave of Deniva. There are those of Evengard among them, plotting our destruction, including the Marshal Amuro Jenitzen herself. We must strike them first!"

The riled up Dark Elves needed few words of encouragement. They started striking their armor with their swords.

"Girt your loins and gather your arms! The Drow march for war!"

The Drow called out "death to Deniva" as they rushed to the nearest armorer for weapons and chain. In a matter of moments, they were fully prepared for war and formed ranks. Abaddon and Virgus walked out of the cavern, leaving Palias to his command.

"Of course, you know that if the Empire fails to agree…" commented Virgus.

Virgus stopped himself as Abaddon smiled. The haughty look on his ally's face was all that he needed to know.

"You had no intention of keeping such an agreement."

"The world of man is of little use to me. The walls that you have created for us have no form of siege. By the time the Empire could move to strike against us, I will have already accomplished our goals."

"I don't see why we have to let these fools fight. My army would be more than effective in dealing with the Denivan rabble."

"In a chess match, you should always let the pawns die first. Alia will serve me well and these idiots will keep charging the walls of Deniva even after the last one is long dead. Did you convey my message to Valadrim?"

"He marched out of Central Acadia this evening. A large host of Demonkin accompanied him."

"My prince, I beg your patience for a just a bit longer, but rest assured victory is finally mine!"

Abaddon laughed.

Bishop's Residence, City of Antiquity

"Si Vis Pacem, Para Bellum!"

Inscribed on the entrance to the Titan Military Academy

Bishop Wulf knelt on a stone kneeler in front of the Blessed Sacrament in his private chapel. His eyes were closed as his breaths intensified. Tears were falling from his eyes and in that moment the bishop received the stigmata. Peter Wulf had received very few visions in his lifetime and they were always preceded by the stigmata. His visions, however, needed to be interpreted as they did not have the clarity of those received by Garrett Greensage. In his mind, the bishop witnessed four standing towers. The first tower preceded the other three and it was the only one not engulfed in fire. A wounded eagle sat on top of this tower but still continued to call out a "war cry." The other three towers featured shattered stone versions of a dragon, a unicorn, and a wolf. His eyes opened quickly and they were red as well. Argus came running into the room. Concerned over the appearance of the stigmata and resulting seizure, the captain held his leader tightly. The bishop finally stopped praying and the bleeding ceased immediately.

"It's happened again?" asked Argus.

The bishop composed himself. Staring at his hands in awe, the bleeding did not stain nor drip on any of his clothing. The wounds were almost cauterized completely and displayed no sign of infection.

"I'm sorry to cause you such alarm," expressed the bishop. "It's been quite some time since I had an experience like this."

"What did you see?"

"During my prayers, I saw a terrible vision. There were four towers and three of them were engulfed in flames and crumbling. A lone eagle remained on top the last tower with shattered bodies of a dragon, unicorn, and wolf below it."

"The eagle is the sigil of Titanus. The dragon belongs to Napolitan, the unicorn to Evengard, and the wolf to the Tribes. Bishop, if those animals have shattered—"

"Then it is possible that I've seen the Kingdom of Titanus as the last defender of the West."

The bishop attempted to calm himself down, however he couldn't help but see the concern in his loyal captain's eyes.

"What do you need of me?" asked the bishop.

"The last of our scouts has returned to the city. He was sent to spy on the developments in Central Acadia."

"Good, I need to see him. Once we are confident in our security we can safely move Cedric back to Rhinegard. Perhaps Arch-Bishop Langely will know more of the vision I witnessed."

Argus and Wulf left the room for the front door of the residence. The Kablisha had gathered in a circle. A scout knelt in the streets exhausted from his ordeal. A close examination of his face would have led someone with knowledge to know this was the scout that was killed by Valadrim. Ignorant of his fate, the bishop and captain approached as if nothing was out of the ordinary. The scout prostrated himself when the bishop approached him.

"Your Eminence…" said the scout.

Wulf knelt down by the scout and lifted his face to his. The bishop took time to give the man some water.

"Rest now, brave one. What news do you bring?" asked Wulf.

"Bishop, I was discovered," pleaded the scout. "The Nephilim know of our plans."

"Oh God, how could they?" asked a concerned Wulf.

"Abaddon is very cunning," continued the scout. "He had the wizards search for a distortion in the forest. I was barely able to escape with my life. They wanted to use our magic to break the barrier."

"This man needs aid, bring him to my home at once," ordered the bishop.

The Kablisha nodded and went to lift him.

"If they know, plans must be made to move him immediately," interjected Argus. "Every rotation he remains here will bring torment for both our peoples."

The scout smiled as he listened intently to the conversation at hand. A small winged imp was hidden carefully under his sleeve with a message tied to him.

"Yes," agreed Wulf. "You must summon Wilhlem back here, it is the only way out."

The scout determined that this was all he was going to get. He reached under his other sleeve and slowly slipped his hand towards a knife on his belt. A quick scream and a shove knocked Wulf to the ground before Argus could react. The scout went with his knife towards the bishop's throat but something stopped his hand. Argus covered the bishop in order to protect him from a further attack. The crowd gathered was screaming "assassin," but the attack was already thwarted. Staring in terror, the scout realized the one grasping his arm was none other than *La Morte Angelus*. The Titan prince squeezed the hand so tightly that the wrist of the scout snapped like a twig.

"Cedric Rhone, it's not possible!" screamed the scout.

The scout knew his life was finished so he let the imp under his arm to fly up. Cedric threw the scout to the ground and pulled out his crossbow from his side. Cedric took aim and fired, striking the imp through the chest. The Titan prince moved back to the scout and snapped his neck before he had a chance to flee. Quinn and Mesmara came running up with a platoon of soldiers to protect the bishop.

"Cedric!" demanded Quinn. "What did you just do? Why is our kinsman dead?"

Cedric drew Ragnarok and placed it at the throat of the scout. The sight of the sword was enough to have the Kablisha soldiers step back.

The Titan prince started his "Saint Saber" chant. The holy energy from the blade of the sword traveled to the body of the scout. As the energy passed to him, the dead body shook. The true form of the scout was revealed to be a duco-matios.

"The Nephilim did find your scout," explained Cedric. "The same energy force that creates this barrier blinds you to the transformation of the duco-matios or else you would have spotted this agent easily. We have to prepare as if all of our secrets have been compromised."

"It's worse than you can possibly imagine!" screamed a frightened Argus. "Search the body!"

Mesmara patted the body down. She searched every pocket and sleeve leaving no area undisturbed. Cedric witnessed the concern growing in the eyes of the maiden warrior with each touch. Quinn pulled off the face-dancer's boots and shook them. Neither of the two could find what they were looking for.

"Uncle, the amulet is gone," cried a tearful Mesmara.

"What amulet?" asked Cedric.

"The amulet that allows us to move in and out of the barrier," explained Argus. "It works based on the spell branch of mysticism and allows for the mark and recall spell."

"You mean to tell me that all I had to do to get out of this prison is to rip one of those necklaces off of you?" exclaimed Cedric.

"This is hardly the time to discuss such trivial matters."

"You're right. What's our situation?"

"The Nephilim wouldn't have taken the amulet unless they knew how to use it. Oh, God!"

Argus ran to the walls of the city. He climbed a set of stairs two at a time until he reached the top. Cedric, Quinn, and Mesmara took off after him and the company filled in on their defensive positions along the walls. Argus adjusted his scopes and looked about eighteen to twenty miles away from the city. Cedric took a pair as well and focused on the area. The warriors saw an army of Demonkin consisting of about one hundred thousand goblins, twenty trolls, and two hundred Nephilim Warriors lead by Valadrim. The vanguard was taking their time making their way through the barrier and causing the forest creatures to flee. A group of goblins set up a camp, meaning an attack on the morrow before first light.

"They're crossing the barrier," exclaimed Argus.

"I thought you said the barrier was unbreakable."

"They can do anything with that amulet if they wish. We're sitting ducks! Our militia wouldn't stand a chance against that many troops."

Argus took a deep breath and stared at Cedric Rhone. The Kablisha captain struggled mightily with what he had to do next. There was no way the City of Antiquity would withstand more than one wave of attackers before the walls fell to the vanguard. The people in the city would have no chance to flee far enough into the forest to escape the enemy.

"Cedric, come with me," demanded Argus.

Cedric read the actions of the captain well. Argus was prepared to fight and no doubt the Titan prince would stand by his side after what they had done for him. The two went back to the center of the town square. The whole city was gathered in the immediate area waiting to see what was going on. The Kablisha that were outside of the walls came fleeing into the city at the first sign of the vanguard. The militia tightly sealed and barred the doors of the city to shelter them the best they could against an oncoming attack. Argus looked at his people with a heavy heart. He stared into the eyes of his bishop for comfort. The simple nod of Wulf told Argus that he had his full support no matter what his decision was.

"My Kablisha kinsman, the rotation that we have long feared has finally come," announced Argus as he took a moment for the people to absorb what was happening. "Demonkin and Nephilim are marching towards the City of Antiquity as we speak. I estimate we only have until dawn on the morrow before they descend upon this city. All military personnel report to the gate immediately. All others gather your families and prepare to evacuate the city into the deep forest."

The people protested and screamed. They didn't want to abandon the City they had lived in for so many revolutions. There was also the issue of the hundred or so men and women who would be marching to their death under Argus' command. The debate was going nowhere fast and Argus didn't have a lot of time. Cedric saw this happening and pulled out his sword. A second "Saint Saber" set off a wave that instantly silenced all of the murmurs, fears and doubt.

"We have to buy enough time for all of you to escape; there is no other way," continued Argus. "We also have to give Wilhelm von Angelhardt the necessary time to come and get Cedric Rhone away from here."

Cedric's smile fell from his face. He turned to Argus with utter defiance and disbelief.

"Wait a minute—if you're going to fight those bastards, you need every warrior you have," exclaimed Cedric. "This isn't a lost cause Argus; we can win this battle!"

"Don't argue with me, Cedric, you're getting out of here! I will accomplish my mission to keep you safe and hidden. I don't care that Titans never retreat, this is a war you can't win!"

"This isn't about hiding me anymore, Argus. War has come to your people and it's time for me to make good on my debt."

"This isn't about honor!"

"I think we would both agree that my record in unwinnable fights is quite sterling. I've already told you that I'm reporting for duty!"

Argus walked over to Cedric and put his hands on both of his shoulders. He looked the prince straight in the eyes with tears forming in his own. The Kablisha captain could not believe the determination he saw in the warrior's face. However the Kablisha were not without honor; Argus would never allow Cedric to waste his life in their defense.

"Cedric, I beg you, the time will come when it will be your responsibility to save us all. Just hide now! Please!"

He sighed as he stared at the people with whom he had lived for five revolutions. Warriors were busy embracing their families for a final time. Many of the children and wives were crying heavily at the sight of their fathers leaving them. "Daddy, I don't want you to go" and "Please don't go" were the prevalent choice of words. Men and women got their weapons and armor ready for battle, but didn't have the spark of a winning army in their eyes. Cedric knew they never had a chance without him and enough people had died for him already. His stare almost burned a hole right through Argus' face.

"Argus, no one throws me my sword and tells me to run!"

Cedric stepped back and clicked his boot heels together. He made a long and exaggerated salute towards Argus before turning on his heel. He comforted a few of the children standing there before walking back into the Bishop's residence. Those same children perked up at the thought of this invincible warrior standing side-by-side with their fathers and mothers. Argus knew that his only hope for stopping Cedric was Wilhelm von Angelhardt getting here in time to take him away. Mesmara approached him.

"We've raised Wilhelm von Angelhardt. He said he must take care of one thing first and then he will immediately come to take care of Cedric," explained Mesmara.

"Maybe he can talk some sense into Cedric. Why can't that stubborn divikin ever look at the big picture?"

"I think he already has, Uncle."

Argus was frustrated with Cedric's defiance, but needed to see to the safety of his people. The only hope he had was that Bishop Wulf would keep them together. The Kablisha captain went over to his Bishop for the last time and knelt down before him. The bishop soon joined him on one knee and Argus offered up one last confession. The bishop took the time and patience to listen before offering him absolution. Wulf gently kissed Argus on the forehead and offered a blessing over him.

"We'll do our best to protect you, but I can't guarantee how long we'll be able to hold out," declared Argus. "You must move quickly."

"Argus, I thank you for your sacrifice," expressed the bishop.

"May the Hand of God be with you!"

"Godspeed, Argus!"

The Bishop turned to his frightened people who had gathered in the center of the city. There were many that still couldn't understand what was going on. However their holy leader was their strength in this time of trouble and he wouldn't let them down.

"Come, children of the Kablisha, we haven't much time."

Bishop Wulf and the Kablisha people began moving slowly through the back posterns of the city. The long train of children, women, and elderly was moving slowly as the warriors hurried to the Gate.

CITY OF THE TREES, ARUDIN FOREST

"Since you refuse the sanctity of our protected lands, we
have no choice but to ask your people to populate the Arudin
Forest. The High Elves of Evengard have placed you under the
protection of the Crown of Titanus. You will join the Dwarves of
Lion's Peak as part of our vassalage system. As our vassal you
must pay us an annual tithe and be prepared to take up arms
when we call upon you. Rest assured that we will never ask
your people to die for a cause where our finest soldiers would
not take up arms first. Those that serve the nation of Titanus
are greatly rewarded; those who wish to do you harm will die.
These are the words of the King."

King Leto Rhone, Accord with the Wood Elves

Gerard and four of his underlings were on guard duty in the trees twenty
meters from the city. Gerard continued to twitch and stroke his beard.
The forest was telling him that something was wrong even before he could
see it. The Wood Elf commander's ears picked up the sound of horses
beating their hooves against the trail. As a precaution, the five elves on
duty drew their bows. Gerard breathed a sigh of relief when he was finally
able to make out Christian and Colin on approach; however, he was not
pleased to see their condition. The elves on duty blew their horns to signal
the remainder of the clan to arms. Archers took up hidden positions in
all of the trees covering the road ahead as Rosa raced to the center of
the camp. Christian and Colin pulled up their horses in the center of the
village and drew quite a commotion. Christian dismounted first and saw
Rosa had water waiting for him. The operative appreciated her labors and

downed the canteen. Colin was disappointed that no one had provided such sustenance for him and had to walk over to a well to draw his own water.

"What happened?" asked Rosa.

"We were being pursued by Acadians," answered Christian. "I didn't want to stop until we reached the cover of the deep forest.

"Yes, I know. I tried to send word to you that they passed through the forest a few rotations ago. It was a large train with Templars at the head of the column."

"Well, let's just say we had a first-hand encounter with those Templars," added Colin.

Christian put both of his hands on Rosa's shoulders and stared into her eyes. She blushed slightly at all the attention, but could see the look of fear in Christian's eyes.

"Rosa, I need you to muster whatever troops you can give me," demanded Christian.

"Why?"

"He's going for Cassandra—Abaddon is moving to attack Deniva as we speak."

"That's crazy, Khan would never allow that. He couldn't run the Empire without that money."

"He would if he thought he could get territory in the West and Port Talus."

"Abaddon will never allow that to happen. Once he has Cassandra, we're all doomed!"

"Khan can't see through that trap."

"Wouldn't it make Edenia too nervous to see Demonkin sacking Deniva? They would know they're next!"

"It won't be the Demonkin. Abaddon is cunning; he's going to use the Drow as fodder."

"Alia Drathan is ambitious enough to walk right into that trap. What are we going to do?"

"Rosa, if you don't help us the entire hope of the West is going to die and Cedric will have made a sacrifice for nothing."

"I wouldn't let that happen. My people lament for his death and we always knew there was a time where we were going to have to make a stand. However, I cannot march this army without the permission of a Titan royal family member. Can you speak for Princess Cecilia Rhone in this matter?"

"Absolutely!"

"I'm sorry, Christian, but you know as well as I do certain formalities have to be observed. I cannot deny such a request with the necessary permission; however, there is a small favor that I am going to require."

"Another favor?" inquired Christian.

"You'll really love this one," smiled Rosa. "You see, I'm getting a little tired of being left behind and waiting for you to come home to me dead. If you're going to fight, then I will lead my people into battle personally."

"Rosa, this isn't a good idea! You don't know what we're up against. I love you too much to put you in harm's way!"

"So it's okay for you to race off into danger? I'm asking a lot of my people. We are going off to die for a city whose merchants have treated us with utter contempt, and the queen of nation that has long wanted us wiped off the map. It's not enough just to save Cecilia and her son, even if he is the heir to our vassal lords. If the Wood Elves see how worthy a cause I stand for, their morale shall be encouraged. I told you this was not going to be easy, but you need me, Christian!"

"There may be a little Titan in you yet. Cecilia is always clamoring about how women will stand to the death with the man they love. Since you placed me in such a difficult position, I have no choice but to accept your terms. We will test the theory of the Vanadis."

"You won't be disappointed."

"I'm afraid you will be."

"Why's that? The good guys always win."

"It may cost all of our lives just to keep Cassandra from the enemy's hand," said Christian as he shook his head.

"Yet you would try to convince my people to fight without me?"

Rosa could see the fear in the eyes of her lover. Her intuition told her that Christian was preparing to make his last stand at Deniva. Even with their strength, the Wood Elves could not possibly contain the Drow. She put her hands on his shoulders and pulled herself up to kiss him. Rosa would do anything to make Christian's plan work even if it meant lying to people she had been entrusted to lead. Christian couldn't help but smile at the look in Rosa's eyes. She was right to persuade him; only Rosa could get her people to fight for this "lost cause." The judge let go of Christian and went over to where Gerard was standing. The hardened Woof Elf commander had already mustered his army as if anticipating the command of his leader. The Wood Elves did not possess the stoic nature of their High Elf cousins and there was a sense of foreboding among their ranks. They knew that many of them were not going to return if they fought the Dark Elves; however, they wanted revenge for the sins committed against their ancestors revolutions ago.

"My lady, our love for you is strong," pronounced Gerard. "We are sworn to follow you to whatever end."

"It is with a heavy heart that I must ask all of you for a grave sacrifice," started Rosa. "Ready twenty cohorts of our forces to march to Deniva immediately! Prince Cecilia of Titanus calls for aid and the Wood Elves will heed her call."

"As you wish! Will Prince Marisol be at the command?"

Rosa looked back at Christian, who shook his head. He didn't want this business started again among the elves. Christian had welcomed the relative silence of the past five revolutions without rebel outcasts demanding that he return to Evengard to reclaim his birthright.

"Prince Marisol and Princess Landon shall ride at the head of the column! Elf and Titan shall stand side by side together this rotation!"

The Wood Elves started to cheer. They ran over to Christian and hoisted him up in the air. He was extremely displeased as they carried him around the encampment. Colin looked over to Calvary perched on his shoulder.

"I guess it beats a boring parade review," joked Colin.

Calvary called out an eagle laugh as Colin tossed him a piece of dried meat. Rosa appreciated the love and respect her people had for Christian. However, she had duties to attend to as well. She sought out her younger sister, Vanessa, who waited for her holding a brown package. Vanessa had dyed her hair red just like her older sister when they came to live among the Wood Elves. The green-eyed and freckle-faced girl had a bright smile on her face even though she knew her sister was riding into danger. Vanessa took the time to hand the package to her sister while Rosa stripped herself of her green dress. She had pair of green tights on her lower body along with a bustier that served as an under covering. The High Elf lady donned the vanadium mail in the package first and tied it around her waist with a brown belt. She put a green coverall on top of the mail, which was held in place by a second belt.

"Be careful, sis," said Vanessa.

"You're in charge while I'm gone. I want you to take the remaining cohorts and our people to the safety of the trees."

"Will do! Just try to come back alive with your betrothed! Don't forget about your promise to make me your maid of honor!"

"Don't you worry; I'll bring Dulles back even if I have to chase him into the fires of Hell."

Vanessa winked at her sister. Rosa grabbed a golden bow with vanadium ridges for a comfortable grip along with a quiver carrying a large amount of arrows. She took two daggers and slid them onto her outer brown belt. The last thing she took was a golden circlet with a sapphire stone on the left side of it rather than in the center. A long golden pheasant feather attached to the sapphire marking the symbol of House Landon. When she placed this circlet on her head, her hands started to glow in soft white light as if her archery skills had just increased. The Wood Elves released Christian so he could get on his horse. Scoping up Rosa with one hand, the she-elf flipped up and landed sidesaddle behind him. She grabbed him tightly around his waist as Gerard and his armies started to climb the trees at an astounding pace. The cohorts grabbed at the sturdier branches in the trees and prepared to move. Colin rode over to Christian with concern all over his face.

"What about horses?" asked Colin.

"We don't have enough horses," retorted Rosa. "We're rangers, not cavalry."

"How are we going to make it in time? Deniva's too far even for a forced march."

"Don't worry, Colin," teased Christian. "We're lucky if we're going to be able to keep up with them."

Colin watched with amazement as the Wood Elves started jumping from tree to tree with amazing acrobatic skill. They never lost their pace as they grabbed one branch of the tree to the next. In no time, they had gotten well ahead of the two horses. Christian just laughed as he and his assassin companion broke down the trail to follow them. It was if the Arudin Forest had come alive to aid the allies as tree branches and other blockages were pulled away by forest creatures, speeding the way for the coming relief. Christian just prayed that they would be able to make it to Deniva in time.

CASTLE TITAN, TITANUS

"In the tenth revolution of the reign of King Robert the Wise,
Lucifer's minions transported directly into the Cathedral
district of Rhinegard led by one of the 'Daughters of the
Prince.' The people of Titanus concluded that this attack was a
Nephilim plot to assassinate the King. I am using this report
to disclose the true reasons for such an attack because I fear
no Titan will believe me. A comrade of mine going by the
name Francesco Angelino needed to penetrate the barrier of
Terminus Mundus in order to undertake an important mission
in Hell. When he returned from his mission, dark minions and
their leader chased him into our city mistaking my aura for
his. The resulting battle caused the King to be wounded but I
rallied the King's Cavalry to victory. The King's Cavalry had
their black cloaks smeared in red blood and became known as
the Scarlet Riders. The 'Daughter' leading the attack fled, and
has not been seen in Titanus since."

Eighth Report, Wilhelm von Angelhardt

Civilia was sitting on her throne clearly irritated. She tapped the steel
side of the throne very loudly as if she was intentionally trying to be
obnoxious. The room was empty save for two royal guards standing on
either side of the throne. Wilhelm knelt before her with his head bowed
down. Even though Civilia had a pretty good idea what he was going to
ask, certain formalities still had to be observed.

"Why did you request a private audience, Duke Wilhelm?"

"I must beg of you a favor, your Highness," pleaded Wilhelm.

"If you're willing to get down on a knee before me, I hesitate to grant such a favor."

"My lady, the time has come for me to retrieve your son from Kablisha imprisonment."

"You didn't need to beg my permission for that request. What's really going on?"

"I fear that it comes at an ill time; the City of Antiquity is under attack. Nephilim Commanders and their Demonkin slaves march to eradicate the Kablisha."

The queen hadn't anticipated this. Though Titanus had no love for a nation that abandoned them in the time of King Frederick, they had no desire to lose them as well.

"Can we do anything to help them?"

"My transport abilities are quite limited; we could not provide enough soldiers to aid them nor can we penetrate the barriers."

Civilia took a deep breath and closed her eyes.

"Wilhelm, the only hope for the Kablisha is my son. I doubt that you could drag him from such a desperate battle even if you tried. You are commanded to offer any assistance that he deems necessary."

Wilhelm shook his head in disbelief. He had not expected such a reaction from the queen, but in the end understood where she was coming from. Wilhelm reasoned that if anyone could save the Kablisha it would be Cedric.

"I will hold off notice that my son isn't dead until he is safely in these walls. I don't want to make any premature celebrations."

"I grant leave to your wisdom and prudence as always."

"I doubt you would go through all of this just to save the Kablisha. I know your opinions of them. However, you saved my son's life, so what favor must I grant you?"

Wilhelm stood and signaled to a dark corner of the room. Meekly walking out of the corner of the room, Nadia held her head down submissively. The two royal guards snapped to attention and pointed their spears forward. Civilia stood and drew her saber.

"You dare to ask the one request I cannot grant?" screamed Civilia. "This thing has a capital sentence in this country!"

"Your Highness, the identity that I have kept secret for these ten thousand revolutions will be compromised when I openly declare my loyalty against the Nephilim. Abaddon and all of my enemies will use anything they have against me."

"That woman is evil!"

"I will not deny what she did."

"My grandfather was a kind and gentle soul!"

"He was not the target of the attack, your Highness," cried Nadia. "It was a terrible mistake…one I have paid for dearly."

"I won't mince words with a liar and a coward."

"Then mince words with me, your Highness," interrupted Wilhelm. "I have kept certain information secret from the Titan Royal Family out of necessity. However, I cannot keep silent anymore. I was responsible for bringing Nadia here."

"What do you mean?" questioned Civilia.

"A companion of mine was given a terribly difficult mission to infiltrate Hell and bring someone out."

"I know the scriptures and traditions well, Wilhelm. No angel can rescue you from Hell once you give into despair."

"This was a special case," recounted Nadia. "She was one of us but didn't accept my father's will. Even if the midst of unspeakable torture and torment, she invoked hope over despair, and the bravest angel I've ever known came to her rescue, a true guardian angel."

"I helped him, your Highness, and because of this, Nadia led a capture squad into Titanus because they traced my signal instead of his. I am the one who put King Robert's life in danger. Do not punish Nadia for my sins."

Civilia was moved by Wilhelm's pity. She closed her eyes and shook for a second at the thought of begging to be released from Hell. The queen wondered what kind of an angel, even a guardian, would willingly partake in such a dangerous rescue mission and entertained the thought of recruiting him for the war effort.

"I believe you, Wilhelm, and Titanus knows the price we all must pay sometimes for aiding a fellow soldier," said Civilia. "No matter the target, she caused the death of many brave Titans and innocent civilians."

Nadia threw herself down on her knees. She took out a dagger and sliced the skin just above her breasts. It was just at the surface and not deep so a line of red blood simply trickled out. Civilia was stunned by this action, but understood what it meant. In the early rotations of the kingdom, an act of penance by a Titan was often accompanied by a wound above the heart. It was supposed to show contrition for past actions.

"My queen, I plead for sanctuary!" asked Nadia.

"Damn you!" shouted Civilia as she threw her hands up. "You planned this, Wilhelm! You know that the law states I cannot refuse a plea for sanctuary in these hallowed halls!"

"Actually, she did this herself," corrected Wilhelm. "I would never stage such a show for your Highness—it wouldn't be honorable."

"I knew she couldn't be trusted."

"I do not beg you to overlook my past because I can never undo what I was. However, I pose to you this question. Is it easier for the righteous to remain righteous, or for the unjust to continually seek redemption?"

"Nadia has provided countless services to the Divikin since her conversion, and there are also personal reasons."

"I do not wish to be bored with the details of your sex life," dismissed Civilia as she replaced her sword. "I cannot deny her plea for sanctuary; however, I will not allow her to remain in the castle. I will make arrangements to bring her to the Basilica and put her in the care of the bishop. Those are my terms."

"Your Highness, if you place me in the Basilica, I'll be powerless," pleaded Nadia.

Smiling deviously, Civilia had planned to accept Wilhelm's terms but the queen knew how to turn this to her advantage. She was not going to have this "thing" running around her castle. Besides, if she left the sanctity of the Cathedral, Nadia would have some serious problems with the rest of the Titan population.

"That's right. I never said I trusted you, but I will grant you sanctuary as I've given you my word."

"Well, that's okay, then."

"I thank you, your majesty. I fear I must depart now because I can risk no further delay for your son's sake. I will make this up to you."

"You already have, Wilhelm. Godspeed!"

Wilhelm nodded. He kissed Nadia goodbye and left the throne room. A relieved Nadia turned to thank Civilia.

"Your majesty, may I trouble you for a moment."

Civilia stood from her throne and started to leave.

"You may use the dining facilities if you're hungry and you may use the guest services if you chose to refresh yourself," announced Civilia. "An escort will arrive in some time to take you to the Cathedral and transport anything you may need. While you're my guest here, I don't want to see you and I certainly don't wish to speak with you. This is a country where actions prove worth; if you want my respect, I demand that you earn it."

A dejected Nadia stood alone with tears running down her eyes.

"Your Highness, allow me to fulfill one last duty to someone I love and then I will adhere to any sentence you have for me."

Surprised by the request, the queen stopped her gait. Civilia stared into the eyes of the demoness and her worst fears were confirmed. Losing her breath for a moment, she regained her resolve.

"Perform your task, Nadia, but the second it is over, I want you in the Basilica and dressed like a nun until the final battle begins."

Nadia threw herself at the queen's feet and thanked her.

Royal Castle, Deniva

"It was originally Wilhelm von Angelhardt who ordered the conquered Dwarves to forge the Legendary Weapons of Terminus Mundus for the Divikin and Elves: Ragnarok, the Gottin-Speer, Gungir, Enhancer, and the Artemis Bow. When the humans came to prominence in the West, the Dwarves forged weapons for them as well. Two sister weapons, the sword Excalibur and the Ivory Mace, were forged from the same sacred ore found deep in Lion's Peak. This allowed a human to use the gift of the Saint Saber Magic reserved only for Divikin. The Dwarves, however, botched the creation of the Ivory Mace and it was lost to Terminus Mundus in order to prevent its curse from spreading to an unfortunate warrior. Excalibur is still called the 'Sacred Blade' today."

Elf Scholar Demetrius

In the training center, Joshua and Valentine approached one another. Joshua was no longer the wide-eyed teenager of five revolutions ago. He had matured into a young man, and filled out his body nicely due to the intensive weight training program Ethan created for him. The young Paladin wore a custom plate mail designed for his large size over a chainmail shirt. He held a steel tower shield in his right hand. It was tall and bulky for a Paladin, but Cagius felt training with a larger shield would only make him stronger in battle. Valentine and Joshua both carried blunt metal blades in their fighting hands. Valentine opted for a buckler so he could still use his speed. Joshua would have intimidated most men, but that never bothered Valentine. The assassin just stared him right in the eye and looked like he was ready to go for the kill. The difference now was Joshua wasn't afraid of the assassin's tactics and realized he would see the same lust for battle in the eyes of his enemies. Walker and Cagius stood on the side of the room watching. Cagius had his arms crossed over his chest but Walker was on the alert in case he needed to intervene.

"I hope we don't have to restrain Valentine again," quipped Walker.

"He's the only man alive that scares me with a blunt blade in his hand," added Cagius.

"Well, boy, are you ready to finally take me down?" taunted Valentine as he licked his lips.

Joshua pushed his shield forward. He had finally accepted the fact that a Paladin was a defender first and an attacker second.

"Strike me if you can," goaded Joshua.

Valentine nodded and relished his position as the aggressor. The assassin struck at him with his blade but Joshua had gotten much better. The young Paladin anticipated every one of his teacher's moves and used his tools to defect each blow. Valentine used his buckler as a weapon, but Joshua was ready for it. He either leaned back to avoid the attack or simply dodged out of the way. The young Paladin waited for his opening after carefully studying his Master's techniques. Joshua spun and bulled Valentine over with his shield. The assassin was not one to be quickly vanquished and attempted to sweep Joshua's legs out. However the tall apprentice anticipated the attack and jumped back to avoid it. Valentine got back up and went on the attack again.

"It's difficult for me to stand and watch this," observed Cagius. "It's as if I see a ghost."

"He reminds you of Julius?" asked Walker.

"He carries many of his same natural abilities."

"But what?"

"Julius never used his shield as a ram or possessed the force necessary to make an attack out of it. Valentine has trained him well."

Joshua shifted his feet and waited for Valentine to come at him. As Valentine missed with a lunge he knew he had left himself in a precarious position. Joshua waited and swung hard with his shield. The maneuver disarmed Valentine when it struck his wrist. Joshua twirled his sword in his right hand and positioned it so it was at Valentine's throat. The assassin allowed himself a smile.

"The duel is mine!"

Cagius stared at Joshua and took full scope of what had happened. He knew that it wasn't Julius that he had learned his style from. The aggression of his attacks and his ability to adapt to the situation could only have come from studying Cedric's style. The Dragoon wondered how Joshua could have learned so much about the sword master, but that was another discussion. Valentine was beaming with pride at his apprentice's victory.

"Well done, boy," complimented the assassin.

Joshua took his sword away from Valentine's throat and let it hang at his side.

"Every time I've beaten you, we've moved to the next level," recounted Joshua. "I'm ready for anything else you have."

"There is nothing further I can teach you. I'm quite confident now that you can survive an encounter with an opponent in battle. My work here is done."

Cagius and Walker clapped appropriately. Joshua nodded approvingly as the two warriors approached him. Cagius gave him a hearty slap on the back.

"I think it's time you received your legacy."

"My legacy?"

"Yes."

The men walked over to a sealed chest in the room. Cagius took a key on a chain out from around his neck. He opened the chest and Joshua saw glowing objects from within.

"Eventually you will be formally given a knight's title and have permission to forge your own insignia on your plate mail," explained Cagius. "However, these treasures will increase your ability in battle."

Cagius took out the Sacred Shield first and handed it to Joshua.

"The Sacred Shield carried by the Paladin to defend the weak."

Cagius took out the War King's Crest that was affixed to a green cloak and Julius' war crown.

"The War King's Crest and War Crown are the marks of a Royal Defender."

Joshua looked confused by the award.

"Even if my father was Prince Julius Imperia, my mother was simply a lowly born maid," countered Joshua. "I do not have to right to such treasures."

"Your mother was no mere maid, Joshua," explained Walker. "She was noble born of the Elf House of Yannis. Felicia served an important role as a deep cover bodyguard of Queen Cassandra. Your mother gave up so much to fulfill that noble mission."

"Thus your mother and father could never have openly been together," interrupted Valentine. "It would have led to war."

Cagius took out Excalibur. Joshua looked at the sword in awe.

"I know that sword. It's my father's legendary weapon, Excalibur."

"A holy sword forged by the Dwarves—however, unlike its sister weapon, the Ivory Mace, it does not bind the user. This sword was forged to protect the human race and was gifted with the innate power to use Saint Saber Magic. While the blade has its limitations, it passed to my brother when it was deemed that he would be a defender of men as First Tribune of the Napolitan Imperium. This is a heavy honor and burden, Joshua, do you accept?"

Joshua bowed his head and took the sword with reverence. He drew it in a single motion and held the sword to his eyes. A blue light glowed on the blade of the sword as if testing Joshua's worthiness.

"The blade has accepted you as its owner," exclaimed Cagius. "Kneel!"

Joshua gave the sword back to his uncle and knelt down. Cagius took Excalibur and tapped both of his shoulders.

"In the absence of my father Caesar Constantine, I, Prince Cagius Imperia, heir to throne of Napolitan, and Legate of the Dragon Legion, knight thee, Joshua Imperia, to be given the title of Knight of the Dragon Heart. Rise, Paladin!"

Joshua rose and got his sword back from Cagius. He placed it back in the hilt.

"Thank you."

Joshua grabbed his uncle and hugged him. Cagius was struggling in a bear hug of his taller and stronger nephew. The sound of alarms began to ring throughout the castle.

"Now what?" asked Walker.

"It certainly isn't the alarm for a fire," commented a troubled Valentine. "It sounds like we're under attack."

Valentine's prognostication brought fear to his companions. The four ran from the training room up the stairs to the courtyard. Merchants and citizens were pouring into the castle courtyard in utter panic. They were screaming loudly for the protection of the margrave and concerned they were going to die. The four could see the nearby farmers and those that lived outside the castle city running into the gates as the Denivan mercenaries attempted to get them all to safety. Ethan stood in the middle of the crowd trying to give some hope and order, but many just stared at him gravely and demanded he do something. Robespierre and Selim were both in full battle gear and had their garrisons mustered. Walker went to his kinsman to try to get some explanation for the impending chaos.

"Robespierre, what's happened?" asked Walker.

"The outlying villagers spotted an army marching on the city," explained Robespierre. "I sent my own scouts out to confirm the reports. Walker, the Dark Elves are marching on us. They set up siege materials in the outlying farms and sure as hell look like they're ready for an all-out assault."

"In the past we had our problems with the creatures of the Underdark," interrupted Selim. "However, King Dennis brokered a peace deal with their queen, Alia Drathan, and their raiders haven't bothered us since."

"What are they doing here then?" asked Walker.

"I guess someone is going to have to find that out," volunteered Ethan.

The Denivan knight walked over to the stables and took the reins of his horse. Ethan took a deep breath and calmed his nerves before getting on the beast.

"Hang on, you speak only for the interests of Deniva," commented Robespierre. "I've got just as much a right to be out there as you."

"I must concur with my Acadian colleague," agreed Selim. "The Imperial Garrison must be represented as well."

"I can't guarantee your safety," retorted Ethan.

"What does that matter?" teased a laughing Selim. "As an Imperial Officer, if I die then the entire Empire goes to war."

"I would imagine that her Highness wishes to be kept alert to these events," added Walker. "Robespierre, do you have any closed helmets I could use?"

Robespierre nodded and directed Walker to put on the helmet and armor of one of his Knights. The closed helmet completely covered his identity. Ethan called out two of his mercenary guards to carry a white flag of truce and the banner of Deniva. Selim had two of his Janissaries carry the flags of the Empire while Walker bore the banner of the Order of the Lion for Robespierre. The delegation rode through the streets and out of the city gates as refugees flowed into the city. Cecilia had gotten word of the alarm late and was just leaving the castle. When she saw she was too late to stop Ethan, the Vanadis simply ran up the stone steps to the bridge above the castle gates. Malcolm followed her with his bow in hand and gracefully leapt up the stairs to take up position behind her. The elf archer was ready to draw at a moment's notice and probably could buy a few seconds for the delegation to escape.

"Malcolm, if you would be a dear, please make sure that my son doesn't wind up fatherless."

"I'll do what I can, Cecilia."

Cecilia took out her scopes while Malcolm used his keen eyesight to spot the same target. The Dark Elves stood behind their siege lines and were dug in for the long haul. Cecilia realized that this was simply a feint since she studied the tactics of the Drow in school. It would be an all-out rush on the city when they did decide to launch their assault. She spotted Alia standing at the front of the siege lines with two bodyguards and then turned her attention towards Rene Palias.

"Damn peacock!" uttered Cecilia. "Who let you out of your cage?"

"You don't suppose Abaddon has anything to do with this?" suggested Malcolm.

"It has to be. We deceived ourselves into believing we'd be safe here in Deniva forever."

"What are we going to do? Can we risk moving her?"

"I don't know. We'd better be certain first."

Ethan and his delegation approached the middle area between the Dark Elf siege lines and the city of Deniva. He took the white truce banner and put it down in front of him. Alia got into her spider drawn chariot with Palias. Focusing his gaze past the chariot, Walker counted two hundred and fifty cuirassiers serving as the personal guard of the peacock. The sight of the coming chariot absolutely revolted Ethan who never liked the crawly ones.

"I hate spiders!" exclaimed Ethan to the humor of his comrades.

The spiders pulled up short when the nerves of the horses begin to tick up. However, the delegations were certainly close enough to make out what they were saying to one another. Palias locked eyes with Robespierre and the two looked at one another with great animosity.

"Oh, this is rich!" commented Palias. "One of the little bastards is looking to play war. Where is Lord Delan?"

"I fear the captain had been placed under arrest," responded Robespierre. "It's a very serious crime to engage in treason against your king."

"Acadians should stand with Central Acadia!"

"Now is not the time to hash out the internal politics of your country. I am Alia Drathan, High Priestess and Queen of the Dark Elves of the Underdark. I believe your party knows my War Master Rene Palias of Central Acadia."

"I am Ethan de-Milly, son of Margrave Dennis, the ruler of the border province of Deniva. As per the Treaty of Deniva, I would introduce the Garrison Commander of the Alliance Lord Captain Jean-Luc Robespierre and the Imperial Pasha Ataturk Selim. I speak in the name of my father and must ask why you unilaterally broke our treaty."

"You do deserve an explanation. I fear that a benefactor has made me an offer that only a fool could refuse. Unfortunately that means breaking all agreements and setting up the siege lines you see before you. We would be swarming you as we speak if not for the generous offer of our benefactor."

"Since you have employed Rene Palias as your war master, I can only assume that such an offer comes from Maximilian Luminas."

"We come on behalf of our Lord Abaddon. Our master has need of one of the Denivan exiles, and I am under orders to deliver Princess Cassandra Acadia to him at once."

"We hold no Acadian princess in our city."

"Don't be coy with me, Lord de-Milly, we know she is protected by your city walls. If you fail to deliver her to our lines by sunset, my people will attack your city and destroy every last living being. Once you return to your castle, no one will be allowed to leave the city save for the princess. If they do, they will be killed immediately."

"You don't understand. There is no princess in this city, but the queen of Central Acadia herself. As a margrave, my father has no authority to hand over one of the sovereign lords of our border province. I know that you have effectively cut off the attack of one of our allies by that infernal shield, but we are protected by the Empire as well. You wouldn't dare risk bringing their wrath upon you."

"Sultan Khan has great interest in the financial prosperity of Deniva; one communication and the standing garrison at Edenia will be here well before nightfall," noted Selim.

"I wouldn't be so sure, Selim," countered Palias. "I am to relay to you this message: a pact of non-aggression has been signed between the Empire and Central Acadia. You are to lead your garrison and imperial citizens out of Deniva immediately to travel to Edenia. The sultan wishes that none of his people be harmed in this attack."

"You lie!" ejected a dumbfounded Selim.

Palias took out a copy of the treaty that Luminas and Khan had signed. He handed it to Selim to review. Ethan's concern grew.

"Is what he said true?" asked Ethan.

"This is Sultan Khan's signature," nodded Selim. "I'm sorry, Ethan, but I have no right to be here."

Selim turned on his horse and started to slowly ride back to castle. Ethan focused his attention back on Alia.

"I will convey your message to my father," said Ethan. "I am sure that you will receive an answer soon."

Palias laughed at Walker and Robespierre as they turned around. Ethan was mumbling to himself on the way back. He knew the castle was not suited to withstand a direct siege and there was no doubt that the merchants would quickly revoke the hospitality shown their guests with an army standing outside their gates. There was no escape and Ethan didn't have enough men to provide a proper defense. Ethan moved with speed towards the gate and his companions could sense his apprehension. The only comfort for the Deniva knight was when he stared up at the castle gate and spotted his wife tightly holding onto her spear. He knew that if he was going to make a last stand, he'd have at least one person standing with him. When the delegation passed, he pulled the guards aside.

"Allow no one to pass through the gates save for Selim and his company; it's too dangerous for any civilians to be outside now."

Those in earshot panicked at the sound of this, but Ethan wouldn't allow himself to be stopped by the masses grabbing at him. The knight simply pushed his way to the castle courtyard. Walker and Robespierre dismounted once the crowd passed. Cagius and Valentine came over to get some more information.

"What's going on?" asked Cagius.

"We've been ratted out, boys," commented Walker. "Palias is standing at the command of a hundred thousand Dark Elves and demanding that we turn over Cassie immediately."

"This is why I hate the first rotation of the lunar cycle," quipped Valentine.

"Well, it's not going to be easy getting out of this one," joked Cagius sarcastically. "Any chance for an escape?"

"Robespierre spotted snipers all around the wall; they'll be on top of us in no time if we tried to break through," suggested Walker.

"What about the Empire?" asked Valentine. "I'm sure Sultan Khan is not going to be happy if his primary source of income is cut off."

"Apparently Luminas has come to some agreement with Khan in order to attack Deniva."

"This is bad; if he knew this was happening Christian would have given us some warning."

"Then we have to assume Christian and Colin have been cut off," surmised Cagius. "Or worse..."

"I think once Ethan delivers those terms to Margrave Dennis and the merchant class, we're going to wear out our welcome," assumed Valentine as he licked his lips. "Give me twenty minutes, and be ready to run."

"What the hell are you talking about?"

"I'm the most expendable of all of us. I'll hit the camp and take out Palias. The resulting chaos should be enough to get the queen out of the city."

"No one is going to sacrifice anything yet! We'd better get inside before they start eating Ethan alive."

The men walked back into the reception room of the castle. There was an overflow of people trying to get into the throne room and the remainder had shoved their way into the outer rooms. Ethan's words to his father had the impact the others had expected. Fear and panic had taken hold, justifying the fears of the Alliance exiles. There was a lot of yelling going on and Dennis was slumped on his throne.

"This is insane!" screamed one of the merchants. "We never asked for any of this."

"We offered them our hospitality," said another. "We can't abandon them."

"Without the Empire, no one is going to defend us," said the first merchant. "We can't rely on the Alliance. I agree with you on hospitality, but we can't hide them here."

"I knew if we let political prisoners in here this would happen," commented a third merchant.

The yelling and screaming had grown out of control. Dennis decided that he finally had enough and called for Ethan.

"Son, if you'd please," requested Dennis.

"Of course, Dad!" said Ethan with a smile.

The Denivan knight drew his axe and struck the floor. The impact of the legendary weapon caused the marble floor to crack and the sound caused a deafening silence in the room. Dennis rose to speak and Henrietta took his right arm to support him.

"My family was given a sacred responsibility. We were named Margrave of a border province by the Treaty of Titanus and the Empire," announced Dennis. "I am charged with her defense and her safety. However, my duty is not simply to this city, but to its overlords as well. I no sooner would have the authority to hand over the Queen of Central Acadia than I would to hand over the Sultan of the Chinotal Empire..."

Dennis was interrupted when Cassandra entered the room in a light blue and white gown with the Royal Crown fixed atop her head. She knew well the tradition that when facing judgment she should endeavor to look her best. While there was concern in her eyes, it was clear that she had made a decision. The other exiles stood with her like retainers. Determination filled their faces and they were prepared for a final stand. Despite their justified concerns, those gathered in the room could not help but feel sorrow for the young Queen and the misery which followed her. Dennis was horrified by this display and was not prepared to go down that road.

"Your Highness, please do not fear that Deniva would ever disregard the sacredness of hospitality. We gave you the tokens and will stand by them to our end."

"There is no need, Margrave Dennis," started Cassandra. "I have five thousand troops at my disposal and some of the finest warriors in the world. We'll make our stand against the Dark Elves and spare the good people who sacrificed so much to keep us safe and welcome these long five revolutions."

"Your Highness, I would never imply..."

"I'm far too important a commodity in this war to sacrifice myself, but I am willing to take a stand—and if necessary, die—for what I believe in," said Cassandra. "Your people have endured far too many sacrifices for us already. I will not ask for their lives."

Cecilia was the first step forward with her spear and Amuro followed with her sword. One by one the royals came forward with their weapons raised. Robespierre and his Knights soon followed. The Denivans were awed by the display of courage. Many had expected the Queen to beg for use of the walls but never to fight on open ground. The hearts and minds of the populace were swayed.

"I cannot allow this," pronounced Dennis. "As I said, this is my responsibility, the Margrave my family has built. To hell with the Empire if they refuse to defend us, all of the resources of this city are at your command, your Highness."

"Father, we have extremely limited resources," commented Ethan. "We may have about a thousand battle-ready mercenaries along with the Alliance garrison. Even if we had the Imperial garrison we'd be vastly outnumbered. While our walls would easily break the first few waves of Drow attacks, they are not designed to maintain a siege for long. However, if it is your will to defend this city, I will lead its defense."

A messenger ran into the room out of breath. His appearance broke the rising tension.

"Your majesty, we've spotted an army approaching from the southeast."

"Are they friend or foe?" asked Ethan.

"Lord DeVries is leading them with a red-headed she-elf at his side."

The warriors ran for the gates of the city as merchants crowded the windows. They could see turmoil breaking out in the Dark Elf encampment at the appearance of the new army. Palias got up on a rock and put a pair of scopes to his eyes. He spotted the snipers that they had positioned in the areas around the city lying dead with arrows in their chests. Wood Elves were busy accumulating the arrows from their bodies. Christian, Rosa, and Colin headed to the front gates of the city deliberately crossing the Dark Elf encampment to show their numbers. Alia rode up to Palias in her chariot and spotted the concern in his face.

"Why have the Wood Elves come to defend Deniva?" demanded Alia.

"The Wood Elves are allied vassals of Titanus," explained Palias. "DeVries must have called them in to fight for Deniva."

"Our surrender ruse will not work now that they have an army."

"Then this will be a great rotation; we'll take care of all of our problems in one fell swoop. Call back your snipers; we can't risk losing any more unnecessarily before the battle."

"But General Palias, if we stop spying on the posterns, there is likely to be an escape."

"DeVries didn't bring an army here just to escape. When the sun sets, we'll storm their gates."

Christian dismounted to the cheering populace of Deniva. Many of the Wood Elves found themselves being embraced and kissed by citizens as they entered. Unfortunately, many of them felt that the appearance of another army would simply drive the Dark Elves from the fields. The exiles knew better, but at least they knew they had a fighting chance. Cecilia was the first to approach Christian. He gave her a quick salute and she smiled when she answered it.

"When the Dark Elves arrived with the news from the Empire, we feared for you both. I'm glad that was premature."

"It wasn't easy getting out of there, your Excellency. I knew that our soldiers would be coming up short so I made sure I called in some reinforcements to aid us."

Christian helped Rosa down from his mount. She walked forward to Cecilia and curtsied. The Wood Elves snapped into formation and saluted her in unison.

"Princess Cecilia Rhone, I, Rosa Landon, leader of the Wood Elf nation, have come to fulfill our oath of fealty to the Kingdom of Titanus. My people and I are willing to fight and die under your command."

"We are honored to have you."

Cecilia answered the salute before walking over and kissing Rosa on the cheek. The elf leader smiled and patted the Titan princess on her shoulder. Cecilia let go and turned back to Dennis.

"Margrave Dennis, the Kingdom of Titanus will honor the treaty in lieu of the Empire's treachery. We will defend the margrave from this Drow threat!"

The citizens threw their arms up and cheered as tears came to Dennis' eyes. Ethan walked over to Amuro who was busy scratching some notes down on a piece of paper. She stared at one part of the wall and made an uncomfortable face.

"I guess if you're going to treat this as a military operation, you're still the commanding marshal of the Alliance Army," commented Ethan.

"I don't really want to pull rank on you in your own city, Ethan, but experience prevails over heart here. I think you'd better get your father. He's not going to like what I have to say."

The commanders of the Wood Elf forces left with the royals and the high-ranking merchants. They marched slowly toward the courtyard of the castle where King Dennis and the leading members of his court were standing. Dennis had the chief news agencies present in the city so he could address the citizens of his city. A nervous populace was huddled around every television and radio they could find. Many were holding onto each other in utter fear and wondered what this bizarre elf army could do for them. Ethan walked over to his father and whispered something into his ear. The king seemed distressed at first but turned to Amuro with resignation.

"My son informs me that in our situation you are to serve as our military commander," said Dennis. "I may be disappointed that my son is not going to lead us, but your reputation is well-earned. What do you need, marshal?"

"The walls are aesthetically pleasing and difficult to scale, but there's nowhere to station our archers," explained Amuro. "It looks like we're going to have to set up barriers along the city corridor. I'm going to need to use your city and the castle as our defense."

The citizens gasped in horror at this thought. They weren't fighters and had no idea how they could withstand such an assault.

"I feared you would say that," answered Dennis.

"The rear posterns prevent entry for the Dark Elves; they are going to have to come through the main gate," pronounced Amuro. "Vice-Marshal Walker is quite familiar with Palias' battle tactics and they always involve a massive swarming attack without giving the enemy a chance for respite. This can work to our advantage. In order to coordinate a massive retreat of our size, only certain groups of people can retreat through the rear posterns at a time."

The grumbles of the citizenry suddenly turned to one of confusion. They had expected a call to take up arms and never dreamed they would be asked to flee.

"I don't understand, marshal," commented Dennis. "Why are we running?"

"The people of Deniva have no reason to waste their lives in this war. They never asked for this when they graciously took us in as refugees. I would never dream of asking them to sacrifice their lives in such a reckless and desperate battle. The armies will defend the city and hold off the enemy as long as we can. This way the civilians can make it to the safety of Edenia. Abaddon's hand will have grown far indeed if the Dark Elves dare pursue you into the Empire. Besides, we know who that bastard really wants. We'll retreat in waves with priority going to weakest members of the city first."

If Amuro ever wanted to run for Emperor this was the time. The citizens of Deniva fully endorsed her plan through their cheers and clapping. The she-elf marshal did have a caveat to her plan that she still had to explain. The defense of Deniva wasn't going to be easy and she needed every strong citizen she could find to work to the last minute. Amuro took her sword out and began to mark a poor representation of the city of Deniva in the sand. Cecilia stared at this with an irritated look on her face. After a few minutes of Amuro's clumsy drawings, she screamed and took a small laptop out of her riding pack. It brought up a three-dimensional representation of the city and enemy positions. Marshal Jenitzen smiled and knew that this was going to help make her point much better.

"Before we begin our retreat, I'm going to need your help. I need every able-bodied person to start gathering heavy items: wood, metal, carts, sandbags. We need everything we can use to build strong barricades throughout the city. The idea is to continually funnel the larger attacking force into our strength. Our army is range heavy and it's going to be difficult to stand toe-to-toe with an attacking melee force for too long. I propose three such barricades with a final defense point set in the castle."

Amuro used a touchscreen to show the four points in the city she wanted to use as defense points. The first point was only a few meters from the main wall. The second point retreated midway between the wall and the merchant's circle. The third point was at the merchant's circle and the last point of defense was the castle wall itself.

"The castle walls have the best defensibility for a last stand. It will also give us the most time necessary to complete the retreat. I have pre-determined the order of retreat for every citizen in this city. My sister Saria will coordinate the waves. If you try to use force or bribery to hasten your retreat, I'll kill you myself. I affirm to the populace of Deniva, I will be dead before a citizen of this city fails to get out. We'll be sending provisions with you, but do not burden yourself with anything that will weigh you down. You must move quickly! Do you object, margrave?"

"Our lives are in your hand, marshal," announced the margrave. "If it is any comfort to the citizens of the Castellan, know that I will remain until the last retreating wave."

"Since I have your blessing for the defense, I, Princess Amuro Jenitzen of Evengard as Marshal of the Allied Forces of Deniva, declare martial law. I name Princess Cecilia Rhone of Titanus and Prince Ethan de-Milly of Deniva as my Vice-Marshals. Prince Cagius Imperia, Lord Jonathan Walker, Lord Jean-Luc Robespierre, and Lord Christian DeVries will complete the command staff of senior officers. Cavalry units will leave their mounts in the stable or they will be used in the retreat. Knights and heavy mercenaries will take up positions in front of the archers. You'll serve as their shields in the coming battle. I'm sending each of you a list with the officers, soldiers, and civilians under your command. Your duty is to work on the barriers until the great horn sounds. When that happens drop what you're doing and prepare yourselves for battle. Do not exhaust yourself on the barricades; food and water will be brought to you regularly. The civilians are going to have to carry the weight of building the defenses because we simply must have every able-bodied person ready for the fight. It's not the time to be a hero! Stay fed and hydrated. We're burning daylight, people! Let's do this!"

Alerts went to everyone in the city. Those scheduled to work grabbed whatever they could carry to form a barrier. Children and the elderly went to the hospitals and churches where they aided those too weak to move to the retreat preparation areas located at the posterns behind the castle. Soldiers took off their gear and armor in order to aid with the preparation of the defenses. Selim stood outside the imperial barracks with a sour look on his face. He watched merchants and civilians gathering whatever they could for the barricades. The soldiers behind him took down the imperial standard and flags. An Imperial Mamluke rode over to Selim and saluted him.

"We've assembled the whole army and are ready to march out. When you're ready, Pasha, we can pull out."

Selim ignored his subordinate for a moment. He instead focused on Ethan dragging a cart full of equipment for use in the barriers. Ethan turned his gaze and stopped.

"Selim, what are you doing?" asked Ethan. "You've got to get your troops out of here so we can barricade the gate."

"Deniva has been my home for far too long," retorted an embarrassed Selim.

The Pasha looked down at the imperial insignia on his uniform. Selim had never doubted the wisdom of his sultan before, but his own sense of honor was going to get the better of him. He remembered the kindness and rewards shown to him by Margrave Dennis time after time. There was no way Selim was going to leave his home. He got off of his horse and turned to his troops.

"I know that you have served many revolutions under my command. However, I cannot retreat from this city in its hour of need. There is no oath that binds you to my next action. Our sultan has condemned the Margrave of Deniva, but I can't allow my home for the last twenty-five revolutions to fall so easily. Those of you that wish may stay with me and defend it. If not, please ride safely back to the Empire and may the Saints watch over you. Please give the sultan my reasons for my final act of disobedience."

The Imperial vice-captain got off of his horse and stepped forward. There were many in the garrison who believed he was ready to ask him to surrender himself. However the vice-captain simply saluted his superior officer.

"I think I speak for us all when I say that we are proud to defend this city with you, Pasha."

"You heard that wretched elf—let's get to work."

The Imperials joined in the work. Selim grabbed onto the cart Ethan was pulling. The two shared a laugh with one another and got to work. Amuro watched it all, perched on the castle wall with a pair of scopes. She smiled at the coming together of sworn enemies. Saria approached her sister nervously. She shuffled her feet and twitched her shoulders as Amuro turned to her.

"Sister, are you sure?" asked Saria. "I don't know if I can handle this responsibility."

Amuro took her by the shoulders and spotted the lie in her eyes right away.

"You never could lie to me! Saria, this isn't combat training! This is war! I know you've trained hard and you're a good fighter but I can't afford any amateurs. Every link in the chain must be strong."

"I don't want to leave you to fight here alone," pouted Saria.

"Don't look so depressed, you have an extremely important mission! Keep that bright smile of yours shining because the retreating waves are going to need hope."

Saria worked hard to put the most beautiful smile on her face. Amuro thought to herself that there was no way to be in a bad mood seeing it.

"That's the annoyingly cheerful smile I was looking for! Now go and do as I tell you, I am your commanding officer and older sister, after all."

"Just be careful, sis," cried Saria as she kissed Amuro on the forehead.

"I've faced worse odds than this; we're going to be just fine!"

Saria went back to the castle and started to comfort the young and elderly who were in the first retreating wave. Amuro's smile left her face and a serious countenance overtook it. Malcolm was behind her.

"I don't think you should have lied to her," commented Malcolm.

"Do you want me to mope around here knowing we don't have a chance? Yes, Malcolm, I know. This city is going to serve as the mausoleum for Marshal Amuro Jenitzen and her entire army."

"Even with the elves, we're still vastly outnumbered. It may take us to the last man just to make sure one wave can retreat, let alone the whole city. What if our calculations are right and we can't hold them?"

"Then we all better pray really hard!"

"We used up our allotted miracle when he died saving us in Castle Acadia."

Amuro got choked up and cried. Malcolm put his arm around her shoulder to comfort her.

"I won't let Abaddon take her, Malcolm. Cedric gave everything to keep her safe and I will not do anything less. I just don't believe it. Five revolutions ago we were dead, and yet, during that rotation...when Thomas was born, I felt something. I can't explain it, but it was like a small fire at first that built up to a wildfire spreading everywhere. Couldn't you feel it?"

"I felt power that rotation. However, it wasn't a power of destruction."

"Exactly. It was for good. I know that feeling well; it's the same feeling I would get when I rode into battle with Cedric and Julius, a true feeling of invincibility. I guess the Father kept me alive at Verian so I could save these people tonight. All right, I had my cry. Get back to work, Malcolm!"

"No 'sweetheart' this time?"

"The time for jokes is over!"

Christian caught the attention of the two when he cleared his throat.

"I hope I'm not interrupting anything," teased Christian.

Amuro shuttled Malcolm away and turned to Christian.

"I don't know how you managed to get us an army, Christian, but I'm sure glad you did."

"You can show me some appreciation by granting me a little favor."

"What?"

"I think I might have a way of overcoming some of our defensive deficiencies. However, it's going to involve tunneling under one of the walls."

"I can't wait to hear this idea."

The two walked off. Struggling to lift a sandbag onto one of the carts, the young prince Thomas felt another hand working on it to ease the burden.

"What are you doing?" asked his mother.

"I'm aiding in the defense of the city as ordered by the marshal."

"Get ready to get out of here; you're leaving with the first retreating wave."

"But Mom!"

"No arguments! You're a Titan—you have to learn to grin and bear it! There may come a rotation when you are going to have to avenge what happened here! It's a burden, but it's the way we are."

"We can still be ruthless if you let us!"

Cecilia smiled and got down on one knee. She hugged and kissed her son. Tears were coming down from her eyes.

"Pray that we will see each other again. I need you to remember that you might be the only heir to the throne, so you're going to have to be extra careful."

"I will, Mama."

"Now off with you, and say goodbye to your father."

"Yes, Mom."

Thomas went on his way.

Bishop's Residence, City of Antiquity

"Meanwhile, the Lord said: Do not fear them, for I have delivered them into your power. Not one of them will be able to withstand you. And when the General made his surprise attack upon them after an all-night march from Gilgal the Lord threw them into disorder before him. The Elves inflicted a great slaughter on them at Gilgal and followed them down the old forest paths, harassing them as far as Azekah and Makkedah."

The Ancient Scriptures, Book of the General 10:7-10

Cedric was dressed in his under tunics, chainmail, and boots. On his knees praying, the sword master ended his pleas with a large and deliberate sign of the cross. Time being of the essence, he quickly suited himself in his plate mail and riding cloak. Rapping on the door to announce his presence, Wilhelm entered the room and bowed deeply before his dressing prince.

"My lord, I am bound to ask, what you are doing?"

"For every action there is a season. I've been away from this all far too long, Wilhelm. I believe that now is our time."

"You intend to fight for the Kablisha?"

"Argus doesn't stand a chance unless I take command."

"You're not wrong. Only with your tactics can they defeat this darkness."

Cedric took the time to put on his paladin gauntlets as Wilhelm studied his former pupil. He had seen this sign of thoroughness many times before, and for a second he felt sorry for the Nephilim and demonkin raiding the Kablisha territory. They didn't know the storm that was coming for them.

"You'd better get ready yourself," commanded Cedric.

"So I'm drafted now? You're quite taken by these people."

"I must confess that it really doesn't matter where the next battle took place. I am sick and tired of being on the defensive in this war. I want that fallen angel's head mounted on my wall before the end of this!"

Wilhelm clicked his heels together and bowed to Cedric Rhone. He held up his right hand and called forth a halo. It covered his arms, body, and finally his head, calling forth his armor. Concealing his weapons and wings temporarily, the fallen angel did not suffer the poison running through his body. Cedric put Ragnarok over his back, his new crossbow on his hip, and grabbed his repaired Rising Moon Helmet, which he kept under his arm.

"I appreciate this, Wilhelm."

"It's time we make a stand against these bastards. If we keep retreating, we'll never win anything. You have to confront evil when it rears its head."

"You don't confront evil, Wilhelm, you destroy it!"

"Always the same! Besides, your mother put me under orders to back up whatever actions you saw fit."

The two laughed as they went to join the other Kablisha warriors. Argus looked at the approaching warriors with disappointment.

"Dammit, Wilhelm, you were supposed to talk some sense into him," screamed Argus.

"Why are you so eager to die, friend?" asked Wilhelm.

"I will not fail my mission."

"You won't, but we're fighting for the survival of your people, not simply to let one person go free," countered Cedric. "You need all the help you can get. What's the position of the enemy?"

"Since I can't scare you away and I dare not challenge you, we found them encamped at the Gilgal crossing," explained Argus. "My warriors and I will set up an ambush when they make their push for the city. Demonkin have very low morale; if we kill enough of them they may run and we'll only have the Nephilim to deal with."

"Did you say Gilgal?" recounted Cedric as he licked his lips.

"Yes, it's what the elders of our people call it."

"I know that name! Get me the scriptures!"

"Well, we need all the prayers we can get," teased Quinn.

A Kablisha soldier handed him a copy of the scriptures. As Cedric started to read it, he noticed it only contained the Gospels and letters.

"No, I need the Ancient Scriptures. Please hurry."

"The Ancient Scriptures?" asked one the warriors. "What good will that do? We're taught most of the stories in there are myths and allegories."

"Myth was once history! I'm telling you there's something in there!"

Mesmara searched her pack and found a copy. She handed it over to Cedric though she had no idea what the Titan prince was thinking. Leafing through the pages, the sword master scanned the text, slapping the book at the passage he was looking for.

"At Gilgal there was a secret path that the general used to sneak his army behind the enemy and get in position for a strike at first light. The enemy was caught completely by surprise and it was a slaughter. If we find the path described in the scriptures, we get behind their lines!"

"We don't have enough soldiers for a raid," claimed Argus.

"We don't need the extra soldiers," commented Wilhelm. "Cedric, if you turn to the book of the Judges, you'll find an elf judge faced a similar problem. Despite the fact we're vastly outnumbered, a small elite force could easily sack the camp. In their arrogance, the Nephilim will never expect an ambush."

"It's better than my plan," acknowledged Argus as he wiped the sweat from his face. "If we're going to die anyway, I'd rather die on the offensive."

"We'll move in three teams. One hundred soldiers with me on the right flank, one hundred soldiers with Argus on the left, the last group with Wilhelm. After we cross the forest path of Gilgal, we'll break into those positions. Everybody got it?"

The Kablisha warriors didn't know what to think. Many weren't prepared to defy Argus and chose instead to defer to his judgment. Argus could see this happening and decided to cast his lot with the Titan prince.

"Yes, sir," said Argus.

Quinn and Mesmara led the warriors behind them in a series of cheers giving full support to their new temporary commanding officer. Pushing through the troops, Florence had dressed herself in a field cleric's uniform complete with a small silver mace and many packs of potions. Though he wanted to object, the sword master couldn't shake the feeling that the beautiful cleric's services may be needed before this was over. He allowed her to stay with the troop, and Florence was overjoyed.

"Double time!" ordered Cedric. "Let's find the general's path."

The defending force left the safety of the city and headed for the cover of the forest. Argus walked next to Cedric as they made their trek through the forest's path.

"It's going to be dark soon, Cedric," suggested Argus. "I don't see how we're going to able to find this mystery path of yours without torches."

"If we light torches we'll give away our position," replied Cedric.

"We can't go stumbling around here in the dark!"

"Don't worry, I'm going to find us some help."

Argus was puzzled by Cedric's last statement. The Titan prince approached a patch of flowers on the forest floor. He knelt down to the patch and began to scan each bud with his eyes. He smiled and gently rocked one in the middle. An annoyed pixie emerged from the flower bud wearing a small green tunic. She had short green hair and big blue eyes. The pixie fluttered up towards Cedric.

"You big meanie!" chided the pixie. "What's your problem?"

"I need the help of the forest," pleaded Cedric. "I'm looking for the secret path near the Gilgal Crossing."

"Sure, I know of that. Why?"

"An army of demonkin has entered the forest; they've made their encampment there."

The pixie's face filled with fear.

"Don't worry, little one," assured Cedric. "I've got a plan, but we've got to get as many of your friends as possible to help us."

"No problem!" boasted the pixie. "Per the alliance with the sylphs, we are at your beck and call, Milord."

The pixie let out three high-pitched whistles. The Kablisha Warriors stared in awe as the Fae of the Forest rose from the plant life, water, and earth around them. Even Wilhelm couldn't believe the respect his prince received from the beings of Terminus Mundus.

"Follow us!" cried the pixie.

The Fae led the warriors through back trails along the forest. Branches magically receded when the warriors came upon them and hidden trails cleared. After two thousand meters, Cedric slowed his party. He could spot campfires in the distance and knew that the Fae had led them right behind the enemy. The Titan prince smiled as he knew once again God had delivered his enemies to him.

CITY OF DENIVA, TWILIGHT

"The Elves are strong and proud warriors. They have won
countless battles where the odds were against them. However,
there is one jinx that they have never been able to break. No
Elf Commander has ever successfully led a defense of a city
under Siege. Not even Brooke Run or the City of Antiquity are
immune to this jinx. I don't care how decorated the Commander
is, never trust an Elf to defend a city."

General James Darius

The final hours of daylight could be seen in the distant horizon. In a
matter of hours, the citizens of Deniva had turned their merchant city
into a fortress. Barricades laden with traps were set up at every street,
alley, and corner not on the main road. Pikes were placed in front of these
barricades as well to dissuade the Dark Elves from tampering with them.
They were also placed all around the walls so any Drow who jumped from
the wall would suffer instant death. The main door to the city was braced
with the heaviest beams and timber available. Calderon even donated the
marble sculpture on top of his building to the door's defense. Civilians
placed the finishing touches on the established chokepoints with every
piece of furniture, good, or equipment they could find. Amuro walked over
to the last of the civilians, already dressed in her armor. She smiled at them
and put her hands on the shoulder of one of them.

"You've done more than I could have ever asked of you," thanked
Amuro. "You need to see to the safety of yourselves and your families.
This is our battle now."

The civilians put their final loads in place and ran for the back posterns.
Many passed Amuro with the words "good luck" and "thank you." Calderon

looked at Cagius and gave him a "give them hell" look while pumping his fist. Cagius tapped his spear to his helmet in salute. Amuro's defense force was stationed between two six-story buildings where the street was at its widest. Wooden stakes lined the ground in front of a heavy infantry front. This line consisted of the heavy-armored Knights of the Order of the Lion and Imperial Mamelukes. Nordice mercenary pikeman and Imperial Janissaries covered the flanks. Cecilia, Cagius, Joshua, Walker, Valentine, Christian, Colin, and Hippolyte commanded the front lines. The Wood Elf archers took position on the higher ground in the rear. Malcolm was in the direct middle of this unit and assumed full command over his woodland cousins. Rosa stood behind this unit with a bow in her hand guarding Cassandra. Amuro had made Cassandra don a vanadium breastplate over her sorceress uniform for extra protection in the battle. Gerard had taken two units of archers on top of the six-story buildings. Barricades had been set up to allow for extra protection while they were sniping. Hippolyte had convinced her sister to take up position with these archers above the fray. On the other side of the city, Saria coordinated the organized retreat. There were still four caravans of civilians she needed to clear. The beautiful high elf stared at the setting sun and knew she was running out of time. The prior caravans had proceeded without incident. Wood Elf snipers kept any Dark Elves from harassing the caravans and Palias had decided hours ago it was not worth losing any troops chasing the sick and elderly.

Amuro walked back to her position in the center of her defensive positions. Her elf hearing could pick up the sound of heavy breathing among the soldiers in her command. Many started to wipe the sweat beading up from their brows and the she-elf Marshal decided it was time for an inspirational speech. Amuro allowed herself one last deep breath.

"I know none of you want to be here," teased Amuro. "I know you want to hear me babble even less so I'll make this quick. In a matter of moments this city is going to be swarming with Dark Elves. They are reckless in battle and will incorporate suicidal attacks to gain an advantage. Our task is to give the civilians enough time to escape to the Kaiser Pass. We've got to be able to hold this city until first light tomorrow, only then can we order a general retreat. For now, we must kill whatever comes over those walls. I could keep going but there's really only one thing left to say… fight for your lives!"

Everyone chuckled as intended by the brief moment of levity.

"Now stay cool, there'll be plenty of time for panicking when the fighting starts," ordered Amuro.

Christian walked from his position to where Rosa was standing. She smiled as he approached.

"You know what you have to do," said Christian.

"Don't worry, I'll stay with Cassandra as long as I can," replied Rosa. "It's funny that Amuro hasn't mentioned the 'jinx' to the defenders yet."

"As daylight lingered, Cecilia pondered whether or not she should relieve Amuro and assume command. The Titans have a much better track record in these cases. However, she didn't want to embarrass her friend. I guess that jinx will have to be broken some time."

"Yeah. Good luck, and stay safe."

Rosa gave him a quick peck. Cassandra tapped her on the shoulder.

"What jinx?" asked Cassandra.

"It's not really important, your Highness. You see, no elf commander has ever successfully defended a city against an attacking force."

"Wait a second, what about Hayden Marisol at the City of Antiquity?"

"Unfortunately, your Highness, the true history of the battle shows the city was completely breeched and overrun. The elves and Kablisha had fled the city and were only saved by Ulyssess' timely arrival."

Cassandra's face completely sunk at the revelation. She stared intently at Amuro who tried to maintain her cheerful disposition. On the other side of the walls, Dark Elf swordsman began to form ranks behind banners. Female Drow battlemages and archers filled in behind them. Alia's spider-drawn chariot made its way to the front of these lines while Palias rode a horse next to her. Two giant spiders began to draw a siege tower towards one of the walls. Palias stared at the setting sun with great anticipation.

"Well I guess those bastards are going to fight it out after all." said Palias as he turned to Alia. "If she was coming out, she would have done so by now. Order all of your divisions forward!"

"Don't you think we should leave some in reserve?" requested Alia. "Perhaps if we were to attack in waves instead…"

"They have a small defense force that's based mostly on ranged weaponry. We need to overwhelm them with massive amounts of troops to gain a quick advantage. My cuirassiers can finish the rest."

"Abaddon did place you in command. We will do as you say."

"And remember, Cassandra Acadia must be taken alive!"

"My people are well aware of this. What of the other royals?"

"Kill them all! This war ends here!"

Alia nodded and raised a war baton high in the air. The Dark Elves squatted into a running stance with swords in their teeth. The echoes of warriors drawing their swords sent a chill through the defenders behind the walls. Standing among the troops with the banner of Deniva held high, Father Giovanello offered a final blessing for all the troops.

"O God, I beseech You, watch over those exposed to the horror of war, and the spiritual dangers of a soldier's life. Give them such a strong faith that no human respect may ever lead them to deny it, nor fear ever to practice it. By Your grace, O God, fortify them against the contagion of bad example, that being preserved from vice and serving You faithfully, they may be ready to meet you face to face when they are so called through Christ our Lord. Sacred Heart! Inspire them with sorrow for sin, and grant them pardon. Mother of God! Be with them on the battlefield during life and at the hour of death, and grant that they may live and die in the grace of thy Son. Saint Joseph! Pray for them. May their Guardian Angel protect them! Saint Michael the Archangel, defend us in battle, be our protection against the wickedness and snares of the devil. May God rebuke them, we humbly pray, and do thou O Prince of the Heavenly Host by the power of God cast into Hell Satan and all evil spirits who prowl about the world seeking the ruin of souls."

Cecilia screamed "Amen" but no one else in any of the lines said anything. The Vanadis grew extremely irritated by this. She turned around and faced everyone in the defense. In that moment, the Titan princess inspired more fear in the army than any Dark Elf force. A resounding "Amen" was said by everyone in the defense.

"That's better!" screamed Cecilia.

The Vanadis took a moment to twirl her spear. She started to beat the handle of her staff against her breastplate.

"Come on, you underground bastards, which one of you is worthy to slay the Vanadis?" rallied Cecilia. "I feel awful sorry for all your grieving widows singing their lamentations this evening."

Cecilia's actions began to whip up the morale of those around her. Cassandra bowed her head and whispered a final prayer.

"Sanctus Espiritus…redeem us in our solemn hour…"

Alia seemed puzzled by the screams of the defenders coming from inside of the city. She started to see the slightest drop of fear in the eyes of her soldiers. However she dismissed this quickly and dropped her baton.

"All attack!"

Eyes glowing from their queen's command, the Dark Elves screamed a horrible yell and ran for the wall. Soldiers carrying battering rams sprinted for the main gate while others carrying ladders went for the walls. The giant spiders dragging the Siege Tower reached the right wall. The sounds of the moving army could be heard by the defenders. They silently awaited orders from their Marshal.

"This is it!" screamed Amuro. "Malcolm, let them have it!"

"Bows!" screamed Malcolm.

The archers pulled out their arrows and loaded.

"Do not waste your arrows!" commanded Malcolm. "Every shot must hit a target."

Drawing his bow first, Malcolm fired quickly. His arrow sailed over the wall and struck one of the Dark Elves carrying the ladder in the chest. The elf keeled over and the ladder with him. The Wood Elves and even Amuro herself stared at Malcolm who uncharacteristically managed a small smirk. Thud after thud, the battering rams went to work on the gate with a relentless pounding but the reinforced barricade held. Heads peaked over the top of the walls as the primary waves of Drow finished their ascent. While the wood elves were ready to fire, Malcolm raised his hand to stop them.

"Hold!" commanded Malcolm.

The others looked on anxiously, and Amuro had a noticeable bead of sweat forming on her forehead as she watched the ominous siege tower opening on the right wall. Dark Elves swarmed the wall.

"God, I hate being right all the time," commented Christian.

The Nightblade took out a remote control in his hand and pushed a red button. The walls of Deniva began to shift and ropes started to snap off of hooks. The wall Christian had dug shifted and collapsed directly onto the siege tower. The weight of the stone easily crushed the wooden devices the Drow had put together. Dark Elves trapped on the walls and towers were hurled to the ground, impaled on the spikes below or succumbing to fractured skulls against the hard ground. Their limps bodies and the collapsed tower served to seal the breach. The gruesome sight brought comfort to the defenders, and Christian's thinking had spared them the fury of the opening swarm. Undeterred by the Nightblade's ingenuity, more waves of Drow swordsman ascended the walls. These maneuvers did not allow for the coordination of units and often a swordsman would find himself alone in an isolated area of the wall. Malcolm didn't wait long to take advantage of this opportunity with a command of "fire at will!"

The wood elves narrowed their line of sight to focus on a single target each. They lacked the precision and coordination of the High Elves, and Malcolm was growing irritated when they didn't fire in unison. However, they were dead on with their accuracy and their arrows rang true. Drow were thrown either on the wall or to the streets below with arrows in them. A lesser force may have decided to regroup, but the brave and persistent Drow managed to form makeshift ranks using shields and debris as cover. No matter how many bannerman Malcolm managed to kill, another would rush to pick up the banner. Two Divisions of Dark Elves made it to the street level.

"Prepare for single combat!" ordered Amuro.

The two divisions broke into a full sprint towards the lines. Ethan shifted his weight, raised his axe in the air, and screamed "Deniva!" Cecilia giggled to herself at the thought of her husband imitating her brother's infamous battle charge. Thrusting her spear forward, the Dark Elves flung themselves into the defensive lines. The Vanadis and Hippolyte each caught one on their spears. Ethan buried his axe downward and nearly split a Drow swordsman in half. Cagius set up a shield wall in the center of the line using the shields of the Order of the Lion as cover.

Despite their lack of training and discipline, the Napolitan prince had managed to make them a poor man's version of the Dragon Legions. The Imperial troops held the left flank with their dervishes and bucklers. The first two undermanned units of Dark Elves didn't stand a chance. Every swordsman was killed in a manner of seconds, hacked to pieces by the professional soldiers defending before them. Amuro scanned her lines and checked them quickly. They suffered a few scratches and bruises but no significant injuries or deaths. She took a quick breath before she returned to her command duties.

"Pile the dead!" ordered the Elf Marshal.

Ethan and his mercenaries moved quickly. They started arranging Dark Elves bodies on top of one another. Archers covered them from behind and above. The layers of bodies created a second barrier that Amuro hoped would prevent the Dark Elves from throwing themselves into the lines.

"They're coming again!" screamed one of the Wood Elves on the roof.

"Reform the ranks!"

The soldiers ran back into position, took up arms, and readied themselves for a second wave. The distraction of the first wave had allowed multiple units of Dark Elves to get into position. The Elves charged simultaneously and Amuro feared the attack from the successive waves would swamp defense points. Malcolm ordered his archers to let loose successive volleys. The impact of the arrows along with the Dark Elves leaping in the air would often send those hit hurtling backwards. Joshua took a few deep breaths as he gripped Excalibur tightly.

"Remember your training," ordered Valentine.

"Yes, sir."

Dark Elves came leaping towards them. Valentine responded by jumping onto a dead body and met his foes mid-air. He crashed into the first Dark Elf with both of his short swords. The assassin found himself in the middle of a group of Drow but it hardly mattered. Parrying, spinning, and stabbing his foe, Valentine readied a back kick that knocked the last invader away from his position. Joshua would have admired his mentor's work if didn't have his own problems. A Drow came flying in and hit hard against his shield. Joshua flung the swordsman to the ground and finished him off with a kneeling stab. The young Paladin worked himself back into fighting position just as a second soldier came at him screaming, "die!" Joshua kept his shield up high and managed to block three strikes. He bulled the invader with his shield and stabbed him in the gut.

"No, you die," said Joshua arrogantly.

Joshua took a second to admire his kill to his detriment. An arrow flew in and hit him in the shoulder plate. The large Paladin winced in pain for a second while his Uncle laughed at him.

"Are you going to take it out or stare at it all night?"

Joshua ripped it out without any effort.

"If it came out that easy it didn't get through the chain. You didn't even get winged, but you shouldn't be too worried because a good scar gets a lot of sympathy with the ladies."

Joshua smiled at his uncle's advice. Christian found himself stumbling back as an arrow hit his left shoulder. He looked around and spotted Dark Elf Archers firing down from the walls of Deniva. The half-elf screamed "archers" and Cagius had his men throw their shields up to block the incoming shots.

"Leave them to me!" shouted Cassandra.

"Don't use any fire spells," advised Rosa as she fired a shot. "The Drow can almost completely resist the effect."

"Thanks."

Raising her staff in the air, Cassandra chanted in her native tongue. Shining blue light filled the orb of her staff. Particles of snow fell from the sky around the position of the enemy archers while a blue magic circle formed underneath them. Cassandra pushed her staff forward shouting, "Cold Blaze!" Ice geysers exploded from the magic circle ensnaring all of her intended targets. As the fog passed, a masterpiece of ice sculptures was all that remained. The weight gave in on the roof and the whole battalion shattered against the floor. The attack horrified many in the ranks of the defenders as the Wood Elves were unaware at how powerful a sorceress they had on their side. The queen didn't shed a tear at this and crushed the skull of a Drow swordsman who leapt through the line at her.

The Drow regrouped once more, seeing that their first two strategies weren't working. Two units sprinted along the sides of the street using the buildings as cover. They neared the defense lines and jumped onto the walls of the buildings. The Drow pivoted off of the walls, spinning in the air and crashing down into the lines. It was as Amuro predicted; these swordsmen were deliberately sacrificing themselves to distract the defenders from firing on the main force. This allowed more of the units to have a clear route for their attack runs. Ethan called out to the mercenary force behind him. The Denivan mercenaries had originally hailed from the Nordice Provinces but were thrown out of the tribes for various reasons. They banded together and sold themselves off as a mercenary company before coming in the permanent employ of the margrave. These warriors were axe and spear fighters. Ethan knew they had to create separation, and long arcing attacks were the best way to do it. Cecilia and Hippolyte hopped up to join the company as well. Hippolyte followed Cecilia's lead and grabbed the far end of her spear. In unison, the spear-women twirled wildly in wide circles, intentionally breaking the tight units of their foes. Ethan and the company did the same with their axes. Hippolyte was caught in the open when a Drow swordsman attempted to crash his spinning attack on her back. Cecilia reached into her boot quickly for a dagger and threw it at the Drow. It caught the attacker in the chest who landed harmlessly behind the tribal chief. Body convulsing behind her, the wolf girl chided herself for being so close to death.

"You can keep that!" screamed Cecilia as she tipped the top of her spear to her crown.

Offering a wink to thank the Vanadis, Hippolyte took the dagger out of the body and used it to slay another charging Drow. After a few minutes, Cagius whistled the troops to fall back. The Order of the Lion went forward in a shield wall to relieve them with Imperial Janissaries covering them. Selim held his sheath forward as a blocker and kept his dervish in his right hand. When he blocked a sword strike with the sheath he was able to duck under and spin with the dervish to cut the elf's head off. Robespierre noticed how the Imperial's style of fighting was more of an art than a form of combat. After a few minutes, Robespierre tagged Selim and took over the primary position. The imperial sighed and steadied himself, thankful for the respite.

"Bet you wish that you took the Drow offer and rode the garrison out of here," teased Robespierre.

"Yes I do, but even I couldn't leave an enemy in a position like this and keep my honor," replied the Commander.

Robespierre laughed and killed another Drow. Dennis watched the battle from the parapets of the Castle Gates. He was constantly wiping his brow with a cloth he kept in his hand. The old Margrave was not a battle veteran but studied war long and hard. Witnessing his troops holding their own, his gaze was drawn to the thousands of Drow breaching the walls of his city.

The king turned quickly to the rear posterns where Saria was doing her best to move the evacuees as quickly as possible. It was clear that the elf maiden was taking much longer than she had anticipated. Dennis could feel the presence of Keiko fluttering next to him.

"Well, dear one, we're still alive," commented Dennis.

"It is very early in this battle, your majesty," said Keiko.

"We're throwing them back easy enough."

"That's only because they cannot flood through the main gates yet. They've been working on that door with multiple rams for a long time, and it's going to fall. When it falls, we will be swarmed."

"Maybe it would be a good time to see how Saria's doing then."

Keiko nodded. The sylph beat her wings and flew down from the castle parapets to the rear posterns. Saria hardly noticed her as she focused all of her attention on evacuating the civilians. Keiko coughed slightly to grab her attention.

"What's the status of the evacuation?" asked Keiko.

"I need more time," pleaded Saria. "I can get them through the gates fast enough but it is a long road to the safety of Edenia. The elderly and the children are moving slower than I anticipated."

"Okay. The second the evacuation is complete make sure you send word to your sister. She has orders for you."

"Okay," said Saria meekly.

Keiko flew back up to Dennis who held the walls of the castle tightly. He was watching his son in the middle of the fray. Ethan flipped a Drow over his back. The Denivan knight slammed the axe into the middle of his chest. In a fluid motion, he pulled the axe up and caught another in the midsection.

"I wish my son wasn't fighting this battle alone. I know I wouldn't last five seconds in that battle—not at my age and with all my ailments. Still, I should be standing with my son."

Keiko smiled and held Dennis at his shoulder.

"No, my margrave, you're rationalizing now because you're just as terrified as the rest of us. No one wants to be down there but from those who have been given much, there is much to be expected. The masses and their elitist taskmasters always complain that aristocrats live in the lap of luxury and that wealth must be equally distributed, no matter how hard someone works or how talented they are. In truth it has always been different; these aristocrats will shed their last drop of blood to protect the common populace."

"Your people really are amazing, Keiko. I think it's time for another round of prayers."

In the middle of the battle, Amuro caught a foe across his midsection, spilling the purple blood of the Drow upon her sword and cloak. Hair frazzled, the elf maiden's face was covered in sweat, dirt, and Drow blood. Amuro's ears picked up the sound of wood beginning to break. She turned her eyes towards the gates and adjusted her keen sight. The commander saw her worst nightmare come to pass as punctures from a battering ram showed.

"Damn, I thought it would hold longer," commented Amuro as she turned to her banner carriers. "Retreat! Retreat to the second defensive point!"

The banner carriers swung their banners wildly as they ran back to the central market circle of the city. The archers in the buildings and on the rooftops caught sight of this first and immediately retreated. When they got back into position, they launched cover fire for their allies. Rosa turned to Cassandra who had just used a dirk to slit the throat of another Drow.

"You need to get out of here, your Highness."

The queen nodded. Cassandra chanted a spell, covering herself in a blue light. In a flash she disappeared from the spot she was in and reappeared in a plume of smoke at the market circle. Jumping on top of the fountain, Cassandra served as the rallying point for the soldiers. In the front lines, Cecilia swung her spear in an arc taking out two more. Ethan screamed at her.

"We've got the order to fall back."

"I hate running!" screamed Cecilia as she thrust her spear into chest of another elf. "Fall back! I'll cover you!"

Cecilia chanted, swung her spear, and brought up her defensive wall. She knew she had about thirty seconds before it would give out since the Drow were slashing at the shield and firing arrows at it. The appearance of the defense wall resonated quickly with the front lines. Running towards the second defense point, Amuro continued to bark out orders at Gerard, Minerva, and others providing cover for Cecilia and the troops below.

"Gerard, get yourselves out of there!"

"Retreat!" screamed Gerard as he acknowledged the command.

The Wood Elves bounded across the rooftops, but Minerva took the time to fire off two last arrows. The arrows counted as she hit the commanding officer in two units of the Dark Elves. The wolf tribe archer turned and found herself in the rear of the retreating Wood Elves. She was still surprised at the great nimbleness the Wood Elves possessed. Effortlessly bounding to the next building, Minerva had to prepare to make the same jump. Before she could take off, a blast of fire blew the ledge of the building away, killing three archers in the process. The wolf princess turned to see a battlemage flanked by two swordsmen approaching her. Sweating as she drew arrows from her quiver, Minerva aimed quickly and miraculously struck the wizard in the heart before she fired off another spell. The swordsmen were undeterred and charged her. Hippolyte screamed when she saw this.

"She's trapped!"

"I'll get her, Hippolyte!" volunteered Walker.

Walker ran to the edge of the building just as Cecilia's shield frizzled out. The Titan princess sprinted down the street from the market circle, passing Walker along the way and encouraging him to get moving. Malcolm yelled to the archers to give cover fire for Walker. The Lord Knight slung the Oath Shield over his back and held out his arms.

"Jump, Minerva!"

"Are you crazy?" screamed Minerva. "It's a six-story building!"

"I'll catch you!"

Minerva stared at the collapsing shield and the charging swordsmen.

"Oh well, I had a good run."

The wolf princess leapt off the building and her sister covered her eyes. Walker braced himself and caught her perfectly in his arms. Minerva opened one of her closed eyes and saw the smiling face of the Lord Knight. She swooned and immediately kissed him.

"My hero!"

"No time for that, soldier! We've got to move!"

"Reform the lines!" screamed Amuro.

The melee infantry took a defensive position so the archers could fall behind them. Bursting from the pounding of the ram, debris came flying from the gates. Frenzied warriors swarmed the streets of the city, but Amuro's ingenious plan had worked. The traps activated all over the city, causing rocks, debris, and false doors to funnel the attacking force into one narrow pass the royals could defend. Malcolm and his command unleashed flight after flight of arrows at the charging foes. Despite hundreds of them dying in seconds, the Drow remained undeterred and the melee lines were ready to meet them. Staring at the configuration of the circle, Christian licked his lips. Assessing four unspeakably dangerous scenarios, he went with the worst idea.

"Cassie, bring down the blacksmith!"

Christian might as well have told the young queen to kill herself. Shaking her head and hands with trepidation, a second command from Amuro telling her to "do it" told Cassandra she had no choice. Muttering a slight prayer that her actions wouldn't result in the death of her defenders, the rune mistress' hair frizzled a bit as it became charged with electric energy.

Calling forth "Storm Bolt" after her elven chant, a huge bolt burst from the heavens and rattled the foundations of the blacksmith. Collapsing to right, the shattered building took down the buildings in the circle around it in a domino effect. For a moment, Cassandra wondered what possessed Christian to unleash such destruction, but her faith in the Nightblade paid off. The eight buildings falling to the ground in the market square created a tidal wave of rubble, stone, and debris crashing down against the incoming enemy troops. The Drow that ran for the market square rather than retreating to the gates survived the worst of it. Most of their comrades were not so lucky, and when the waves of destruction finally settled, Palias and Alia found the loss of life from the first group of attackers was for nothing as rubble blocked the main gate. The eight thousand Drow who had survived the collapse of the buildings in the market square found themselves severely outnumbered by the defenders of Deniva. Valentine licked his lips and smiled.

"Break ranks! Charge!"

The melee infantry pushed forward and caught their aggressors in the trap. It truly was an awesome sight as the Order of the Lion and the Imperial Garrison fought side by side slaughtering their foes. The entire surviving front column was laid to waste to the delight of the cheering defenders as arms and hands of buried Dark Elves twitched in the rubble.

"Reform the ranks!" ordered Amuro. "I don't want to lose everything we gained so far."

The melee fighters hurried back into position and cut the celebration short. Everyone appreciated the quick breather, as they knew it was only a matter of time before the Dark Elves found a way around their latest obstacle. Despite the mood of those around him, Ethan fell to his knees in disbelief at the state of the city around him. Reassuring him, Cecilia put an arm to his shoulder.

"Oh my God... what were we thinking?"

"Husband, I thought you wanted to win this battle."

"I didn't realize this defense would involve us destroying half the city."

"Considering our enemies would choose to destroy it all, it isn't a bad trade."

Amuro looked at her command. She had lost few but every loss felt like a hundred lives were lost.

"We need water and food—let's a take a respite while we have a chance. Cecilia, Cagius, Malcolm, come with me—we've got to anticipate their next maneuver."

The command was obeyed. Palias shook off the feeling of disbelief at the main gate. His army was still trapped at the starting point despite the brilliant tactics he offered them at the beginning of the battle.

"What the hell happened?"

Alia leaned over to one of the elves. After a few words, the Dark Elf Queen steadied herself.

"They say that the half-elf sorceress called down a bolt that collapsed the building. It was apparently the cornerstone building that took down the entire center market."

"Destroying their own city to preserve the victory… that sounds like a Titan plan."

"It will take some time to take care of this obstruction…"

"What about the buildings?"

"We can't move enough troops across them in time. We'd be easily exposed to their archers."

"Then we dig ourselves out! We've got a man's job ahead of us."

Palias got off the chariot and joined the other Drow in removing the stones from the obstruction. His cuirassiers dismounted and joined the effort as well. The obstruction was too compacted to tunnel through; the Drow sought a means to get around it.

DIETRICH RHONE MEMORIAL SCIENCE HALL, TITAN ACADEMY

"Science is a process of elimination; it's the eliminating part
that takes the most time."

Doctor Martha Heinrich, Annual Orientation Lecture

Down in the depths of the basement of the science hall, a large oval room had been transformed to house the bane of all experiments in Titanus. A model city was displayed in the center of the room surrounded by an active tachyon barrier. Two revolutions into their experiments, Martha had perfected the science of creating the barriers. The trick was trying to destroy them. Eventually a design was settled upon, a large white cannon with a disk attached to the front of it, and a single rod sticking out of it. Noticeably distraught over the failure of her tachyon cannon yet again, Martha crossed her arms under her breasts. Restraining herself from kicking the cannon, the brilliant scientist organized her thoughts.

"What the hell did we decide to use in the last experiment?"

"Seismic activity, doctor," replied a scientist as she went through her notes.

"What about atmospheric changes... let's simulate during a thunderstorm."

"Right away, doctor..."

The scientists near the cannon made the necessary adjustments. Upon completion of their work, they gave their superior a thumbs up. Martha pointed her finger forward.

"Fire away."

The cannon went off. When it first made contact with the shield it appeared to make a dent, but the joy was short-lived. As it had done so many times before, the beam refracted. The good doctor screamed, crumbled up a piece of paper, and threw it at the barrier.

"Not even something as simple as that works! How many times have we failed?"

"Eight hundred sixteen, doctor."

"Damn."

"I am sorry, Lady Heinrich. If you feel that I or any member of this project is not satisfactory..."

"It's not your fault...well not too much of it. I would put a little of the fault on me and most of it to you and others."

The scientists appreciated the levity. Looking up as she slumped into her seat, Doctor Heinrich noticed odd configurations on the ceiling above.

"What did we use this room for before we changed it?"

"It was the planetarium."

"Oh yeah...I used to like this room. I remember when I was a little girl running around here. I'd sneak down here at night and hack the system so I could stare at the stars. Virgus would scold me for hours..."

Crying a little bit at her beloved mentor who had fallen, Martha pushed a button on her seat. The room went dark and a picture of Terminus Mundus appeared on the screen surrounded by its three moons. Mundus appeared as a sapphire, flawed only in its center by the stretching continent of Gaia. The three moons continued to give off the same hue often seen in the night sky on a clear night.

"Alpha, Beta, Gamma. That's what you get when you let elves name the satellites surrounding the planet—there's no romance in that. I bet there is life out there that gives satellites better names. I always wanted to call them Michael, Gabriel, and Raphael. I guess I thought that way it would be like they watched over us like archangels."

Chuckling a first, Martha cut herself off. She bobbed her head back and forth for a bit as she bit her lower lip. The scientists observed as she computed mathematical algorithms just by moving her lips. Finally, the doctor tapped abruptly against the padded arm of the seat. Overcome with sudden enlightenment, she screamed for a pencil.

"Doctor Heinrich, are you all right?"

"Get me a pencil and some paper."

"Of course."

Not wanting to raise the ire of the doctor anymore, her trusted assistant handed her a pencil from her pocket and some paper from her clipboard. Computing calculations at an accelerated rate, she burned through her resources in no time. Demanding more, Martha laughed sinisterly to the amazement of her subordinates.

"Very clever, Tattenburg, but you're no match for the greatest genius on Terminus Mundus! You should have never taught your pupil everything you knew!"

Observing the calculations in earnest, the scientists in the room could see Martha using the formula for the gravitational constant over and over again. They understood what she meant to do. When Martha finished, she jumped up in the air.

"Adjust the gravitational fields on the weapon to reflect the pull of the three satellites during the equinox."

Working with renewed hope, the necessary adjustments were made. Martha gripped the back of the chair in front of her tightly and shouted the command to fire once more.

As the cannon fired, the blue shield buckled as it had done hundreds of times before. Yet, this time a bulging bubble exploded in the center of the tachyons. It took fifteen minutes for a chain reaction to sever the bonds and dissipate the field. Crying tears of relief, Martha grabbed her assistant and the two embraced one another. Everyone in the room cheered, kissed and hugged one another.

"Raise a second field and do it again," ordered Martha.

They repeated the experiment and the same results were realized. Martha tested it once more just to be sure and to her delight it worked a third time.

"All right kids, we'll pop a few bottles of some good wine tonight, but we need to get to work on a much larger version of the cannon. We have to have it ready to go by the equinox of the growing cycle."

"All hail the greatest genius on Terminus Mundus," teased her assistant.

"Damn right! I always told you the process of elimination leads to any scientific solution. If she wasn't at Hawkeye tonight, I'd call Civilia now, but she'll have to wait until tomorrow morning."

Deniva

"The Titans created the Order of the Valkyrie in order to strike
fear in the hearts of the primitive human race. The winged
goddesses who the primitives believed to be the servants of
Odin himself became the premier lance cavalry in the world.
The most sought-after title was that of 'Vanadis,' the goddess of
war herself. This command position was passed only when the
prior Commander either relinquished their post in combat or
fell in battle. The first Vanadis was a noble named Freya who
died heroically in battle. However, her divine attenuation was
so strong, her powers remained within the Gottin-Speer which
was used as a summons when the Vanadis was overwhelmed."

"Rise of the Valkyrie," The Titan Battle Manual

Anxiety and sweat dripped from the brows of the defenders as the hours passed painfully slow in Deniva. The sound of tunneling was all around them and it was only a matter of time before their foe reached their position. Trying to maintain morale, Amuro approached her command one at a time. A simple smile and some of her natural empathy gave her soldiers the will to keep on fighting against these overwhelming odds. She noticed Christian twitching nervously against the walls of a destroyed building.

"Christian, I came over to thank you. That really bought us some time."

"Unfortunately, marshal, that's the last time we can use that trick. I'm out of walls and buildings we can destroy."

"Is there any other strategic fall back point?"

"We've got one last defensive chokepoint. However, if that's overrun, we're going to have to fall back to the castle."

"Deniva's Castle isn't necessarily defensible…"

"Neither is the rest of this city, but we've held so far. "

"Castle it is, then. I guess we'll have to fight them from room to room. Carry on."

"Don't be so mopey and hard on yourself, Amuro," praised Cecilia. "You've done a marvelous job so far, just keep it up."

"Just try not to destroy any more of the city than we have too," pleaded Ethan.

"I will try my best, Ethan."

At the rear posterns, Saria and Keiko prepared to dispatch the last train of refugees bound for Edenia. Dennis joined the last caravan of his people.

"Margrave, are you prepared?" respectfully asked the elf maiden.

"Yes, young one. It was encouraging to see such a sweet face in these horrid times."

"Well Saria, I think's it time to call your sister," informed Keiko.

Saria tapped her communicator and made contact with her sister. There was nothing she could do to hide the sadness in her voice, but her elder sister would not let her fall into despair.

"Hey sis, you do everything I told you to do?"

"Amuro, are you all right?"

"We're fine, for now…I assume the evacuation is finally over."

"It will still take a long time for them to reach the safety of Edenia."

"I know, sis… I want you to take Maiden and travel personally with Dennis to safety. It wouldn't be good for relations if something happens to the Margrave."

"Maiden is your mount, sis. You know I love her but I couldn't…"

"I think she's going to need someone to take care of her. You're the only person I could ever trust."

"I won't leave you," cried Saria.

"I told you to follow my orders! This is my last one. If I have to give my life for this country, I am going to be damned sure the margrave lives to tell the treachery of Central Acadia and the Chinotal Empire. Use your gifts well and make them hear and see."

"I will, Amuro. I promise you I will."

"One apple per rotation—she prefers the braeburns. Make sure you don't overload Maiden with sugar cubes, it's not good for her…no matter how much…"

Amuro broke down and couldn't say anymore; the thought of losing the mount she raised from childhood overtook her. Saria signed off knowing this and approached the beautiful winged unicorn. Seemingly knowing what was about to happen, Maiden thrashed angrily, as if demanding to join her partner of many revolutions in death. Seeing this, the young elf maiden sang an elvish song and calmed the rage within the mount. Saria gently stroked the face and neck of Maiden and the beast allowed her to climb upon her back. Changing her tune to a soft lamentation, she bid her sister a final goodbye before joining Dennis and the others in the caravan. They passed through the posterns guarded by mercenaries and some of the wood elf rangers injured in the first wave who could no longer fight in the defense. Keiko remained behind treating the wounded in her makeshift field hospital behind the castle walls.

In the streets, Amuro wiped the tears from her eyes and swallowed hard.

"We're clear."

The uneasiness of Christian and Valentine was soon noticed by the others. The Napolitan assassin put his ears to the ground and the Titan operative followed suit. They looked at one another in fear and ordered everyone to silence. Amuro glided over without a sound. When the two picked their ears from the ground again, Christian grabbed her arm.

"Marshal, they're moving the army underneath us. We've got to move back to the last chokepoint now; there is bedrock underneath there, they can't break it."

Amuro signaled to her command to fall back. Wrapping cloaks around their bodies, they tried to move as quietly as possible. Cassandra teleported herself back and Rosa quickly took up her guard position.

The elves below the ground caught wind of the defender's movement. Dark Elves burst from underneath the city through newly created holes. The rubble that had impeded the progression of the Dark Elves into Deniva was sucked down into the depths of Terminus Mundus.

A first flight of arrows shot into the hole and the gurgling sound of death was heard. Yet, the Drow were relentless and poured out of their mounds like ants fleeing a colony. Attempting to cover her soldiers in retreat, Cassandra invoked an arrow wind spell but a new horror was unleashed. The Dark Elves cloaked themselves in a light green aura of counter magic. When hit with the spell it reflected back on Cassandra's position. Dumbfounded by this new power, Rosa threw herself in front of the young queen to protect her. In doing so, she suffered severe lacerations to her shoulders and back. Cassandra grabbed her and tried to stop the bleeding.

"Rosa, what happened?"

"Counter magic, your highness. The Dark Elves are masters of it. The spell reflects all magic attacks unless aligned with the holy element."

The sorceress used her minimum knowledge of healing magic to bandage her protector's wounds. Cagius rallied all of his shield fighters together to form a phalanx. Despite the efforts of the Drow to perform suicidal spinning sword attacks, they held true. It bought Amuro a few minutes to regroup from the shock attack.

"Amuro," called Ethan. "We can't hold this chokepoint. Our best bet is to hunker down in the castle until we can retreat."

"Ethan, if we retreat, we'll be disorganized and slaughtered."

"Hang on, marshal, I think I've got an idea," interjected Malcolm. "It's a tad unconventional but it might work with some discipline."

"Really, Malcolm, you're doing much better. Okay, I've got nothing better so go for it."

"Gerard, get me fifty archers in two lines. I'll take first line and you get the second one."

"Yes, Vice-Marshal Fenidor."

The Wood Elves formed the two lines. When one was taken out by a Dark Elf archer, Minerva fell in perfectly. The first line knelt down and drew their bows with Gerard in command. Malcolm stood with the second line in firing position. Amuro ordered Cagius and phalanx to fall back.

Malcolm's line fired and struck the coming enemy. They dropped back two paces and knelt to draw as Gerard's line stood and fired. They mimicked the first's line movement as they stood to fire again. They repeated the attack over and over again as the infantry fighters protected their flanks. Even Amuro couldn't believe how well her lover's tactic was working.

"Wow…I think Malcolm changed warfare. I think I'll call it the thin elf line. All right, soldiers, the defenses are breached! Fall back to the Castle."

Despite the coordinated retreat, the defenders lost all of their ground. In one fatal, brilliant blow, the Drow made up for all of the losses they had suffered so far.

"We shouldn't have missed that!" cursed a running Christian.

"Kill now," demanded Colin. "Talk later!"

Colin sliced through two more Drow as Christian unleashed the trap spikes from his remote underneath the charging enemy lines. Using the last of his tricks, the Nightblade threw down the device. Hippolyte whistled and Stryker came charging in. Ripping into the throats of two enemies, the wolf tribe leader loaded two wounded on the wolf's back as they moved to retreat. Stryker stayed on Hippolyte's heels. Drow mages blasted magic into the remaining dilapidated buildings, forcing the retreating troops to run around a gauntlet of falling stone. Still feeling the wounds from before, Cassandra supported Rosa as they retreated. Despite her pleas to leave her behind, the burden of carrying her protector negated the queen's ability to use teleportation magic. Archers fired down on the defenders from above, flying in on both sides. Walker took an arrow right in the hip; Joshua grabbed him and lugged him back.

"I've got you, Walker!"

"I feel like we danced this dance before. Don't worry, I can walk; let's get out of here."

Robespierre and a member of the Imperial Guard hit the Castle Gate doors. They pushed them open quickly and stayed on them. As retreating soldiers passed, they tapped them on the shoulder doing a number count. Malcolm got on Robespierre's right side and continued to fire at the coming enemy.

"Come on!" encouraged Robespierre to those in retreat.

Cecilia swiped with her spear and took out two more enemies. She took an arrow in the arm and ripped it out effortlessly. The princess threw it back at the charging soldiers and struck an incoming enemy in the eye. Determined to be the last one to fall behind the safety of the castle wall, she scanned the battlefield for Cassandra. The queen continued to aid Rosa covered by two Order of the Lion Knights. Drow charged in and drew the knights into combat as the women moved away. Unbeknownst to her, a piece of collapsing building descended, about to crush the two. Seeing the young women in danger, Selim rushed in and pushed the two out of the way. Cassandra hit her head against a large chunk of building and Rosa passed out from her wounds. The falling rubble struck Selim right on the base of the spine. As a wall of stone collapsed around the two, Cecilia tightened the grip on her spear and screamed for the queen. Fearlessly charging towards them, Cecilia cut through two Dark Elf warriors before being struck on the right arm. Undeterred by her wounds, she made for the queen's position. As the Alliance forces cleared the gates, Christian stopped by Robespierre.

"What's the final count?"

"Sir, I can't account for Selim, Cassandra, Rosa, or Cecilia. I don't think they made it."

"What the hell are we waiting for?" demanded Ethan. "Let's get them."

"No, Ethan. You know this castle; you have to array the defenses. Malcolm, get archers on that wall and cover us. We have to spare the minimal amount of troops possible in a rescue. Walker, get two knights and saddle five horses. Colin, you're with me."

"Christian, this better go more smoothly than our last rescue."

The five were soon ready to ride. Amuro grabbed the reins of Christian's horse.

"I'll keep it open as long as I can, DeVries. However, I cannot risk this final defense... not even for Cassie."

"Marshal, if the defense is going to be compromised, seal the gate! We'll be dead by then anyway, and know I will have personally taken care of Cassandra at that point. May God have mercy on my soul."

As they rode out, Cassandra shook her woozy head. Stroking her raven hair away from her eyes, she felt blood rushing from her skull. Rosa was on her knees trying to get back to her feet. Tears came to the queen's eyes when she spotted Selim breathing heavily on the ground with the stone fragment still crushing his spine. Cassandra lifted her staff, chanted "air cutter" and used a blast of wind to slice the stone.

"Thank you, your highness," acknowledged Selim.

Cassie took his hand.

"Pasha Selim, I'm so sorry... thank you."

"I don't suppose... a sorceress who dresses in black... is much of a healer."

"Not for wounds this serious."

"I don't know what's more ironic...an imperial saving the life of his sultan's chief adversary...or a queen filled with such mercy that she cries...over an enemy..."

"You are no enemy of mine, great Pasha."

"It wasn't about protecting you at first... it was about protecting Deniva, about fighting for something that I believed in... but you... if I could, I would have followed you..."

The first platoon of Dark Elves entered the area. Rosa drew her bow on the ground and fired a shot killing one. Still standing, Cassandra grabbed her staff and swung it like a weapon.

She knocked over one Dark Elf and stabbed him through the chest with the sharp point of the bottom of her staff. For the second, Cassandra went into a handstand and grabbed the elf between her legs. She twisted quickly and snapped his neck. The changing equilibrium made her woozy and she fell to her knees. Dark Elf archers readied arrows enchanted with green glowing light. They shot both Rosa and Cassandra. In seconds, eyes fluttered and maidens collapsed into a deep sleep.

"That's the girl, and a treat for Queen Alia as well. That girl is a highborn elf. Get them back!"

The clashing of a spear and the screaming of "Titanus" caught the platoon's attention. Leaping through the air, an already bloody Cecilia thrust her spear into the platoon commander's heart. Ripping it out, she took another dagger from her waist and slit the throat of an enemy putting his hands on Cassandra. She kicked another in the chest and crushed his throat by stepping on it with her gold-tipped boot. Initially startled, three

Drow charged her, and the Vanadis performed a long, arcing swing with her spear that sliced them all through the midsection. Two unenchanted arrows caught her in the chest; Cecilia threw her spear into the chest of the archer. A Drow swordsman took the opportunity to slide his sword between the steel breastplates of the defenseless Vanadis. It ripped into her chainmail and sliced up her midsection. The enemy smugly expected a gasp and a crestfallen look to overtake his opponent. Cecilia just laughed and spit her own blood in his face.

"It will take more than one lucky hit to kill the Vanadis!"

Grabbing him around his neck, she twisted quickly and snapped it like a small branch.

Another swordsman came in for a deathblow from her side. Cecilia turned too late to get out of the way.

"Cecilia..." shouted Selim.

Selim threw his dervish in air. The Titan princess caught it with her right hand, spun around and sliced the enemy's head off. The Pasha finally slipped into death with a smile on his face. Cecilia continued the fight by throwing the dervish into the chest of another archer before falling to her knees from her wounds and exhaustion. She crawled desperately to her precious spear as a second platoon came upon her. Breathing heavily, the Vanadis glowed in the same otherworldly light her brother had when death was overtaking him during his fight against Abaddon.

"Cedric, I'm sorry...this I all can do to keep Cassandra safe. I feel what you must have felt against Abaddon and I'm not afraid. If this is my time, I accept God's plan and I pray he watches over my son. By my rank as Vanadis, I summon the spirit of the first of her name. Freya, vanquish these enemies and restore the honor of all the Valkyries!"

Jamming the spear into the earth, thunder crashed in the heavens above. Descending from on high, the body and soul incarnation of a Valkyrie with a flaming sword and wings joined the fray. The beautiful avenger had long brown hair and burning green eyes. When she landed, Freya paid homage to Cecilia's courage and honor before taking over the battle. Shouting a deafening war cry, the first vanadis swung her holy sword in long arcing strikes. Heads were separated from the bodies of the Dark Elf platoon before they could even raise a defense. Despite their fighting prowess, they were no match for the heavenly force. As Christian and his group approached the scene, they witnessed the slaughter.

"Christian, I've seen that depiction in books," stammered Colin. "That being is Freya."

"Divikin gain mysterious powers when they approach death. Cedric was said to be able to carry all of the powers of light and darkness to his sword. Cecilia has the power to summon Freya."

Walker and his men tended to Cassandra and Rosa as Christian went running to Cecilia. Colin knelt down next to Selim and checked his pulse.

"Thank you, Selim. Thank you for being here."

The Titan operative checked his princess for a pulse and breathed a sigh of relief when he found life within her.

"My lady, I shall not fail you."

Gathering the maidens on horses, Christian turned to Freya and offered a final salute. The angelic incarnation answered, and created a pillar of divine flame to aid in his retreat as she returned to the heavens above.

"I wish we didn't always have to come in so hard!" commented Colin as they rode for the gates.

Covered by archers on the walls and towers of the castle, any enemy that came close to the five riders suffered instant death. As they passed the gate, Ethan, Joshua, and Cagius slammed them closed. Soldiers took two giants beams and plugged them against the gate to prevent it from being rammed. Everyone else grabbed everything not nailed down in the Castle—furniture, planks, or beams—and built another line of barricades. Gently, Ethan went over to Christian's ride and lay Cecilia down on the ground. Amuro and the others gathered over her with grave concern. Ethan's tears fell on his wife's face. Not wanting to be pitied even in her state, Cecilia tried to sit up.

"I'm not dead yet…" murmured Cecilia.

Fluttering to her position, Keiko used whatever white magic she had to close her wounds.

"I don't have the knowledge or magic power to heal her. If we don't get her to a cleric, she's going to die."

"There's no cleric within a hundred kilometers of us!" screamed Ethan.

The burly ax knight was comforted by Amuro, who tried to put a brave face on the scenario.

"She's our best fighter, Marshal…how can we lose her?"

"Cecilia's out of the battle, Ethan, and I'm afraid we lost Cassandra's magic also."

While Rosa had recovered from the enchantment on the arrows, Cassandra remained unconscious due to the concussion she suffered from colliding with the building. Nervously, Walker believed her skull might be fractured more severely. Seeking answers, Christian climbed one of the towers to get a bird's eye view of the city. His worst fears were witnessed as Dark Elf warriors infested the city. Flanked by Palias' cuirassiers, Alia brought her chariot into the city. Palias bore a smug look across his face as he deemed the battle to be over.

"All troops forward! We dare not now allow any respite for these traitors."

Fear, doubt, and despair filled the minds and hearts of the defenders. Amuro felt it happening and felt powerless to stop it. She understood how all of her ancestors must have felt when they failed at preventing a siege. Looking to her friends, she knew they would follow her to the end, but one look at Cassandra made her think clearly.

"All right, my brave defenders, I'm not going to lie to you. As you can no doubt surmise, this defense is the only thing that stands between us and the civilians. There is no vow or order that I can ask for or give to keep you here. The rear posterns remain unblocked, so anyone that wants to get out of here may do so. Those that are directly under my command will take my orders now. Robespierre!"

"Yes, marshal."

"Muster a division of your knights; they are to escort Cassandra out of Deniva. Lady Rosa will send some of her divisions to accompany you and hide you in the safety of the forest. Joshua, Hippolyte, and Minerva will join you as well."

"Wait a second, Amuro," said Hippolyte. "My sister and I are not running!"

"This isn't about bravery anymore, Hippolyte! This Castle is going to become a graveyard very shortly. The Chieftain of the Wolf Tribe must live through this battle in order to make those son-of-a-bitches pay for what they've done to your people!"

"I don't believe you brought us behind these walls without a plan. I know you too well, marshal."

"Fine. It will be dawn soon. When light strikes, the drow will weaken. We can strategically retreat out of the city at that point and hound them like rangers and hunters in the forest."

"This is an act of courage I have not seen since the Terrace River... there is great nobility among the 'steelbellies' after all..."

"Or incredible stupidity..."

"My sister and I stay, Amuro. You'll find we'll be quite helpful for hit-and-run tactics in the forest."

The vice-captain of the Imperial Forces came over to Amuro.

"Marshal Jenitzen, our Pasha is dead, our two captains are dead, and we've lost half our command."

"You've done more than I could ever ask. I thank you for standing with us. Go quickly! There isn't much time."

"If you think that a true Imperial soldier would dare run at the behest of an Alliance Marshal, you are sadly mistaken. We stand with you to the end!"

"Ethan, would you dare risk taking Cecilia out of the city?"

"If we move her now, she's going to die, Amuro. We might need some time for Keiko to stabilize her wounds before we can move her."

Keiko stayed next to Cecilia's body and desperately tried to save her life.

"Not even a thousand Titans could ever match your spirit, Milady. It isn't time for you to die yet."

Walker handed Cassandra's limp body to a knight on horseback. He tied her to his body so she could maintain her balance on the horse despite her current state. Her protector kissed her on the forehead.

"It disgraces me that I was not there to protect you from this. However, I hope this final defense will serve as proper penance. It's my duty now to take up Cedric's vow. They'll never touch you."

Cagius saluted Joshua who answered.

"I am proud to call you the son of my brother! I have faith that you will one day sit on the throne of Napolitan and restore the courage and traditions of our people...just as he would have..."

"They will know of your bravery, uncle."

"Of course they will, because I intend to go out in full regalia with banners flying. I will make my end an end to remember! Every maiden will write and sing songs of Cagius the Undaunted for all eternity. Take that, you so-called immortal beings of Terminus Mundus."

Joshua laughed and gave his uncle a quick hug. "Good luck."

Christian slid down a ladder and went to Rosa.

"Thank God you're all right."

"I failed you, Christian. I couldn't protect her."

"Don't you dare let that be the last words between us. Time for you to go!"

"I won't bear losing you," insisted Rosa. "When we die...we will die together!"

"You elves are a stiff-necked people. I know no words of reason will talk you out of this."

"Elves can be very stubborn, even those without red hair."

"Stay close to me!"

"I intend to. After all, you're the one that needs protection."

The two laughed. Robespierre formed a contingent to guard Cassandra as they made for Edenia. The remaining troops remained behind, hoping that Amuro's plan could buy them some time. Malcolm could see his Marshal needed some reinforcement.

"Your choices surprise me, Amuro. What made you save Joshua?"

"I had to make sure there would be a living heir for every throne. Thomas can rule Titanus, my sister can take Evengard, and Joshua can rule Napolitan. It might not be the grandest triumvirate to defend our young Queen, but they're the best we have left."

"Logical to the end."

"I'm glad you approve."

"Unless, of course, if you feel I am more suited to sit on the Evengard throne..."

Amuro looked with scorn at Malcolm.

"A joke, marshal…did I fail at my attempt at humor?"

"More than you can imagine."

Cagius and Walker set their infantry into a line behind another set of barricades. The archers took positions on elevated levels behind them. Everyone took a deep breath and waited for the inevitable. Ethan stared at everything and shook his head. He went to Christian for guidance.

"Amuro put on a brave face for everyone. We're not getting out of here, are we?"

"I'm sorry, Ethan. There's no escape."

"Is there anything left we can do?"

"Yeah…pray for a miracle…"

Gilgal, Forest of the Eternal Spring

"He divided the three hundred men into three companies and provided them all with horns and with empty jars and torches inside the jars. 'Watch me, and follow my lead,' he told them. 'I shall go to the edge of the camp and as I do, you must do also. When I and those with me blow horns, you too must blow horns all around the camp and cry out, For the Lord and for Gideon.'"

Book of Judges, the Ancient Scriptures 7:16-18

Readying their swords and armor, the resting demonkin prepared for the dawn raid against what they believed to be the unsuspecting population. Though well organized, there were a few spats involving orcs bumping into one another. In the center tent of the camp, Valadrim and his Nephilim officers plotted the strategic attack on the City of Antiquity. The eerie silence of the forest proper made the commander uncomfortable. Yet, these doubts were put to rest as he reminded himself of his foe.

As they prepared for war, Cedric had split his force into three positions above the camp. Though the size of the camp was overwhelming, the Kablisha warriors were not afraid. Inspired by their new commander, they lay perfectly still on the ground, ready for their final orders. As he tugged the rosary in his hands, Cedric tapped his communicator.

"Well, Wilhelm, here we are."

"Cedric, I have to admit, I never thought I would take part in biblical war reenactments. Did you take care of everything else I asked you to?"

"Sure did. On the mark… over and out. Argus, how's it going?"

"We're holding... I don't know why we didn't strike before they formed ranks for battle. We could have caught them off guard."

"It's psychological warfare. You always panic the most when you feel you're completely safe."

"I'm going to trust you. The animals are in place for your mark."

"Great. Take positions."

Argus signed off and put his troops in place. Wilhelm followed suit. The Titan prince tugged his rosary beads and concluded his prayers. Placing his hand on top of the ridge, the fairy from the flower before came up to his ear.

"Lord Rhone, the will-o-the-wisps are in position."

"Thanks for all your help. Crossbows!"

The warriors picked their marks with the crossbows and even the sword master got the chance to test his present.

"All right, my little friend, let's shed some light on this darkness!"

The fairy nodded and her wings glowed in a bright translucent light. Above the camp, wisps materialized in the night sky. In a coordinated ballet, they danced above the enemy, illuminating the area. Transfixed by the actions above, the demonkin wondered what had brought about this sudden display. From the forest, thousands of birds called in a single sonic boom, further disrupting the encampment. Even the Nephilim officers didn't deny something was afoot after these two displays. Cedric signaled the three positions to launch the assault. Every single warrior screamed "For God and Prince Cedric Rhone!"

They unleashed a barrage on the enemy and all of the Titan prince's predictions came true. Armor and weapons merely sent the demonkin into the panic. As the hundreds fell to the ground, footmen turned from position to position seeking to identify the source of the attack. In retaliation, demonkin battalions slaughtered one another believing them to be the ones behind the sudden slaughter. Valadrim and his officers rushed to get them back into ranks but fear had consumed them. Ripping Ragnarok from behind his back, Cedric determined he couldn't hold back his troops anymore. The Kablisha were determined to slaughter the evil that dared to destroy their homes and families.

"Forward!"

The Kablisha switched from crossbows to swords and charged down the ridge into the panicked camp. Cedric enchanted Ragnarok with saint saber as he went first into the camp. Picking out an ogre for his first target, the sword master separated his head with one mighty blow. Not knowing if this was flesh and blood or a specter from the world beyond, the Demonkin agreed that *La Morte Angelus* was sent from Heaven to make them atone for their sins with fire. Screams of *La Morte Angelus* permeated throughout the entire camp. In every Kablisha warrior, they saw the face of their great enemy. Dying ogres flattened battalions of goblin footmen.

Wilhelm used his crossbow when his group first hit the encampment. As a fell beast approached him, he switched to his spear and drove it into the beast's mouth where the path to the brain was tender. Dispatching the beast, the goblins swarmed him, and the fallen angel moved to his tower shield and Devil Slayer. The heavenly blade certainly lived up to its name. Argus and his group came in with saber swords. They were very efficient at cutting off the heads of their enemies. Dismayed by the full retreat of his forces, Valadrim lost all sense of judgment. He and his officers killed their own troops to force them to remain behind and fight. The Nephilim lifted a dying goblin from the ground, seeking an answer to his cowardice.

"Why do you flee?"

The dying creature kept screaming *La Morte Angelus* over and over again. When he tired of his squealing, Valadrim cast the soldier to the side.

"Cedric Rhone is dead, you fools! Now form ranks and destroy these upstarts who dare to attack us."

In was then that Valadrim noticed fear seeping into the eyes and expression of his compatriots—a fear no Nephilim had dared show in five long revolutions. Turning his gaze to the blazing fires in the middle of the camp, the silhouette of the Rising Moon Helmet shined clear in the flames and smoke.

"No… I won't be deceived," justified Valadrim. "He's dead… he has to be dead!"

Emerging from the smoke, the Nephilim cast their eyes upon the black blood soaking Cedric Rhone's master plate. Glowing from their enchantment, the paladin gauntlets illuminated his body so that his eyes bored into his enemy's souls from behind the helmet.

"By my prince… my eyes deceive me… Cedric Rhone is dead!"

"That's right Nephilim, I was dead but I found it painfully hard to sleep peacefully in my grave when Abaddon's spirit haunts Terminus Mundus. There will be plenty of Nephilim who will die here, but Valadrim, you are mine!"

"Fine. Kill him!"

Refusing to disobey their commander, the Nephilim rushed forward, but Cedric made no move against him. As if summoned from the fire, Argus, Wilhelm, Quinn, Mesmara, and a whole host of Kablisha warriors engaged the Nephilim in battle. Other Kablisha shot arrows into demonkin as Cedric stepped deliberately towards Valadrim. Gripping his sword, the Nephilim commander refused to back down. The two engaged in combat, and on the first blow Cedric knocked Valadrim back with an upswing of Ragnarok. Valadrim spread his wings to get his balance back and landed on his feet. Just as he had rebounded, the Titan prince was on him again. The sword master severed the right wing from the Nephilim's body. Sprouting dark red blood from the fresh wound, Valadrim screamed in intense pain.

"This is just what I needed, Nephilim, something to take all of my pent-up aggression out on!"

Cedric sliced hard and chopped off the sword hand of Valadrim. Not knowing where to clutch his bleeding wing or stub, the Nephilim pulled the exposed bone of his arm to his chest. Swinging Ragnarok upward, the Titan Prince knocked Valadrim flat on his back, twenty meters from his position. Kicking his heels against the ground, the Nephilim desperately tried to crawl away from *La Morte Angelus*. For a moment, the angel of death truly had wings as the sword master went for the kill strike. He leapt in the air and drove the blade into the center of the Nephilim's chest. Valadrim choked up blood and gasped for air. Cedric Rhone's strike had been carefully calculated. He made sure to just miss Valadrim's heart to bleed some last tidbits of information out of him. Staring his fallen foe in the eyes, the Titan prince twisted the blade.

"Give Lucifer my regards and tell him that he'll have to walk this planet himself before I allow his minions to ever take Cassandra from me."

Laughing and spitting blood at his tormentor, Valadrim was defiant to the end.

"You think you've defeated us... no, Cedric Rhone... you cannot stop what is coming...Cassandra belongs to us; she's always been one of us. I may die here, but I will savor knowing that the one you love shall bring this world to ruin…"

Concerned by the tone and defiance of his dying foe, Cedric grabbed Valadrim's head at the temples. Knowing what he had done to the compatriot before, the Nephilim wailed, screamed, and with his one remaining hand tugged at the sword master's arms.

"No… I won't let you!"

"I will never tire of the arrogance of your race. If you had just kept your mouth shut, I would have eased your passing…but I guess I must thank you for this."

Valadrim's eyes faded to a blank white as he screamed in agony. He felt it—every memory, every ounce of information Valadrim held flowed into Cedric. No matter how much resistance he offered the spell was too powerful, and he unwillingly told the sword master everything he needed to know. In his mind, Cedric saw it. He saw the Dark Elves marching on Deniva and the Defense that the Royals had mounted. He saw all of the plans that Abaddon and Luminas had made and feared for the fate of the Royals. Valadrim's tongue rolled out of his mouth and his head slumped over. Mesmara gagged a few times at the sight as Quinn embraced her and turned their heads from the wretched scene. Argus remembered his trepidation of Cedric Rhone's actions and the dreaded powers he could unleash on the world. Letting go of the brain-dead husk, Cedric called for Wilhelm.

"What do you require, your Excellency?"

"We have to go Deniva now!"

"Why Deniva?"

"The Dark Elves have the city under siege… it may already be too late. However, I just have a feeling that if Amuro was in charge, she did everything right."

"I understand."

"Cedric, catch!" yelled Argus as he tossed the amulet around his neck to Cedric.

"What's this?"

"The Recall amulet we spoke of. It will compensate for Wilhelm's inability to teleport you over that great a distance. We have one made for every city on Terminus Mundus. It will take you right to the castle courtyard of Deniva. Your internment among our people is over. Praise God that it was in the plan to send you to us for this hour."

"You're going to be handle the rest of this?"

"We've broken them. It will be easy to finish them off now. The Old Forest will help us!"

Argus went over to Cedric and embraced him as a brother.

"Never without you…we never could have done this without you. God bless you, Cedric Rhone, and God bless the Alliance for confronting this evil. Whenever you need us, the Kablisha are at your command."

Cedric hit Argus on the arm before he joined Wilhelm.

"Argus, I don't confront evil! I destroy it! Where's Florence?"

Running through the battlefield, Florence joined Cedric and Wilhelm.

"What do you command of me, my Lord?"

"Florence, can you possible leave for Deniva temporarily?"

"There isn't a single casualty among the Kablisha, and Mesmara is more than capable of handling the minor scratches."

"I can feel my sister's life is in grave danger. I need your help to save her."

"You have nothing to fear, my Lord. You're going into a war zone, and there is no cleric assigned to Deniva. You need me."

Embracing the cleric as thanks for her assistance, tears welled up in Florence's eyes. She knew this was as close as she was ever going to get to her true love, but the feeling of warmth coming from him was worth it.

"We can't waste any more time here. Florence, Wilhelm, let's go!"

Cedric and Florence grabbed the amulet around their necks as Wilhelm chanted the teleport spell. They disappeared in a flash of blue and white light. Unnerved by the twitching brain-dead body of Valadrim, Argus cut off his head in a final act of mercy. The Kablisha commander picked up the stolen amulet with the tip of his sword. Once again, they remained safe behind the barrier. Quinn awaited orders.

"Quinn, create a task force and fan out. Drive the Demonkin across the barrier and deal with the stragglers. The fools that fled into the Old Forest will be dealt with accordingly. If the enemy desires to leave the barrier, let them go! I want Abaddon to know what happened here and remember that there is still fight left in the Divikin."

"You've got it, commander. Two divisions with me!"

The Kablisha remaining in the encampment tracked down every demonkin who still clung to life. They chopped off every single one of their heads. The demonkin and Nephilim who fled into the deep forest soon found themselves entangled in vines and branches. Those that ducked the first wave found jaguars leaping from the trees and devouring them. Wolves hunted down wounded stragglers. Wasps and hornets stung them repeatedly. Even those that dove into the water to escape the land beasts found their fate sealed by river and lake predators nipping at them. As dawn came over the land, the army of the Nephilim and Demonkin was but a few stragglers fortunate enough to the escape the barrier.

GATES TO THE CASTLE, DENIVA

"Pray for miracles because miracles require faith!"

Old Titan Proverb

Vigilantly, Amuro kept staring at her watch and the sky above. Never before had the elf prayed so hard that night would give way to dawn. Cecilia was placed on a stretcher as Hippolyte and Minerva prepared to lead the first battalions of troops through the posterns per Amuro's orders. Determined that the Titan princess' best chance of survival was with the Wolf Tribe Chief and her sister, the selection for the first wave of retreaters was obvious. Wood Elf snipers took turns climbing and descending the walls. The Dark Elves had given up trying to scale them, favoring three rams working the courtyard door at once. Splinters formed and the beams were knocked out of place. As she paced, the Elf Marshal gripped Enhancer tightly. Only leaving their positions to reinforce the fallen beams, her brave soldiers formed a full defense behind a barricade near the posterns. Remaining undefeated to the last they gritted their teeth and had their weapons ready for the inevitable. Amuro rallied them once more.

"When the door breaks, and it will break," rallied Amuro, "There shall be no more restrictions concerning how you fight. Break ranks, kill as many as you can and when possible retreat through the posterns. Those of you like me who must remain behind, die knowing that every elf we kill will reduce strength of their forces. We will give our comrades the time they need to escape and continue the fight."

Crying harder than ever before, Amuro found her courage once more. The empathy from her body exuded hope to those in her command.

"It has been an honor to serve as your commander. I am sorry for how I failed you…"

The defenders would have none of that. Walker stepped up.

"Defenders of Deniva! Attention!"

Everyone stood and faced Amuro.

"Pay homage to the elf marshal who nearly pulled off the impossible when there was no hope. I say thee, Amuro Jenitzen, the bravest elf I have ever had the honor to serve."

The soldiers banged their weapons against their armor and offered her full homage and salute. Malcolm stepped forward and embraced Amuro tightly. Despite his distaste for public displays of affection, he kissed her fully one last time. The soldiers returned to their positions for the final assault.

"We are proud to stand with you to the end," praised Malcolm.

"You know, Malcolm, Cerwin was wrong about you. You never were a putz."

The sound of the rams penetrating the gate shocked Amuro to reality. Drawing Enhancer, she positioned herself in front of her command.

"Full retreat now!"

Initially startled by the command, the troops moved back as Amuro heroically pushed forward. As the gate came smashing down, Amuro unleashed her entire arsenal of offensive magic spells. No longer fearing for her life, she held nothing back. Evoking wind and earth spells from her left hand, the first drow swordsman through the gate was sliced across his stomach by her sword as dirt flew into the air and bolts came crashing down. She slaughtered two more opponents before being knocked down. Her sword cast to the side, she threw one last earthquake spell at her attackers before her magic well ran dry. Despite killing a score of troops, the elf Marshal witnessed her end. A single charging drow swordsman, weapon drawn back, positioned himself to sever her head from her body. Closing her eyes and begging Yahweh for forgiveness, Amuro heard the sweetest sound in the world. As the rays of Primus bathed the golden spire of Castle Deniva in divine light, a sword blade intercepted the drow's attack. Not wanting to open her eyes again, the Evengard princess could hear the gurgling death sounds of her drow attacker and felt its blood stain her body. A frightening war cry covered the landscape, concurrently with the light of dawn, weakening the Drow. When the marshal saw the world again, she saw a single knight holding a claymore high in the air.

Though his back was to her and he was covered by the radiating light of the morning dawn, Amuro could make out a silhouette.

When the she-elf was a young girl, her favorite scripture was the story of the pillar of fire that held back the Nephilim from slaughtering her people. The incarnation before her eyes, a single knight now held back the entire enemy force. The weakened bodies and carcasses of his foes piled up around him. Inspired by the knight's actions and overcome with a force that made them feel invincible, the defenders of Deniva screamed a war cry to join him in battle. Filled with fear and grief, their dark elves foes climbed over one another to retreat.

"Marshal Jenitzen, are you all right?" asked Wilhelm.

The high elf princess blinked and in her stupor recognized the face of Cedric's mentor Wilhelm von Angelhardt. A second woman, a cleric, hovered over Cecilia. Christian, trying to absorb all that had happened, recognized the familiar face.

"Wait a second, I know you," said Christian. "You're Florence... but your supposed to be among the Kablisha."

"Colonel DeVries, I am glad to make your acquaintance and would love to continue our conversation," greeted Florence. "However, Lady Cecilia's wounds are mortal, and if I don't move quickly I will not save her life."

Clapping her hands together, she generated a large, golden magic dome that covered the whole of the Vanadis's body. Amazed by the healing power this cleric possessed, Ethan watched joyfully as his wife's breathing normalized.

"Lord von Angelhardt... but... how is this possible?" demanded Amuro.

"Get your troops together... we're not out of this yet," said Wilhelm as he rushed to the join the other knight.

"Wait, who's that knight fighting them..."

She stopped as the first rays of dawn subsided. The defenders basked in wonder and awe. There before them bravely fighting off hundreds of drow side-by-side with them was the one sword master they had thought was taken from them. The Rising Moon Helmet was undeniable, but Christian only believed it when he saw Cedric turn his face back to Amuro. Cheers and tears of joy were cried among the loyal defenders. Robespierre and the knights who abandoned the city earlier charged back in through the posterns.

"You disobeyed my orders!" shouted Amuro angrily. "I told you to get Cassandra out of here."

"I am sorry, Marshal," replied Robespierre. "But we met a woman on the road and she told us to come back and fight. Deniva was going to be a shining light in the war against the darkness and we would be necessary to grant you a final victory. I believed this woman and that is why I came back."

Already overwhelmed by the appearance of her dead comrade, her comrade's mentor and a mysterious cleric, the Marshal believed what Robespierre was telling her. Wilhelm took a position next to Cedric.

"It's got to be now, Cedric!"

"Let's do this!"

In tandem, the two warriors chanted the holy war spell in the ancient tongue as Ethan, Walker, Cagius, and the others protected them. The echo was deafening and upon hearing it, Alia turned her chariot and rode out of the city. Unaware at what had happened, Palias and his guard followed her, shouting at the Drow Queen to return to the front. The first wave of retreating Drow were shouting *La Morte Angelus* at the top of their lungs. The Drow had already harbored a great fear of Cedric Rhone for his actions he had taken against them, the demonkin, and the wild men. Fearing an invincible specter from beyond, Dark Elves dropped their weapons and fell back from the gate. Both warriors ended the chant with the "Holy War" call. Doubling the firepower of the divine assault, the shockwave covered the whole walled city. Every Drow trapped in its powers fell to the ground. Alia just missed getting hit with the attack as she cleared the city with some of her troops, but when she turned back, she saw her entire army lying before her. The Dark Elves who fled with her returned to the Underdark. Despite having the wave pass over them, Palias and his men were unharmed by the attack. Neither the enemy nor the defenders could understand the power displayed to them.

A deep breath was all Cedric and Wilhelm needed to recover. The sword master rushed back to Florence to check on his ailing sister. A brief smile from the cleric who loved him was all he needed to know his beloved sister was all right. As the Titan prince stood again, a tearful Christian grabbed him in tight hug.

"It's damn good to see you! You really cut it too close this time!"

"I missed you too, buddy. What's the situation?"

"Well, I would say roughly you just laid waste to about sixty or sixty-five thousand Dark Elves ready to break down that door and slaughter what's left of this command."

"They aren't dead, Christian."

"What are you talking about?" demanded Amuro. "They're all lying there in the street."

"Take notes from your own scriptures, Amuro. Even as far as they have fallen, elves are still the chosen of the Father just like King Saulides. I cannot kill them while wielding the powers of God. However, I was able to stun them, so I'll have time to get to Alia Drathan."

"Alia's protected by Marshal Rene Palias and two hundred and fifty of his knights," informed Walker.

"The holy war spell won't have worked on them either, Cedric," interrupted Wilhelm.

"Amuro, this is still your command, but I need your help. You've got to take out those knights to give me a chance with Alia."

"It is you, isn't it? I'm not dying and we didn't both get sent to some kind of afterlife where we constantly fight battles for all eternity?"

Cedric took a sip of brandy from his flask and handed it Amuro. Though the she-elf hated the taste of the Titan prince's preferred libation, she needed it. A single sip and she accepted the present as reality.

"Come on, we pull this off and you're the first ever elf to successfully defend a siege attack. They'll be singing stories of the beautiful warrior maiden of Evengard in all the forests of Terminus Mundus."

"You're definitely Cedric Rhone; no one can flatter me like you. Robespierre, how many horses do we have?"

"Fifty, marshal."

"I can offer fifty riders, Cedric. Fall in behind us and do what you have do!" offered Amuro as she turned to her command. "I need fifty volunteers to ride out and do battle with two hundred and fifty Acadian knights."

More than fifty were willing, so Amuro had to choose. Walker, Robespierre, Ethan, Cagius, Joshua, and Hippolyte were among the selected, including both Order of the Lion Knights and Imperial Mamelukes.

"Malcolm, take the archers and form a perimeter around the cleric's field hospital. Infantry, take your positions at the shattered gate once we ride out. If we lose the tactical advantage, take the wounded with you and get out of here. Malcolm, you're in charge—I trust you to do the right thing!"

"Absolutely, marshal. I believe the phrase 'give them hell' is in order."

"That it is."

Lacking Maiden, Ethan made Amuro mount Myst. Cecilia's warhorse was more than happy to take on a decorated rider and exact some revenge of her own. The riders set themselves up in columns of five with Cedric bringing up the rear. Amuro took her place at the head of the column with Enhancer drawn as Wilhelm, now in command of the infantry, had them part ways to let them through. The screaming war cry and gallop made like the sound of thunder as the column spread through the city. On the outskirts of the city, Palias tried to settle Alia down.

"What was that?" asked Palias.

"The powers of creation…" stammered Alia. "It is a punishment brought upon us by Yahweh. He has called forth his divine warrior, *La Morte Angelus*, to exact his revenge for failing to hear his word. We're all going to die here."

"You're not making any sense. Cedric Rhone is dead!"

"No…I saw such an attack in my nightmares…I know the face of the one who possesses such power…it is *La Morte Angelus*!"

A knight came upon Palias.

"A small cavalry force is riding through the city to our position. I estimate about fifty, Marshal Palias."

"I'll give these rebels credit, they certainly take advantage of every opportunity. Ride out with me, we'll meet them in battle and end this!"

The Acadians formed ranks as Palias went to the front of the column. With a quick slash of his sword, they charged into battle to meet Amuro's smaller force.

"Okay, Julius, this one's for you!" shouted Amuro. "Let's show them what we're made of!"

Pushing her fist forward, Amuro led her riders into battle against Palias's knights at the main city gate. Riders on either side were tossed from their horses in the initial collision. Walker specifically rode his horse towards Palias's position. He tackled the older marshal from his mount. A swift draw of Sigmund and Walker drove the blade into the traitor's heart.

"Pin that medal on your chest, peacock!"

Approaching the battle scene, Cedric knew he couldn't waste time mowing through the turmoil of a cavalry battle. The sword master stopped Jericho and whispered into his ear.

"Old friend, I'm afraid we're going to have to do something crazy in order to accomplish the mission. From my perspective, I'm not too happy about it, but I defer to your better judgment."

A mighty snort came from Jericho's nose. The albino horse beat his front hooves into the ground before turning to two wooden slanted beams. Cedric shook his head negatively and ordered his warhorse to stop but Jericho sprinted without prodding. The horse and rider galloped up the wooden beams and Jericho leapt from one part of the collapsed rubble to the next. Ascending the wall on the stone steps as Cedric bounced in the saddle, the colt found the collapsed siege tower from the beginning of the battle. He carefully descended the destroyed mechanism to solid earth once again. Relieved that the nightmare was over, the Titan prince spotted his target Alia. Seeing her most feared enemy, Alia ordered her chariot to retreat to the safety of Underdark. All would be lost if the Drow queen escaped him, so the sword master spurred his horse. In a full charge, Jericho easily overtook the lumbering spiders. Cedric stood on top of his saddle and leapt at the chariot. Unable to land directly on it, the prince was forced to grab the rung on the back of the vehicle. Seeing him dragging behind them, the spiders rolled over every large rock for ten meters to shake the determined warrior loose. Alia started beating him with her whip, but the sword master pulled himself onto the chariot with considerable effort.

The moment he got on, the Drow Queen kicked and punched at him, but Cedric endured every blow to accomplish his mission. As he had done to Cassandra over five revolutions before, the prince grabbed her on either side of her head.

"Let me go!" demanded Alia.

"This isn't your will, Alia Drathan. Like a colony of insects, Abaddon knows that your people must obey your every command. I will draw his poison from you and put you on your own path again!"

Since the events five revolutions before, Cedric's golden aura had become stronger than the black aura of Abaddon surrounding Alia. Polarizing forces pushing against one another, Cedric planted a kiss on the Dark Elf queen's lips. Her aura flowed into his body and when the Titan prince had taken it all in, a barrage of feathers burst around him. Releasing her from the kiss, his recent enemy fainted against the side of the chariot. The sudden stop of the chariot flung the two from the back. The Titan prince landed first and caught Alia before she hit the ground. Muttering a silent prayer for his safety, the warrior was grateful that Cassandra hadn't witnessed the kiss. Waiting an appropriate time, the sword master took water from his cantina and woke the queen. Embarrassed by her antics and actions, Alia scampered away from the sword master and back onto her chariot.

"Alia Drathan, you are no longer bound to Abaddon's will, nor can you be bound by his dark sorcery again."

"It would have been easier for you to kill me."

"No, it wouldn't have. Your successor would have remained corrupted by the dark angel's power, and thus I would have been forced to fight a costly war I can't afford right now."

"You are wise, Prince Rhone. I am in your debt. Whatever you desire of me, if it is in my power, I shall grant it."

"Then please go home and trouble us here no longer."

"Your desire shall be granted."

Alia knelt before Cedric as he picked himself off the ground. As Jericho trotted over to Cedric's position, a few retreating Acadian knights that survived being killed or captured by Amuro raced past him. However, his attention turned to a single duco-matios disguised as a dark elf. Forced to reveal his true form to the divikin, the demonkin cowered in fear.

"Fear not, foul creature, your death is not at my hands this hour. I know you are going to report all of this back to your Master, so tell them this: I am here and I am coming for them."

Not willing to test the proclamation, the duco-matios hurried away. Recovering from Cedric and Wilhelm's devastating attack, the Dark Elf warriors staggered to their feet. Each of them grabbed their heads as if recovering from a terrible migraine as the glow in their eyes dimmed. Pulling a horn from her chariot, Alia blew it three times to signal a retreat. As quickly as they attacked, the Drow left the city without the malice and wroth they had brought with them. It was surreal for the defenders to see the vicious battle end in a strange way, and it took them a while to start celebrating. As Cedric walked back to the gate, Amuro stood waiting for him.

"Congratulations, Marshal Jenitzen, you broke the jinx."

Cedric put out his hand to offer his homage but the elf princess kissed him passionately and stuck her tongue in his mouth. Releasing him and blushing fully, Amuro fanned the heat down around her for a few minutes as the Titan prince stood dumbfounded.

"I'm sorry if I made you feel uncomfortable, Cedric. That was on my bucket list and I really thought I was going to die here. I affirm I will never tell Cassie about this…or you sister for that matter. That was wonderful—now I realize why Cassie's so flustered every time she kisses you."

Returning to her brave defenders, Amuro was crying out shouts of "victory" to her celebrating troops. Florence approached Ethan.

"Lord de-Milly, I have good news. Your wife is doing just fine. Though her wounds were grave…well, from my experience treating Rhone siblings, they have an indomitable will to live."

"I'm not surprised. I thank you, Mistress Cleric."

"Well, I did owe a favor to an old friend."

Florence winked at Cedric, but the sword master picked up what the cleric said to Ethan.

"Did she say 'wife?'"

"Oh my God, how could you ever have known? Cecilia and I have been married five revolutions. My sincerest apologies, sir, for not seeking your permission!"

"Congratulations. This and everything around us calls for a celebration."

Cedric opened his flask and took a drink. He passed it to Ethan who joined him. The much smaller Titan prince put his arm around his brother-in-law.

"From the rotation you arrived at our military academy, I couldn't have thought of a better and more honorable man for my sister to spend the rest of her life with. My advice to you on how to court her was all the permission you ever needed to marry my sister."

"Thank you, Cedric, that means a lot to me. Even with all the help you offered me those revolutions ago."

He rubbed his jaw.

"I just wish I listened when you told me not to ever try to buy your sister a drink."

"There is one thing, though. If you ever cheat on my sister, I will hunt you down, gut you, and have Jericho drag you from one end of Gaia to the other."

"Yes, your excellency."

"Not that you ever will, but you know it's a traditionally protective older brother thing."

"And I always thought Cecilia was the overprotective one."

"You should see what I did to this one noble who groped her at a dance. The best way to instill fear, Ethan, is to keep your actions quiet. After everything with Cecilia, I know God won't give me a cross I can't bear. There's no way I'm ever going to sire a daughter."

All of his friends still in the city wanted to greet Cedric appropriately. Everyone embraced him and said how happy they were to see him alive. For the first time in five revolutions, hope was on the lips of all around the Titan prince. Wilhelm felt it in the air. It was like a raging wildfire and nothing was going to stop it. Cedric Rhone, long thought dead, had come home to destroy evil.

CASTLE TITAN, TITANUS

"A Titan warrior believes that service to God, country, and
family are the three most important things he must defend
in his lifetime. Therefore the terms 'retreat' and 'surrender'
are an anathema to our vocabulary. Think of us as fanatical
warmongers all you want, but I ask you now to join us in
battle to preserve the hour when all beings of goodwill are
finally free."

King Frederick the Great on forming the First Alliance

Entering the room holding some folders, Martha skipped happily past
the royal guards and did the full circle around the garden in the center
of the room. Civilia did not notice nor care of the antics of her chancellor.
She was severely hungover from her surprise morale visit to Fort Hawkeye
the night before. Though divikin, she did not possess the high levels of
tolerance to alcohol her offspring did.

"My queen, I have marvelous news!"

Civilia raised her eyes from her throne. Taking notice of the expression
of her chancellor's face, the queen knew it was not a monotonous, routine
visit. She hadn't seen Martha this happy in revolutions and Civilia's hope
exploded.

"Martha, do we have our weapon?"

"I figured it out! We can take down the barrier."

"What's our timeframe?"

"I have to wait for the equinox at the start of the growing cycle.
After many failed experiments, I discovered that just like tidal forces,

the gravitational pull of the three satellites can bend and flex the tachyon field…"

Civilia was rattling her fingertips hard against her throne. Martha noticed immediately and bit her lower lip.

"Martha, I have a nasty hangover. Let's pretend that I know nothing about science. Explain the situation to me."

"I created a cannon that uses gravity to punch a hole through the tachyon field. The giant hole sets off a reaction that breaks every link in the tachyon chain. After a few minutes, the whole shield blows up."

"It sounds beautiful."

Martha punched her hand in the air. Civilia got off her throne and walked down to Martha. She gave her a hug and a kiss.

"Thank you for all of your hard work."

"My pleasure, your Highness! There is nothing more wonderful in life when all of your hard work pays off. Oh…"

Martha reached into her pocket and took out a pill.

"Take this, it's an experimental pill that should help you with your hangover. I was developing it for myself… I didn't want to repeat the embarrassment of that royal gala five long revolutions ago. Stupid football comment…"

Civilia took a deep breath and swallowed.

"Has it only been five revolutions, Martha? I often think back to that fateful night—the last time I ever held Stephen in my arms. Everything that has happened to us since was the result of that night. Yet, despite my hangover, when I woke this morning, I had the same feeling of joy I experienced when I woke the morning of the victory parade. We had just won the war and I thought in that one moment, after all our hard work, we could finally have one moment of peace. When I was growing up I was versed in the philosophy of the previous kings and queens of Titanus. Every event must happen in its own time, but there are things that remain universal and those are what we must preserve. Every generation must face their own challenges. I am not the first queen of Titanus burdened with difficulties; every ruler who sat on this steel throne before me had a moment to shine. Yet, all the great ones acted the same, even Braden in his final action; when the challenge arose, they all confronted them.

Despite the lies the Acadians have created about us over the revolutions, the Titans never saw themselves are warmongers filled with bloodlust. Our bloodlines told us there was good and evil in Terminus Mundus. When evil rises, it is the duty of the good to confront and destroy them at every turn…"

In her mind's eye, Civilia saw the defenders gloriously celebrating their victory in Deniva. The chanting of the name of Cedric Rhone echoed across the plains, and faintly on her throne, Civilia could hear it.

"There is no shell we can hide behind when there are those that wish to destroy us. A call to arms must be answered. Though borders may be strong, we have to live with the dangers of the world around us. Compromise does not bring safety, it brings defeat and weakness. It will only embolden those who hate you to take more and more from you. If every problem could be solved by negotiation, I would gladly talk until I collapsed. However, I know better. When an enemy shows us ruthlessness, we respond in kind. That is why my ancestor Ulysses chose his words carefully in our coat-of-arms: We can still be ruthless if you let us!"

Across the Acadian plains, the Kablisha warriors were celebrating their victory wildly. Argus planted Valadrim's head on a pike just outside the barrier. It led the way to a pile of smoldering Nephilim and Demonkin bodies, warning those that the Kablisha were no longer a people to be trifled with. Just like in Deniva, they chanted and praised the name of Cedric Rhone.

"In the end we must hang onto to the three virtues: faith, hope, and love. Our enemies lack the kinship, friendship, and brotherhood to ever destroy those three things we hold dear. Cedric performed the first act of faith against an overwhelming opponent; he managed to destroy Abaddon. I swear that I will have the courage of my son who saw evil and knew that he couldn't run away. And now he shall give us a second act of hope, since he returned to lead us against the evil that lingers behind."

"Civilia, are you saying…" stammered a teary-eyed Martha as if a veil of despair had been lifted from her.

"I'm so sorry for having to deceive all of you, Martha. Cedric has been in hiding among the Kablisha these past five revolutions. It was arranged, but Wilhelm broke their trust to tell me. I had to keep it secret, but that time has come to an end. We're no longer going to hide and fall back from this darkness. We'll be charging forward once more and vanquish this evil from our lands. It will not be easy or quick, but it shall be done."

Civilia put her arms around Martha.

"We could never have done this without you, Martha."

"Without me?"

"You've delivered us the weapon that will end the arrogance of our foes. Those cowards will have to make a decision to stand with evil or fully retreat from it. I believe they will choose the former. The greatest battle in the history of this planet is coming, and I am proud to have the greatest genius on Terminus Mundus at my side."

"Well, if you put it that way, your highness, I am just happy to have played my part. However, I caution you, all of my theories and experiments are worthless until that barrier comes down."

"Spoken like a realist; that is why you're my chancellor and my friend. Come, Martha, you've earned yourself a drink."

"And I'll be happy to take it."

The two retired to Civilia's inner chambers.

FIELD HOSPITAL TENT, CASTLE DENIVA

"Twins normally have an intense bond beyond what a normal brother and sister feel. However, in my studies of Cedric and Cecilia, I have observed a bond that almost borders on telepathy. They have the uncanny knack to sense when the other is in danger or safety. If such a bond exists as children, it will be interesting to witness how it develops past puberty."

The journal of Martha Heinrich, over thirty revolutions ago

Nestled in the midst of the ongoing celebrations, Cedric pulled back the canvas of a tent. Florence was out of the room washing up after doing all she could for her two royal patients. As he entered the makeshift field hospital room, the sword master noticed two cots. The cot on the left had Cassandra still sleeping soundly with her head bandaged below her raven hairline and her arms crossed over her chest. The Gottin-Speer and Cecilia's bloody armor lay next to the other cot. The sheet was pulled over the body all the way, indicating death.

"Oh Cecilia, I promise to never forget your sacrifice," joked Cedric as he took a slug of brandy. "The battle of thunder between Freya and you in the heavens shall be the words of legend. If one of the Rhone twins had to be taken from Terminus Mundus, we're probably better off with me still being here and you on the way out. Watch out, Heaven, when you design her robes, you've got one busty maiden incoming. I hope those are proper funerary rites."

Cecilia pulled back the bed sheet angrily and sat up.

"Not even close! You could at least pretend to be heartbroken!"

"I'd have to accept the fact I didn't feel that you were alive first. Here, you deserve a slug of some contraband. Try not to drink it all, it's the last I have right now."

Cedric grabbed a broken chair from the barricade and took a seat next to his sister. Cecilia drank liberally from the flask before handing it back to her brother. He shook it to make sure some was left before capping it and putting it back in his cloak.

"I'm not talking to you!" pouted Cecilia.

"What did I do now?"

"Listen, brother, I don't want you to get the impression that I thought you were dead. However, you could have at least sent me some form of communication over the past five revolutions. Do you know how much work and effort I had to put in to keep this ragtag bunch together?"

"And what a marvelous job you did, sis. Thank you."

Cedric kissed his sister on her forehead, but she still pouted.

"Yeah, and what did you do? Here I have to risk my life to save your girlfriend, and then our big hero comes charging in at the end and gets all the credit for winning the battle. It's just not fair."

"Are you finished yet?"

"Just indulge me with one more rant. As for your girlfriend, I'm starting to get worried. Here I get gutted, shot full of arrows, and dragged from one end of the courtyard to the other. Yet, I'm sitting up in bed talking to you. She gets one bump on her noggin and she's out cold for hours. What a wimp! Okay, I'm done, you can wake up sleeping beauty now."

Cedric moved to get up but stopped himself.

"So you really didn't think I was dead when everyone else did?"

"Think? I didn't need to think. Well, at first I was crying, praying, and cursing the Acadians to hell for all eternity, but I had to take one last pass before riding to Deniva. Standing there at the barrier on that fateful rotation, I felt your soul still burning strong and I knew we were going to get through this Denivan Exile or anything else the dark angel threw at us. Seriously though, how did you get out of Central Acadia?"

"Wilhelm pulled me out right before I died."

"I take back everything bad I ever said about the duke. And did you kill that dark angel bastard?"

"I destroyed his physical form, but they say his soul still haunts this world."

"Damn, well I should have expected it when the Dark Elves came to attack us. Don't let your obnoxious, angry sister hold you up any longer—wake her up!"

Wondering silently to himself why his sister suddenly seemed so deferential and nice concerning his girlfriend, Cedric stood. As he walked over to Cassandra, Cecilia turned in the bed, rested her elbow on her propped-up pillow and sat up to watch. Her brother kept pestering her to turn around, but the Vanadis insisted on seeing this moment. Resigned to the fact he wouldn't dissuade her, Cedric returned his attention to Cassandra. Sleeping, she resembled her angelic form rather than the demon within. The Titan prince remembered the last kiss they had shared, even if it was attached to a spell he used to repress her succubus soul. Since then he had dealt with Florence stealing her kisses in his sleep, breaking the spell on Alia, and even Amuro sticking her tongue down his throat. Genuflecting next to her cot, the Titan prince moved to press his lips against her. Just as he reached her, Cassandra jumped up and pulled him down to her lips.

"You were awake this whole time!" exclaimed an exasperated Cecilia. "What a lamp weasel!"

Cassandra held onto Cedric for a long time and wouldn't let him go. Not that he was complaining, but the Titan prince finally forced her to release him.

"It's been a long time, Cassie."

"Four revolutions, eight lunar cycles, twenty rotations, six hours, five minutes, and thirteen seconds!"

"It's like she's a living countdown clock," teased Cecilia.

"I never tire of her citing such statistics, sis. Cassie, I can't tell you how much longed for the taste of your lips."

"I believed her, Cedric. When Nadia told me you weren't dead, I believed her."

"So you believed the words of that evil witch before mine? Some best friend you turned out to be."

"What do you mean by 'best friend'?"

"Your sister and I came to understanding while you were away, Cedric."

"I'm less convinced now that she is going to destroy the world and everything I love. Besides, I didn't think I ever saw anyone love someone as much as the queen loves you."

"Well, this explains a lot. You know I prayed for a long time that you two would get along, but now that I've got want I want, I'm not sure I want it anymore."

The three in the tent had a hearty laugh, but outside the tent Florence stood crying. She screamed "rats," and silently walked away.

CASTLE ACADIA, VERIAN

"Even the most carefully planned political calculation can be met with utter disappointment. Unlike chess, the problem is that the pieces never seem to do as you wish."

Count Maximilian Luminas

Despite the joyous celebrations in Deniva, Titanus, and among the Kablisha, the throne room of Castle Acadia was as a funeral parlor. The rebels had been summoned by Abaddon and King Luminas to hear the tales of what had happened in the west. A single Nephilim stood before his fellow officers covered in blood. They had been the lucky few to escape the wrath of the Kablisha and the old forest. The duco-matios, whose life Cedric had spared, recounted his tale as well.

"Where is Lord Valadrim?" demanded Abaddon.

"My Lord Abaddon, he is dead."

"Dead? What happened?"

"We were ambushed in the forest as we prepared to march on the City of Antiquity. Whether there were hundreds or thousands or tens of thousands, I will never know. In the fires we saw him, his eyes burning like an avenging angel. I thought it was an apparition or the fire had merely deceived my eyes… but I have no doubt now who it was."

"Stop speaking in riddles!" commanded Sharon. "Who led the Kablisha force that killed Valadrim?"

"Prince Cedric Rhone…"

The mere mention of his name blanketed the room with fear and silence. Even Abaddon was at a loss for words as the throbbing in his chest returned. Only the duco-matios next the Nephilim dared to challenge his statements.

"Impossible! Cedric Rhone turned the tide of the battle at Deniva. He broke Abaddon's hold over Alia and rendered the entire Drow army impotent with one swing of his sword."

"Are you telling me that Cedric Rhone was with the Kablisha and Deniva?" contemplated Luminas. "Are you mad? The kilometers between the two lands are too great. He would have had to cross the barrier!"

Overtaken by madness, the nobles in the room screamed and begged their king for answers. Even the Nephilim and Demonkin looked to Abaddon to offer them protection from the sum of their fears.

"The Lord of Titanus has returned to punish us for our sins!" uttered a noble.

"His powers cannot be contained by the grave!" shouted another as if possessed by sudden madness.

"Listen to yourselves—this is madness!" reasoned Jonas. "We tested the DNA from the blood and his helmet was gone... Cedric Rhone died here."

Abaddon let loose a burst of power from his body to stop the frightened masses. Shaking the floor, he sought to take control of the situation.

"There is a way Cedric could have crossed the barrier," declared Abaddon. "The amulets that the Kablisha use could have been rigged to travel to Deniva. I have been watching the eyes of my subordinates this entire time and I assure you they speak the truth."

"But the helmet!" challenged Jonas.

"Jonas, you recovered a helmet, not the body of Prince Cedric Rhone. I was such a fool to deceive myself for so long. He held breath in him when he finished me off; I assumed he would die. The Kablisha obviously pulled him out of the castle before you got there. Five revolutions... this is the deception of Krystos, I'm sure of it, but I don't remember him being this cunning, unless... no, it cannot... Nadia... why would you do this to me? How could you betray me?"

Abaddon wailed in agony as his astral spirit faded into and out of reality. This only raised the fears of those in the room that the Titan prince was soon to arrive.

"Cedric Rhone is alive and if what my subordinates testify is true, he's stronger than we could ever imagine. There is only one attack I know that could have had that effect on the Dark Elves. It is the power of "Holy War," a divine magic that can incinerate the strongest of Prince Lucifer's manifestations, let alone Demonkin and Nephilim. I didn't think it was possible for a divikin to use such a power since it is a weapon of Heaven, however, I will not place anything past the Titan sword master. We're in for a world of trouble."

"Doctor Virgus, what of our barrier?" inquired Celius.

"The barrier is holding… for now."

"The barrier is not meant to be our offensive weapon, it was meant to give us time to destroy the royalists," interrupted Abaddon.

"Lord Abaddon, considering these new developments and failure of our offensive campaigns, it would be wise to merely wait the royals out," suggested Celius.

"You can't wait Cedric Rhone out!"

"Cedric only controls Titanus for now, if he can even get home," reasoned Sharon. "In order to march on Verian, he needs to put a coalition together and the history of Alliance coalitions holding together is spotty at best."

"None of you understand the Titan prince. Cedric Rhone is coming for us. He saw our weakness during the battles against the Kablisha and in Deniva. He is going to launch a holy war against us because he believes he was born to save Cassandra. That divikin is not going to shirk at his goals, even if he has to walk in here alone and half-dead. The question now becomes what are you willing to do to stop them?"

Everyone in the room seemed to be looking for answers from someone else. Luminas stood with the answer.

"All of you begged me… you all wanted King Stephen thrown off of his throne. When the Nephilim came to us with their plan, all of you rushed to be the first names on the list. Now, at the first sign of trouble, all of you want to pretend you had nothing to do with it."

Sharon and Jonas both stood at the side of Luminas. He was happy to have their unabashed support at least.

"I want to fight," rallied Luminas. "I want to do something that I believe in for once, and that's to meet this enemy head on. We'd never coexist with this enemy. All they can think of is making us pay for our supposed 'crimes.' We are fighting for our survival. Perhaps Cassandra would be merciful...but not Rhone, he'd sooner see us all hang."

Luminas walked down to Abaddon and bowed his head.

"We can't do it alone, so if you have some ingenious plan to get us out of this mess, I'm more than willing to hear it."

"It's a dangerous time, Maximilian Luminas, and perhaps in these times we have to put aside our minor differences to settle the big picture. I have an idea on what might save us, but it will require sacrifices on all of our parts."

"Very well," answered Luminas. "Then we stand together until victory...or death..."

"Victory or death!" became the chant first from Abaddon until it resonated with everyone standing in the room. They resigned themselves to fact they were beyond salvation at this point and no forgiveness would come from the heart of the Titan warmonger they feared.

"We've trusted you this far, my liege," pledged Jonas. "Everyone in this room is willing to follow whatever decision you make."

"We'll see this through to the end," said Luminas.

"Good, I was sick and tired of listening to this bellyaching of chickening out. You have my sword."

"I know."

Sharon stepped down and kissed Luminas. She pulled him aside.

"There is something else you should know. Virgus was successful in transferring your DNA to my egg. I am carrying your child."

A bright smile came across Luminas' face and he hugged Sharon tightly. Abaddon walked away from the others and grabbed his chest.

"A reminder, Cedric—do not think that I forgot our last confrontation. I know the pain you feel as well. Our destinies are intertwined and our grand finale for the soul of Terminus Mundus shall be glorious!"

CASTELLAN OF DENIVA, TWO ROTATIONS LATER

"The Lord lives! Blessed be my rock! Exalted be God, my savior!
O God, who gave me vindication, made peoples subject to me,
and preserved me from my enemies, truly you have exalted me
above my adversaries, from the violent you have rescued me.
Thus I will proclaim you, Lord, among the nations; I will sing
the praises of your name. You have given great victories to
your king, and shown kindness to your anointed and his
posterity forever."

The Ancient Scriptures, Psalm 18:46-51

In the husk of the ruined city in the Margrave of Deniva, the golden spire remained a bright contrast to the night sky. The sound of music filled the canyons of rubble as a bonfire blazed high into the evening sky. A convoy from Edenia returned with King Dennis and many of the powerful nobles, businessmen, and traders of Deniva. While they were there to survey the damage and make determinations on rebuilding, they joined the celebration of victory over the Dark Elves. Saria rode Maiden into the city with Thomas sitting in front of her. Cecilia went over and grabbed her son off the winged unicorn.

"Mommy!"

The mother embraced and kissed her son many times.

"How is my brave little boy doing?"

"I'm all right. Miss Saria kept up with my lessons while we were gone. She really is a beautiful singer."

"I'm happy to hear that. Now I have someone important you have to meet, so you'd better be on your best behavior."

Thomas nodded as she set him down. The two walked slowly over to Cedric. Cedric and Cagius were discussing the finer points of Kablisha culinary cuisine at the time.

"So let me get this straight," reiterated Cagius. "You're telling me the Kablisha have this thing they call 'pizza'—bread, cheese, and tomatoes."

"Well, essentially. You see, they roll the bread out before they bake it," explained Cedric. "Then they put the toppings on and bake it in the oven."

"And it's square?"

"Yes."

"I think you were right to come to me with this. Now, what if instead of a square we roll it into a circle and stretch it with olive oil. We substitute marinara sauce for tomatoes and use fresh mozzarella cheese. Then we'll bake it in the brick oven. I'll call it Napolitan-style pizza."

"My mouth is watering just thinking of it."

Cecilia cleared her throat to distract her brother from his new culinary appreciation. Upon seeing his Uncle for the first time, Thomas was caught between awe and fear. The Titan prince extended his hand to his young nephew.

"I'm your Uncle Cedric. Your father said you look a lot like your mother, and now that I see you, I'd say you're about her spitting image, save for the hair color."

"You're Prince Cedric?" asked a puzzled Thomas. "The great warrior who killed an angel? I don't believe it."

The young boy couldn't get over how short his Uncle was. He was expecting to see someone like Joshua or Cagius.

"Thomas! Don't say such things about your uncle," chided Cecilia.

"But Mom, I have to think this is a joke. He's wearing a skirt!"

Riotous laughter broke among Cedric's comrades and friends at the young boy's blunt statement. Cecilia turned a deep shape of red and nearly slapped Thomas across the face.

"In her efforts to teach you history, your mother has obviously neglected to tell you of our own family history," lectured Cedric. "When

Ulysses became our first king, there were two types of Titan War Lords: Heartlanders and Highlanders. While the Heartlanders resembled the modern Titan, the Highlanders were farmers and miners who wore battle paint and war kilts, like this one, into battle. Ulysses donned a war kilt when he was crowned King to honor the traditions of both Heartlanders and Highlanders. My grandfather Justin reintroduced the kilt after the tradition had lapsed for many revolutions and so I wear it to honor his victories and that of our ancestors."

"It sounds made up," countered Thomas.

Cecilia gave Thomas a slight slap on the back to stop talking.

"Mom is certainly going to love this little one," teased Cedric. "I bet she's dying that she hasn't been treated to a meeting with her first grandson."

"I guess she would," surmised a worried Cecilia. "If I had told her…"

"What do you mean, if you told her? Christian briefed me that you've been communicating through Andres regularly."

"Yeah, but the whole issue of your daughter getting married and having a child is very personal. I just didn't feel it was appropriate to write such a thing in a message. Suppose it got intercepted and misinterpreted."

"You didn't know the code word for 'marriage,' did you?"

"There was that as well…but mostly the first thing…"

Ethan reported to his father. Dennis was overcome with grief at the destruction of his once beautiful city. Seeing his son alive and well made the Margrave forget the damage to the materialistic world. He embraced his son tightly and cried.

"I am sorry, Dad. In order to save the city, we practically had to destroy it."

"Don't worry about it, Ethan. We've got more than enough money to begin repairs in order to get our trade infrastructure up again. As for the rest, I'll make sure the Titans and the other loyal alliance members offer restitution for keeping their queen safe at all cost."

"That's my Dad."

"I'm just glad you're alive! Now, I was able to smuggle some Acadian Whiskey back with us from Edenia. Apparently King Archibald did not agree with Sultan Khan's decision to wipe us off the map."

Dennis ordered his servants to uncover the wagons.

"To the loyal defenders of this city, to our staunch allies from the west and our new allies in the Arudin Forest! I want to reward your bravery with this small token. On this rotation, all of Terminus Mundus knows that we made a stand here, in the ruin of this beautiful city. We fought evil and we kicked its ass."

The Defenders and their companions cheered and yelled. Dennis filled mugs and passed them out to everyone there. It took some time but finally everyone got a glass. Amuro found a stone step to get up on and raised her glass.

"To the fallen that died defending this city, to those who survived to give us victory, and to Pasha Selim, perhaps the most honorable Imperial I've ever known."

Everyone shouted "Here here," and took a sip from their glasses.

"We all know that this victory was only the beginning," added Cedric. "In a simultaneous battle halfway across the plains, the Kablisha defeated a large army of demonkin attempting to destroy them. Abaddon seeks to bring an end to all of the goodness that we believe in. Well, we pushed back that Fallen Angel bastard on this rotation! The victories at Deniva and in the City of Antiquity will resonate throughout the West. Hope was kindled here today—a fire that will rage until Abaddon and his puppet king are driven from our lands. It is a long road for all of us, but celebrate this rotation, my brave warriors."

Everyone cheered and clapped like mad. Many of them started to chant, "Cedric!" The Titan prince allowed himself a smile and took a drink. Cassandra grabbed him around his waist.

"You have a gift," complimented Cassandra.

"Unfortunately, Cassie, making a few charismatic speeches isn't going to do us a lot of good if we don't win. Then again, you did always see something in me, even before we realized the only thing standing between this world and Abaddon is me."

"Permaneo Eques Ordinaris! I have something for you."

Cassandra reached into her pocket and pulled out Cedric's rosaries. She put them in his hand.

"I kept these for you, but I figured you'd probably want them back now that we're going to have to fight a bunch more battles against overwhelming odds."

"These look like they've been repaired a few times," said Cedric, examining them.

"About that…" replied a blushing Cassandra. "You see, relics and I don't necessarily have a good relationship…"

In the midst of the celebration, Saria sung a canticle of victory. When she finished, two soldiers grabbed fiddles as Cagius kept rhythm with clapping. Saria sang a contemporary tune, which riled everyone up. The couples danced away among the rubble. Malcolm tried to escape but Amuro grabbed him. As they started to dance, Amuro was stunned at how good Malcolm was.

"Malcolm, I've never seen you dance before. You're so good."

"Just because I choose not to do something doesn't mean I can't do it."

Hippolyte looked eager to dance with the others, but Colin was nervous. Every time he stepped to her, he took a step back. The Wolf Tribe Princess got impatient and danced with Thomas for a few moments. Christian walked by the duelist with Rosa on his arm. He gave his a companion a wink and whispered in his ear.

"Never waste a genuine opportunity."

"You're just a fountain of good advice."

Colin nodded. He begged Thomas' pardon, took Hippolyte's hand, and led her out. Everyone danced, laughed, and drank the night away.

Prince Cedric Rhone thought lost had returned to his friends. Throughout the west, hope was spreading like wildfire as rumors of victory over Abaddon were spoken out of the shadows for the first time in five revolutions. Yet, Abaddon and King Luminas had reaffirmed their Alliance. The rebels of Central Acadia saw to improving their defenses as all-out war with the Kingdom of Titanus was inevitable. All eyes turned to Martha Heinrich who worked around the clock to make her theory to take down the barrier a reality. Faith and hope blanketed the west, but all beings of goodwill had to embrace one another to vanquish evil. The Denivan Exile was coming to an end; the Saga of Terminus Mundus was far from over.

EPILOGUE

CASTLE ACADIA, VERIAN

"Among the items we found in the treasure troves of the Dragon Masters was the Libro Mortuorum. The goals of our enemies concerning this book were unclear, though I deem it possible that they meant to raise dead dragons. The elves secured this book first, but Cerwin feared its temptations immensely. Though he was incorruptible, he felt an elf mage may attempt to learn its secrets. The book is most dangerous because it plants a seed of corruption in the soul of its wielder. That seed will germinate until it strangles the soul and blooms the user into a servant of darkness. Now that it is the hands of the Wizard Guild, I find myself wishing we had destroyed it."

Von Angelhardt's Sixty-Seventh Report

In the bowels of Castle Acadia in Verian, Luminas met with Abaddon.

"Why have you summoned me?" demanded Luminas. "I thought our arrangement was quite clear and we're going to work together."

"I'm not backing out of our deal, Maximilian. However, an incident has risen that will work to the best of our interests. In order to legitimate our claim on this throne, it would be imperative that you would have a figurehead to secure the weak-willed."

"Who would you suggest?"

"The legitimate heir, of course, Princess Marie Acadia."

"She'll never do it. The girl is weak and won't stand against the sister she loved and respected."

"Do you think so? Come with me!"

Luminas followed Abaddon through the blackened corridors. Guided to an observation window, the two watched a training session below them. Clad in long black robes with a black feather protruding from the shoulders was Marie. Attached to her waist was the Libro Mortuorum with a belt made out of leather and human bone. In her hand was a black rod that had a flail and mace on one end of it and a crystal skull on the other end. Marie's eyes showed an unnatural pallor to them and her smile was turned to one of evil. It was as if her original personality had been wiped away in favor of a soul of pure darkness. Chanting in a foul tongue, she created a black summoning circle in the center of the room marked with a red pentagram. A full battalion of skeletons in armor bearing swords and shields were summoned. The skeletons turned to their new mistress and obediently knelt before her. As she unleashed a maniacal laugh, Luminas smiled with approval.

"She's become a Necromancer. I didn't think she had it in her."

"It was best suited to her talents... she blames Cedric for both the disappearance of her sister and the death of Julius. It took time, but it was easy to brainwash her in order to do my bidding. Once she legitimizes your occupation of the throne, the royals will hold no sway with the Acadians on the fence. Norville Warrington will never agree to it, but he is a little fish. If, Marie, you and I stand together, Cedric Rhone shall receive his eternal reward."

We hope you enjoyed *The Denivan Exile,*
Book 2 of *The Saga of Terminus Mundus* series by
Michael Mazzaro.

For additional titles by this author and others, including
Book 1, *The Legend of the Last Knight*, please visit our
website and online catalog at:
http://www.signalmanpublishing.com